RIVER
OF
LIES

RIVER
OF
LIES

A DETECTIVE
EMILY HUNTER MYSTERY

JAMES L'ETOILE

OCEANVIEW PUBLISHING
SARASOTA, FLORIDA

ISBN 978-1-60809-589-6

Published in the United States of America by Oceanview Publishing

Sarasota, Florida

www.oceanviewpub.com

10 9 8 7 6 5 4 3 2 1

Behind every great fortune lies a great crime.

HONORÉ DE BALZAC - 1834

RIVER
OF
LIES

CHAPTER ONE

IT WOULD BE easy to float away in the darkness and let the current pull her under, too. She'd thought about it several times before—in her "dark times," as her ex-husband used to call them.

Lisa's life hadn't turned out the way she'd hoped. Abusive parents, a failed marriage, the booze—so much booze—all swirled together to set her on this path. Losing her apartment finally put her out here. Now this. She thought she'd escaped, but running from her past hadn't worked. The ghosts of years past had stripped everything away. Lisa had nothing left, not even hope.

The tug of the Sacramento River on her legs was tempting, and the spring snow runoff numbed Lisa's thighs as she waded out.

Lisa closed her eyes and pictured herself lying back and allowing the river to put an end to it.

"Momma?"

Lisa's eyes shot open.

Glancing over her shoulder, she spotted the faint outline of her daughter standing on the riverbank. The eight-year-old wore a thin blue T-shirt with a unicorn on the front, a threadbare pair of jeans, holding a stuffed bunny with one ear missing. The girl's face registered confusion.

"Baby, go on back to the tent," Lisa said.

Lisa felt her daughter would be better off without her. The mother's sins cast a damning shadow. But she couldn't abandon Willow. Not like this. Lisa knew what it was like to be an orphan in an unfriendly world. The future of an eight-year-old alone in a homeless camp wasn't the life Willow deserved.

"Momma, what are you doing?"

Lisa's eyes welled. She didn't need to tell her daughter the world was a hurtful place. She'd keep the secrets and not let her know there was nothing worth living for—for now.

"I'm coming, baby."

Lisa turned and waded back toward the bank. Her daughter spent the last two years in one homeless camp or another. The tightly packed shelters made Lisa's claustrophobia itch.

Lisa reached for her daughter and grabbed her, lifting the girl into a tight hug. Tears streamed down Lisa's cheeks. Not because Lisa wanted to end her suffering. She'd considered that option before. The tears came from nearly making Willow an orphan and leaving the innocent girl behind in a homeless camp. Willow couldn't fight off the predators who lurked in the darkness—like they did tonight.

From the river's edge, the camp spread a quarter mile in either direction. There was never any official count because people came and went, died, were arrested, or simply disappeared from the camp. Lisa guessed there were over two hundred people living here in the city's forgotten shadows.

It was time to move. When the camps get too big, bad things happen, and people talk.

Lights flickered from small campfires and lanterns throughout the settlement. Lisa thought they looked like fallen stars. She hugged Willow a little closer and followed the trail back into the camp.

She unzipped the fly on their tent and scooted inside. Their belongings—a change of clothes, a towel to share, and two children's books—lay on one end of the nylon dome tent. A pair of sleeping bags took up most of the space. Lisa knew they were lucky to have them—others didn't.

"All right, sweetie, let's get you settled in for the night."

Willow wiggled into her sleeping bag with her stuffed rabbit. Lisa grabbed a book, *The Mouse and the Motorcycle*, one of her daughter's favorites. The eight-year-old could recite most of the story by heart.

Lisa opened the book when a loud commotion erupted outside. It wasn't uncommon in the camp. Fights over property, drugs, or imagined slights fed by drugs, alcohol, and glitchy mental health were a daily occurrence. Lisa learned the best thing to do was stay out of it and never get involved.

It sounded like the usual dustup until the screams began.

"Stay here, Willow."

Lisa crawled to the tent flap, zipped it open, and poked her head out.

Fire.

Flames erupted on the far side of the camp. It was always a risk in the cardboard condos and plastic tarp shelters along the riverbank. This was different. At least six structures were ablaze. People were running, backlit by the orange and yellow glow. The evening delta breeze fanned the flames, igniting another dozen tents.

The cheap nylon shelters went up like dried rice paper.

"Baby, get your shoes on."

"What is it, Momma?"

"We need to—"

Lisa spotted two men in the chaos, both outlined by the flames behind them. They weren't running. One set the next row of tents ablaze. The second man wielded a baseball bat and swung the aluminum cylinder at anyone who came near. A sickening *tink* sound echoed among the rows of tents when he bounced the bat off a man's shoulder.

Lisa grabbed her daughter's hand, pulling her from the tent. The girl's eyes grew large when she spotted the fires.

Willow pulled away and ducked back into the tent.

"Willow Marie, don't you pull away from me. Come here. We need to get away."

Lisa felt the heat from the fire. It was spreading fast, and the flames jumped up into the trees within the camp.

Bending into the tent, Lisa found Willow gathering her stuffed animal and the books.

"Come now, we need to—"

Tink.

Lisa fell flat on the ground. The rounded end of the baseball bat shoved at her ribs. Dazed from a blow to the head, she didn't move. Lisa registered a man's boot stepping over her.

The flames grew closer.

Willow's fear backed her into the far corner of the tent.

Lisa's ragged voice called to her daughter. "Willow. Listen. I need—I need you to run. Hide. Go to the safe place—the rock where we hide things. Stay until I come for you."

"I don't want to go. I'm scared."

"I know, baby. You have to be brave. Take Mr. Bunny and go, now."

Willow clutched her stuffed animal, the book, and stepped through the tent flap.

"Momma, you have an owie."

"I know, baby. I'll be okay."

It was a lie. Lisa knew she was far from okay. She could feel the pressure in her head building with each heartbeat.

"Go to the place we talked about, honey. Go quick."

Willow's eyes welled. She didn't budge, frozen in fear before a scream from someone nearby broke her from the trance. Another row of tents went up in flames.

"Go."

Willow hugged her bunny and trotted toward the river. Lisa lost sight of her through the smoke billowing through the camp.

She tried to get up and couldn't move her legs. She crabbed forward using her arms, inching away from the burning camp.

Her tent flashed, and the flames consumed it in seconds. The melting fabric, plastic and nylon fibers fell on her. The molten material burned through her clothing and ate into the flesh on Lisa's back.

The pain seared into her. Screams around her meant she wasn't the only one. The two arsonists headed in the same direction Willow had fled.

"Stop them," she cried. No one could hear over the chaos of the burning camp.

Lisa now wished the water had brought a calm end to everything. She didn't expect this—the fire, searing flame, and torture. Part of her believed she deserved this fate for the pain she'd caused. Willow didn't. The girl didn't understand. Now, Lisa worried about what would happen to her sweet little girl. Mr. Bunny would not be enough.

The last thought before the flames ate at her pant legs. *I've failed you.*

CHAPTER TWO

DETECTIVE EMILY HUNTER was unlocking her front door when she felt the caress against her leg. The unexpected ambush from the shadows on her dark porch made her jump.

"Dammit. What are you doing here?"

Her admirer pressed against her.

"You need to stop. I'm not your midnight hookup."

A pair of piercing yellow eyes stared up at Emily, judging her for the late evening.

Emily pulled her key from the door and the black cat sashayed through the opening and trotted to the kitchen.

Emily followed, placing her purse on the kitchen table and kicking off her heels.

"What?"

The cat looked from Emily to a spot on the floor.

"You don't live here. You aren't my cat. Doesn't Mrs. Rose feed you?"

The black cat was well-fed, and Emily knew she used the neighborhood as a buffet, sampling the offerings from house to house.

"Fine."

Emily grabbed a bowl and a bag of dry cat food from under the counter. She kept the stash because she first thought the cat was a stray. Feeling sorry for the poor thing caught out in the rain, Emily brought her in, toweled her off, and now the cat rarely ventured far. Emily knew she was pegged as an easy mark for cat-extortion.

She placed the bowl of food in front of the cat, who shot Emily a look proclaiming, *This is the best you've got? The neighbors gave me tuna.*

"Eat up and be gone."

Emily took off her earrings and placed them on the counter. She closed her eyes and recounted the date she had this evening with Brian Conner. Brian was also an officer with the Sacramento Police Department, and they'd met six months ago at a crime scene. Yes, the height of romance.

They'd been having a good time until Brian got called in. She didn't get the details, but it sounded like another disturbance call—the type where they needed as many uniformed officers on duty as they could grab. Managing a social life as a cop was difficult, doubly so when both of them were a phone call away from another crime scene. This time it was Brian who needed to cut the date short. Which left Emily home alone with the cat.

Emily unpinned her shoulder-length brown hair and was about to change from the dress she'd chosen for her date, on one of the rare occasions she wore one, when her cell rang.

She hoped it was Brian calling to tell her he was on his way over, but it was the Watch Commander.

"Hunter."

"Hey there, Em, sorry to bust up your night," Lieutenant Terri Williams said.

"Nothing to bust up, Lieutenant. What you got for me?"

"Mass casualty event at a homeless camp off of North 7th."

"I know the one. It's a big camp on the river, right?"

"That's the one. Another fire tore through the place. That makes the third camp hit in two weeks. Needed a three-alarm response to put the place down."

"Mass casualty?" Emily said. Burn victims were among the worst crime scenes. Charred bodies found huddled in a closet—they were difficult to see and impossible to forget.

"That's the report from the Fire Battalion Commander on scene. Don't have any idea if we're talking homicide here or not."

"Simmons and Taylor have lead investigating the attacks on the homeless camps."

"This comes from the chief. He wants you out there."

"Let me guess, the chief is getting pressure from the mayor . . ."

"No wonder you're his favorite detective, Hunter."

"Doubtful, but I'm on my way."

After hanging up the phone, Emily headed to her bedroom and changed out of her emerald green dress, hanging it in the closet. The evening with Brian left her with a comfortable, warm feeling before it was cut short. *Better luck next time.*

She dressed quickly—dark pants, a button-down shirt, and a dark blazer, her typical work attire. She pulled her brown hair into a tight ponytail and shut off her bedroom light.

The cat was waiting at the back door. "Oh, you're done with me, too?"

Emily opened the back door and waited while the black cat leisurely set out into the backyard.

On the way to her car, she called her partner, Javier Medina. They'd worked together for nearly two years, with Emily as the lead detective as she had more time in-grade. Although Javier had more time in the department, he never resented her holding the senior position.

He picked up on the first ring. "Please tell me we have a case," he said in a low tone.

"Bored on a Friday night, Javi?"

"I wish. I'm at Mom's and I'm getting the third-degree about where my life is, and she set me up with another one of her friends' daughters. Please tell me we have a gruesome murder to attend to."

"We have a rollout. Homeless camp off North 7th."

"I was just listening to the news. Another arson? Why are we rolling on that?"

"The chief's orders. I'll swing by and pick you up."

"I'm over at Mom's. Come rescue me."

* * *

Ten minutes later, Emily knocked on the midtown home. Javier seemed ready to bolt out the door. He stood on the step and began to close the door behind him. Javier was four inches taller and four years older than Emily, and he had that slight graying in the temples of his short cut dark brown hair. He blamed the gray hair on Emily.

"Hey, hey, what's the hurry? I want to say hi to your mom."

She pushed past him, leaving him waiting on the front steps, shaking his head.

"Mrs. Medina, how are you?" she called.

"Emily," the thin older woman said. Her salt-and-pepper hair pulled back into a bun while she diced peppers, tossing them in a pot simmering on the stove.

"I need to steal your son away, but I wanted to stop and say hi."

"I'm glad you did. How's your mother? Is she adjusting to the assisted living facility?"

Emily bit her lip. Placing the retired schoolteacher into assisted living was the hardest thing Emily had ever done. After a series of incidents, including walking away from home, Connie Hunter couldn't take care of herself any longer. Since the placement, well, it was a struggle—for everyone.

"She's safe, and that's the most important thing. Half the time she's angry at me for putting her in a 'home,' as she calls it. I didn't have any other choice."

Lucinda Medina put her hand on Emily's arm. "I know you didn't, my dear. You made the best decision for her. Please tell her I said hello, would you?"

A petite, olive-skinned woman popped into the kitchen with a curious look in her eyes. She wore a short skirt and tight top emphasizing her toned, athletic body. Her dark hair draped over one shoulder.

"Hi, I'm Emily. I guess I'm the one responsible for taking Javier away tonight."

"I'm Jenny. Nice to meet you. Javier talks about you."

"He does, does he?"

Javier grabbed Emily by the elbow. "Come on, partner, crime awaits. Bye, Mom. Bye, Jenny."

He rushed Emily out the door. "What did you say before I pulled you away?"

*   *   *

Emily got behind the wheel and Javier jumped into the passenger seat. She backed her blue Crown Vic out of the drive and pulled away.

"She seems—nice," Emily said.

Javier knew it best to stay quiet.

"So, is she a badge bunny or something?"

"What? No. What would make you ask that?"

"Well, I mean there's her—and then there's you. She is so out of your league."

"Oh, shut up. She is not."

"Really? Then why the mad rush to get outta there?"

"I know my mom. She'll try to have us engaged or something before the night's over."

"You could do worse."

The flashing red lights blossomed ahead. The river access road was jammed with fire engines, tankers, and pumper trucks feeding hose lines down the embankment to the river's edge.

The engine crews had set up spotlights to illuminate the smoldering camp. Smoking husks of makeshift shelters seemed otherworldly in a dystopian sense. Stark, bleak, and unforgiving.

"I don't like the looks of that," Javier said, pointing at five ambulances parked at the access road.

Across the road from the ambulance crews, a large gathering of displaced homeless watched their belongings turn to ash. A pair of them pointed at a gurney loading into the rear of one ambulance.

Emily found a place to park near a black and white Sacramento Police SUV. Two uniformed officers were keeping the former camp dwellers away from the fire crews.

"Let's find the battalion chief and see what they know," Emily said. "Then talk to these folks before they disappear."

"I'll start with the campers," Javier said and headed toward the edge of the homeless refugees. The shock of what had happened to them was wearing off, and anger was poking through. Shouts blamed the city for allowing the fires to occur, for insufficient shelters, and for ignoring the invisible people.

Emily spotted a public information officer from the fire department speaking with a small knot of reporters. She avoided the media circle and skirted around them, overhearing bits and pieces of the PIO's statement, including the words *arson*, *injuries*, and *investigation ongoing.*

The white helmet identified the battalion chief standing at the edge of the smoldering remains.

"Hey, Chief," Emily said.

Battalion Chief Tommy Mercer turned and nodded. "Detective, this is escalating. The folks who escaped got out with nothing. We got burn injuries and blunt force trauma."

"They get trampled?"

"The doctors will have to verify, but we got reports of a guy attacking them with a baseball bat as the fire spread through the camp. Pretty brutal stuff."

"How many injured?"

"Sixteen. The first wave was triaged and sent off to the UC Med Center or the burn unit. This place went up like a tinderbox. Some were trapped in their tents."

Emily took in the remains of the sprawling community. Blackened husks of plywood, pools of charred tent fabric, and the sight of children's toys strewn in the ash made her feel sick.

"Hey, Chief," a firefighter halfway to the riverbank called out. "Got one."

Another burn victim? Emily thought, but the way the firefighter reacted told Emily there was more than a scorched camper.

Emily followed the battalion chief down the embankment, careful to avoid steaming melted plastic and smoldering tree limbs. Her feet crunched through the blackened grass, and ten feet from the firefighter, the smell hit.

Burnt human flesh.

Emily raised her forearm over her nose. She'd encountered burn victims before, but this one was fresh and severe. A plastic tent had melted and coated the dead with a blue and red cocoon.

"You find any other bodies?" Emily asked.

"We have one more row of tents—or what used to be tents, but this is the only one—so far," the firefighter said. The color had drained from his face.

Emily bent closer to the charred body. She stopped covering her nose and focused on the task.

She wouldn't move the body until the medical examiner was on scene. But this victim—the way it lay face down felt odd. Posed, perhaps. What Emily could tell is that the victim didn't burn to death. He was shot in the back of the head.

CHAPTER THREE

EMILY REASSIGNED A uniformed officer to secure the scene. She wasn't sure what there was to secure. The camp had been trampled by the fleeing homeless, by streams of water, hoses and boots of the firefighters. She set up a perimeter fifty feet from the body in all directions and hoped it was enough.

Javier joined Emily near the melted tent. "Just the one?"

"They're finishing up. For now, he's our one and only."

"Witnesses report two men. One lighting the fire and another with a ball bat as they worked their way through the camp."

"The ME could say otherwise, but this doesn't look like a bat injury."

"Not unless they make Louisville Slugger in a .38 caliber," Javier said.

"You recall anyone reporting two suspects at the earlier homeless camp fires?"

"I haven't read those files so couldn't say."

"Me either. Looks like we've been reassigned. The Watch Commander said the order came from the top."

"You know Simmons and Taylor are gonna love getting their case pulled."

"Well, we can't worry about hurting their feelings right now. These attacks are definitely escalating. There were women and children here."

"There's no official head count, but the best the witnesses can guess is that there were about a hundred eighty people living here. No actual problems and get this—they had their own security."

"They needed more."

"They were the two first victims assaulted. Both taken to the Med Center."

Emily circled the body, keeping a distance from the corpse. The tent with the dead homeless victim was the last one charred. Three more rows of tents were trampled, but untouched by the flames.

"Why'd they stop here?"

"Maybe they got spooked after they did this one?"

"Possible. Took it one step too far and split."

"None of the witnesses mentioned the assailants running off. They were 'whooping it up' when they ransacked the camp. And no one mentioned a gunshot."

Emily spotted the white van from the medical examiner's office at the access road. The police department's crime scene technicians arrived in a separate van.

A thinly built crime scene tech lugged a pair of heavy black nylon bags to the edge of the yellow taped perimeter.

"Got here as soon as possible, Detectives. Three mom-and-pop store robberies in midtown and a drive-by in South Sacramento."

"You cover all those alone, Linc?" Emily asked.

"Lopez had tickets for the Kings. Miller and Ripp called in lame."

"You saved the best for last, Linc," Javier said, opening his arms to the devastated homeless camp.

"Oh, great. I can feel the hepatitis from here. Where do you want me to start?"

Emily told him to get a few photos of the body before the medical examiner started her examination.

Linc set his bags down in a patch of unburnt grass and removed a bulky 35mm camera. He began snapping off a series of photos of the body and the adjacent debris.

"Hey, Detectives." Deputy Forensic Pathologist Dr. Elizabeth White joined Emily and Javier. Dressed for business in a disposable light blue HAZMAT suit and protective booties, the medical examiner took stock of the scene.

"I'm going to wrap this up quickly here. I need to peel all the molten material off our victim, and I'd prefer to do it in a controlled environment."

Dr. White moved in and directed one of her staff to the opposite side of the body.

"Let's see what we have here. Third-degree burns upper torso and both arms. Typical pugilistic muscle contraction from extreme heat."

"Does that mean they were alive when the fire swept over them?" Javier asked.

"Not necessarily. I'll need lab work, blood gasses, and lung tissue to verify which came first, the fire or the wound to the occipital bone."

"Small mercy," he said.

"Let's roll him, toward me," Dr. White said.

She and her assistant repositioned the charred body from its face-down position until it rested on its right side. The front of the victim was untouched by the flames.

"Okay. We have a white male, approximately fifty years of age. No exit wound from the apparent gunshot to the occipital portion of the head noted on initial exam. This partially answers your question, Detective. He was face down when the fire got to him."

The dead man's damaged face was vaguely familiar. Emily couldn't place when she encountered the homeless man. But she'd seen that face before.

The doctor and her assistant rolled the victim on his back. "I'd usually take a liver temp because it's protocol, but the residual heat in the body will throw off the results. You have a good fix on the time the fire broke out, right?"

Emily nodded. "About an hour ago."

"I don't want to take any shortcuts here." Her assistant handed a long temperature probe. She ran a gloved hand below the rib cage of the dead man and inserted the probe.

As many times as Emily witnessed the procedure, it always made her wince. One more violation of the victim.

"Huh. That's odd," Dr. White said.

"What?" Emily asked.

"The temp. Even considering the heat. You can feel the heat radiating from the body. The liver temp is lower than I would have thought. I'm reading ninety-four degrees. If you figure the usual one-and-a-half-degree heat loss per hour after death, our estimated time of death would be three hours ago. With the heat exposure, I'd be willing to say four to six hours."

"He was shot well before the camp was set ablaze," Emily said.

"Seems safe to say so, yes."

"Any identification on the guy?" Emily asked.

The doctor ran a flat hand around the pockets, careful to avoid accidental needle sticks.

"Don't feel anything. I'll let you sift through what's left of the tent and see if you can find a wallet or ID." She examined a charred, burnt fist. "Won't be able to live scan for prints. I'll need dental to compare for a match."

"Homeless aren't typically up to date on their dental exams, if we even knew what dentist to ask."

"John Doe, it is."

She directed her two attendants to prepare the body for transport. A clear plastic tarp went on the ground next to the body and the attendants lifted the stiff, charred body onto the plastic sheet. The tarp was folded over the dead man to ensure any trace evidence, in this case melted debris from the tent, was preserved.

The encased body was secured into a black zippered body bag before the two attendants lugged the remains up the embankment to their van.

Movement near the river caught Emily's attention. At first, she thought it was a firefighter bending over to pick up an object at the river's edge.

"Check it out," Emily said.

It wasn't a firefighter. It was a small girl. She was peeking over a boulder on the shoreline.

"How did she get down there? I'll chase her off," a uniformed officer said.

"No, I've got it," Emily said. "Javi, mind going through what's left of the tent to see if we can find a clue to tell us who we've got?"

"Sure, can't wait to dig around."

Emily ambled down to the river, careful not to spook the girl.

The child held fast behind the rock and when Emily got within ten feet, she squatted down. "Hi, my name's Emily. What's yours?"

The girl didn't respond but edged warily around the rock to cast an eye on Emily.

"Do you live here?" Emily asked.

She ducked behind the rock once more.

"I'm not going to hurt you. Do you have someone here? Can I help you find them?" Emily hoped it wasn't the charred remains of the man they'd bagged up.

"Momma—I want my momma," a slight voice called out from behind the rock.

A slight wave of relief washed over Emily, confirming the girl's guardian wasn't the dead man.

"Okay, I'll help you find your mom. What's your momma's name?"

"Momma."

Emily thought about going to the rock and approaching the girl, but she would probably skitter off into the thick brush encircling the camp.

"Tell me what your momma looks like so I can help you find her."

"She's really tall. She's pretty, and nice."

Emily's heart melted a bit.

"There's a bunch of people up there waiting. Your mom might be there. Come, let's go see." Emily stood and extended her hand, waiting.

A moment later, the girl appeared from behind the rock, clutching a worn stuffed animal under one arm.

She grasped Emily's hand, and Emily felt the small icy fingers grip hers.

"Let's go see what we can find out about your momma. What's your name?"

"Willow. And this is Mr. Bunny."

"Nice to meet you both. Can you tell me where you lived?"

Willow pointed ahead two rows into the charred camp.

Emily nodded to Javier. "I'm going to take Willow here to find her mom."

As they walked to the access road, Emily asked, "How did you two get separated?"

"Momma told me to run and hide when the bad men came."

"You were a good hider. Did you see the men?"

Willow nodded. "Bad."

At the access road, Emily walked Willow to the edge of the homeless group huddling at the barrier.

"I'm looking for this girl's mother."

No initial response from the gathering. Emily thought they were afraid to come forward.

"Does anyone know Willow's mother?"

A bushy red-haired woman pressed to the front of the crowd. "I know her," she said, her lips caught on the blackened stubs of meth-damaged teeth.

"Do you know her mom's name?"

"Lisa. Lisa Larkin. What's you gonna do with the girl?"

"Know where her mom is?"

"She got hurt down there. Got herself took off to the hospital."

Emily bent to Willow. "Did the bad men do something to your mom?"

Willow nodded.

"You can leave her with me. I can care for her til her mom gets back."

"I can't do that. We'll get her taken care of and find her mom."

"Care? What a crock of shit. Gonna dump her in foster care is what you're gonna do. Won't do nobody no good."

"Anyone know the man we found down there?"

Silence reappeared at the mention of the dead man. The homeless weren't going to fill in the blanks for Emily.

Javier returned to the access road. He removed his gloves and dropped them in a biowaste container set at the edge of the perimeter.

"Got nothing there to tell us who he was. Hey, who's this?"

"This is Willow, and her mom is getting taken care of in the hospital."

The unspoken message was the kid's mom is one of the badly injured victims sent to the trauma center, and she's alone.

"Hi there, my name's Javier."

She hid behind Emily.

"It's okay. He's one of the good guys. Javi, you get everything you could?"

"Yeah. It's not much, but I ran into the arson investigator down there and he's going to give us his preliminary report in the morning. Off the top, he said it's like the last two burns—an accelerant was used to get this started, then it takes off on its own."

Emily nodded.

"Let's go find your mom."

CHAPTER FOUR

THE UNIVERSITY MEDICAL Center was the Level I Trauma Unit in the region. Neighbors had long gotten used to the helicopter landings on the hospital's roof, depositing accident victims and broken downhill skiers. It was also the repository for shooting victims and overdose cases.

Emily expected a Friday evening overflow crowd in the emergency room waiting area. She was not disappointed. They entered the lobby to face a tense standoff between two rival gangs.

Emily recognized one player decked out in blue—blue track pants, blue puffer jacket, and blue ball cap. Mika Hyde, a shot caller in one of the local Crip gang sets, was chest to chest with a larger man wearing a red bandanna and red T-shirt.

The families in the waiting room, holding blood-soaked compresses to injuries, or passed out from whatever they ingested, didn't seem phased by the loud display. Another night in the city.

Emily turned to Willow. "You stay with Javier for a minute. I'll be right back."

Willow clutched Mr. Bunny tight, and Javier led the girl to the information desk.

Emily sidled up to Mika. "What's the problem here, Mika?"

"Hey, Detective."

"What's this, Mika? You bringing your cracker-ass girlfriend in to bail you out?" the other man said.

"Too Loose here forgot where he at. One of mine and one of his went at it, and here we are," Mika said.

"Hey, both of you step back. The hospital is neutral ground. You know that. You got a beef with one another, take it outside. Now. Do I need to get some officers here to shake you down for weapons and whatever else you all might be packing?"

"Too Loose? Hear me?"

"Yeah, I hear you. Whatever. This ain't over, Mika."

Emily gave Mika a hard look that said, *Don't push it.*

Too Loose and three red-clad thugs stormed out of the waiting room.

"Mika, how's your mom? She managing after her heart attack last month?" Emily asked.

"Doctors say she'll be okay if she rests. But you know her. She's back to work in the bakery."

"If she knew you were out here doing this, she'd worry, and it wouldn't be good for her, you know?"

"Yeah, I know."

"Who you got in there?" Emily said, pointing at the emergency room door.

"Lil' Tommy. Needed a couple stitches is all. He'll be fine."

"Good. Get him and go home. Hear me? Your mom don't need this grief."

Mika glanced over at Javier with Willow.

"Who's the sprout?"

"Her mom got caught up in a fire at one of the homeless camps. We're here to check in on her."

"Man, that's a raw deal. Them fires is getting outta hand. We've started having our people watch the camps. They got no place to go and then someone does this to them."

"You be careful. There were two guys at this last burn and it got violent. You see or hear anything, you call me, okay?"

Mika nodded as Javier waved for Emily.

"What'd you find?" she asked.

"They have three women in the burn unit from the camp fire without identification. Willow gave the nurses a description and they are going to look and try to identify her mom, Lisa Larkin."

Willow nodded.

"They said someone would be out to talk to us," Javier said.

Emily scanned the waiting room. The overflow crowd meant no one was going to come and update them soon.

"Come with me," she said and started pushing them through the crowd to the elevators. She ushered Willow and Javier inside and hit the button for the second floor.

The burn unit included its own ICU, and the second floor was warmer than the lobby. Emily remembered being told the last time she was here that the higher temperature was necessary because burn victims can't regulate their own body temperature.

Emily approached a nurse's station after asking Javier to stay near the elevator with Willow.

She pulled her badge and identified herself to the nurse at the counter.

"The little girl over there—we think her mother is one of the unidentified burn victims brought in from the camp. Any chance you can check? I'd like to have someone give the girl a once-over, too. Need to make sure she's all right after this."

Emily gave her the description Willow had provided, minus the tall and pretty characteristics the girl recited.

"This might be easy. Only one of the three is white. The other two are Black. Let me go see where they are with her."

The nurse strode down the hallway, ducked into a room, and popped her head out, motioning to Emily.

Emily put a palm out to tell Javier to stay put, and she joined the nurse at the threshold to the patient room.

"The patient's burns aren't severe. The attending doctors debrided and cleaned the burns—mostly on her back and legs. Her primary medical issue at this point is blunt force trauma to the head. X-rays show a small fracture, and we're concerned about swelling and brain bleed at this point."

Lisa lay face down with a wire frame around her lower body, keeping the sheet from touching the raw, sensitive skin. A tube snaked up the side of the hospital bed and entered the woman's throat. A light bandage lay atop the wound on the back of her head. A shaved section of scalp showed around the edges.

"I take it she's unconscious?"

"Yes. She's been that way since we admitted her."

"Momma?" a weak voice from the hallway sounded.

"Sorry, she got away from me," Javier said.

Emily took Willow's hand.

"Is this your mom?"

Willow nodded. "Is she okay?"

"She's resting now and they are taking good care of her."

Willow eyed a chair in the corner of the room. She pulled away from Emily and plopped on the chair. She was so small and vulnerable. Her legs swung under the seat, swaying to a sad internal song.

"You can spend a minute or two with her, then we need to let her rest," Emily said, giving the nurse an eye.

The nurse nodded and backed out of the room.

Javier edged close to Emily. "What are we gonna do with the girl? Want me to get someone from the hospital to call CPS?"

"I know we need to get them involved, but my God, this kid has gone through enough, don't you think?"

"She can't stay here."

"Willow, do you have any family we can call? Anyone who can come and be with you and your mom? Grandparents, maybe?" Emily figured it was a long shot.

Willow shook her head. "Momma said her parents aren't around anymore. We're not supposed to talk about it."

"Before you even think about it, Em, you cannot take her home with you. She's not a stray."

"I know, I know." She pulled her phone from a pocket and scrolled through her contact list. Emily tapped on one and stepped out into the hallway.

"Hey, Patty, it's Emily. I got a big problem with a small package. Her mom is over here in the burn unit ICU and she doesn't have anyone or anyplace to go. She's been through enough for one day. You think you could help?"

Emily returned to the room. Willow was asleep in the chair. The girl didn't even notice a nurse fussing with her and cleaning a slice on the web of her right hand. She applied a bandage and gently put the sleeping girl's arm down.

"Only a minor cut. Looks fine otherwise."

"Dammit, Javi. Why do I feel like such an ass?"

"About this? I don't know. You usually have lots of other reasons—totally legitimate reasons."

She smacked him on the arm and noticed a large plastic bag tucked under the patient's bed.

Ducking down, she reached under and pulled the plastic bag from under the bed. Inside, the remnants of Lisa's clothing and personal items were sealed up tight. Partially burnt, Emily could see the straight lines where they were cut off of the patient.

Javier leaned on the doorframe, tapping notes on his phone. He preferred the electronic method and the no-mess, no-clutter approach.

"What are you gonna do when your battery drains and all your case notes disappear?"

"You know this is the way to go. Don't hate. Besides, these notes get transcribed into the case files when we get back to the office."

"I'm just sayin' either your battery will fail or the network will go down, and then where are you? Besides, some defense attorney is bound to subpoena your phone to compare notes, and she's gonna stumble on all those selfies you take in the bathroom."

"One time. I did that one time."

A slight knock on the room door.

"Hi, I got here as soon as I could." Patty Thompkins stepped inside. A slight Black woman in skinny jeans and a thin insulated vest. The ever-present reading glasses hung on a gold chain around her neck. Emily could never pin down her age, but guessed she was in her fifties, but looked no more than forty.

"That was quick," Emily said.

"Is she our girl?" Patty asked, tipping her head at Willow, still sound asleep on the chair.

"Her name's Willow. and she and her mom were living out at the river when the place got torched. Mom got hurt and there doesn't seem to be anyone else."

"Okay then. I can take it from here."

"Where will she go?"

"I'll get her tucked in at the Receiving Home. There are a handful of girls her age. Give her a chance to be around other kids while mom gets better. I'll let her sleep for a while. No rush to get her moving. I've got this, Emily. You guys can get going."

"I don't want to abandon her," Emily said.

"You're not. I'm here."

"Can I check in on her at the Receiving Home?"

"Of course. And I'll let Willow know."

Emily bit her lower lip and nodded. She gathered the bag with Lisa's burnt and shredded clothing.

On the way to the car, Javier said, "You got pretty attached to the kid."

"Yeah, I kinda feel for her, you know? I thought what it would be like to be her age, alone with her mom, living in a tent by the river. Those camps—they get—you have to be tough to survive. I hope Willow has a shot at some kind of life after this."

* * *

When they returned to the detective bureau, Emily dropped the bag of partially burnt clothing in a paper evidence bag, sealing it closed.

Emily saw the light on in the lieutenant's office. Newly promoted Lieutenant Larry Hall was a twenty-year veteran on the job, had worked in every division, from patrol to vice, and took to the lieutenant's role like he was born to it. It didn't come easy, and it didn't come without some grumbling in the ranks. Hall was Black and gay, a bridge too far for some of the old guard.

"Knock-knock," Emily said.

"Hey, Hunter. I heard you took the call for the camp fire tonight. How'd it go?"

Hall pushed back in his chair, his six-three frame stretched under his desk.

"We have one death. Over a dozen transported for treatment. Could have been much worse. The ME is preliminarily calling it a homicide. Looks like he was killed before the fire started. Gunshot to the back of the head."

"Sounds like an execution. Let me guess, no one saw or heard the shooter?"

"Nope. We have reports of two white guys setting the fire and assaulting the homeless residents with a bat. Put sixteen in the hospital with a combination of burns and blunt force trauma."

"This is what? The third arson of a homeless center? We've made no progress on a solve. They are getting bolder with the physical attacks. If it were a straight up murder, we'd call it a serial. In some ways, it would be easier."

"I hear you, Lieutenant. We don't have enough coming in to warrant a tip line. Most of the city feels like, if it's only happening to the homeless, then it doesn't matter."

"And the NIMBY folks aren't losing any sleep over it."

"We have a couple of threads to pull, but the arson and the shooting might not link up. Maybe we'll get lucky with ballistics. If not, there isn't much to go on," Emily said.

"You need more help? I can assign another detective or two."

"Not right now. Besides, I think Simmons and Taylor are gonna be pissed they got pulled off this one as it got more interesting."

"They had their shot at this one. The chief is getting outside pressure to get this under control. You know what that means."

"The mayor is a lot of talk about shelters and services, but we still have two thousand people camping out in places like the tent city on the river. She just got elected and hasn't done anything."

"And you can say your piece in this office—but it stays here."

"Yeah, I get it. You know me, I'm always politically correct," Emily said.

"I know exactly, Detective, hence the warning," Hall said through a grin.

"Lieutenant, I'm hurt."

"File a grievance."

Emily chuckled. "Don't think I won't. I'll keep you posted, boss. What do you want me to say to Simmons and Taylor?"

"I gave them the news. They're to give you all their case information this morning."

"How'd they take it?"

"You don't need to be concerned about it. What you do need to be concerned with is the corner office wants my best on the case, so they're gonna expect results—no pressure."

"Your best?"

"You must have misheard me, Hunter. Go get a solve on this one, would you?"

Emily pressed off the doorjamb. "Will do."

Javier was finishing downloading his notes. "The lieutenant getting heat from on high?"

"He is. We need to do our jobs and get this murder pinned down."

"Doesn't it seem like the two aren't connected? The fire and the murder?"

Emily plopped into her chair, a relic handed down from other detectives. "The fact they didn't burn the last row of tents bothers me. Maybe they got spooked and split? I don't want to write off a connection yet. I'd feel better if we had evidence one way or another."

"Done."

"What's done?" she asked.

"My case notes. All entered into the file."

"I'm going to do mine the old-fashioned way—" As soon as she said "old-fashioned," she regretted the word choice. "I meant the right way."

"I heard you the first time. What do you need me to do?"

"Go home and get some rest. Maybe Jenny and your mom have your engagement party planned."

"You are a mean-spirited woman, Hunter. But, yeah, I should see what I have left of my life."

Emily waved him off and caught up on her case notes. It took her longer than she thought, and she considered Javier's new-fangled approach more than once. Even though she was younger than her partner.

She took the evidence bag of Lisa Larkin's property to a long, open table. After covering the table with brown craft paper, she sat the bag on the surface.

Donning a pair of purple nitrile gloves, Emily opened the bag and arranged Lisa's clothing, a necklace, and shoes on the paper. The burnt odor from the clothing was strong. Emily hoped it was only material and plastic and not human flesh.

The sum total of a woman's life lay in front of her. Emily used a pair of forceps to pull the material apart, looking for some sign of what—and why—she was targeted. It could be as simple as Willow thought it to be—Lisa was attacked at random, solely because she was in the way.

Emily would have to dry the clothes. They were wet. She didn't remember the fire department's hoses trained on the tent.

She laid the pants out and checked the pockets for loose debris: drugs, keys, money, but she found a single waterlogged business card. It was smudged and nearly unreadable, but the bottom edge of the card was legible. A phone number, and a name, Pete Bell, River City Foster & Adoption Services. An appointment written in ink on the back said Lisa was to have met with Bell a few hours before she was attacked.

Lisa was thinking about giving up her daughter.

It was late, but Emily dialed the number on the card. She held the phone against her shoulder and she finished sorting through the items on the table. Nothing else to shed light on her attacker, or why—until she spotted a soot-covered lump caught in the rolled cuff of her pant leg.

The phone went to a recorded message. Bell was unavailable. Leave a message. Emily hung up and would try again in the morning.

She unrolled the pant leg, working around where a chunk of melted blue material clung to the fabric. The short cylindrical object was familiar. A brass .380 caliber shell casing.

CHAPTER FIVE

WHAT WAS THE probability of a brass casing, the same caliber as the one apparently used to murder the victim found in the camp, ending up in Lisa's clothing?

Emily slipped the metallic shell into a small evidence bag, making a mental note to have the lab geeks run the shell through NIBIN, the National Integrated Ballistic Information Network. The national system held over four-and-a-half-million pieces of evidence. It wasn't uncommon for a single handgun to tie to multiple shootings.

"How did this end up with you, Lisa?"

Had her burn victim become a suspect?

It was closing on midnight before Emily secured all the evidence away and left the detective bureau.

During the short drive to her midtown refurbished Victorian home, Emily couldn't get Willow off her mind. The kid was not off to a good start in life. Homeless, scraping by in a camp on the river, witnessing what happened to her mom, all combined to create a toxic foundation.

She pulled up to her place, and as she unlocked her front door, she felt a familiar rub against her legs.

"You again? Isn't it a little late for you to be out?"

A pair of yellow eyes stared back at her.

Emily opened her door, and the cat slipped in ahead of her.

"Oh, yes, please. Come in, won't you?"

Emily locked her gun away, changed, and fell into her bed. She felt a slight weight curl onto her legs. The cat hadn't ventured into her bedroom before, let alone onto her bed. Emily was too exhausted to protest the feline trespass.

What seemed like minutes later, her phone rang. Emily glanced at her bedside alarm: 5:50.

She grabbed her phone and held it to her ear. "Hunter."

"Miss Hunter, this is Tina Johnson at Western Care."

Emily's heart froze at the mention of her mom's assisted living facility.

"Miss Hunter?"

"Yes, yes. What's happened? Is Mom all right?"

"We've had a bit of an incident. She's okay. But we think it would help calm her down if she could see you."

"Incident?" The last incident involved a claim her mom threw a plate at an in-home caregiver—which led to the agency calling the police on her seventy-year-old mother.

"She's very agitated. Confused, actually. She's asking for Robert. Do you know who that might be?"

Emily did. But she didn't want to tell them her mom was asking for her husband, who died twenty years ago.

"I'll be right there."

Emily quickly showered, changed, and carried an unhappy cat to the front porch.

"Go home!"

Emily selected Western Care Assisted Living with the help of Javier's mother. She used to work at the facility and swore they were the best in town. The first few months, they were. Connie was adjusting. Her memory loss had slowed its pace of decline. Three months ago, the facility was bought out by a large health care chain.

Emily started getting emails from their corporate office about the changeover, ensuring her that patient care was their number one priority. The facility developed new treatment plans to address specific patient needs. The only things Emily noticed were a gradual decline in her mother's condition and a monthly cost increase.

Emily found the front door of the facility unlocked at half-past six. The policy required the door locked until the day shift came in and the entrance was monitored.

She made it all the way to her mother's room before she spotted anyone from the facility staff. She didn't know this one—there was so much staff turnover.

"Excuse me? Is there someone I can talk to about my mother, Connie Hunter?"

The woman shrugged. "Try the break room." She wandered off, nose down in her phone, before Emily could ask where the break room was.

She heard a loud laugh down the hallway and figured that's where they were. First to look in on her mom.

She pushed the door open, and the lights were off. A shadow in the room's corner caught Emily's eye. Her mother was sitting in a chair, rocking back and forth slowly, humming an unfamiliar tune.

Emily flicked on a bedside lamp, casting a yellow glow to the room. Her bed was unmade, but Emily's heart sank when she saw the wet stain on the sheets.

"Mom? How are you doing?"

The rocking continued, but Connie flicked an eye open. "Oh, hello, dear."

A slight pang of relief swept through Emily. She knew who she was.

"How was school?"

And there it went. Connie had lost touch where and when she was again. A major lapse like that hadn't happened in over a year.

"Hi, Mom. Can you look at me for a minute?"

"Whatever for, dear?" Connie didn't look up and kept rocking.

Emily put her hand on her mother's arm and stopped the rocking. The touch roused Connie from wherever she was.

"Hi, honey. Can I get you anything?"

"No, Mom. What can I get for you?"

"I'm fine. I'm getting ready for your father to get home from work."

And there it was. Emily felt her heart breaking.

"Mom, Dad's not coming home tonight. Let's get you back in bed, and we need to change your clothes."

Emily found a nightgown in her dresser drawer and took her mother to the bathroom to change. She cringed at the rash from lying in her own urine.

"Mom, let's get you comfy on the sofa while I get someone to change your sheets."

"Don't bother them, dear. They get angry when I ask them for too much."

"Oh, they do, do they?"

Emily got her mother comfortable, then marched down to the break room where she pushed in and found six staff members sitting around a table, a deck of cards in mid-deal, and an open box of donuts.

The staff person closest to the door, a skinny, bleached-blonde with dark roots about three inches in, put her cards face down.

"This is a private area. You aren't supposed to be here."

"You're supposed to be out there," Emily said, hooking a thumb back toward the rooms.

"They're all asleep, anyhow. How'd you even get in here?"

"The woman in 105 needs some attention."

"Oh, her. She always wants something."

Emily felt her blood pressure boil.

"Get up off your ass and go take care of her."

"Who do you think you are? You don't get to come in here and tell us how to do our business."

"Actually, I do. I'm paying for that woman in 105. I pay your salary—and it's not to sit around and play cards while residents need help."

An olive-skinned woman at the far end of the table started to get up.

Emily pointed at her. "You, sit down. I want you to do it," she said, looking at the loudmouthed blonde.

"I don't have to do a damn thing. You need to leave. This is private property. Don't make me call the police on your ass."

"Don't bother." Emily pulled her jacket aside, displaying her badge as she pulled her radio. "10-Adam-24, Silver-6."

The radio crackled to life. "10-Adam-24."

"Adam-24, please respond to Western Care Assisted Living to take a report on elder abuse."

"10-4, en route."

A pair of women at the far end of the table shuffled away from the table and snuck out behind Emily.

The bottle-blonde remained defiant and seated. "Is that supposed to scare me?"

"Last chance. You gonna go take care of Connie Hunter in 105?"

"Pfft—she can wait until the day shift comes on."

Emily had had enough and was fuming at the lack of concern over a helpless old woman. If her mother experienced this, Emily knew she wasn't the only one.

"Stand up."

The bottle-blonde shot up from her chair. "What, you wanna get tough, bitch?"

Emily's hand snaked out and grabbed the woman's arm, spinning her around and bending her over the table. Handcuffs snapped on and everyone else in the room left. Patting the employee down, Emily felt a hard object in her front right pocket. She reached in and retrieved a meth pipe and three baggies of yellow-tinted crystalline powder.

Emily dragged the skinny blonde to the lobby and parked her on the sofa facing the front doors.

The automatic doors opened and two uniformed officers entered. The handcuffed woman's false bravado fell with each step they took.

"I need this job."

"Shoulda thought about that before, don't ya think?"

"Detective, what do you have for me?" A stern Officer Brian Conner stood with his arms crossed.

"Princess here is in possession of a controlled substance, and we have her for elder abuse." Emily showed him the pipe and baggies.

"Could you have your partner sit on her for a second while I talk with you?"

Brian jutted his head toward the handcuffed woman and his partner, a six-three, thick-necked man with a face that could have been carved out of granite, stepped next to the detainee. "Start getting her info, would you, Tucker?"

Emily led Brian around the corner. She grabbed his arm. "I am way out of policy on this one. Elder abuse—I mean it is—but I took her into custody based on my emotions. And dammit, she pissed me off."

"You did find her in possession."

"Only after I put her in cuffs for personal reasons. That evidence will never be admissible. I screwed up, Brian. Now she'll walk and probably take it out on my mom and the others who live here."

Emily spotted two of the employees from the break room coming out of her mother's room. Both sheepishly locked eyes with Emily.

"We're sorry, Miss Hunter. Your mother is all taken care of. Janice—well, she runs the night shift and told us if we didn't go along with her way of doing things, she'd make it hard on us."

"Her way of doing things?"

"Put everyone to bed, then party time. Now we can finally do our jobs again."

Emily wasn't sure how sincere the woman was. If she hadn't interrupted *party time*, would her mother's care have resumed?

The two women scurried away, and Emily entered her mom's room with Brian. Connie was dressed for the day, her bedding changed, and the room was tidied up.

"Oh, hello, honey. It's nice to see you again."

A faint blessing of dementia meant Connie couldn't remember the unpleasant events of the evening.

"Hi, Mom. I wanted to drop by and say hello."

Connie squinted at Brian next to her. There was a tint of confusion in her eyes.

"You remember Brian? He's helping me with a few things."

"He's a pretty one."

Brian blushed.

"Yes, Mom, he is. But we try not to let him know that."

A quiet knock at the room door. The door slid open, and a woman slipped into the room. Her eyes widened when she spotted Brian in his uniform.

"Um . . . Miss Hunter, may I have a word? I think there's been a misunderstanding."

"The misunderstanding is this was a care facility. First, I get a call saying there was an incident involving my mother, then I get here and I find the facility unlocked, my mother in distress, and all the staff are having a blowout in the break room. How can we trust you?"

"We take this kind of thing very seriously."

"So. Do. I. What do you think your corporate people are going to think when I tell them about drugs and elder abuse in this place?"

"I'm sure that's an overreaction."

Emily wished she had another pair of handcuffs.

"Come on, Mom, we're going for a drive."

CHAPTER SIX

THE NEXT TWO hours were consumed with getting her mother home and settled. A call to Javier and his mother was at Emily's place, ready to spend the day with her mom.

"You're a lifesaver, Mrs. Medina."

"Nonsense. This happens. I haven't spent much time with Connie since she moved to Western Care. As soon as Javier told me what happened, I called a friend in their corporate offices. I think things are about to get wild over there at the facility. About time, too."

"Thanks for sitting with her today. I'll figure a solution for the long term. But for today, I think she's worn out and should sleep. I can't thank you enough."

Lucinda Medina shooed Emily out of her own house. "Go on now. Keep my boy out of trouble."

Emily met Javier at the address listed for River City Foster Care and Adoption Services, a small storefront in North Sacramento, off of Bearcut.

The social service agency was tucked next to an auto repair shop and a check cashing establishment. Javier was waiting in his car when Emily arrived.

"Mom doing okay?" he asked.

"Thanks to your mom, yes."

"I hear you arranged a date with Officer Conner over the radio."

"I did not."

"It has a desperate vibe to it. That's what everyone is saying."

"If they are, it's because you started the rumor."

Javier shrugged.

Emily pushed into the office. The small waiting room was only deep enough for a desk and two chairs. The desk was empty and there was a hallway to the rear.

"Hello? Anyone here?" Emily called out.

"Be right there," a high-pitched voice called out from the hallway.

A woman popped out into the lobby, entirely too bubbly for this time of the morning. Her blue tinted hair and tie-dyed peasant blouse overpowered the small space.

"How can I help you? I'm sorry there wasn't anyone here to greet you. We usually have all the bases covered, but it's so busy right now and—are you two cops?" The rambling fell to a silent pause.

"Detectives Hunter and Medina. We're looking for Pete Bell," Emily said, referencing the name on the worn business card she found in Lisa's clothing.

"I'd like to talk to Pete, too. We were supposed to do some outreach today. But here I am and he's nowhere to be found. I'm sure he'll come traipsing on in any moment now. That's how he is—a free spirit and—"

"Outreach? Where do you do outreach at and what kind of services do you offer?"

"We focus on getting vulnerable youth off the street. We meet at the shelters, the food pantries, and the camps like the one on the river. Although, from what I hear, there was a terrible fire at a camp last night. Is it true? I hear it was a bad one. Was it? I had people come by while I was opening up and said some hate group burned the place up. Can you imagine? I don't know what the world is coming to these days. When I was—"

Emily glanced at a photograph on the wall. "Is this Pete? Pete Bell?"

The photograph featured three men, one Emily recognized as the former mayor, a rotund man with thinning gray hair, who still believed he was the Savior of Sacramento. If there was a photo op, or a cause of the day, Mayor Stone would be there, with a plastic smile on his face.

The other two men, Emily couldn't place.

"That's Pete on the right with Mayor Stone and his homeless advocate, Jensen something-or-another."

"Where was this taken?"

"I think it was last year at a fundraiser for the mayor's homeless awareness initiative for shelter bed expansion in the city. We need more beds to get the unhoused off the streets—"

"What is it you were supposed to do with Pete this morning?" Emily asked.

"It's a follow-up from a contact he made yesterday, I believe. A vulnerable young person and we have a chance to get her off the streets and into a stable environment. He met with the mother and after some convincing, Pete got her to agree to talk with us today. Imagine? Another Willow?"

Emily tensed. "Willow?"

"Yes. Can you believe it? Another Willow. I thought it was a sign because that's my name, too. I don't run across very many Willows."

Emily snuck a look at Javier while this Willow droned on about the origin of the name and how her mother thought it was such a lovely way to embrace her inner spirit that would bend but not break.

Emily unpocketed her phone and snapped a photo of the ex-mayor, Pete, and his aide, Jensen.

"Thanks, Willow. I think we have what we need for now. When Pete comes in, have him call me. I need to speak with him about Willow and her mother. They were caught up in the fire last night."

Willow's hands clutched her chest. "Are they all right?"

"No, I don't think they are. Have Pete call us the minute he comes in." Emily gave her a business card.

Once outside, Emily glanced at the photo on her phone again. "There's an agency to pull kids out of homeless camps? I mean, sure, the people need lots of help, but why those kids? Who pays for these services? Where do they go?"

"I get it. You remember I was a foster kid, right? My birth parents got deported and left me on this side of the border. I fell into the system and it's not pretty. I mean, I'm sure it's better than living under a tarp on the river but foster homes—a lot of them—treat the kids like property and cash the county checks."

Javier paused and cast a glance toward the burnt-out camp. "Smell that?"

There was an acrid, musty smoke blowing over from the former campsite. Emily wondered if the smoldering ruins had reignited in the drought-stricken dry grass.

"Let's make a pass and see what's going on."

They got in their cars and headed for the camp less than a mile away. They parked near the 7th Street access road where a single fire engine was working, but what surprised Emily was the sight of a pair of small tractors plowing up the camp debris into a single pile. Tents, clothing, plastic bags, and human waste, all scraped up from the campsite and gathered into burn piles.

Three ten-foot-tall stacks of camp remnants were arranged on bare earth of what was the homeless community. One of them was ablaze. A pair of firefighters stood ready to douse the flames if they threatened to jump the dirt containment lines.

"So much for walking our crime scene again," Emily said.

"It was a mess when we got here last night. We got all we were going to get. The fire, the water from the hoses, and the people who lived here trampled everything. We're lucky we even got a body out of here before they did this," Javier said.

"Makes you wonder why they jumped on this so fast."

A city vehicle was parked at the mouth of the access road. A man sat on the hood of the car, wearing the required white hard hat and orange reflective safety vest. He watched the activity from his perch.

"Morning," Emily said as they approached the white city vehicle.

"It's morning, I'll give you that," the man in the orange vest said.

"I don't recall the city ever moving this fast to clean up a homeless camp," Emily said.

"We just go where they tell us. Had this one listed as a priority when I got in this morning. I'm Tommy. Tommy Franklin from City Development."

"Detectives Hunter and Medina."

"Fellow city servants." Franklin gestured to the cleanup operation. "I mean, I get it. This site was a mess. Hypodermic needles, condoms, trash, not to mention the human shit threatening to spill into the river. Imagine the outrage then. The salmon run threatened by the human waste runoff. Not exactly the image our good mayor wants to project for the city."

"The smoke this is putting off can't be healthy," Javier said.

"Which is why I'm sitting upwind. Mostly agricultural land to the north of us. Besides, the city issued an exemption for the burn operation today. Can't say I've ever seen them do that before."

"No offense, but efficiency isn't the city's strength," Emily said. "I've never seen a public works project move in less than twelve hours for cleanup. We had levee breaks a few years back, and it took days to mobilize a work crew."

"I hear you. This crew got assigned out here. I wanted to see what the deal with this one was. There's a dozen others that are just as bad. The state crews evicted and took down camps under the freeways and those are still sitting there with piles of garbage. They're all an environmental hazard. This one was bigger, I'll give it that."

The second pile of refuse ignited. Flames and dark smoke erupted from the pyre. While the trash and debris burned, Emily couldn't help but think it was the last tangible property some residents possessed. The aluminum frames from a pair of backpacks and a grocery cart melted under the heat.

Emily watched them liquify and drip into the pile. The push to clean up the site so fast bothered Emily. She understood the political optics of getting rid of the unsavory side of the homeless epidemic, but this felt rushed. Someone wanted to make sure the camp's secrets were permanently locked away. Maybe it was her jaded view of politics and politicians. Maybe there was more to it.

CHAPTER SEVEN

"No."

"But, Lieutenant, this smells," Emily said.

Lieutenant Hall sipped his coffee and placed it down on his desk. "Detective, this coffee smells. I know it, you know it, hell, even the plumbers who have to snake out the sinks know it. But the thing is, it's our coffee. It's what we've got. Same with the mayor's office—it stinks, but it's the one we've got. And like it or not, the mayor gets to call the shots when it comes to city resources and what projects get priority."

"This was a crime scene less than a day ago."

"And what purpose would the mayor have in letting a camp lay in ruin? You're not suggesting the mayor wanted to hide evidence and had the camp destroyed, are you?"

"I don't know."

"You best know when you go down this path. In here, in this office, we can talk and speculate on all the different angles. But if you take a run at the mayor, I won't be able to protect you."

"I don't need protection. I want to know why evidence was destroyed. I need to find out why a scene was sanitized as quickly as it was."

Lieutenant Hall sighed. "I'm not going to dissuade you, am I?"

"I won't poke anyone with a sharp stick, Lieutenant."

"The fact you'll have a stick at all is what worries me. Go as far as finding out who signed off on the permits to move dirt out there. No further. No contact with the mayor's office."

Emily hopped up from her chair. "Thanks, LT."

"Don't thank me, Hunter. Be calm and composed."

"When am I not?"

The lieutenant suppressed a laugh and pointed to the door.

When she returned to her desk, Javier waved and continued to talk on the phone.

"We can be there in ten minutes." He hung up.

"We got competing protests going on over at City Hall. The Shelter For All Coalition and some anti-homeless group are going at it. Only some verbal jousting right now, but the Watch Commander thought we might be interested."

"Why not? We need to look into the camp cleanup permits, anyway."

Emily and Javier were headed to the door as Detectives Simmons and Taylor entered.

Simmons was a barrel-chested man who acted six-five, but was five-seven on a good day. He started shaving his head once the gray hairs outnumbered the brown. Detective Taylor was younger, good looking, but full of himself. He had a reputation for chasing after female cops and had made several plays to Emily with such great come-ons as, "I'd like to put you in cuffs," and "We should get together and let me frisk you." Who could resist? When Emily told him to pound sand, Taylor wrote it off to her being another lesbian cop.

"You here early to poach another case, Hunter?" Simmons said.

"I work the cases they give me. Maybe if you did the same, the chief wouldn't reassign your cases," she said.

"Well, you can have the camp arsons. No one cares what happens out there. We got us real cases to work on."

"Last night's burn turned up a homicide. You guys run across anything that might have said this was coming? What about threats, beefs, or warning these attacks were escalating?"

"It's a homeless camp. Who cares? Half of 'em are whack jobs who should be locked in a mental ward, and the rest are drug addicts or criminals. As long as they keep the violence to themselves, no one's really hurt."

Emily wasn't sure if Simmons was baiting her or not. "There's women and children in the Med Center who might not share your opinion."

"Ah, the city will throw them a few dollars in a settlement, and they'll be right back out there."

"Would you leave your case files on those arsons on my desk?"

"Sure, no problem. My advice is get the lieutenant to close them. They aren't worth the time and you're never going to pin them on anyone. Even if they knew who started the fires, those people won't talk to us about it."

"Wonder why."

"What?"

"Nothing. Just thinking out loud. We gotta run," Emily said.

"Yeah, we need to let Butch and Sundance go fight crime," Taylor said, emphasizing the word *Butch* while glaring at Emily.

Emily felt her fists clinch, her nails digging into her palms.

"Simmons, Taylor—in here," Lieutenant Hall called.

"The rainbow coalition is in full bloom today," Taylor said as he walked away from his partner.

"Hey, Hunter. I'm sorry for my partner—what he said. He gets outta line. But these cases, don't bust a grape over them. They ain't going anywhere." Simmons trod after Taylor.

As they pushed out the door, Javier turned to Emily. "To be clear, I'm Sundance, right?"

"Ass." She smacked him with a backhand to the shoulder.

*　*　*

A ten-minute drive put Emily and Javier a block away from City Hall. César Chávez Park sat across from the city building, and on a typical day it served as neutral ground where city employees, local government workers, and a transient vagrant population shared the space. Today was far from typical. The park was overrun with homeless who'd set up camp. Dozens of tents and cardboard shelters had been erected in the pre-dawn hours.

Posters and hand-drawn signs proclaimed the park was a safe zone for the unhoused with slogans like, RIGHT TO EXIST, WE'RE NOT INVISIBLE NOW, and FREE HOUSING.

Emily estimated a hundred people milled in the park.

"You figure these are the people who got burned out last night?" Emily said.

"Maybe. Don't see any familiar faces—the ones I interviewed. Where did the tents and shelters come from?"

"Check it out." Emily pointed across the street to the south of the park, where J Street traffic snarled to a standstill.

Protesters linked arms and moved against traffic chanting some indecipherable slogan. The signs translated the noise. SAVE OUR

CITY, NO ROOM FOR DEADBEATS, and the one grabbing Emily's attention, BURN 'EM OUT.

"Oh, this ought to be interesting," Javier said.

A line of uniformed police officers in riot gear, helmets, face shields, batons, and the telltale green- and orange-colored shotguns loaded with less-than-lethal rubber rounds. The officers walked a parallel path with the protesters, keeping them from spreading the disturbance. The department learned direct intervention and kettling, the practice of cornering protesters into a small area, blocking off exits, often escalated the disturbance.

The hundred protesters amped up their chants when the new homeless camp came into view. The line of officers kept the two groups apart. But the chants grew louder. Among them, "Burn them out—burn them out."

A handful of homeless campers formed a picket line, a weak line of defense if the protesters broke free of the police.

The protesters marched past the camp turning right on 9th Street, against the flow of traffic. They circled the park in front of City Hall when a Molotov cocktail landed in the center of the park.

The glass bottle shattered when it hit a cement pathway. It missed a cluster of tents by a few feet. The gasoline in the cocktail erupted into a pool of flame sending the park dwellers scattering amid screams and panic.

Four uniformed officers pushed through the protesters and grabbed the man who tossed the Molotov cocktail. Most of the nearby prote protesters stors backed away from the assailant who now lay face down on the street under an officer. Three officers kept the crowd off the arresting officer. No one moved to intervene.

The officer cuffed the bomb-thrower and pulled him to his feet. A worn, olive drab military surplus jacket, stringy, dirty blond hair, and a scraggly beard made the man look like he could have been on the other side of the protest. He pulled against the officer and yelled, "Save our city!"

"What's the chance this guy's our burner?" Emily asked.

"That would make it easy—so it's not gonna happen," Javier said.

Emily found the sergeant and the officer who held the bomber. The man was clearly agitated, sitting on the curb, rocking back and forth.

"Dude, what brings you out today?" Emily asked.

The man kept rocking and glanced up at Emily. "Gotta clean the streets, man."

"You got a name?"

"I don't gots to share that with you. As a sovereign citizen, I don't recognize your authority."

"Oh, God, one of them," Javier said.

The man glared back at Javier. "You're part of the problem, coming here taking jobs from citizens."

"I come from Los Angeles, so I can see where you might have a point there," Javier said.

A confused look crossed the man's face.

"Emily, this guy's not bright enough to plan any of this, let alone light the fuse on a Molotov cocktail."

Emily looked to the arresting officer. "You pat him down?"

He nodded. "Nothing on him. No lighter, if that's what you're asking. Could have dropped it out there on the street. He's the one who tossed it. I spotted him and he smells like gasoline."

"Who do you think wound his clock?" Emily said.

"No telling. He's definitely not the mastermind here."

"Get him booked and have the jail run livescan on his prints. Most of these sovereign citizen types are hiding a warrant or some other nonsense in their past."

"On it. Lucky for me the jail is walking distance," the officer said. "Come on, Sparky."

A change in the crowd's attitude in the park drew Emily's attention. Their gaze tracked to the front of City Hall, where a maintenance worker wheeled out a podium on a dolly.

"Oh, they are not serious," Emily said.

"Never let a crisis go to waste," Javier said.

At the northwest corner of the park, the opposing sides faced off, yelling at one another. A police line in the middle of the street continued to separate the factions.

The squeal from a microphone shot from portable speakers placed near the podium. Heads turned in the direction, and the mayor strode through the City Hall doors to the podium. Mayor Ellen Carsten was less than a year into her term after a landslide election against her scandal-ridden predecessor. She'd been viewed as a moderate during the election, but since then, her policies took a more conservative bent. Some viewed the sudden change as politics as usual, while others considered her policy shift as a betrayal.

She adjusted the microphone down to meet her five-five height. Behind her, the city council members fanned out in a rare show of unity.

"This ought to be interesting," Emily said.

"Who is she speaking to? There's only one news camera there."

"Citizens of our city. We have witnessed yet another attack on the most vulnerable members of our community. My administration and your city council will not tolerate the continued victimization and hate directed at our unhoused population. The hate turned deadly last night when a man was killed during an attack on one of the camps in our city. Our prayers go out to a man who didn't choose to live in a tent along the river—he had no option.

"His life—his legacy—will not end in a homeless camp. We have enacted an emergency ordinance banning all camping along the rivers in our city. The dangers to the inhabitants of these camps are too great to turn a blind eye."

Shouts erupted from the homeless protesters occupying the park. "Where are we supposed to go?"

The mayor raised her hand toward the park. "I have signed an order to establish five hundred new shelter beds to serve as temporary housing for our citizens in need. We've identified three shuttered hotel properties which can be opened quickly and each of our supervisorial districts will share the burden of siting and distributing the new additional shelter beds."

"Who's paying for this shit?" a voice called out from the mob.

"Another government handout!"

The mayor pressed on. "The better question is who's paying for the cost of these camps now? The burden on our mental health services, medical providers, and social services is overwhelming. We cannot allow this to continue. The shelter programs will provide wraparound services to get people back on their feet and out into the mainstream. We'll have more information for you shortly. Until these new beds are established, I'm ordering the city to lift the inner-city camping ban—except for the dangerous riverside encampments."

The mayor turned and strode back inside City Hall.

A man remained and swaggered to the reporter on scene for her exclusive. Emily recognized him as the third man in the photo she'd copied at the foster care establishment.

"Let's go get a word with Jensen."

"Didn't the lieutenant say to stay away from the mayor's office?"

"Technically, we're not going into the mayor's office. This guy's outside on the sidewalk."

"I doubt Lieutenant Hall will see the difference."

Emily and Javier stood back while the mayor's staffer finished up with the reporter. As they finished, Jensen turned on his heel and headed back toward the city building.

"Excuse me, Mr. Jensen?" Emily said.

He pivoted, expecting a follow-up from the reporter, and frowned when he found Emily and Javier.

"Yes, do you need a copy of the mayor's address? Which news service are you from?"

He handed a single sheet of paper bearing the city letterhead. A list of bullet points the mayor was to cover in the "impromptu" address.

"Mr. Jensen. I'm Detective Hunter and this is Detective Medina."

"Oh, detectives. How can I help you?"

Jensen tugged on his suit jacket. Emily noted the cut emphasized the man's trim build. A pair of emerald cuff links matched the color of his eyes.

"Mr. Jensen, we're investigating the fires in the camps."

"Good. As the mayor said, we need to do more to protect the unhoused community—sometimes, it's protecting them from themselves."

"I don't recall her saying that."

"As officers of the law, you should be the first to admit the camps, like the one on the river, attract a certain element. Predators go where the vulnerable live. The mayor's policy initiative interrupts the cycle. No more large, uncontrolled encampments where the weak and disadvantaged are victimized."

"I don't see that on her talking points either."

Jensen smiled. "Listen, the mayor has been outspoken in her position on services and shelter space for the unhoused. This city holds the dubious honor of the highest percentage of unhoused living on the street. Is that someplace you can be proud of? Is that a place where businesses want to invest?"

Emily recalled the photo at the foster care office. "It isn't often a new mayor will keep staff from an outgoing administration. Especially, one with—issues?"

Jensen smiled again. He was a man who knew how disarming his smile was, Emily figured.

"Mayor Carsten is a political outsider. It's probably her greatest strength. It's also a deficit, if she ignores how the game is played. I'm fortunate to help her bridge the gap. I've been in the game for over ten years. I'm ideologically more aligned to Mayor Carsten than I ever was with Stone. I'm committed to helping her achieve her vision. She's good people, Detective."

"What about those who don't want to live in a shelter? You can't force them inside."

That smile again.

"Listen, they can't care for themselves out there. Whatever happened in their lives to result in squatting in a camp under inhumane conditions in some *Lord of the Flies* reenactment, we have the responsibility to change that. You're not going to let a child run out into the freeway—we can't let people who can't make decisions choose to continue down this self-destructive path. We're better than that."

"Are we? I'm not sure taking someone's free will away because we don't agree with their choices is the right path either," Emily said.

"Someone has to be the adult in the room. Waiting around for them to make their own decisions only means more incidents like last night's fire."

Emily felt the man was honest about his convictions, but one man's beliefs weren't necessarily another man's desires.

"The camp—the one on the river—we stopped by the scene this morning and city crews were in cleanup mode. How did it happen so quickly? I know city government isn't always quick to act."

"Public health. What was left of the camp was a danger to public health. If people returned, they'd repeat the cycle. Listen, Detective, it was nice to chat. Please call me if you have any developments on the unfortunate death out there. It's an example of what the mayor is trying to prevent."

"Murder."

"Excuse me?"

"The man was murdered."

"I was told he was trapped in the fire." Jensen shook his head. "His death served as a catalyst to make positive steps to deal with the issue. Oh, which reminds me—can you tell me the man's name? The mayor would like to name the foundation in his honor."

"No. Not yet."

"Thanks, Detective." Jensen strode into the recesses of City Hall, leaving the two opposing protest groups still chanting and posturing at one another. A hint of his cologne lingered behind.

Emily watched him retreat until Javier bumped her with his hip. "Pull it together, Emily. I feel like I just watched an episode of *The Bachelor*."

"Oh, shut up."

"I think Officer Conner may have some competition."

"Just because he has a nice smile doesn't mean I'm getting all weak in the knees."

"Noticed, did you? He is listed as one of Sacramento's most eligible. Number 7, if I recall."

"And how would you know that, Javi?"

"I know things. And you know another one on the list," he said, straightening his lapels.

"No way."

Javi looked hurt. He fished out his cell and tapped in an address in the phone's web browser. He held his chin up and thrust the phone to his partner. She snatched it from his hand and stared at the screen.

"You? How do they figure you're a 'most eligible'? And who wrote this anyway?"

He tried to take the phone back and Emily turned away.

"You're number 48? Three of the guys ahead of you on this list are dead."

"Doesn't matter. I'm one of the city's most eligible. You should treat me accordingly."

"Wait a minute. This was written by the reporter you dated last year."

"So? And she's a journalist."

"You were dating this woman, and she ranked dead guys ahead of you?"

"You're missing the point. I'm. On. The. List."

"Oh, I've got you on a list all right."

Emily's cell phone vibrated in her pocket. She handed Javier his cell and answered hers. "Hunter."

Hello, Detective. It's Dr. Pixley. I'm getting ready to open up your victim from last night. You'll want to see what I found."

CHAPTER EIGHT

THE SACRAMENTO COUNTY Coroner's Office wasn't too far from the Department of Motor Vehicles on Broadway. Both were where people went to linger, some more permanently.

The coroner's building itself was deceptive. Smooth brick and concrete, smoked glass windows concealing a waiting room where no good news found the families and friends who gathered within. The place was a vortex of grief. Emily avoided the front entrance where a mother sat gripping her husband's hand. The story they were about to hear from the medical examiner would change their lives forever. There was no going back, no second chance. A life was over.

Emily drove to the rear entrance where funeral homes picked up remains for memorial services. It was more businesslike back here. There was a job to do, and everyone did their part in a respectful and dignified way.

There were empty gurneys parked in the hallway, and Emily followed a path she'd trod many times before, past the open bays of the autopsy suite to the one room reserved for murder cases, a smaller space, which hoped to keep the secrets and pain contained.

Emily knocked on the door and stepped inside. Dr. Sharon Pixley made notes on a laptop on a movable stand.

A strong odor of burnt flesh hit the detectives when they entered. Dr. Pixley, the chief forensic pathologist, glanced up and caught their reaction.

"Yeah, he is a bit of a stinker. Partially cooked," the doctor said.

Under the bright operating theatre lights, Emily saw more of the body than last night's spotlights allowed. Still partially draped, the man's head stuck out from the sheet, bits of gray and brown hair charred and matted on his head.

Emily circled around the table. "May I?" she asked pointing at the sheet.

"Be my guest."

Emily gently pulled the sheet down to reveal more of the man's body.

Exposed tissue facing up was burnt. Dark sheets of blue and red plastic melted to his charred clothing and skin. The man's chest, hips, and tops of his thighs were pinkish-gray, but unburnt.

"What do you see, Detective?" Dr. Pixley asked, pushing the laptop stand away.

"When we first saw him last night, he was face down. You've managed to remove most of the melted material—the tent and tarp covering him. His back and one side of his face were—are—burnt, while his anterior surface underneath was preserved. Tells me he was in this position when he died."

"Very good. Lividity—heat will make a mess of it, too—supports he died face down as well."

"There's the gunshot wound to the back of his head . . ."

"That's where things get complicated. This is not a wound pattern from a firearm."

Emily and Javier drew closer to the body and Javi leaned in. "It sure looks like one."

Dr. Pixley flipped an X-ray film onto a backlit white panel. The image of a skull glowed on the screen.

"Old-fashioned X-ray film instead of the image on my laptop. Made it easier to see this. Remember when we said it didn't look like there was an exit wound?"

"Right. Did you find one?" Emily said.

"No exit wound." The doctor traced a fingertip on the image starting from the back of the skull. "Widest at the entry point, then narrows to a taper. No bullet or bullet fragment."

"If it wasn't a gunshot wound, then what caused this?" Emily asked.

"I'm going to pour a cast before the brain tissue proteins break down even more as time elapses. If I wait too long, there'll be too much liquefaction to make any determination."

Dr. Pixley pulled open a bottom cabinet and removed a pair of bottles. "Think of it as a two-part epoxy, but this one hardens quickly. Where is—yes, this will work."

She withdrew a small funnel, inserted it into the mouth of the wound, careful not to drag it across the eggshell cracks in the skull. "Hold this."

Emily donned a pair of gloves and held the funnel with both hands, the tip hovering over the gaping hole in the man's head.

Dr. Pixley poured the two bottles together and shook them, starting a catalytic reaction. She gently poured the gray slime into the funnel.

"It's getting warm," Emily said.

The doctor stopped pouring when the substance filled the cavity and began overflowing. After she set the bottle on the counter, she placed her hands over Emily's and lifted the funnel straight out.

"While we give it time to set, let me show you some interesting tidbits I found."

Emily and Javier followed the doctor to another room. Scraps of melted plastic tent fabric, clothing, and dark burnt lumps, which took Emily a moment to recognize as a pair of shoes.

"We've been operating under the assumption our recently deceased friend in the other room was caught up in the fire that swept through the camp, frying him in his tent. But, as we've come to understand—"

"He was dead when the fire got to him," Emily said.

Dr. Pixley nodded. "And now we have this." She gestured to the charred display.

Emily leaned over the table and examined the exhibits. The plastic was melted onto the bits of clothing, confirming the victim was inside the tent when it caught fire. Same with the shoes. They were cut from the victim's corpse because the heat had baked the leather and melted the shoelaces on the low-rise boots.

Emily stood back and bit her lower lip. "You took these from our victim?"

"We did."

"He didn't live in the camp," Emily said.

"How can you say that, based on this mess?" Javier said.

She closed in on the table and pointed at the shoe. She picked it up in her gloved hand and held it in profile for her partner. "Unless our victim mugged someone and stole these shoes, I don't see someone living in a river camp wearing six-hundred-dollar Varvatos boots."

"You can tell the brand from—from this?" Javier said.

"Enough to know these aren't what you'd expect to find on a guy living in a tent down by the river."

"I didn't catch the boot, but the clothing backs up your theory, Detective. The fabric is thin and probably a wool blend of some sort. We can see a patch of it which escaped the flames. It must have been underneath him."

Dr. Pixley used a small set of forceps to lift the fabric scrap, holding it under the light.

"It looks like a dark blue pinstripe—like a suit," Emily said.

"My thought as well."

"What was a banker doing out on the river?" Javier said.

Emily snapped off her gloves and tossed them in a biohazard bin by the door.

"How tall was our victim?"

Dr. Pixley turned to a computer on a nearby center and tapped in the information to pull up the John Doe's case file. "The heat shrunk the tissues somewhat and made an exact measurement difficult, but we estimated our man was six-foot-one. Why?"

Emily fished her phone from her pocket and found the image she was looking for, laying it on the counter next to the computer. The image of Pete Bell, Ryan Jensen, and the former mayor. The ousted politician was taller than the other two men and wore a dark blue pinstripe suit.

Emily tapped on the image. "I think we found our victim—it's Mayor Stone."

CHAPTER NINE

"THE FORMER MAYOR?" Javier said.

"Should be easy enough to confirm. I've got enough tissue left uncompromised by the fire and dental for comparison," Dr. Pixley said.

A timer sounded off on the doctor's watch. "Ah, our casting should be ready."

The detectives followed the chief pathologist into the autopsy suite where Mayor Stone's charred remains lay.

The gray slime had hardened into a rigid plastic blob on the surface of the dead man's skull.

"Time to find out if our arts and crafts project worked."

Dr. Pixley grasped the hard plastic button protruding from his head and wriggled the cast until a slurping pop sounded as the cast withdrew from the dead man's head.

The rigid, hardened plastic mold was six inches long with a slight downward arc. Bits of brain matter clung to the edges of the plastic. Dr. Pixley took the mold to a sink and washed the debris from the casting.

She plopped it down on the examination table. "I think we've found the manner of death—clearly a homicide. The cause of death was massive brain bleed from a penetrating wound deep into the brain structure. I'll be able to confirm as much after I open him up. Speaking of—I'll be doing it this afternoon, if you want to observe."

"One of us will be here, Doc."

Dr. Pixley dropped the casting in a plastic bag and handed it to Javier.

"I'll see you then."

"Why the quick turn on the autopsy? I mean I appreciate the priority and all, but you have other cases ahead of this one, I'm sure," Emily said.

Dr. Pixley stripped off her gloves and leaned against the counter. "Outside pressure to get this case off the table. I don't like it when some political weasels tell me how to do my job. I got a call from the county administrator who got a call from the mayor's office who wanted this case handled quickly. Faxed over an order to have the remains cremated as an unknown indigent person. We need to keep the identity of this one under wraps."

"Yeah, we'll try to keep it from leaking on our end. I guess the unknown indigent might be known now," Emily said.

"I'll get to work on confirming the victim is the former mayor. I'll need dentals for comparison. Is that something you can help me with, or you want me to send one of my techs around?"

"Let us take a shot at it. We'll need to loop in the next of kin if it might be the mayor, anyway. I'll try to collect a DNA sample from a comb or toothbrush."

"All right. We'll compare notes this afternoon when I open him up."

"Sounds like a deal," Emily said.

As the detectives walked through the back halls to the loading dock, they heard the backup *beep-beep* of another body delivery. Life and death go on.

"You think our stiff is the former mayor? I mean, I feel a little bad he might be dead, but the man gave us a ton of grief in the past."

"Yeah, he did. Tried to keep his mistress out of prison for killing her husband."

"As I remember it, he wanted you fired. I don't remember him looking like that—heavier, like a tick ready to pop. You sure it's Mayor Stone?"

"I'm almost certain it's him. Same size and round shape as Stone. It's his face for me. Someone threatens you like he did—that face burns into your memory. The pricey boots seem like him, too. The thing I can't wrap my head around is why the former mayor was hanging out in a homeless camp."

"Why would someone drive a spike into his skull? That's what this thing looks like. One of those old-timey railroad spikes." Javier turned the bagged plastic cast of the murder weapon in his hand.

"Why would someone want to kill a corrupt, womanizing, influence-peddling political? Gonna be a long list."

"A certain detective I know might be on that list as well."

"Hey, I'm not going to shed any tears if it turns out to be John Stone, but my issues with him ended after he got his ass booted out of office in the last election."

"Who else had an axe to grind? Or a spike to drive?"

"When the media gets wind of this, it's gonna get wild. Simmons and Taylor dodged a bullet on this one."

"Doubt they'll see it that way. Taylor loves the spotlight."

"We'd better go let Lieutenant Hall know we might have an ID on our John Doe. Oh, and call your mom while we drive—check in on her and make sure she's okay with my mom."

"You call her."

"She's your mother."

"She's watching *your* mom."

"I'm driving."

"Never stopped you before. Hello—use hands free."

"You're impossible, Javi. It's like you're avoiding your—you are. You're afraid to talk to your mom. What did you do? You know I'll get it out of her."

"Nothing."

Javier turned his face to the window to avoid Emily. But she caught the blush running up the side of his neck.

"What did you do?"

Emily called up the number for her home where Connie was spending the day with Javier's mom. She put it on speaker and moved the phone to her left so Javier couldn't grab it.

After the first ring, Javier's mother answered. "Hello?"

"Hi, Mrs. Medina, it's Emily. Wanted to check in and see how things are going."

"Hello. We're having a good day. She's up, dressed, and we're having some tea."

"How does she seem?"

"There's a little confusion on why she's here and not at her home. There's some disconnection with what's going on with her and her memory—the short term is a struggle for her. Say, she should have her medication. I don't think you got them when you left the facility. You might have to stop by her place and grab it. It's important to slow the memory loss. If she's been missing it, it might explain the recent issues she's having."

"Javier and I will stop on our way back to the office."

"Is Javier there with you?"

Javier shook his head and waved his arms begging her not give him up.

"I'm going to meet him at the office. Anything you want me to pass on?"

"Yes, tell my son to call that sweet girl, Jenny. She's willing to give my boy another chance after he darted out on her last night."

"In fairness, we did get called out to a crime scene."

"My son needs to call her. He's a good man, but my God he acts like he's never been around a woman before."

"Yeah, he's not the most sophisticated man-about-town. What is it with him?"

Javier glared at Emily. "Stop," he mouthed.

"I blame it on—"

Javier grabbed the Crown Vic's siren control and flipped it, emitting a loud squelch from the car.

"Goodness, what was that?" Mrs. Medina asked.

"Gotta run after a guy who doesn't know who he's messing with," Emily said.

She disconnected the phone and couldn't suppress a grin.

"You think that's funny, don't you?" Javier asked.

"Kinda. Yeah."

"Mom won't get any rest until I take Jenny out on a proper date."

"So, what would be so bad? She seemed nice. You act like you're fifteen."

"Like I said the other night. I know. I'll handle it. I don't need you and my mother playing matchmaker."

"I could do it. I can set you up."

"God, no."

"Why?"

"You'd have me paired off with some tatted-up roller derby enforcer and I'd be afraid to turn my back on her."

"Don't knock it if you haven't tried it."

Emily pulled the Crown Vic into the Western Care parking lot and ran into the office to pick up her mother's prescriptions before they headed back to the office.

CHAPTER TEN

"WHEN WILL DR. Pixley have confirmation?" Lieutenant Hall asked.

Emily sat forward in the chair. "She needs dental comparisons or DNA samples to verify. Once she has them, it won't take long—"

"Won't take long until the media get wind of this, you mean," Hall said.

"Yeah, Dr. Pixley will try to keep a lid on it, but with someone with this kind of notoriety, it's going to open a can of complications for us. We need to find out why Stone was hanging out in a homeless camp, for starters. You and I both know his elitist ass wasn't any Mother Teresa. The fact he was in the camp at all means it was for a self-serving reason—and that reason got him killed."

"Maybe. But we need to take it one step at a time, Detective. Let's find out what he was doing before we condemn him. I've got no love lost for the guy. But are we going to have any issue with you investigating his death? Less than two years ago, you uncovered some of his campaign funds originated from organized crime, and it was a major reason he lost his reelection bid."

"I can manage this."

"If I get any blowback, I'll have to reassign the case back to Simmons and Taylor. The current mayor wants my best on this investigation, and you need to show her you're up to it."

Emily nodded.

"What do you need from me?" Hall asked.

"The first thing I have to do is get Dr. Pixley the dental records and locate a DNA sample. Which means—"

"The wife. She's not exactly your biggest fan."

"Nope. Which is why I might need your help to keep her from blowing up. When was the last time you did a next-of-kin notification?"

*　*　*

Lieutenant Hall, Javier, and Emily stood on the doorstep of the mini-mansion in Sacramento's exclusive Fab 40s district. The former mayor's home was a massive Tudor-inspired home with two wings and a four-car garage.

Emily pushed the doorbell. When she didn't hear a response, she pushed it again.

"I'm coming. Hold on a second," a voice sounded over a doorbell speaker. She hadn't bothered to check the doorbell camera, evidenced by the look on her face when she threw open the door.

Emily thought her expression showed surprise, but the Botox and cosmetic surgery procedures muddled the emotion.

"You," Mrs. Stone said through clenched teeth. "What do you want?"

Lieutenant Hall edged forward. "Mrs. Stone. May we have a moment of your time? I'm afraid it's important and concerns your husband."

She cast her eyes at the lieutenant. "Haven't you people done enough? You ruined his career, damaged his reputation beyond repair, and now you want a moment?"

Emily bit her lip to avoid a harsh response. It was the mayor who sank his own career, not the woman in front of her.

"Please, ma'am, may we come in? It's important."

"Fine, if it'll get you out of my life." She stepped aside and pulled the door open.

The living room was in disarray. Shelves emptied, boxes on the floor, and a bag of foam packing peanuts leaked onto the hardwood.

"What is it you want from me?" The woman wore a pair of teal yoga pants and a tight tank top. She fidgeted with the end of her blonde and gray ponytail while she spoke. Her slim figure lost in the great room.

"I don't think there's any easy way to say it, so I'll lay it out for you. A man was murdered last night, and we need to determine if it was your husband or not," Hall said.

Emily watched for a reaction, and all the woman did was slump her shoulders and sigh. "It would be like him to get himself killed when we've got all this work to do."

"What work is that?" Emily asked.

Mrs. Stone's eyes locked onto Emily. "Because of you, we've lost the house. We're moving. Somewhere your scandal will let my husband earn a decent living. This is all your fault, Detective."

"I seem to remember it was your husband who took campaign cash from a prison gang—not me."

"In any case," the lieutenant interrupted, "we need to know where Mr. Stone went for dental work and we need you to let them know we need his records."

"His dentist? What would you possibly need—oh . . ."

"If you would give me his toothbrush—or a comb . . . "

The slight woman shivered as the reality of the situation set in.

"Mrs. Stone, I know you think little of me, but can you tell us if your husband had any reason to be around the homeless camp out near North 7th?"

"The fire. That's what this is about. And you need his dental records?"

The lieutenant nodded.

"All he said to me last night was he was going out. Needed to meet with someone. I assumed he was having another fling. Unless he was trolling for a gal in the homeless camp, I have no clue why he would be there. No, wait. He mentioned low-income social services, or a service center of some kind. I'm sorry, I only half listened. I was busy getting our things packed."

"He ever mention River City Foster Care and Adoption Services?"

"I know he received calls to show up at fundraisers and events, but those trickled off recently. There was one man who kept asking him to sponsor, or support, programs. I don't remember what it was. The guy showed up here about three weeks ago, and the two of them talked about some children's day camp."

Emily fished her cell out and pulled the photo up of Stone, Jensen, and Pete Bell. She held it to Mrs. Stone.

"Yes. Yes. Him."

Emily pointed at Pete Bell from the River City office. "You're certain?"

Mrs. Stone scowled. "No. Not him. Him." She tapped Jensen's image with a manicured nail.

"Do you know him?"

"No. I don't make it a habit of nosing in where I don't belong."

"If we could get the name of your husband's dentist and his toothbrush?" Lieutenant Hall said.

She trod off without a word to the three detectives.

"They're selling the place?" Javier said. "Gonna make a killing in this market."

"Hunter, dig around and find out when the house went up for sale. See if the wife had an insurance policy on the old man," Lieutenant Hall said.

"Will do."

Mrs. Stone returned with a white pharmacy bag and held it out to the lieutenant. He handed the bag to Emily, and she confirmed a toothbrush, a hairbrush, comb, and a diabetic test kit.

"Mr. Stone is diabetic?" she asked.

"He is. Takes a blood sample twice a day to check his levels. The needles in there should have his blood on them, should you need them."

"Thank you, ma'am," Emily said. "And, for what it's worth, I'm sorry this is coming down on you. Your husband's dealings were his doing, not yours, and I just wanted to say that."

Mrs. Stone tipped her chin and regarded Emily coldly. "Let me know if it's my husband."

CHAPTER ELEVEN

LIEUTENANT HALL WAITED until the newly minted widow ushered them out and closed the front door. "Hunter, that went better than expected. Based on her reputation for being a hothead like her husband, and blaming you for his downfall, I would have bet we'd walk into a hurricane."

"What can I say? I'm a people person. I was taken by her attitude—like she expected it was going to happen one of these days."

Hall pinched the bridge of his nose and shook his head. "Get those samples to the coroner's office. Let's get the confirmation on Mayor Stone as your victim. I'll brief the chief and the Public Information Officer and try to get ahead of this thing. Any theories why our former mayor was out in the homeless camp at night?"

"We'll try to retrace his movements in the hours before his death. Someone will have seen the man. I have some thoughts, starting with an old watering hole where he and his political cronies used to hang out."

"All right, keep me in the loop, please. Rough water ahead."

Hall got in his Crown Vic and left Emily and Javier standing on the sidewalk.

Javier nodded back to the home. "I kinda feel for her—the mayor's wife. Her life as she knew it—it's gone."

"She didn't seem too busted up over the news her husband might be laid out in the morgue. Kinda like she expected him to turn up dead."

"All the more reason to find out the details behind the house sale and if Mrs. Stone felt the need to get a life insurance policy on her husband, like the lieutenant said."

"Maybe. I don't think she's the type to bash her husband's head in. But she might know who did. We'll have to keep an eye on her over the next few days."

Emily tossed the white paper prescription bag to her partner. "Let's get this to the lab to have them pull a DNA sample from this stuff. But I have a feeling the dentals will be all we need on this one." She passed the note with the phone number for the former mayor's dentist. "Would you call the dentist and have them get the records to Dr. Pixley?"

"Sure, where are we heading? The county crime lab is back downtown," Javier asked.

"The BFS Regional Lab. They might help us figure out our murder weapon. I have a friend there who's a genius at identifying edged and impact weapons."

"The State Bureau of Forensic Services? Isn't that going to get complicated, getting the attorney general's people involved in our case?"

"Nuh-uh. Cinda and I have an understanding. Kind of an information mutual aid thing."

The traffic thinned as they left the city. The BFS Regional Lab sat in an industrial park near the Placer County line. Emily pulled into the parking lot of a building that looked like it housed a software developer.

As they pushed inside, Emily strode to the reception desk hidden behind a plexiglass barrier. Javier hung back a few paces, his phone tucked to his ear.

"Could you let Cinda Walker know Emily Hunter is here?"

The uniformed security officer nodded and picked up the phone on his desk.

Emily joined Javier as he hung up the phone.

"The dental records are on the way to the coroner's office. Stone's dentist didn't seem surprised her patient might be deceased," Javier said.

"Seems to be the consensus, doesn't it?"

An electric lock on a hallway door buzzed and popped open. A raven-haired woman in a white lab coat appeared. She smiled and her blue eyes sparkled as she approached.

"Em, it's been a while." She hugged Emily, her dark eyeliner, dark lipstick, and a silver nose ring seeming out of place in the state lab.

"Cinda, this is my partner, Javier."

Cinda took a step back and gave Javier a once-over. "Nice to meet you." She put her hands on her hips. "What brings you to the neighborhood?"

"I need your help figuring out what killed our victim."

"Ooh, a puzzle. You have an impression with you?"

Emily held the evidence bag with the gray plastic cast from the medical examiner.

"Oh, fun." Cinda tilted her head, studying the object inside. "Come with me."

Emily and Javier received visitors badges and followed Cinda through a warren of hallways.

Emily caught Javier looking at Cinda's black platform combat boots and slim black leggings. She shot an elbow to his ribs.

Cinda unlocked a door, entered, and flipped a light switch.

"You're gonna get a kick outta this, Javi," Emily said.

Two walls of the room were packed with weapons: dirks, daggers, swords, machetes, and impact weapons mounted in rows. There were two hundred different objects displayed on racks and shelves.

"Whoa," Javier said.

"Thank you," Cinda said.

Cinda motioned them to a white Lexan-covered table in the center of the room. "I'll show you mine if you show me yours."

Emily handed the bag with the plastic cast to Cinda.

"Give me a little context here. Where was this taken and what type of wounds are we talking about?"

"One wound—a deep penetrating strike to the victim's skull. This is a casting from the wound track," Emily said.

"Oh, how cool."

Cinda removed the plastic casting and turned it over in her gloved hands.

"Not an edged weapon. We're looking at an implement with a point. Not with a sharpened cutting edge."

She walked to her wall of weapons and held the cast in front of her. Cinda ignored the far left display of knives and axe blades. She stood at a rack of hammers, chisels, and picks.

"The cast has a distinct rectangular shape at the base."

She turned to the detectives. "You have a photo of the wound?"

Emily nodded and flipped through the photos from the medical examiner until she found two of the wound in the back of the victim's head. She handed her phone to Cinda.

Cinda zoomed in the photo. "There you are, you little bugger. Check this," she said holding the image for the detectives. "This is the back of the dude's head. See the slight bruising and abrasion on the entrance at the base? Down at the bottom if he was standing."

Emily squinted. "Oh, yeah, I see it. I would have missed it if you didn't call it out to me."

"There's not one matching at the top of the wound. Tells me the weapon penetrated all the way up to the hilt. Bet ya there were spiderweb cracks around the point of impact on the X-ray. Looks like someone was determined. Wouldn't take too much muscle to make that happen though. But it means this length here is the size of weapon you're looking for."

Cinda paced back to her wall display, farther to the right. "No, not these," as she passed the picks, chisels, and construction framing hammers.

"It's kinda like Goldilocks and the three bears. This one's too small, this one's too wide . . . and this one"—she plucked an item from the wall—"is just right."

She placed the cast on the white table along with a peculiar-looking hammer. The long protruding end was the same curved shape and size as the gray cast from the man's brain.

"What is that?" Javier said.

"This is a twenty-ounce geologist's hammer, or rock hammer. The square stubby side is the chipping hammer, and at this end is the pick. It's square like your casting, and almost the identical size. Your forensic pathologist might find some stainless-steel flaking at the entrance where the weapon met bone. There is some evidence from your cast that says the weapon isn't brand new off the shelf. There's a crack right here, or at least a line where the steel flaked away."

"A rock hammer? Not a thing you see every day," Emily said.

"Miners, prospectors, rock collectors, all use them. Then there's the odd archaeologist. Where'd you find your victim, if I can ask?"

"A homeless camp."

Cinda rested her elbows on the table and nudged the hammer with a finger. "Not much call for a geologist in a homeless camp. Wait, was it near a river?"

Emily and Javier glanced at one another.

"It was, wasn't it?" Cinda said. A wide smile appeared on her face.

"Yeah, the camp was on the Sacramento River. Why?" Emily asked.

"They were prospecting. The rivers are flowing pretty high right now, and the hobby prospectors pan and dredge, looking for gold flake. There's never much, but these guys get a fever. Your victim seem the type to be a claim-jumper?"

"That's not a thing, is it? This isn't the 1850s," Javier said.

"It happens, but mostly it's up in the foothills."

"Not likely. We think it was ex-mayor John Stone."

"No shit? Kinda funny, don't ya think?"

"What's that?"

"Stone killed with a *rock* hammer," Cinda said.

"You really need to get out of this room more, Cinda," Emily said.

"If it wasn't prospecting, what would someone use this tool for?" Javier asked.

Cinda shifted to face him, leaning a slim hip against the table. Her deep blue eyes bore down on him. "You've got several uses.

From someone taking rock samples, excavating a buried object, soil samples, or since you said it was used in a homeless camp, pounding in tent stakes."

"So, we're back to square one," Javier said.

"I wouldn't say that. This is a different tool. It stands out a bit. I'd be willing to bet someone in your camp has seen it or might even know who had it. It might still be stashed out there."

"If the city hadn't rushed to take down the camp."

Cinda squinted. "How come? Seems out of the ordinary."

"Tell us about it. Everything seems out of the ordinary on this one."

"Still, I'd ask around about someone with a tool like this."

Emily snapped a photo of the rock hammer. "If one of our fire victims regains consciousness, I'd like to show this to her."

"Thanks, Cinda. You've been a lot of help here," Emily said.

"It was very nice to meet you," Javier said.

Emily caught a slight quiver in her partner's voice.

"You two take care. Oh, and Em, we need another girls' night soon."

"You got it. See ya, Cinda."

Emily and Javier handed in their visitor badges at the front desk.

"Cinda's—interesting," Javier said.

"She's genius level smart."

"I mean, she's not what you expect from a lab tech."

Emily unlocked her car and they hopped in. Javier buckled his seat belt.

"She single? Seeing anyone?"

"Oh, Javi—you're not wired for that kind of voltage. She'd pop your breakers in a hot second."

"Thanks for the vote of confidence, partner."

Emily drove out of the parking lot and aimed the Crown Vic downtown.

"I need a drink."

"Em, it's barely noon . . ."

CHAPTER TWELVE

Sacramento is a city of neighborhood bars and watering holes. John Stone would have his favorite. There were a couple of drinking establishments near the state capital where the political types would meet and hash out deals, or wrangle committee votes over a bourbon or two.

The city's political animals were territorial, and Emily knew the place to start. The Oak Top was an unimpressive dive bar from the outside, with dark green glass windows preventing pedestrian traffic from spotting their city councilmen day drinking. The Oak Top sat on a corner off of H Street. Close enough to drive out for a quick meeting and quiet enough where these meetings were away from the media and City Hall watchers.

Emily pulled the black lacquered door and stepped inside the darkened bar.

"Not what I expected from the outside," Javier said.

The interior fixtures were deep wood tones and brass. Tables with tall partitions between them lined both sides, booths with leather cushions vibing more like church confessionals than a place to grab a cold one.

Emily spotted a man polishing the bar with a towel. He eyed the detectives but didn't shout out a warm greeting as he continued wiping down the surface.

Three of the tables were occupied with men in business attire leaning into one another. Deals were being made and contracts bought.

Emily stepped up to the bar next to a man who perched on one barstool.

The barman dropped his towel, wiped his hand on his apron, and stepped over. "What can I get you?"

"John Stone come by here recently?"

"We're not in the habit of snitching out our patrons," the man said, crossing his thick forearms. He tossed a pair of heavy drink coasters on the bar. The unsaid message: pay up or get out.

"We're on duty, but I'll buy my new friend here another," Emily said. She pulled a twenty from her pocket and dropped it on the bar.

The older man sitting to her left tossed back the remnants of the amber liquid in his tumbler and slid the glass to the barman.

"Thank you, young lady. What brings a pair of Sacramento's finest into this dive? I'm Michael, Michael Merchant."

"How'd you know we were cops? What gave it away? The swagger and comfortable shoes?" Emily asked.

The old man smiled causing a few wrinkles to deepen. His nose and cheeks were red, marking him as a regular in the establishment.

The bartender poured another double for Merchant.

"I'm in the newspaper business. Or, I was. The paper downsized and decided journalists were a luxury they didn't need when they could buy stories off the wire services. I remember covering a couple of cases you worked as a rookie detective. Everyone was counting you out as the new kid in town and being a woman got under a few collars. Good on you for proving them all wrong." He tipped his glass at Emily.

After a sip, the man continued. "John's a regular here. One of the few places where people don't give him the 'ol stink eye for his problems. If you're in this game long enough, there's gonna be some skeletons in your closet. Johnny had a houseful."

"When's the last time you saw him here?"

Merchant stared at Emily's reflection in the mirror behind the bar. "It's been a couple of days, I suppose. He usually drops in during the lunch rush and gets caught up on what's going down in the city council. You know, who's got polling problems, what cause of the day is in trouble, and what this new mayor is doing to unwind his legacy."

"His *legacy*?" Emily said.

"Yeah, that's the way Johnny takes it. The policies and initiatives he put in place are being dismantled, one by one. He took it as erasing a lifetime of work."

"Some of those policies got him unelected, like his ties to questionable campaign cash."

Merchant took another sip. "There is that. Still, he was bothered by fading away."

"How about the last time you saw Stone? He seem more or less upset by what was going on?"

"I remember him getting into a loud argument with someone."

"Know who it was?"

Merchant shook his head. "No, and it was none of my business. Things get heated all the time. It goes with the territory."

"Hear what it was they were arguing over?"

"Like I said, it was none of my business. It was loud though, more than usual."

Merchant slid his empty tumbler across to the bartender.

"Sorry I couldn't be any more help."

The mirror showed Javier had moved to the back of the establishment. He stood near a table talking with a pair of men. Emily thanked Merchant and joined her partner.

Javier blocked her view of the booth. She was surprised to recognize one man when she got to the table—Ryan Jensen.

"Nice to see you again, Detective. Your partner here was asking about my old boss." A glass of club soda with a lime wedge sat before him.

"Mr. Jensen here was telling me how Mr. Stone likes to come in to feel like he's still part of the goings-on in the city."

"That right? You see him here often?" Emily asked.

"The city council meets on Tuesdays, so Mayor Stone would want to meet on Tuesday mornings to see what was on the calendar, and again on Wednesdays to go over what actions the council took."

"Why was he so invested in what the city council had on their calendar? He's not in office anymore."

"You try telling him. He can't let go. I told him he needs to start playing golf or pickleball. He still thinks he can influence the current council. He'd meet and tell me what the council's position on items should be and would get pissed off when they didn't side with him."

"I understand he got a little heated the other day. Thought maybe the city was trying to erase his legacy."

"Oh, that," the other man in the booth said.

"And you are?" Emily asked.

The man flicked a business card from a suit pocket and handed it to Emily. Morris Fuller of Fuller Investments. A trim man in his mid-thirties with sandy blond hair and dark brown eyes. He extended a manicured hand to her.

"You heard the discussion?"

Fuller flicked his eyes toward Jensen before returning to Emily. "You could say that. It was me he was yelling at."

"What got under his collar?"

"My investors rely on me to get results for them. Mayor Stone has been pushing his concept to revitalize the city with new business and development. The Stone Plan, he called it. This began while he was still in office. New amusement parks, an aquarium, a zoo, high-rise residential housing in the downtown corridor, and luxury condo development."

"I remember talk of the Stone Plan," Javier said. "Didn't the mayor try to take credit for West Sacramento's development along the riverfront?"

Jensen chuckled. "Yeah, he did. That was a fun couple of weeks keeping the two mayors from declaring open warfare. Mayor Stone was a guy with vision. I'll give him credit. His vision, though, was sometimes shortsighted."

"What was he angry about when you two spoke?" Emily asked.

"Mayor Stone was angry I planned to pull the investment group out of the city. None of the infrastructure improvements are moving forward in the city's planning matrix. No infrastructure means little chance for development and translates to a no-win for my investors. I told the mayor we were pulling out."

"And he got upset?"

"You could say that. Threatened to take me and the investment group to court for detrimental reliance and breach of contract. I had to remind him he wasn't the mayor anymore."

"You can guess how that went over," Jensen said.

"Yeah, that's when he blew his top," Fuller said. "He said he had a way to make it all happen and revitalize the downtown area. Begged me to wait. I told him the waiting was over. We need a city receptive to what our investors are looking for. We want to be a partner with a place promising the potential for business expansion. Sacramento isn't that place. Increases in crime, vacant storefronts in your central business corridor, and you can't walk down the street without tripping over a homeless person—these don't paint the picture of a place we want to do business."

"I'm hoping to convince Morris to give us a second chance. The current mayor has a plan to deal with these roadblocks to progress. You saw her press conference on the unhoused initiative. Services and shelters will move the homeless off the streets. Business incentives to revitalize small businesses and attract them back downtown. We're doing everything we need to do to make Morris feel more comfortable when he walks down the street."

"I'll believe it when I see it," Fuller said.

"We've taken down the biggest camp in the city. We're moving forward. You need to meet us in the middle."

"No, I don't. This isn't a compromise deal. My investors demand evidence the city isn't going to change course six months from now. We need to see genuine commitment to making the city a safe place for business. We need assurances you have the workforce we'll need to staff the new businesses."

"What do you need us to do? Hold your investors' hands?" Jensen said.

"Excuse me. How did Mayor Stone take it when you told him you were pulling out?" Emily asked.

"Like I said. He wanted us to stay committed to investing in the Stone Plan. I told him the Stone Plan was dead. He told me I'd regret it."

"Any reason Mayor Stone would be near the homeless camps?" Emily asked.

"The only time John Stone met with homeless people was for a photo op. I know he talked a good game about getting people off the streets into supportive housing, but if you think back about it, he never—and I mean never—had a press conference or an event near a homeless camp," Jensen said.

"I thought he opened a shelter or two? I remember a press conference at one of them," Emily said.

Jensen smiled. "The North C Center. Yes, I remember that one. No one ever noticed during the entire presser, there was not a single homeless person present. We had to keep them away because they're too unpredictable for on-camera events. The public saw the mayor in action, looking out for the downtrodden, even if he couldn't stand being around them."

"Can you explain why the mayor was seen at a homeless camp the other night?"

Jensen frowned. "He wouldn't. I'd say you were misinformed."

CHAPTER THIRTEEN

EMILY PUT A hand up to shield her eyes from the sunlight as she and Javier exited the bar. "Whatdaya think?" she said.

"About Mayor Stone's aversion to homeless camps? If he'd only be there if he had a good reason, we need to find out his reason."

"Exactly. And didn't you find it odd no one asked about Stone after we mentioned he was seen at a camp? The fire is all over the news, Jensen and the current mayor are all over it, yet no one asked."

"Yeah, now that you mention it. It is strange."

Emily moved toward their Crown Vic. "You remember if Stone had a cell phone in the property we picked up at the medical examiner's?"

"I don't remember seeing one listed."

"We can go back over it. Once we get the confirmation on the identity, we can push a warrant for cell phone records. It'll tell us if he made any calls to someone near the camp."

"What we need is someone who can tell us what he was doing out there," Javier said.

Emily started the car. "We need to go over the case files Simmons and Taylor started. Might be something they missed."

A pair of cardboard boxes waited for Emily on her desk at the detective bureau. The thick black lettering on the side marked them as the case files from Simmons and Taylor. The investigation materials on the prior arsons, one box for each fire.

A handwritten note from Detective Simmons: *Don't knock yourself out on these. NHI.* Emily recognized the acronym was a throwback to a different era, when NHI meant No Humans Involved.

"How you wanna split them up?" Javier asked, taking off his jacket and tossing it over his chair.

Emily lifted the topmost box, which was lighter than she expected. She pulled the lid off to find a single pressboard binder lying on the bottom.

"They didn't bust their ass on this case," she said.

The file contained the incident reports from the fire department, the initial reports from the first officers on the scene, and a list of witnesses to the burn.

"They didn't even bother to interview anyone. Most of these witnesses don't even have a last name listed." She tossed the file on her desk.

Javier had opened the second box. "Same here." He held a single thin binder. "They didn't do anything. There's a couple of lines of case notes. Says, 'Witnesses unreliable, unable to identify suspect.'"

"Taylor?"

"You got it. It has his 'no one cares about homeless camp crimes' theme all over this."

"We need to start over, but the witnesses are scattered all over the city." Javier ran a finger down the list of witnesses. "There's no way to—wait. Pete Bell."

"The guy from the adoption services place? What about him?"

"He's on the witness list for the fire last week—the one under the railroad bridge at 18th Street."

Emily glanced over his shoulder and next to Pete Bell's name was his address.

"What's a social worker doing at the scene of two fires?" Javier asked.

"They ever follow up with Bell?"

Javier flipped through the file. "Nothing I can find. Initial entry said he didn't see how the fire started."

"But why was he there?"

Emily jotted down Bell's address. "We should go ask him."

* * *

Emily's vision of a home suited for a not-for-profit social worker was shattered when they pulled up to the address. The social workers Emily knew lived paycheck to paycheck, and it wasn't unusual to pull a roommate in to share expenses.

Pete Bell had found a way around the financial limitations. The neighborhood was once a fringe community populated by gangbangers and sex workers. Investors swept in, bought up properties, forced out the people who lived there, brushed on a quick coat of paint, and doubled the rents. Gentrification made it sound less predatory. But Bell's home stood out as new construction.

"We need to find out who owns this place. Can't be Bell," Emily said.

They stood on the sidewalk in front of a two-story McMansion with a stacked stone face and a three-car garage. The brick pavers used on the home's driveway were an expensive addition, one Emily considered for her much smaller parking pad until she priced the materials.

Emily pressed the doorbell and heard the chimes sound inside.

Javier pocketed his cell phone. "Tax records show Peter J. Bell as the owner."

Ringing the doorbell again didn't get a response.

"How could Bell afford this place?" Javier asked. He edged to a nearby window and pressed his face against the glass. "I can see a television in there, must be sixty inches, at least."

"Excuse me? What are you doing?" a voice called from behind them. A tall, thin man dressed in khaki pants and a bright blue button-down shirt stood on the sidewalk, one hand on his hip and the other holding a cell phone. He was shooting video.

"You know the guy who lives here?" Emily said, taking a step from the door.

The man stiffened and held the cell phone camera, pointing it at the detectives. "I've got you on video. You have no business poking around another person's property."

Emily took another step forward and asked him about the home once more.

"Stop, stop right there. Don't you dare come after me. I'm calling the police." Then he froze for a moment realizing he needed to stop filming to use his cell phone.

"I'll save you the trouble. I'll call for you." Emily parted her jacket and showed him her badge. "Detectives Hunter and Medina. And you are?"

"Clarence White. I live next door—over there." He pointed at a well-manicured front yard leading up to another McMansion.

"Mr. White, what can you tell us about the man who lives here?" Emily said.

"I don't know that it's my place to say." The grin on his face said he couldn't wait to spill the gossip.

"Let's pretend it is."

He figured it was time to put his camera away. "Pete bought the place the minute the developers cleared the lot of the monstrosity that was originally here. Tacky, run-down old tract home. I hear it was a drug house." The last part said in a conspiratorial whisper.

"Pete live here with anyone else?"

"It's not for me to judge who someone brings into their life."

"That's not what I asked. Does anyone one else live here?"

"Oh, oh, no. It's only Pete. I've seen young girls, but no one stays long. Why, is he in trouble? Is he a suspect?"

"What should we suspect him of, Mr. White?"

"I couldn't say. I bet it was some shady secret. Just the other day he had to work late. I know a lie when I hear one. And he wasn't dressed for any work I know of, with those black jeans and a matching black sweater. Looked like a pudgy Jason Bourne."

"He say what he was doing?"

"No, other than he had to work. It was late and the men who picked him up didn't seem like they were working either, if you know what I mean."

"What do you mean?"

"They were dressed the same and seemed like they were going to an underground goth club. I don't judge, but it didn't seem like Pete's scene. I overheard him say he 'needed to find her.' They took off in a black SUV."

"Find *her*?"

"You happen to see him last night?"

"It's not my business."

"But videoing a couple of cops knocking on his door somehow becomes your business?"

"That's different. If our homes start getting broken into, then everything will start falling apart. The bad elements will come back, and we can't have it."

"The *bad elements*? You mean the people who lived here until some rich developer carpetbagged their way in and drove them away? I think the bad elements are here already, Mr. White."

Emily brushed past the self-appointed watchman.

Javier pointed across the street. "You better pay attention over there. They have a scooter in their garage. They're a gateway to inviting the Hell's Angels into the neighborhood. Keep an eye out."

Waiting at the car for her partner, Emily mulled over the observations of Pete with young girls. There might be a reason—the man was a social worker after all. But it stuck with her in an uncomfortable way.

Javier noticed her expression, the bit lower lip and wrinkled brow. "Think he's our firestarter?"

"You got that feeling, too, huh?"

"What would our social worker be doing sneaking around at night, dressed in black?"

"I think I know how to find out."

"Find Pete Bell? Seems like the dude is in the wind after the last fire."

"Might be. We need to talk to the last person who saw him, and I think I know who that was."

CHAPTER FOURTEEN

THE SACRAMENTO CHILDREN'S Receiving Home was always a frantic hub of activity. But it seemed active in a healthy way. Kids running the hallways, playing basketball out on the court, and a double dutch rope contest going on in one of the activity rooms.

One attendant pointed the detectives to Willow. She sat on a sofa by herself watching the older girls spin ropes in opposite directions. Willow clutched Mr. Bunny tight under one arm.

"Hi, Willow." Emily sat down next to her. "Remember me? I'm Emily."

Willow nodded.

"How are you doing here? Meet any new friends?"

"When can I see my momma?"

"As long as she's in the hospital, your mom has people taking care of her. I'll find out when you can see her again."

Willow watched the girls jump rope and ever so slightly bobbed her head in time with the rope.

"You ever do anything like that? I never could get the timing right."

"Sharise let me try. She said I was good."

"Hey, Willow, do you know Pete Bell?"

She shook her whole body in response while watching the other girls.

Emily took her phone and called up the photo with Pete and the mayor. She pointed at Bell. "This man? Have you seen him?"

Willow lowered her face to the photo and squinted. "I saw him and Momma before . . ."

"Before? Do you know this man?"

"He's around a lot. He's not nice. Momma didn't like him."

"What makes you say your mom didn't like this man?"

"They were talking loud and saying bad words."

"When was this?"

"Before my momma got hurt. She said I might have to go away for a while. I don't want to. I want to be with my mom."

"She said you were going away? With him?"

"I didn't want to go away. I told my mom I'd be better if I could stay."

Emily's heart broke.

"Willow, you didn't do anything wrong. Grown-ups say things they don't mean sometimes."

"Momma said I'd be happier somewhere else."

"But your mom didn't make you go after all?"

Willow shook her head. "Momma got mad at him. She, she got real sad."

"Then what happened?"

"I—I don't—Momma said it would be okay."

"After the argument, what happened?"

"The fire."

Javier ducked into the room and jerked his head to the hallway.

One of the older girls holding the ropes called out. "Willow, your turn."

Emily supposed this was Sharise.

Willow popped up from her spot on the sofa and took small, tentative steps closer to the older girls and the jump ropes. Holding Mr. Bunny tight, she stood between the two girls.

"You ready?"

Willow nodded.

Sharise and the other girl swung one rope gently, perhaps a foot in either direction, and let Willow hop over the red cord. She barely cleared the rope with heavy flat feet, but from the smile on Willow's face, she was a double dutch champion.

"You go, Willow," Sharise called out.

Emily took one more look at the young girl and hoped for more happy moments like this in her life.

"What you got, Javi?" she asked as she joined him at the doorway.

"I found two other girls here—a little older than Willow—who say Pete Bell was a regular around the camps."

"Makes sense in his role as a social worker."

"I didn't get *social worker* from what these two were telling me. Bell would cruise the camps looking for young girls and convince their parents to give them up."

"Like he *was* stalking the girls from the camps?"

"Maybe. You wanna talk to them? They're in the library a couple of rooms down."

Emily shot another glance at Willow, giggling with the other girls.

"Show me the way."

Javier led and ducked into a small room lined with bookshelves. A cluster of tables and chairs filled the middle of the room. Two girls at one table scanned open textbooks and made notes on a yellow legal pad.

"Hey, this is my partner, Detective Hunter. I told her some of what you guys said."

The girls looked thirteen, but came off with a twenty-something vibe based on their sense of awareness and the reserved, untrusting gaze in their eyes.

"I don't know if I've ever seen a lady detective before. I'm Lida, this is Cyn."

Emily took a chair opposite them. "Detective Medina tells me you've seen this man around the camps?" She slid her phone with the photo she took at the agency.

Lida tapped on Bell's image. "That's Pete. Gave me a pervy vibe."

"How so?"

Cyn leaned in getting a better view. "He cruises the camps and only pays attention to the girls. My mom had to chase him off. He was telling her how he was looking for the right girl. He'd even pay her to help find one."

"He'd pay to find a girl? Seems odd."

"I know, right? I think he got a few families to give up their kids. He'd come back and give the family a housing voucher, food, even some cash."

"I heard the girls never got into foster care. They got sold on the black market," Lida said.

"Where'd you hear that?" Emily asked.

"One mom—she went to go look in on her daughter, like she had second thoughts. They couldn't find her."

"I heard they got taken to a cult," Cyn added.

"Back up a sec. The mom who couldn't find her kid—where was she told the girl was going?"

"Here. But she didn't."

"A devil-worshipping cult," Cyn said.

"They did not. They got sold to rich white people who couldn't have their own babies." Lida turned in her chair to face Cyn.

"How many times did Bell make a deal to remove a kid from a camp?" Emily asked.

"I don't know, a couple, maybe," Lida said.

"About the same where I was. It was always the girls, never the guys," Cyn said.

"There has to be some record of these placements," Javier said.

"Unless it's to a cult," Cyn said.

"You and your cults," Lida said.

"Cults are a real thing."

"You're a real thing."

"Javi, you get contact information for our two sleuths here?"

He waved his notebook.

"Thanks, ladies."

"No prob. Hope you catch the perv. He kinda vanished when the river camp got torched."

"He did, didn't he? Thanks, and if you think of anything else, give Detective Medina or me a call, would you?"

Emily returned to the activity room and took one more look in on Willow. She sat in a circle with other girls and played a game bouncing a ball between one another.

Maybe the girl had a chance after all.

CHAPTER FIFTEEN

"MAN, EVERYTHING WE turn up on Pete Bell paints a disturbing picture, doesn't it?" Javier said after leaving the Receiving Home.

Emily pulled out and merged with the flow of traffic. "Willow put him at the camp near the time of the fires."

"You think he's one of the two firebugs our witnesses described?"

"Possible. Hard to explain why Bell would do his social worker deal one minute, then burn the place down the next. Unless that was part of his ploy to make people want to give up their kids."

"Bell knew the mayor—the photo we have confirms as much. You think he's good for putting Mayor Stone down?"

"We need to find him," Emily said.

"You think he took off? It's the kind of thing guilty people do."

"Or scared ones. We need to get into his place." Emily hit the turn signal and made a quick left at a stale yellow light. "Let's do a drive-by at the district attorney's office and see if they think we might have enough for a search warrant. It's gonna be close."

"As long as we don't get ADA Marston."

*   *   *

"ADA Marston will see you now." A receptionist led them to an office door on the first floor of the concrete box serving as the district attorney's headquarters. Last time Emily was here, the entrances were blocked with chain-link fencing to hold a mass of protesters from breaking into the facility.

The receptionist knocked on the door and opened it, announcing, "Detectives Medina and Hunter."

"Did we have an appointment?" Lara Marston glanced up from her desk. Stacks of files filled most of the surface making what could have been a child's play-fort around her. Except these building blocks decided which cases moved forward and which victims were left behind. Marston's tapping pen signaled her mood—impatient and itching to get on with her day.

Marston had the reputation of the most difficult attorney on staff. One reason she was kept out of the courtroom and relegated to administrative work. She was prickly on her best day and an obstructionist when she held a grudge. Her grudge with Emily dated back a couple of years when Emily went around Marston to the elected DA herself to impanel a grand jury on a case.

"You're up on the rotation for warrant requests," Emily said.

"You got an affidavit for me?" She shot a hand out, curling her fingers in a hand-it-over gesture.

"I want to run it by you first, so we don't waste time."

"Your time or mine?"

Emily bit her lip and let a few seconds pass. She wasn't leaving until the ADA heard what she had to say.

"All right, all right, go. What do you have?"

"We're working the homeless camp arsons. One murder and a dozen injuries."

"Suspect in custody?"

"Our person of interest is on the run. He worked as a social worker in the camps. Witnesses place him at both camps before the fire. He was seen arguing with one of the victims."

Marston put a hand up. "You haven't made a nexus to the arson or the murder you mentioned."

"He's connected to all of it."

"I need more."

"The deceased and the suspect were well acquainted with one another."

"There's not enough here for a search warrant."

"What else do you need?"

"Bring me an actual connection to a crime and we can talk. A social worker being seen in a camp isn't enough to violate the sanctity of his home. No connection to the murder, no witnesses to say he set the fires, no actual witnesses we can call to testify your man committed a crime. Do I think he's sketchy as hell? Yeah, but go back and take another shot at this one, Detective."

Emily turned on her heel and left Marston's office before she said something she'd regret.

Javier paced after Emily and when they got out of the building, Emily stopped and turned. "Well, that went about as expected," he said.

"She's not wrong. Kinda why I wanted to run it past someone here. If it won't pass Marston's smell test, then it won't fly in front of a jury. I know Bell is the key to this thing." She glanced at her watch.

"You hungry? I'm hungry."

"You're always hungry. Tell you what. Brian has the night off. Call that Jenny girl and meet us for dinner. You can get your mom off your back, and it couldn't hurt to let Jenny know you're one of the city's most eligible."

"Don't you dare mention that. She doesn't need to know."

"That you barely made the list? Oh, honey, I'm sure she's well aware."

"Promise me you'll behave yourself."

"When have I ever . . ." Emily couldn't keep a straight face.

* * *

Emily and Brian sat, tucked away in a booth at a downtown Italian restaurant dominated by a wood-fired pizza oven that gave off a hint of old-world charm, meaning a smoky pallor hung about the place.

"Think he'll show?" Brian asked.

Emily sipped her iced tea. "If he knows what's good for him, he will."

"You threaten him?"

"It's not me he's got to worry about. His mom might be planning his wedding as we speak. She wants grandchildren and Javier isn't getting the message."

Brian took a swig from an amber bottle of a local microbrew. "You ever think about kids?"

"What are you saying, Mr. Conner? You implying I'm not getting any younger either?"

He put his hand up in mock surrender. "I said no such thing. I just think you'd be a good mom is all."

"I haven't thought about it. With work and all. I don't know how I could manage. I can barely keep myself together—being responsible for another human being—I don't know. Seems like more than I could handle."

Truth was, Emily had never been in a position where children—or a family—was a possibility. Keeping a relationship alive was never her strong suit, until now, with the man next to her.

She glanced a quick side eye at Brian. A future? She'd never given herself permission to think about the possibilities.

"Here they come," Brian said.

Emily broke away from the "what might be" to find her partner holding the door for Jenny. Javier spotted them in the booth and whispered something to his date. She giggled at whatever he said and tucked her arm in his.

Emily leaned to Brian. "At least it looks like she came here of her own volition."

"Hi, guys," Javier said, and after a quick round of introductions, he and Jenny sat opposite them.

"Nice to see you again, Jenny. I'm sorry for pulling Javi away last night."

Jenny tucked her long hair over her shoulder and leaned in. "That's the nature of the job. Besides, it gave me time to get to know Lucinda. I'm new to Sacramento, and she and my mother have been—busy."

"Jenny's been getting the full-court press from her mom, too," Javier said.

"What brought you to the city? Family?"

"That was part of it. I was able to transfer my job so I can keep an eye on Mom. She's starting to need a little help. Javi tells me you know what that's like."

Emily stirred her iced tea with a straw. "Do I ever."

"Memory care?"

"That's what it looks like. She's gone beyond what an assisted living facility can provide. It's hard to think about."

"Speaking of thinking. Javi, you give any more thought to what Pete Bell was doing at the camps? "Willow said Bell and her mom were arguing," Emily said.

"What if Willow got it wrong? What if the argument was about something else?"

"Like what?"

"What if it was about Mayor Stone? He was killed before the fires, according to the medical examiner—assuming this is the ex-mayor. What if Willow's mom is the link between Bell and the mayor?"

"Then we better hope Lisa Larkin wakes up soon."

"Or we find Bell."

"Is it always like this with these two?" Jenny asked Brian.

"Pretty much. Once they dig in, they kinda get tunnel vision."

Emily nudged Brian. "Sorry about that. We're working a complicated one at the moment."

"The homeless camp arsons. I saw that on the news. Awful stuff. Before I left law school, I did some internships with community groups servicing those camps. I'd hoped they'd gotten better while I was gone."

"They grow every day. Last census was over nine thousand homeless in the county spread out in dozens of camps. The city's response is a handful of shelter beds—twelve hundred," Javier said.

"The camp under the railroad bridge near 18th—is that one still a big one?"

"Not anymore. It was one of the camps burned."

"Oh no. That's a shame. It's going to hurt Mrs. Whittle. She owns the little store across the street from the park. The camp residents would use their county vouchers at the store for milk, bread, diapers. It was one of the few places they could go. I helped her work with the county to get the vouchers started. She was barely hanging on as it was," Jenny said.

"Simmons and Taylor didn't mention a store in their case notes," Emily said.

"They barely mentioned the fires," Javier said.

"Enough shop talk. Let's order," Brian interrupted.

They split a pizza, and after an hour, Javier glanced at his watch. "Jenny and I have tickets for a late movie. You can come, if you want."

"You two run along. We'll follow up on the market Jenny mentioned in the morning. Pick you up at seven?"

"That works," Javier said.

"Nice to meet you, Jenny. Have our boy in at a reasonable hour, would you? He gets cranky when he doesn't get his beauty sleep. He has that most eligible thing to maintain and he can't do that with dark circles under his eyes."

Javier glared at his partner.

"He's only number forty-eight. I don't think he's got far to fall," Jenny said.

Javier's shoulders slumped.

"I like her," Emily said.

"You're a bad influence, Hunter."

After Javier and Jenny left, Emily started to ask Brian to come over when his cell sounded.

"Conner."

He sighed and flicked his eyes to Emily. He squeezed her hand. "Got it. I'll be there in fifteen."

He hung up, shoved the cell in his pocket. "Watch Sergeant. Late sick calls. I gotta go cover."

"Working a double shift?"

"Looks that way. Sorry about cutting the evening short. It was nice to do something like a normal couple. At least for a few hours."

"I'd like a couple more hours, but duty calls, Officer Conner."

He walked Emily to her car and leaned into a deep kiss. "We'll continue this discussion later."

Emily felt the heat in her chest. "You best continue this later, Bucko."

She watched as Brian walked toward his car. For the first time in her adult life, Emily pondered what a future would look like.

She took a turn toward the river when she left the parking garage. There was something about the way Jenny described the market near the camp. It would be empty this time of night, but a mom-and-pop market would draw a lot of attention from a camp population. A store owner would need to keep an eye on their store with the constant traffic.

And there it was. Emily spotted the black metal box that housed a camera over the front door. If it worked *and* if it saved video footage, it would have a clear line of sight of the fire across the street.

CHAPTER SIXTEEN

EMILY HAD COFFEE ready when Lucinda Medina gave a soft knock on the front door. She decided it wasn't her place to mention Javier's evening with Jenny, and for once Lucinda didn't ask.

"Thanks for doing this. I picked up all of Mom's prescriptions and I left them on the kitchen counter."

"Don't worry, we'll be fine. Keep my boy out of trouble."

Emily pulled to the curb in front of Javier's place at seven. He waited there for her and hopped in the front seat of her Crown Vic.

He snagged a coffee with a big red "S" on the lid. "Thanks for remembering the stevia."

"That's nasty. I tried it by mistake once. I tasted it all day long."

"It takes a refined palate," he said followed by an exaggerated slurp.

"Jenny said something last night—"

"What? What did she say? What did you say? You say anything to Mom this morning?"

"Whoa, whoa. Slow your roll. I was going to say, Jenny mentioned that market near the 18th Street camp. I drove by last night, and she got me thinking about what I would do if I ran a store where the primary clientele were camp residents."

"Open an adjoining methadone clinic?"

"I'd wanna know who was hanging around. There's a camera mounted out front."

Javier sat straight. "You think it caught the arson?"

"Or Bell. He's bugging me. We know he was there, but if we have him on camera—boom—we got him."

"Think he's good for Mayor Stone?" Javier asked.

Emily's cell vibrated in her pocket. She glanced at the screen and showed it to Javier. "Speak of the devil, it's the coroner's office. "Hunter here."

"Hey, morning, Detective, it's Dr. Pixley. I wanted to close the loop with you. The dentals confirm the deceased is John Stone. You want to do the notification, or you want me to send one of our folks out?"

"Thanks, Doc. We'll handle it. We contacted the wife to get those dental exemplars."

"Good. I appreciate it. Oh, another thing. Stone's tox report came in this morning. And we found a couple of things out of the ordinary. First, his liver was shot. He had the reputation for quite the drinker. That wasn't unexpected, but his body showed evidence of a recent wound. I think this is a liver puncture biopsy. Then there's the blood panel. There is evidence of fentanyl ingestion."

"Fentanyl? A lethal dose?"

"Quite so. Completely incapacitating and would have killed him if his skull wasn't penetrated. I'm listing the COD as massive cerebral hemorrhage with opioid toxicity as a secondary factor."

"How would he have taken the fentanyl?"

"Uncertain. Could have been oral, no evidence of intravenous use, or adhesive from a patch—though his epidermal layers were damaged from the fire."

"Thanks, Doc. Javier and I will make the notification now. You might want to alert your public information officer. Once the media gets ahold of this one, you're likely to get some calls."

"Thanks for the reminder. Next time could you bring me someone with a little less media baggage?"

"Hey, we brought you a John Doe. You had to go and identify him."

"The burden of competence."

Emily disconnected the call.

"We need to pay the ex-mayor's wife a little visit and ask about his drug use."

*   *   *

Emily pulled to the curb in front of the Fab 40s Tudor. Mrs. Stone was seeing off a visitor as they came up to the front steps. Her eyes transformed from a welcoming glance to a hard glare.

When the visitor, a man in a business suit, turned to leave, he was so surprised to find the detectives standing behind him that he dropped a sheet from his portfolio. Emily bent and picked it up from the walkway and handed it to him. The document was a service contract with Estate and Heirloom Liquidators. Mrs. Stone was serious about the downsizing.

"Well?"

"May we come in, Mrs. Stone?"

She stepped aside and gestured them in. She wore a different pair of leggings with a loose sweater over the top. Her hair was down and curled. Emily noticed the slightest touch of makeup. Was it for the estate liquidator?

Mrs. Stone closed the door and leaned back upon it. "Tell me what you've come to tell me. It was him, wasn't it?"

"I'm afraid so," Emily said.

She hung her head. "I suspected as much. What do I do now? What are the next steps?"

"Someone from the coroner's office will reach out to you in the next few days and let you know when Mr. Stone's remains are available. You can connect with any funeral home you choose to help you make arrangements."

"I appreciate you telling me in person, Detective. This way I can look you in the eye while I tell you this—my husband's death is on your head."

"I'm sorry you feel that way, ma'am." Finally, some show of emotion from the woman, even if it was misdirected.

"Your vendetta against him sent him down this path."

"Whatever path he took was self-chosen. I do have a couple of questions based on what the medical examiner told us. Your husband's health. Did he see a doctor regularly?"

"You know he was a diabetic. He had regular appointments."

"Other than his diabetic issues, any other medical issues?"

Mrs. Stone's lips thinned, and for a moment, it seemed she wasn't going to answer. "Guess there's no reason for keeping it a secret anymore. John was suffering from liver failure. He was going to get put on the transplant list. It was the last we heard from his doctors."

"I'm sorry to hear that."

"I bet you are."

"Medications? Was he taking anything for this condition?"

"The doctors had him on all sorts of drugs to help slow the liver failure and to control the pain."

Emily's ears pricked up "Pain?"

"Apparently whatever was going on with his liver was quite excruciating."

"We'll need to collect all of his prescriptions as part of the investigation. It's standard practice. Can you direct Detective Medina to where you keep them?"

The new widow thought about refusing for a moment—Emily could see it on her face.

"Why not. It's going to save me from dumping them myself."

She led Javier down a small hallway and left Emily in the living room.

Emily noticed a copy of the estate liquidator's contract on the coffee table. A closer inspection noted the date for an auction and a smattering of items up for grabs. Under the contract, the corner of a file stuck out. From what Emily could read of it, the file held nearly an inch-thick collection of documents for a project called River Gardens.

She started to pick it up, but the shuffling of Mrs. Stone and Javier returning stopped her.

"If that will be all, Detectives . . ."

"Yes, ma'am, of course. Oh, mind if I ask—what are the River Gardens?"

Mrs. Stone's eyes clouded over. "Another one of Johnny's pipe dreams. A redevelopment project to make the city a destination once more."

"Thanks, Mrs. Stone, and we're both sorry for your loss."

"I bet you are. You can see yourselves out. I have an estate auction to get ready for."

Emily nodded and left the widow in the living room.

Once outside with Javier, Emily asked, "You find any prescriptions we need to be aware of?"

Javier pulled an orange and white box from his pocket and shook it. Empty. "Found this in the trash. The medicine cabinet had another half-empty box of fentanyl patches."

"That's a lot of fentanyl. Explains the drug in his bloodstream. But the doc said he was unconscious when he got whacked with the rock hammer. I suppose that's a blessing. Was the dose deliberate or not, is another question."

He hefted a small white paper bag bearing a pharmacy label. "I took any meds with his name on it. Have a blood pressure prescription, a statin, looks like he had some little blue stiffy pills, and his insulin. And those patches."

"Sounds like the typical prescription buffet for a man his age. Still, though, the fentanyl is an outlier. Can't think of a reason for him to crawl into a homeless camp tent and get high when he had a prescription. I mean, he was an absolute troll, but it wasn't his deal."

"It sounds like the last year was rough. You can't know how far he fell. He could have played his doctor for a patsy to get an opioid prescription."

"Anything's possible, I suppose. We might check in with the prescribing. Oh, and we need to find out when the fentanyl patch prescription was filled."

They settled into Emily's Crown Vic when the radio crackled to life. An officer transmitted a body was found in the river near Discovery Park. Emily recognized the officer's voice.

She keyed her radio. "Three Adam-21, Silver-6 en route."

"10-4, Silver-6. Discovery Park off of Garden Highway, southwest corner of the park."

"That was Brian, wasn't it?" Javier asked.

Emily pulled from the curb. "Don't start."

"I'm not starting anything. I'm imagining a nice romantic brunch you and Officer Conner will have as you share case notes over a floater."

"And that right there—that is jealousy talking. I'm telling your mom you're blowing off Jenny. I know she put a lot of effort into her matchmaking effort. Lord knows she has to."

"You wouldn't dare."

"Try me."

Javier changed the course of the conversation. Emily knew it was to avoid her threat to drag his mother into his love life.

"First drowning of the year. It's a little early. Don't usually get the swimmers caught in the current for a couple of months yet. Water's way too cold."

"Could be someone stumbled in from one of the homeless camps in the park. There's a couple of good-sized ones over there."

Emily knew this park flooded during the winter with the seasonal rain and snowmelt, which meant the homeless camps were transient and migrated to drier locations when the water levels pushed them out. But there were always a few stragglers who held out to the last minute. Maybe this body was one who tried to stay a bit too long.

Javier spotted the black and white police vehicle in the Discovery Park lot near a city dump truck parked near a tracked backhoe. The back of the dump truck was mounded with tents, cardboard, and remnants of another homeless camp.

"Looks like the mayor is cleaning up this campsite, too."

"I don't like the way the city seems to be on top of the cleanup efforts in our crime scenes."

CHAPTER SEVENTEEN

A CITY PUBLIC works man wearing the Day-Glo vest leaned against the city dump truck. He puffed on a cigarette and nodded to Emily and Javier as they parked next to the police black-and-white.

"You looking for the excitement?" It was Tommy Franklin, the city employee at the last camp cleanup. "My partner damn near drove over him while we were scraping up the camp remnants."

"When did you guys start cleaning up over here?" Emily asked.

"Yesterday. The city manager's office has us picking up after these animals trash the park. The code enforcement folks chased them off yesterday morning and we're playing cleanup. Needles, condoms, broken glass, and human waste. It's sickening. Had plans to hit the country music festival here in a couple months. Not no more. This place is a toxic dump."

"The officer down that way?" Emily pointed toward the river.

The city man puffed on his cigarette and nodded.

Emily and Javier followed a worn trail toward the riverbank. The sound of the rapid current of the confluence where the American and Sacramento Rivers joined muffled the traffic from the Interstate 5 overpass.

Emily spotted Brian Conner, in uniform, talking with another city employee wearing an identical eye-popping safety vest. Brian glanced in their direction and waved.

Javier caught Emily tucking her hair behind her ear.

"You want me to hang back so you and Brian can have some alone time?"

"Javi, I have your mother on speed dial."

As they drew close, Brian said, "Detectives, this is Carlos Aguirre. He discovered our deceased as he started to burn the slash pile."

Emily stood next to Brian and Javier crept down the embankment. He needed to sidestep because the freshly scraped soil was wet and slick.

"Mr. Aguirre, can you walk me through what you found?" Emily asked.

"Yeah, sure. I was running my rig, grabbing up the camp leftovers. Started over there." He pointed at the west end of the park. Emily could follow the trail of freshly churned soil.

"Didn't see nothing out of the ordinary, then one of them homeless yells and waves their arms. Then I seen a leg poking out when I was about to light the debris. And here we are."

"How far from the riverbank would you say it was?"

"Oh, I'd guess thirty feet or so. Can't get too much closer to the river on account of the rocks and sand."

"You see anyone pull him out of the river."

"It'd been in the river for sure, but it didn't wash up."

"Officer Conner will make sure we get your contact information."

"Can we get back to work now?"

"I'm afraid not. This is a crime scene now. You know—someone died here?"

"There's always someone croaking in these filthy camps. Ain't the first stiff I've pulled up neither. Usually, they're still gift wrapped in a tent or sleeping bag."

"Your sensitivity is noted. Thank you."

Emily followed Javier's path toward the riverbank.

He stood next to a jumble of scraped-up refuse, brush, downed tree limbs, and discarded tent fabric. The pile was three feet tall and easily eight feet long and reeked of gasoline. Emily couldn't see what Javier was taking a photo of until she got within three feet of the scrap heap—a denim-clad leg sticking out from among the garbage collection.

"Up for a game of Jenga?" Javier said.

The body lay buried in the rubble and tangled in all the debris. The lower leg was the only appendage exposed. Mud clung to the heel of a boot.

"Do we have a whole, or just a part?" Emily asked.

"No way to know until we get some of this crap untangled."

"Call it in and get us the manpower to . . ."

Emily circled around the pile and pulled a torn section of blue tarp away from the heap. She yanked on the plastic wedged between dried tree branches revealing the clothed torso of a man. The body was positioned facing away from her, but she could make out the wet and torn jacket.

"We got a male victim here. Let's back off until we get some crime scene techs to work their magic. The area's already been compromised by the tractor driver. But let's play it by the numbers. Hard to tell, but it looks like the body's been in the water."

Javier got on the phone, and Emily waved Aguirre, the tractor driver, over to her.

"You pour gas on the body?"

Aguirre shook his head. "Yeah, that's when I seen what them yahoos were yelling about."

Emily and Aguirre backtracked to where Brian was with the other city worker.

"We'll need you guys to hang out with Officer Conner until he gets all your contact information and statements. We do have a body down there. Gonna need to keep everyone out. Brian, when you're done, can you set up some perimeter tape from there to the trees on the right?" She pointed to the clump of trees and the muddy trail to the river.

"No problem."

"Oh, before you get going, when did you guys get assigned to clean up here again?"

Franklin, the first city man they spoke with, stubbed out his cigarette on the ground. "Like I said, the city manager's office put us on it yesterday."

"Any idea why the rush?"

He ground his boot heel on the smoldering butt. "Who knows what goes on in there. I just go where they tell me."

"Who told you to burn the debris?"

"Lady, I'm just a truck driver. My boss gets an order from his boss, who gets an order from his boss."

"Officer Conner will take your statements; then you're free to go."

Brian separated the two city workers and started taking a statement from the lead man.

Emily took in Brian's confidence, and he caught her watching and smiled. Damn smile of his.

She turned quickly and slid in the slippery soil, nearly landing on her ass. Graceful as ever.

Javier called her over to a spot near the riverbank, twenty yards from the debris pile.

"We've got some drag marks from the water's edge. Someone pulled the body out of the river."

"Yeah, he didn't crawl out on his own. Check it. The tractor swept up most of the trail, but not here. There are footprints in the mud—two sets of them—on either side of the drag marks," Emily said.

"Two people pulled him from the water and left him here. Didn't call anyone, didn't drag him up to the high ground. They just left him."

"They knew he was dead, but still. They couldn't call anyone either because they weren't supposed to be here or were involved with putting him in the water to begin with."

CHAPTER EIGHTEEN

THE PARKING LOT at the riverside park began filling with vans from the coroner's office, crime scene technicians, and the news media crews who smelled a story in the making. Three multi-colored media trucks parked, and news crews prepped the cameras while the on-screen talent adjusted their hair and makeup. The display was unusual for a single floater from a homeless camp.

Emily and Javier held back to the tree line, some fifty feet from the yellow tape Officer Conner had strung up. Down the embankment behind them, the medical examiner's team and the crime scene techs were photographing the leg-laden debris pile. A team of conscripted city public works crews were starting the gruesome task of pulling the sticks, branches, and trash from the tomb.

"I'll go watch them uncover our body," Javier said. "You deal with that." He pointed to the news crews and a black SUV pulling into the parking lot. The mayor's arrival got the media crews hopping, swiveling their cameras away from the riverbank and locking onto the politician.

Ryan Jensen was the first to step from the vehicle, and he grabbed the rear door handle like a doorman. Mayor Ellen Carsten stepped from the SUV and adjusted her tan wool jacket. The stylish buff suede boots weren't about to touch the dust off the asphalt parking surface.

Mayor Carsten took a stride forward and waited until all the cameras and microphones were in place.

Emily sidled up next to Brian at the yellow tape.

"Didn't know elected officials came out to mourn over an anonymous floater," Brian said.

"They don't. I'm curious why City Hall is here at all."

Jensen caught Emily standing at the tape and circled around the knot of media types.

"Detective."

"How did the mayor get focused on this?" Emily asked.

He glanced back to his boss preparing to speak. "Her Honor is saddened by the continued attacks on the city's unhoused people."

Mayor Carsten greeted two of the reporters by name and began. "Our city is defined by compassion. Compassion for those who have fallen on difficult times, and compassion for those in their moment of need. We're here again to say we've failed them. I have failed them. I've learned another unhoused man was murdered here in a Discovery Park camp.

"As I've made clear, these urban camps are unsafe. We only need the evidence of the last few days to prove my point. My executive order bans camping in these parks and public places, including under our freeways, river access points, and bike trails. These makeshift encampments draw those who would prey upon the vulnerable."

A young, raven-haired reporter called out a question, breaking the mayor's focus. Mayor Carsten put her hands up, chastising the reporter as if she were a schoolgirl. "There will be time for questions."

"Where are the homeless supposed to go?" the reporter pressed on.

The mayor's lips thinned as she considered her response.

"I suppose you believe it's all right for people to be victimized, sexually assaulted, and killed as long as it isn't in your backyard. If it doesn't get in the way of your precious yoga sessions, it must be okay then. If a man is murdered out here on the river, it must be acceptable because you can get on with your *mommy and me* classes."

Emily leaned toward Jensen. "Your boss is worked up."

"She is. Can't blame her though. We've tolerated so much violence against this community, and when she makes a bold move to break the cycle, people are left clutching their pearls."

"The reporter has a point. If you're forcing the homeless out, where are they supposed to go? It's like playing whack-a-mole. They're going to move somewhere else."

"Which is why the mayor needs the city council to get on board and pass the Humanitarian Safe Streets Act. We need funding for proper shelters, mental health and drug abuse services, employment readiness training, and childcare so the moms can get back into the workforce," Jensen said.

"What's the price tag of a dream initiative like that? Won't be an easy sell to raise taxes to cover what her wish list will cost."

"It's not a wish list. We have to turn the tide on the unhoused situation in this city. We can't have any more murders like this. It's the price of living in a civilized society. Besides, you heard Fuller yesterday. He and other investors need to see the city is committed to change before they throw their money behind it."

Emily mulled over the talking points. The homeless population was out of control in the city. Neighboring towns were bussing their homeless into the city limits and dropping them off. Then it struck her.

"How do you know this guy was murdered?"

"That's what the public works crew said. After the fires in the camps, it's too much. I gotta go run some interference before the mayor eats this reporter alive." Jensen strode back to the media pack and whispered into the reporter's ear.

Whatever he said to her got her to stop her inquiry, and Emily swore she saw the woman's complexion redden.

Emily turned to Brian and rolled her eyes.

"I haven't heard any one of the city crew guys talking about the body, if that's what you're thinking."

"Well, it leaked somewhere. Before we even know if it's a murder—which kinda pisses me off," Emily said.

"I get it. I know the two public works guys claim they didn't tell anyone but their supervisor. They only told him they ran a dude over with their tractor."

Emily exhaled. "I gotta go give Javi a hand down there."

"You up for dinner later, maybe?" Brian asked.

Emily tucked her hair behind her ear. "I'd like that. Want me to pull something together?"

"Why don't you let me take care of it. You need a break after everything going on."

Emily wasn't used to someone else caring about her, and it left her with an unfamiliar warm feeling.

She nodded before turning back down the embankment. Another slip in a muddy section and she kept her balance and skidded down another three feet. A quick glance back and she was relieved Brian hadn't witnessed her moment of grace.

Javier stood back from the pile and the four workers pulling the debris apart. In between each limb removal, crime scene techs snapped photographs of the reveal.

"Javi, the mayor announced this guy was murdered."

"Nice of her to do our job."

Another thick limb was threaded out of the pile and discarded off to one side. "Hey, Detectives, you should get a look at this," one of the jumpsuited crime scene techs said, pointing a camera into the debris.

Emily and Javier approached from behind the tech, and the tedious process of removing a single branch at a time revealed the man's body—or most of it anyway.

He lay face down in the pile of garbage and leftover camp artifacts. The man's clothing was in better condition than you'd expect from a long-term camp dweller. No duct tape covering holes or popped seams of the newer light green jacket, and the thick leather belt held up a name brand pair of blue denim jeans, instead of a length of rope.

The crimson blossom in the center of his back told a darker story.

"Looks like the mayor was right on this one," Javier said.

With a pair of nitrile gloves, Emily gingerly navigated the pile and patted the rear pockets. "No wallet."

"Could have washed downstream."

Emily straightened and glanced at the back of the dead man's boots. The mud caked on the heels from the drag from the riverbank. But the back of his pants and bloodstained shirt were free of the gray-brown river soil. "Someone looted the body after they found him. He had a jacket on—a heavier one over this light green job."

"Yeah, there's no mud on his backside."

"Might be where his wallet went, too."

Emily backed off the pile while the public works crew continued to dig out the body. She spotted it. One of the city crewmen snapped a photo with his cell phone held down at a low angle, trying to be casual and unassuming.

"You. Hand it over," Emily said pointing at the man.

His eyes grew wide as she strode toward him. He cast a quick glance at the phone in his hand, and before Emily reached him, he pitched it in the river. The electronic device disappeared with a *plunk* in the rapid gray water.

"Dammit. Who were you sending those photos to?"

"I don't know what you're talking about." The Day-Glo vest flapped open and still bore the creases from coming off the shelf.

"Hey, you guys. You know this one?" Emily asked the other work crew members.

"Not before today. He's new," one of them said.

"Let's see some ID."

"I don't gotta."

"Yeah, you do gotta. You're in the middle of my crime scene, contaminating my evidence."

The man paused, and Emily saw his mind working out the possible options. His shoulders slumped, and he pulled his wallet out, withdrawing a license and press badge.

She glanced at them and handed them to Javier. "Run them."

"What are you doing in my crime scene, Mr. Wilton?"

"I have a right to cover a story."

"You should be up there with the rest of them."

"Here is where the story is."

"Where were you sending those photos?"

"What photos?"

"You wanna play it like that?"

"Like what?"

Emily plucked a set of handcuffs from her belt. "Turn around."

"My followers are going to love this."

"You won't." Emily ratcheted the handcuffs on and gripped Wilton's elbow leading him away from the debris pile. She dropped him on his backside against a tree.

"Want to tell me how you ended up here?"

"I can't give up my sources."

"Someone told you there would be a body?"

"They were right."

Javier joined Emily and handed her Wilton's ID and press badge. "Check this out." He handed her his phone, displaying Wilton's Instagram page. His bio called him a blogger and reporter for hire. "Drop a dime and I'll follow the crime."

"Catchy, but you're no reporter. A fake press badge doesn't make you a reporter."

"I'm a respected blogger."

"Says here you have twenty-five followers."

"You can't believe the numbers the social media platforms show."

"I still want to know what you're doing here."

"My job."

"Who's paying?"

"That's confidential."

Javier scrolled down on the Instagram feed and there was a single image of the riverbank, the work crew, and Emily in the background supervising the scene. A mud-clad boot was visible in the posted photo.

"What's not going to be confidential is you going to jail for being stupid."

"You can't be serious." Wilton started to fidget, and the reality of his situation wasn't the express train to stardom he imagined. His eyes widened when he caught a uniformed officer coming in his direction.

"Listen. I got a phone call telling me to be here. Told me to take photos and text with any updates."

"Who was it from?"

"Don't know. Never got a name."

"Sounds kinda sketchy. What made you jump on board?"

"He sent me five hundred bucks."

"Too bad five hundred won't cover your bail on the interfering with a peace officer charge."

Brian jutted his chin at the seated handcuffed man. "Need some help?"

"We need to get him booked."

He pulled Emily aside. "We got a crowd showing up. I gotta ask. Did your victim get shot in the back?"

Emily drew back. "How did you know?"

"I got two tweakers who look like they were former residents. One of 'em's wearing a newer looking puffy jacket with a hole and a bloodstain on the back."

"Are you shitting me? The guy shows up wearing the victim's jacket?"

"I said they were a couple of tweakers. A species not known for their common sense."

Emily whispered to Javier and passed the update from Brian. Javier nodded and started up the embankment at a leisurely pace.

Brian lifted the handcuffed blogger to his feet and walked him up the hillside. Wilton was crestfallen when he noticed the media crews had packed up and disappeared. Even the mayor's entourage had left the scene.

Two uniformed officers stood back from the yellow tape, watching a small knot of onlookers. Emily spotted the dark green puffy jacket as she strode up the hill. The skinny man wearing it had pulled up the sleeves because they were too long. It looked like a kid borrowing his father's clothes.

Emily approached the tape line while Javier circled behind the group. Most of the group were focused on Officer Conner taking the blogger and putting him in the back of a black and white police SUV. Two men, including the one in the puffy jacket, kept their eyes on Emily. The man in the green jacket shifted from foot to foot. Edgy and anxious.

"Anyone here have a statement to make about what happened down there on the river?"

"What happened? The city people said a guy was killed off. Said he was one of us. We'da known if one of ours was attacked."

Emily noted a red ribbon tied around his thin arm. He was an older man—she'd guessed in his fifties—and his natural hair was flecked with gray. The olive drab military surplus jacket was slick from long wear on the street.

"We don't know where he came from, but I think you're right. He didn't live here in this camp. The ribbon on your arm. I've seen them before. What's it mean?"

"I'm part of our community council. We look out for each other and keep the peace when need be. You all don't do much to help our people. Only time we see the po-lice 'round here is when yous rousting us from one camp to another."

"You're not wrong. Anyone here know how this guy came to be here?"

The guy in the green puffy jacket leaned to the skinny guy next to him, whispering a quiet quip ending with a chuckle shared between them. Emily locked eyes with Puffy.

"You got something to say?"

"We was saying dude prolly was swimmin' upstream to spawn." He gave a fist bump to his meth-skinny friend.

"How'd you know he was in the water?"

The smile evaporated on the tweaker's face. He took a step away when Javier clamped a hand on his shoulder.

"Nice jacket," Javier said.

CHAPTER NINETEEN

PUFFY AND HIS tweaker sidekick sat handcuffed at a rickety picnic table at the edge of the parking lot. The green jacket now lay on the table surface between the two men.

"Let's start with how you found the jacket," Emily said.

"I had it for years."

Emily had his wallet, a folding knife, and an empty plastic bag with a yellow residue clinging to the inside on the table behind him. Flipping open the wallet, she pulled out an expired driver's license. "Phillip Monroe. Well, Phillip, where'd you get it?"

"Don't remember. Prolly got it at Loaves and Fishes. They hand out used clothes all the time."

Emily knew the soup kitchen on North 12th. "When did they start handing out two-hundred-dollar designer jackets?"

"You'd have to ask them."

Emily plopped Phillip's wallet down on the table and picked up the billfold Javier removed from the second skinny tweaker. She slid a driver's license out and paused. Holding it up to the man in front of her, she saw no similarity at all. Fifty pounds lighter, different hair color, and no neck tattoo on the license. The name on the license caught her by surprise.

"Javi, take a look." She handed the license to her partner.

"I'll be right back."

Phillip kicked at his partner's leg. "Damn you. I told you to get rid of it."

"You don't get to tell me shit, Phil."

"I hate to step in here, but let's cut through the bullshit, shall we? We know you stripped the jacket off a dead guy down there. You did notice the bloodstain on the back, right?"

"That's from an old—"

"Stop, just stop. You and I both know that's a lie. The hole and the mud on the back from where you dragged him up the bank. Look at your shoes. They're covered with the stuff."

Phillip glanced down at his mud-caked sneakers.

"Walk me through what you saw."

"Screw it. Phil and me was walking up the river like we do most days. Didn't know the camp was gone. This time a day, most people split and go into the city to panhandle and hustle for a few hours. We rummage around and see what we can get."

"You rip off other homeless people?"

"Hey, it's all free-range out here. If it's yours, you keep it. If you don't care enough about it, then you ain't supposed to have it."

"Whatever, so tell me what you found down there today."

"Phil and me was coming out from the overpass and we seen this green thing in the water. It was kinda hung up on some tree root. Anyhow, we get down there and instead of the ice chest I thought someone lost out of a boat, it was this dead guy."

"You found him in the water?" Emily said, confirming the last known location of the body.

"Yeah. Ain't no doubt he was dead or nothin'—like, we didn't have no part in it. You believe me, right?"

"So far. Keep going. What happened next?"

"We pulled him outta the water and—well, Phil took the jacket and I found dude's wallet."

"Where's the wallet?"

"Tossed it in the river. I kept his ID and sixty bucks in cash. It's not like he can use it anymore."

"And you left him there?"

"It weren't like we killed him or nothing. It ain't like that."

"But acting like a couple of vultures, picking off valuables from the dead, is okay with you?"

"It's just things. Why you gettin' all high and mighty about it?"

Javier slogged back up the embankment with the ID card in hand. He nodded at his partner and handed the driver's license to Emily.

Glancing down at the stolen license, the name on the laminated card made everything more complicated. Pete Bell. The homeless camp social worker lay in the mud with a bullet in the back. What led to a do-gooder face down on a riverbank?

CHAPTER TWENTY

EMILY AND JAVIER knocked the mud off their shoes before they climbed in her blue Crown Vic. Pete Bell's body was collected, wrapped, bagged, and loaded into the coroner's van.

"Dr. Pixley's got to deal with exposure to the cold water and the elements to figure out TOD," Javier said, kicking off another clump of river mud. He removed his shoes and tossed them on the floorboard of the rear seat.

Emily shot a glance at the white socks on her partner's feet. She bit her lip when she recognized they didn't match. One was a plain white cotton athletic sock, and the other was a patterned sock with a flamingo motif.

She couldn't help herself and a snort escaped.

"What?" Javier said.

"I never knew you were such a fashionista."

Javier scanned his attire and noticed the unmatched socks. "They're both white. I dress in the dark in the morning because I have this unreasonable partner who expects me to be up and at 'em at the crack of dawn."

"I know you're old and all, but I didn't expect to see you sporting white socks and sandals at work."

"I'm not wearing sandals. And you—you should talk. Your off-work attire consists of sweatpants and a ratty Oleander band T-shirt."

"It's all about being comfortable in who you are."

"I'm comfortable. You're just—how do you expect to land Officer Conner back there? With your personality?"

"What are you saying, Javi? I'm a young, vibrant woman."

"You're only a few years younger than me."

"But you've aged in dog years, Javi. You've become an old, predictable old man. Did I mention old?"

"Is that right? I'll have you know this isn't even my sock!"

"Oh, you rebel."

"It's Jenny's. It got mixed up in the laundry."

Emily glanced at her partner and caught his smirk. "You dog. You had a sleepover with Jenny? Does your mom know?"

"Don't make it sound so impossible."

"You are full of surprises, partner. Speaking of Jenny, we're not far from the market she mentioned. The camera might have caught the action."

"Might be Bell's last act. Think we'd get lucky enough to see who might have had a beef with him? A couple of nights later, he's meeting with Lisa Larkin and that's the last anyone ever saw him."

Emily pulled the Crown Vic in front of Riverbend Market. Greasy windows covered with iron security bars dominated the storefront. Hand-printed signs proclaimed city vouchers and EBT cards were honored here.

The moment Emily opened her car door, she was hit by the charred smell from the burnt brush and grass across the street. The remains of the camp had been cleared away—as she'd seen in the other fire scene—but the stench remained.

Emily and Javier entered the market. A shrill electronic chime sounded when the door opened.

Javier nodded to an older woman with skin like burnished leather from years in the sun. She sat behind a glass barrier, flipping the pages of a magazine.

"Good morning," Javier said. "Detectives Medina and Hunter. You had a front-row seat to all the action when the camp burned."

The storekeeper folded the page of the magazine and put it away under the counter. "Damn shame what was done to them folks. Most of 'em just tryin' to get by. Don't deserve getting run off like that."

"You see how it started?"

"Nuh-uh. I heard people screamin' and runnin' up the hill. It started down by the river. It run uphill fast and tore that camp up something fierce."

"We noticed you have a camera out front. You think we could look at the recording?"

She narrowed her eyes and paused.

"What?" Javier said.

"Like I done told them other cops. I done handed the copy of the recording for that day to the city."

Emily stole a glance at Javier.

"Who from the city?" Javier asked.

"Don't rightly recall his name. Some fire department type, I suppose."

"And you told the detectives? The other officers you mentioned."

"They was here right after. Didn't have to mention nothing. Probably bumped into him in the lot out front."

"Simmons and Taylor," Emily grumbled. "They never mentioned getting any video—did the officers look at the video?"

The storekeeper nodded. "The fire department man said wasn't nothin' showin' who started the fire."

"Guess we'll have to ask around the arson investigators at the fire department for the video," Javier said.

A smile crept over the woman's face. "I said they got a copy. I still got the original. They don't know no different."

She motioned Javier and Emily to a small back office and plopped down at a computer.

She set up the video, and Emily leaned in to watch.

Dozens of people streamed up the hill from the camp. Thick, black smoke billowed from the riverbank. A shiny black SUV slid into the frame. Homeless people flowed from the campsite, running across the road and out of camera view. Two men, both clad in dark clothing, trotted from the camp and jumped into the waiting vehicle.

"Dammit, they're wearing masks."

"Wait for it," the woman said.

The SUV pulled away from the burning camp and she paused the video. In the rear passenger-side window, one assailant had taken his mask off.

Tommy Franklin, the city public works crew supervisor.

CHAPTER TWENTY-ONE

THE CITY PUBLIC works corporation yard off of X Street was quiet in the middle of the day. A gunmetal-blue, metal-sided building served as the offices where the crews received their assignments and checked out the vehicles and equipment needed for the job.

The rolling metal door was up, and two men were talking at a desk in the far end of the building. The metal skin of the structure amplified their conversation about the lows and woes of the Las Vegas Raiders and how the team was stolen from Northern California.

Both men wore the same Day-Glo vests that Emily noted on Tommy Franklin and Carlos Aguirre while they worked at Discovery Park.

"Can I help you?" the one behind the desk sounded, and the tone conveyed less concern for "help" and more of "why are you bothering me?"

Emily flashed her badge. "Detectives Hunter and Medina. You the supervisor here?"

"I am." The man behind the desk lowered his feet from the surface. "What's you need?"

"Want to talk to you about one of your employees, Mr. . . ." Emily found an overturned nameplate on the desk, flipped it upright. "Tannen."

"There's my cue to get back at it. Got PM to do on the claw." The second worker shuffled off to start preventative maintenance on the machine, leaving the supervisor with the detectives.

"Tell us about Tommy Franklin," Emily said.

"Tommy? What's he gone and done now?"

The first box on Emily's mental list—check. Tommy Franklin was, in fact, a public works employee.

"How do you assign crews? How would Franklin know what jobs to cover on a given day?"

"It's not like rocket science or nothing. I get a project list from the boss and assign crews to get the work done. We're a union shop—means crew leads get first pick."

"Franklin a crew lead?"

"Yep."

"Where does the project list come from? Who puts it together? I mean, there's no shortage of work that needs done in the city, right?"

"It's above my pay grade. The director of public works puts the list together and the assistant city manager approves it before it gets passed down to me here in maintenance services."

"Can you show me a list? Today's maybe. Where were crews assigned this morning?"

Tannen sighed and acted put out when he took three steps from his desk and plucked a clipboard off the wall. He handed it to Emily. "Here's the project list for the week."

Emily ran a finger down the page. Line after line of projects, including gutter cleaning in her neighborhood, filling potholes, sidewalk repair, and tree trimming. She flipped to yesterday's list of projects and more of the same. Crew names were listed next to their assigned projects. Today's project assignments showed Tommy Franklin signed up for landscape maintenance in Del Paso Heights.

"I don't see clearing out homeless camps on the lists."

"We don't have work like that scheduled. Those are touchy—got to make sure all the tents are empty. A state road crew ran a tractor over a guy sleeping in his tent. You can imagine the shitstorm afterward. When we got a cleanup, even a small camp, we put lots of manpower behind it."

"Thing is, Tommy Franklin was at Discovery Park today and his crew was cleaning up a campsite down on the river."

"Nah, you got it wrong. Says here he was supposed to lay down new bark in the playground up in Del Paso. Had to replace it on account some yahoo burnt it."

"Franklin was at Discovery Park and I know it because they discovered a body."

"A human body? They didn't—I mean they weren't responsible for killing it, were they?"

Tannen's knees wobbled, and he braced himself on the desk. "Damn Franklin. I knew he was gonna drag us down."

Emily handed the clipboard to Javier. He made the same connection and told Tannen they were going to need to keep the lists.

"Wanna unpack that for me, Tannen?"

Tannen collapsed into his chair, holding his head in his hands. "I knew it. I knew it would come back and bite me on the ass. They was supposed to do the work, and that's it."

"Work not on the project list from City Hall?"

He rocked more, then nodded in response to Emily's question.

"Run down how Franklin and Aguirre were working at Discovery Park."

Tannen sat back in his chair, the springs loose from frequent reclining. "There's always more work than the city can get around to. Sometimes a special request comes in and we get it moved to the top. It stays off the official project list, but we get the crews on-site and get the work done. There's a little extra cash goes along with those jobs so everyone wants them."

"A special request comes in for Discovery Park cleanup and Franklin takes the assignment."

Tannen nodded. "Picks his crew—whoever he wants—in this case Carlos on account of him being a good worker and won't ask no questions. Gets the equipment he needs from the lot and takes care of business."

Javier nodded to the yard and let Emily know he was going to talk to the maintenance man.

"And Franklin got paid off the books for this work. Who paid for the special request?"

"I don't know. The cash comes in an envelope with the particulars. I'm always the first one here to open up the shop—about five thirty. The money and the details are dropped off overnight. I have a lockbox." Tannen pointed to a metal box welded to the front door. A locked metal box, accessible from the inside of the shop. From the outside, it appeared like a typical mail slot.

"Who orders the work done?"

"Don't know—never needed to know. If someone wants to grease the wheel a little, it gets handled first. We only got so many resources to spread around. Might as well put them where they're appreciated."

"You mean where you get paid. What's your cut on the cash coming in?"

"Listen, everyone gets their fair split."

"You're getting paid by the city, like me. Then you take someone's money and use city crews and equipment to do private work. What about the projects that were supposed to get done—like the playground in Del Paso?"

"They'll all get handled eventually. Besides, the way I see it, this way we go where we're needed. Them black and brown kids in Del Paso don't need no playground anyhow. They'll be hanging out on the corners dealing and gangbanging right out of preschool."

"Well, aren't you a little racist ray of sunshine?"

"Just calling it like I see it."

"Me too, asshole. How much did Franklin get for cleaning up Discovery Park? How about the 7th Street camp cleanup? He on that, too?"

"He got five grand. Same for the 7th Street camp cleanup."

"That's a lot of cash."

"The project had to be done quickly, so we got a little more juice."

"Franklin got both projects. Doesn't it make the others jealous, with him getting the special projects?"

"There's only a couple I use for projects like this. Actually, they asked for Franklin specifically."

"How would anyone know who to ask for?"

Tannen shrugged. "Don't know, didn't ask."

"You have any of the written project requests?"

"Have one he got this week."

"Hand it over."

"Do I gotta?"

"You gotta."

Tannen slid open the desk drawer and removed a folded piece of paper, placing it on the scarred surface between them.

Emily used a pen and opened the document. Typewritten, no signature.

"Immediate squatter camp cleanup. Riverside under the railroad bridge at 18th Street. Put Franklin on it."

"When did this arrive?"

"Found it in the lockbox. Don't know when, exactly."

"Where's the cash?"

"What cash?"

"Tannen, you said these special requests always come with cash. Hand it over."

"Tommy got his cut already. All's I have left is my taste. I don't gotta give that up, do I?"

Emily crossed her arms and waited. Tannen pursed his lips, shoved open another drawer, and tossed a thick envelope on the desktop.

"Dropped off like this?" Emily tapped on the typed document.

"Yeah. Like the other times. Never seen who makes the delivery."

"You check every morning to see if you have a special request like this?"

"Well, yeah, I know when to look for them on account of the text messages."

Emily sighed. "Text messages, and you didn't think to tell me about them until now? Show me. Let me see your phone." She put her hand out, treating him like a disobedient toddler. She knew he didn't have to surrender the phone, and she'd have to get a warrant to force him to comply if he refused.

Tannen unclipped a phone from his belt and thumbed the screen until the message popped up. He handed the cell to Emily.

She glanced at the screen. The string of text was short and simple. "Delivery. Make it happen."

"You ever text back or call the number?"

"Never had no reason to."

Emily forwarded the message to her phone and jotted down the number as a backup.

Taking the cell phone back from Emily, Tannen swallowed hard. "So, what happens now?"

"That depends."

CHAPTER TWENTY-TWO

As Emily and Javier pulled from the city corp yard, Javier briefed her on his discussion with the maintenance man.

"He made sure Franklin had whatever he needed for his off-the-books projects. The guy knew it was shady because he disconnected the odometers and hour meters to avoid showing city equipment used for private purposes. Said he's been doing it for four or five years, but nothing on the frequency we're seeing now."

"Was he getting a cut, too?"

"Says he wasn't, but I'm not convinced. I'm sure he was getting his end."

"Franklin was getting his. Did your guy give you an idea how many others were involved?"

"Franklin for sure. He said Franklin always picked a guy who wouldn't question him. Usually a new guy, one who needs the work and less likely to rock the boat. I'm thinking we could lean on Aguirre a bit and see what he's been keeping quiet about."

"If what I'm thinking about works, we might not have to lean on him. I want Franklin and I want the person who's financing this. The more I mull it around, might not be the same person we've been after for Mayor Stone's murder. I don't see the connection.

Some low-level landscape maintenance guy on the take and an ex-mayor don't seem like they'd run in the same circles."

"I hear you. With Bell dead, where does that leave us? If the fires stop, it tends to label him as the arsonist."

"But there were two of them in that video. Franklin and the other one who didn't take his mask off. He moved more athletically and didn't look big enough for Bell."

"Bell's neighbor mentioned Bell getting picked up in a black SUV, right?"

"And they were all dressed in dark clothes. That's not what Bell was wearing when we found him."

Emily pulled into a slot at the police department headquarters off of Freeport and shut down the engine. "The only common threads are the attacks on the homeless camps."

"Each of them have a different connection to the camps. The former mayor, Franklin, and Bell. You think the homeless aspect might be throwing us off the scent?"

Emily pulled her buzzing cell phone from her pocket as they walked into the building.

"Hunter."

"Detective, Chief Clark needs to see you. Don't even think about telling me you're not in the building. I know these things."

Sandy was the chief's personal secretary and had outlasted the last three top cops. If there was a cop equivalent to a mafia boss's consigliere, Sandy was it. She knew where all the bodies were buried and you didn't want to get on her bad side.

"On our way, Sandy. Anything I need to know?"

"The chief got an unexpected visit from City Hall."

"Understood." Emily hung up.

"Shit. That was fast." She hit the speed dial button for Lieutenant Hall.

The lieutenant picked up on the first ring. "Detective, what's up?"

"Got a call from Sandy. Wants us there. Seems they got a visit by City Hall."

"Great. Where are you?"

She knocked on his office door. "Right here."

Lieutenant Hall grabbed his jacket from a hook on the back of his door. "Thanks for letting me know, Emily. Don't know why Sandy didn't give me a ring."

"Habit, probably. The chief's summoned me before—sometimes it's because people seem to think I overstep."

"I find it so hard to believe, Detective."

Javier chimed in, "You've met Detective Hunter, haven't you?"

They arrived at the chief's outer office. Sandy nodded and gestured them to the door. Javier opened the mahogany door and before they entered, Hall grabbed Emily by the elbow and nodded. She knew it was an unspoken thank-you for respecting his position and authority. There were others in the department who didn't offer the same respect because Hall was gay and Black.

The chief sat at a low table to the right. Across from him, sipping coffee, was Ryan Jensen and Mayor Ellen Carsten.

"Lieutenant, Detectives, please join us. The mayor was just telling me she's concerned about the continuing rash of violence directed at the homeless."

"I think we all are, sir. There is quite a bit we're running down, but the two murders we have may be—are somehow—connected to the violence at the camps," Lieutenant Hall said.

"Two murders?" the mayor said. "I only knew of one—John Stone. There's been another?"

Emily wondered how the mayor knew of Stone's demise so quickly. The leak had been inevitable.

"Yes, ma'am. A second victim was found at Discovery Park."

Ryan Jensen set his coffee cup down with a clatter, spilling a drop on the tabletop. "So, it was true. Like we were told. Another murder in the homeless camps?"

"Definitely a murder."

"These homeless camps attract a vile element, and this is the inevitable result. What do you know about this most recent victim?"

Emily felt the political pressure in the room shift with Jensen's comment. The mayor's team would run with any details of the crimes to support their approach to making homelessness illegal. She had to tread carefully.

"We're looking into the victim's background and his association with the camps. He served as a homeless advocate. We're pulling together a profile of his activity and known associates to help us determine the motive for his murder," she said.

"He wasn't another homeless person?" the mayor asked.

"No, ma'am."

"Someone who worked to better the homeless was murdered trying to do his job," Mayor Carsten said.

She turned to the chief. "This is exactly why we need to step up the enforcement of our urban camping ban. They are a cesspool of crime and violence. Good Samaritans like this man, who was trying to help, are murdered. It's no longer an issue of crime contained in the camps."

"That might be premature, Madame Mayor. We're looking into possible criminal activity our victim may have been involved in, taking advantage of the vulnerable people trapped in the camps."

"It proves my point, Detective. The camps lure bad elements. And trapped? Really? Most of those people live there by choice. No one forces them to become drug addicts. No one forces them to rob and kill one another. They are unable to live in civilized society, and it's our responsibility to rehabilitate them and put them in a position to contribute to the community."

Chief Clark seemed to sense Emily's next less-than-politically-correct response coming and said, "They're all citizens of the city, no matter what happened in their life circumstances. Our charge is to keep all citizens safe, no matter where they live. Detectives Hunter and Medina are two of my best, and they'll find out who's responsible for these crimes."

"I'm sure they're fine investigators. My plan to eliminate the camps altogether should be a move you'd support, seeing so much of your best investigators' time is wasted in these squalid pits."

Ryan Jensen added on, "Think of the real crime your people could investigate if they weren't always responding to the camps."

Emily stiffened. "Real crime? You don't think murder, arson, assaults, and human trafficking are real enough?"

Jensen smiled and seemed to enjoy getting a rise out of her. "What we're saying is—what the mayor has been saying all along is—getting people off the street and into shelters with supportive programs will be a cost savings for the city."

"There aren't enough shelters and programs to serve them all."

"It's part of the mayor's capacity building plan. But we also need to be mindful of other counties dumping their burden on us—the whole if-you-build-it-they-will-come idea.

"Isn't that what you're doing? Pushing them out of the city?"

"We can't solve the world's problems. We're only responsible for and accountable to the citizens of this city," Jensen said.

"Speaking of the city, can you tell me how these three camps—
7th Street, Discovery Park, and 18th Street—were cleaned up by
city crews so quickly?"

"And I should thank them for it," the mayor said. "The minute
a camp vacates, we must move in and reclaim the property."

"Mr. Jensen and I have had this discussion before. The city has
never been this quick to act—on, well, anything. We've—"

The mayor straightened in her seat. Her lips thinned and her
jaw tightened.

Lieutenant Hall cleared his throat. "What Detective Hunter's
found is unusual. Special burn permits issued to incinerate the
camp debris, and the clearing of that rubble. Typically, those
approvals take weeks. Air Quality Assurance Board process alone
takes multiple hearings. Yet in these instances, it looks like the
city public works crew took it upon themselves to act first and seek
permission later. The clearing and burning may have eliminated
potential evidence. Not to mention the possible environmental
damage from these activities in a protected watershed."

As the mayor prepared to respond, Jensen placed a hand on her
knee. Emily noticed the strange, intimate gesture.

"We'll look into the matter. Public works crews, you say. Well,
I have to hand it to them. They must be as upset as the rest of the
city over the fact a few people have taken our public areas hostage.
The way I see it, they need to be commended, not attacked. I'm sure
they took all environmental precautions—they are professionals
after all."

Emily recalled debris running into the river and black toxic
smoke from the burn piles. They reminded her of the poisonous
burn pits veteran groups protested. Tannen and his double-dipping
partner, Tommy Franklin, didn't scream professional in any

definition of the word. Opportunist, perhaps. Fraudsters, definitely.

"With the city reclaiming these locations, like you said, what are you planning on doing with them?" Emily said.

"Our citizens will be able to use their parks and river access for recreation again," the mayor said.

Emily flashed on the project file she noticed in former mayor Stone's home. "What's River Gardens?" she asked.

Both the mayor and Jensen fell silent. Mayor Carsten was the first to break. "Where did you hear that?"

"Something I ran across recently. A development project, if I recall," Emily said.

"River Gardens was a plan to revitalize the downtown area and anchor it with riverside condominium development and commercial properties. It comes up every couple of years. It's actually been kicking around for quite some time."

"Mayor Stone was a proponent, as I understand."

"I wouldn't know. I wasn't on the council then."

"But you were, Mr. Jensen." Emily shifted her gaze to him.

"Mayor Stone advocated all sorts of redevelopment projects during his administration. I don't recall the specifics of River Gardens, other than the commercial districts would mirror the feel of the riverside shops and tourist attractions of Old Sacramento."

Emily knew the Old Sacramento district well, with its cobblestone streets, bars, shops, and river attractions like the Delta King steamboat. Artificial tourist trap is what came to mind.

Jensen glanced at his watch. "Mayor Carsten, we need to get moving to the ribbon cutting in Oak Park."

"Which one is that again?"

"The new women's shelter."

"Oh, yeah, that."

The mayor stood from the chair, straightened her skirt, and shook the chief's hand. "Please keep me advised on your progress in this investigation. We need to make sure the citizens of this city know they are safe from the violence centered in the homeless camps."

The chief agreed to keep her in the loop as new developments came to light.

Ryan Jensen paused at the door, glanced over his shoulder at Emily. "I trust your best investigators will focus on the camp-centered violence and not get distracted with city business and whatever Mayor Stone had planned." A grin appeared on the staffer's face and it made Emily grow cold.

CHAPTER TWENTY-THREE

"WHAT THE HELL did he mean?" Emily said after the mayor and Jensen left the chief's office.

"That was a 'stay in your lane' warning," Chief Clark said. "And not a very subtle one. I get the feeling you know more than you let on in front of our City Hall friends."

Emily glanced from the chief to Lieutenant Hall. "I haven't had time to brief the lieutenant yet, sir. Detective Medina and I only now got back to the office."

"Go ahead, Emily," Lieutenant Hall said with a nod.

"The three homeless camp crime scenes. Two involved an attack on the camp residents, burning the tents and shelters. Murder victims were found at two of the locations. In each case, a city public works crew shows up and clears the place out, right down to the topsoil, within hours."

"I'm sorry, Detective. I don't see the connection," the chief said.

"The connection is the public works crew."

Javier pulled a copy of the store video feed captured in the aftermath of this morning's fire. "Two men, these two, lit the most recent fire and were picked up by—there it is—this black SUV. Detective Hunter and I recognized this guy. Tommy Franklin—a city public works employee."

The lieutenant nodded. "Good deal. You might have a lock on the arsonist for one fire. But how do we connect him to the other fires and the two homicides?"

"Javi—Detective Medina—and I met Franklin at Discovery Park, where our second victim was found. Franklin was getting paid under the table to clean up these crime scenes. The projects were never approved by the city, no environmental permits, no planning department sign-off."

"Okay, I'll admit it's odd, but like the mayor said, some city employee takes some initiative and cleans up the city. There's not much to connect your public works crew to the attacks. You've got video of the guy at the scene, but nothing showing him lighting the fires."

"We have witness accounts of two men wearing masks like this starting the fires, and at the 7th Street camp, beating the residents with a bat. I know how unreliable the homeless population is when it comes to testimony. They are hard to locate when it comes to trial and their histories provide enough impeachment evidence for a competent defense attorney. We have messages and money drop-offs at the city corporation yard—directing Franklin to clean up the crime scenes—messages delivered before the camps are burned."

"Who's behind the money?"

"I don't know yet," Emily said, and rubbed the back of her neck.

"How does your Franklin guy connect to Mayor Stone's murder?"

"Admittedly, he doesn't. Witness reports say the attackers got spooked when they stumbled over his body. The coroner says he was already dead when the camp was torched."

The chief sat down behind his desk. "What are we missing? I see where you're going here, but there's a big fat hole, especially when it comes to the two homicides. Are you thinking Franklin is the guy behind them?"

"I don't. I think he knows who's pulling the strings, though. Could be the murderer using Franklin as his personal crime scene cleanup crew."

"Doesn't get you any closer on the murders."

"True, but I think we can squeeze some information out of Franklin while we try to find the connection between the ex-mayor's murder and the second victim, Pete Bell, a camp social worker."

The chief stretched his neck. "Every bit of this feeds into the mayor's narrative about the homeless camps and the violence surrounding them. The involvement of city crews to torch and sweep away any evidence is a troubling twist."

"You think the fire was set to cover up Mayor Stone's murder?" Lieutenant Hall asked.

Emily paced the office. She stopped mid-stride. "Could be the connection we're looking for. *If* Franklin burned the camp, and *if* someone paid him to take care of it, that's the person we want."

"What's your plan?" Hall asked.

"The corp yard supervisor knows we have him dead to rights on running a fraud ring out of the city shops. He's going to give Franklin the message that he's done getting special assignments to get rid of the camp debris. No more money. Should make Franklin angry. If he's angry, he'll make a mistake."

"You going to follow him?" the chief asked.

"We're watching for another money drop at the corp yard. I'd like to have surveillance on his place, too. He might realize we're onto him and try to lay low."

"Do it," Lieutenant Hall said. "The city facility doesn't have any expectation of privacy there. We don't need a warrant."

"Might be a little more complicated for city cell phones. The supervisor gets a message from a number before each drop. I'd feel better with a warrant for them because of the whole two-party consent issue. Might apply if a text leads to a phone call."

"Good point, Detective. Let's draw up a quick affidavit and get it filed."

"Keep me in the loop on this one," the chief said. "Especially as it concerns our City Hall friends."

Emily nodded and left the office with Javier and Lieutenant Hall.

"Man, if this bleeds over into Mayor Carsten's homeless cleanup initiative, it's gonna get ugly," Hall said.

"Lieutenant, I'm sorry to blindside you like I did. I never intended to go around you."

"Emily, don't worry about it. I know you didn't plan on it. The chief gets to ask whatever he wants, and our job is to answer him—directly."

"Still, I don't mean to undermine you."

Lieutenant Hall stopped in the walkway. He leaned in and spoke barely above a whisper. "Emily, you and I share a common experience here. Despite our records, our experiences, and commendations, there are those here—in this building—who want to see us fail. They cannot accept that a Black gay man, or a woman, can do the job. That goes for you, too, Javier. We know there's a culture at work here—they expect us to be incompetent and they will try to sabotage us so they can prove their point. We compensate for that by exceeding expectations, not because we can, but because we have to."

"I know you understand, Emily. I've seen you deal with it before. I have no question that you have my back. I hope you know I have yours, too."

"We do, Lieutenant."

"All right then, let's get these warrant affidavits wrapped up."

"Yes, sir."

Emily and Javier met at her desk. Javier glanced at the lieutenant's office. "I didn't know he felt it like we do. I mean, he's been in the job for twenty years."

"For some, that's not enough and it'll never be enough. The same people who bemoan identity politics are quick to use identity to expect him to fail."

Javier lowered himself into his chair, pulled his keyboard in, and started in on the affidavit for a trap and trace for Franklin's number and the number Tannen provided. "I know this won't give us the content of the call or message, but it will show all numbers coming to and from them. Hopefully, it will give us a fix on who's making those payments."

Emily accessed the DMV records for Franklin and jotted down the address. She prepared the affidavit for a search warrant at the address shown in the DMV file. He was on video running from the fires. A defense attorney could argue their client was fleeing along with everyone else in the camp. It wasn't like they had a photo of him with a torch in his hand. They needed a smoking gun.

CHAPTER TWENTY-FOUR

EMILY AND JAVIER parked a half block from the address Franklin listed with the DMV. A second-floor apartment off Whitney Avenue near American River College. The small apartment complex consisted of a dozen units on two levels. Javier did a quick walk-through into the complex courtyard and tagged Franklin's unit as the corner unit on the left front.

The windows were dark in Franklin's apartment since they'd arrived an hour ago.

"You know, Franklin as the shooter makes sense. He gets the camps emptied, burning, beating with a bat, or shooting to fulfill the mayor's vision of a homeless-free city. It's twisted, but I can see why someone might go there."

"I put in a call to Dr. Pixley. She's gonna call us when Bell hits the table—tomorrow, she thinks. She's getting backed up. If we can get the slug, we can run it on NIBN. Maybe we get lucky and get a pop. Best we can do without the gun, anyway."

Javier peered at the window with a pair of binoculars. "Still like to know who paid him to do it. Think he's the type to roll on his benefactor if we take him down for the murder and arson?"

"We can hope."

Javier's phone sounded with the Pat Benatar refrain "Hit Me With Your Best Shot." Emily sniggled at the pop music ring tone.

"What? She is a rock icon." He accepted the call. "Medina. Oh. Hi Mom, didn't recognize the number. Um, yeah—yeah, I can tell her. No, Mom, I don't need you to do that. Yes, Emily's here with me."

He held the phone to her. "She wants to talk to you."

"Hi, Mrs. Medina."

"Hello, dear. Two quick things. I noticed Connie seemed a little more confused today. She wanted to leave. When I asked her where she wanted to go, all she said was home. I was cleaning up after dinner and found her medication. She's not taking it. She's trying to hide it in her napkins. Found two other little stashes like that. We need to figure out a way to make sure she knows it's important to take them.

"Secondly, I heard from friends saying Western Health fired the director and four or five staff members at the facility. Apparently, Connie wasn't the only one they neglected. It makes me angry they could do that to Connie. I could spit."

"I'm not surprised. I feel for the residents there. I don't think I'd feel comfortable sending her back there—no matter who the new director is."

"Emily, honey, I think it's time to consider something more than supportive care or assisted living. It's time to think about specialized memory care facilities."

Emily put the cell phone to her forehead. She let out a deep breath. The time had come, Emily knew it. But to hear someone else say the words cut at Emily's soul. Connie fought going to assisted living, comparing the facility to a dump where old people went when their families got tired of them. Now this. Getting her to go into a memory care facility, especially when she couldn't even mentally process the idea, would be a battle.

"I knew this day was coming. Brian's been helping me with a list of possible facilities. His mom went through the same thing. He knows the struggle."

"He also knows what this is doing to you, dear. Don't be afraid to lean on him. It doesn't make you weak."

"I know . . ."

"If you share the list you and Brian have been working on with me, I can tell you if I know any of them, and maybe Connie and I can go on a field trip and happen to drop in."

"You think she's willing to go along?"

"I can be persuasive. Just ask my son. Speaking of—would you tell him to call Jenny? Her mother has been nagging me. She's a nice girl, and I think my Javier likes her. I don't know what his problem is. Make him listen, Emily."

"Yes, Jenny is a nice girl," she said, looking at Javier, who winced at the direction of the conversation with his mother.

"I'm sure he'll get ahold of her. He probably wants her to wait and realize he is one of the city's most eligible bachelors."

"Oh, I'm aware of that nonsense."

"I know. I think he's put out over barely making the list at all."

"Would you stop winding her up?" Javier whispered.

"Get him to listen to you, Emily. Drop the list by when you have a chance, and I'll get Connie used to the idea."

Emily agreed and disconnected the call, handing Javier the cell.

"So, mommy dearest doesn't know you and Jenny had a sleepover."

"No—and it's none of anyone's business."

"Well, maybe it wasn't so memorable for her. She didn't tell her mother you'd 'reconnected.'"

"You are an evil—we have movement. Anything from the team at the corp yard?"

"Nothing," Emily said.

A light flicked on in Franklin's apartment. Javier keyed the radio and connected with the officers who parked behind the complex. They were going to coordinate the takedown to cut off any escape route Franklin may have and limit the risk to residents in the adjoining apartments. They opted against evacuating the apartment complex because Franklin would have smelled that effort and snuck out.

Emily and Javier slipped on their ballistic vests, tightening the Velcro tabs on the side. Emily grabbed a green-colored shotgun from the rear of the SUV and gently lowered the lid.

They sprinted across the street and entered the front of the complex. At the same time, two uniformed officers came into view from the rear of the building. The officers cut to their right and climbed the stairs to the second level, while Emily and Javier took a matching set to their left.

The detectives arrived first, since Franklin's apartment was in the front of the building. The officers drew close, and their heavy footfalls were going to give away their approach.

"Oh shit. It's Stark," Emily whispered to Javier.

Officer Robert "Bobby" Stark was a thirty-year veteran on the job. At six-three and three hundred pounds, Stark was imposing and intimidating. Brash, loud, and opinionated—especially when it came to his beliefs about women on the job. He'd earned a suspension or two for running his mouth about how female officers should be at home making a sandwich for their husband, not in a police uniform. He'd come close to getting canned after he didn't respond to calls for backup assistance from female officers. One of them was Emily.

She'd been the first unit on the scene of a domestic violence call. Husband and wife were slugging it out on the front lawn. The call came in from a neighbor, probably one of the half-dozen people gathered on the sidewalk cheering the combatants on. No one was trying to break it up.

Emily called for backup, waded through the crowd, and ordered the couple to stop. The drunk husband—Emily could smell the booze on him—spun around and tried to shove Emily. He stumbled and missed her, falling on the lawn. The wife jumped at the opportunity and pounded on her downed spouse, pummeling him with both fists.

Emily grabbed her by the collar and pulled her off of him. The husband responded by taking a drunken swing at Emily. "Nobody touches my woman."

Temporarily aligned, the two faced off with Emily, yelling, spitting, and threatening to kick her ass. Emily kept her distance, waiting for her backup to arrive.

The wife lunged, holding a small blade. She'd not pulled the weapon on her husband, but tried to cut Emily. Emily caught the glint of the steel and pulled a pepper spray canister from her Sam Browne belt.

An orange cloud enveloped the woman and sent her into a coughing fit. She dropped the weapon, fell to her knees, and gagged.

The thing about pepper spray is it's carried by the wind, so the onlookers who encouraged the front lawn domestic squabble caught a little of the effects of the chemical agent as it wafted in their direction. They coughed and started to back away.

Emily handcuffed both of the combatants and shoved them in the rear of her patrol vehicle. Usually, you'd separate the two, but her backup, Stark, never responded.

Now, Stark pounded down toward Franklin's apartment door, not even trying to hide his presence.

"The captain sent us to make sure some real cops were here in case you fuck this up."

Emily knew the captain didn't send him. Stark was lazy and incompetent, and the only reason he was at her location was to mess with her.

"Stay out of my way, Stark."

Emily knocked on the door. A slight rustling emanated from within the apartment. Emily knocked again. "Mr. Franklin. Open up. Police."

A scuffling sound from behind the door, with the lock turning. The door opened a crack. The face peering out wasn't Tommy Franklin.

A wide-eyed Tannen, Franklin's boss, stared through the opening.

CHAPTER TWENTY-FIVE

"Tannen, what are you doing here?" Emily said.

Tannen opened the apartment door. "Prolly same as you, looking for Tommy."

Emily peered past Tannen into the apartment. Either Franklin was a slob, or Tannen tore the place apart in a frantic search.

"Franklin wasn't into the whole Martha Stewart thing, was he? Better step aside. Stark, cuff him up."

Emily slipped inside the apartment. It was a small space. Open living room and kitchen. A door to the right hung open, revealing a bedroom. A bookshelf in the living room bore evidence of being ransacked. Papers, books, and a couple of framed photos lay on the worn olive-green shag carpet.

Stark shoved Tannen on the sofa to cool off while Javier checked the bedroom.

"No one else is here," Javier said.

Emily pointed at the clutter on the floor. "This your doing?"

Tannen slunk into the sofa.

"Where's Franklin?"

"If I knew, I wouldn't be sitting here."

"Fair enough. Wanna tell me why you're in a hurry to find him?"

"Not especially, no," Tannen said.

From the back room, Javier called out for Emily. "Hey, come check this out."

While Stark stayed with Tannen, Emily joined her partner in the small apartment bedroom. It was furnished with hand-me-down college dorm furniture. Nothing matched, and it was all worn to the inch of useful life.

Javier stood at a closet, a small one. "Franklin didn't pick the place for the ample storage. Not that he needed it." Javier slid the closet door open, and it was completely empty. Not so much as a warped metal hanger on the rod inside.

"It's the same with the dresser. Empty. All of it."

"It's like Franklin didn't live here. If he packed up and split, he'd leave some trace behind."

"Same in the bathroom. Cabinet is empty."

Emily looked for herself. She drew back the stained shower curtain. "Huh, nothing. Not even a half-melted bar of soap."

Same in the small kitchen. The cabinets were empty. There was a six-pack of a local microbrew, or what was left of it, in the refrigerator.

"Looks like he's into your hipster beer," Emily said.

Javier pulled a bottle from the shelf and examined the label. "Been here for months. This brewery puts a date on the bottle when they brewed the batch. Check it out."

Emily leaned in. "Eight months ago."

"Odd, don't you think?"

Emily turned and surveyed the apartment. She took a stride to the tossed contents of the living room bookshelf. The framed photograph on the top of the heap lay face down. Turning it over, it sent a shiver through Emily.

She extended it to Javier. "Look familiar?"

The photo was a wider angle of the picture she'd found in the foster care headquarters. Mayor Stone, Ryan Jensen, and Pete Bell were side by side. But in this version, Tommy Franklin was next to Bell.

"What do you make of this?" Emily said.

"Our boy Tommy had a connection to Bell . . ."

"Sure enough. Was the connection worth killing him?"

They returned to Tannen sulking on the sofa. "What do you know about this apartment? Kinda obvious Franklin didn't live here."

"It's the address I had for him."

Emily held out the photo to Tannen. "Recognize any of the men with him in the photo?"

Tannen squinted as he examined the photo. Emily saw his eyes widen. Recognition.

"Which one you know?" she asked.

"All of 'em. Had no idea Franklin knew the mayor and these guys. Never said a word about it. Musta wanted to keep it on the down low."

"How do you know these guys?"

"Well, Mayor Stone, on account of him being the mayor and all. The guy next to him was his PR flack while he was in office. The guy next to Tommy, Bell—well he's a strange one. Supposed to be some kind of kid counselor, but the only times I seen him, he was doing more than counseling, if you know what I mean."

"No, I don't. Spell it out for me."

"Bell is a strange ranger. I don't got no proof or nothing, but them young girls he kept talking to, there was no counseling going on. I overheard Tommy on the phone talking to someone, probably Bell, and said something about how bad he wanted to find this new girl."

"What was special about her?"

"I dunno."

"How'd you get in here?"

"Tommy keeps a spare key ring in his locker. I needed to get in touch with him. I got a new text message."

"You're just now mentioning that little detail?"

"I was gonna call you."

"Why don't I believe you?"

Tannen shifted on the sofa, handcuffs rattling behind him. "Listen, okay—the text said tomorrow, Franklin needed a cleanup crew at Miller Park."

"Miller Park? That's on the Sacramento River," Javier said.

"And a huge homeless camp on the south end near the marina," Emily said.

Emily straightened and glanced at her watch. She let the seconds bleed away. There was going to be another homeless camp attack—tonight.

CHAPTER TWENTY-SIX

STARK AND HIS partner took Tannen for booking. The veteran patrolman wasn't happy about wasting his time with paperwork for a trespassing charge.

"Get it done, Stark," Emily said, knowing, in this case, Tannen would be on the street before Stark finished his report.

Emily and Javier searched the apartment and uncovered no evidence of cameras or photographic equipment hidden in the nooks and crannies of the small bedroom.

"What do you make of Tannen's story—Bell's extracurricular activities?" Javier said.

"There's not much there. The girls at the Receiving Home said Bell gave them a pervy vibe. Now he's looking for a particular girl?"

"Or a particular type . . ."

"What do you think about Tannen telling us about the new text message?"

"The one about Miller Park?"

"Yeah. On the surface it's a cleanup order, like the others. Telling him where the cleanup was supposed to happen means he'd burn the camp down hours before."

"Simple, but kinda slick. Whoever sent the message could claim they were only calling to get a camp cleaned up. Nice way to get some plausible deniability," Javier said.

"Franklin didn't receive this message; does it mean the camp won't get hit tonight?"

"We can't take the chance. I'll call the Watch Commander and see if we can get a unit or two over there to sit on the camp."

"Good idea, Javi. Need to figure out where Franklin's hiding. I need to go home and relieve your mom. She's been a miracle worker. She's got a way of getting Mom to stay level. I know it's only a patch and Mom's looking at a memory care facility—but Lucinda is helping to get Mom on board with the idea."

"I know she doesn't mind spending time with your mom. She'd stay for as long as you need it. Go home, get some rest, and we'll hit it fresh in the morning."

"I need to call Brian—"

"Or you could hit *that* tonight."

Emily smacked her partner with a backhand to the shoulder. "Ass."

Part of her thought maybe Javier had a point. She chased a blush away before her partner noticed.

Emily dropped Javier at the office and she drove home, thinking about the connection between Franklin and Bell and the .380 shell in Lisa Larkin's pantleg. Did she shoot Bell? The weapon, though, was probably tossed in the river after it was used.

Emily pulled up to the house and heard soft music wafting in from the kitchen. After storing her firearm in the safe and hanging her jacket, Emily found Lucinda and Connie at the kitchen table. Teacups in front of them, heads dipped in quiet conversation.

"Hello, ladies," Emily said.

"Oh, hello, dear. I was waiting up for you," Connie said.

Lucinda's brow ticked up, giving away an unspoken concern.

"You didn't have to do that, Mom."

Connie scooted her tea closer to her, gathering it in both hands. "You know how your father and I worry when you're out late on a school night."

Emily felt her heart break. This wasn't a simple infection interfering with her mother's thought processes. This was dementia lurking in shadows, erasing swaths of memory and replacing them with loops of old conversations, along with faded and reconstructed memories. Mom wasn't going to recover from this. There was no cure or silver bullet. There was only the continuing spiral downward. When would Emily become another familiar, but unrecognizable face?

Emily patted her mother's hand. "No need to worry, Mom." A single tear tracked down Emily's cheek.

Lucinda pushed away from the table and lifted the teapot, carrying it to the sink. "Emily, could you help me for a moment?"

Rinsing out the teapot under a stream of tap water muffled their conversation.

"She's had a confusing day. Not bad, mind you, but she slipped a bit into old memories and connections. I think it's time you get a doctor to evaluate her and see if they think scans are a good idea to see if the disease is progressing faster than we thought."

"The disease. Alzheimer's. It was easier to wrap my head around Mom having memory problems . . . or just dementia."

"I know, dear. I took Connie by a memory care facility today. I hope that's not what wore her out. They do that, you know—have episodes when they're stressed, or tired."

"What did she think of the place?"

"She didn't say much. She seemed to take it all in."

"She have any idea what the little tour was about?"

"I think she did. It's hard to read her when she gets quiet."

Lucinda shut the water off and dried out the teapot.

"Mom, it's time for you to get some rest. Lucinda needs to go home."

"Are you taking me home, dear?" Connie asked.

"You're staying with me. We have the guest room all set up for you, remember?"

Connie's eyes glassed over. It was clear she remembered no such thing.

Lucinda gathered her coat and purse. "What time do you need me in the morning?"

"I need to pick up Javier by seven thirty. I can put it off if we need to."

"Nonsense. I'll be here by seven."

Emily hugged Lucinda. "Thanks for doing this."

"It's my pleasure. Connie is a dear friend, and this is what you do for friends." She shrugged on her jacket. "If you want to thank me, tell my son to call Jenny. That girl will not wait around forever."

"I think he already has."

Lucinda's eyes widened. "I've heard nothing from Jenny's mother. Why wouldn't Javier tell me? That boy . . ."

"I think they are taking it slow to get to know each other." Emily kept the discovery of the "sleepover" to herself.

"I need to light a candle for my son."

"He needs all the light he can get."

Emily bid Lucinda goodnight and locked the front door. She considered changing the locks to the kind with the interior key on the dead bolt to prevent her mother from wandering off. Locked in like a prison.

Emily got her mom settled for the night and tucked in. She knew it was inevitable. Mom needed a safe and supportive environment, and she couldn't rely on the sainted nature of Lucinda Medina forever. Connie Hunter needed a true memory care facility. The fact she was even thinking about it jolted Emily.

She poured herself an Irish whiskey and plopped on the sofa in the dark, alone with her thoughts. With the slight veil of a decision made, Emily felt one weight lift, but another pile on. Which facility and how much would it cost?

Emily pulled her cell from her pocket and placed it on the side table next to her. Glancing at it twice before picking it up, she hit a speed dial button.

Brian Conner picked up on the first ring. "Hey there. You're calling late. Is this one of those booty calls I've heard about?"

"You wish," she said, curling up on the sofa.

"I do."

"Needed to hear your voice. It's been a day."

"Same here. Wanna tell me about it?"

"These homeless camp fires are getting more complicated. We have a city public works guy good for the fires, and it's looking like he's on the short list for shooting Pete Bell. He was getting paid to torch the camps, but the connection to the murders isn't solid yet."

"I know. I'm sitting out here at Miller Park."

Emily sighed. "I was hoping you could come over."

"So, this *was* a booty call?"

"I guess you'll never know."

After a pause, Emily told him about her mom's memory lapses and deteriorating condition. "I don't know what to do. I know she needs care. I felt bad enough moving her into assisted living, and you saw what happened there. Now it feels like I'm throwing her away."

"I get it. I do. I felt the same thing when my mom needed memory care. Remember? You know you're making decisions in her best interest—decisions she can't make anymore. It's a crappy thing to happen, and it's hard to watch. I have the list of facilities we looked at whenever you're ready for it."

"I think it's time." The words came out softly.

"Why don't I stop by tomorrow, and we can go over it together."

"I'd like that." She cleared her throat. "What's happening at Miller Park?"

"Nothing going on out here. The camp has put up their own security. Couple of guys at the edge of the camp looking for people who don't belong. I think there are a couple of local street gang types who joined in."

Emily flashed back on Mika at the hospital, telling her they'd been watching out at the camps. "Be careful. If Tommy Franklin got the message from his benefactor, he might try to take the place down. The gangbangers have their heart in the right place, but they don't have the best decision-making skills."

"So far, so good. Don't want to jinx it. But I think you'll have a good night's rest."

Emily said goodnight and hung up the phone with the warmth from his voice lingering behind.

Rinsing her glass in the sink, Emily felt a presence. On the job, it was called situational awareness—officers need to know what was happening all around them, assessing threats, and identifying avenues of escape.

Emily spun toward the glass sliding door to the backyard. There, out in the darkness, she was being watched. Surely the glass was thick enough to stop a break-in.

Enough of this. She strode to the door, unlocked a heavy dead bolt, and flung the door aside.

"What are you doing here?"

The black cat sat there with its judging yellow eyes.

"Does Mrs. Rose know you're out again?"

The answer came in the form of a less than sleek brush against her leg as the plump black cat strutted past her and into the kitchen.

Emily closed the door against the damp, cool air.

"What?"

The cat—not her cat—strutted and parked expectantly at the kitchen counter. It cast its eyes in Emily's direction and yawned.

"Fine. But you need to find a cat soup kitchen somewhere else . . ."

Emily opened the cabinet, leaning around the cat to get to the door. She pulled out a small white bowl and a fresh bag of dry cat food. The cat started munching away as she poured crunchy nuggets in the bowl.

"You're welcome."

A soft purr came through in between the crunching.

Emily finished tidying up, hand washing the teacups and her whiskey glass. By the time she dried them, the trespassing cat was at the back door.

Sliding the door open for the cat, Emily watched the contented critter amble out onto the patio and disappear into the dark, without so much as a glance back.

"You're welcome!"

Emily locked up the door, gathered the cat bowl, and stacked it away until the next time the portly creature needed a midnight snack.

And it was after midnight when the visions of her mother's memory care saga and the search for Tommy Franklin finally subsided enough to let her catch a few hours.

CHAPTER TWENTY-SEVEN

LUCINDA MEDINA ARRIVED a few minutes before seven while Connie was still sleeping. Emily directed Lucinda to a fresh pot of coffee and let her know about the list of memory care placements Brian was going to share with her.

Leaving Lucinda with a hug, Emily was grateful she had such a caring, generous person in their lives. If not for her, there was no way Emily could care for her mother and keep up with the demands of her job. She would have to ask for a leave of absence—or quit outright. Knuckle-draggers like Stark wouldn't let it pass—the fact a woman couldn't do the job because her personal life got in the way. It didn't matter Stark had three divorces under his belt.

Emily pulled to the curb in front of Javier's place. Her partner slipped out the front door, and Emily saw a shadow flash in the doorway and a slim arm wrap around Javier's waist, pulling him in for a kiss. A raven-haired woman dressed in one of his shirts, long sleeves rolled up, raised up on her toes and quickly disappeared inside.

When Javier got in the car, he found a steaming hot coffee waiting for him.

"Oh, thank you. I needed this," he said.

Emily pulled from the curb. "What? Didn't get much rest last night, partner?"

Javier's jaw tightened and a pink blush crept up from his collar. "Thanks for remembering the stevia."

"I keep telling you the stuff is poison."

"Better for you than sugar," he said with another sip.

"And speaking of sugar . . ."

Javier slammed his eyes shut and shook his head. "It's not what it looks like."

"Oh really? Because it looks like you and the young lady—and she is young, Javi—are getting quite familiar. You should call a repair service about the heating in your place, because the poor girl looked like she was so chilled you needed to lend her a shirt."

"Dammit. We're taking it slow."

"That ain't slow, Javi. Your mother and I were talking about this last night."

"You didn't say anything about Jenny, did you?"

"She's under the impression you never called the girl back. Far be it from me to tell your mother her precious son is living in sin."

"We're not living together."

"Could have fooled me. She looked pretty comfortable when you left your place just now."

"She needed a place to crash while her apartment is being fumigated."

"Aren't you the gentleman. I guess her clothes needed fumigating, too."

"You're projecting here. You wish you were 'fumigating' someone."

Emily's laugh was cut off by her cell phone tone. She pulled it from the console and tapped the speaker button.

"Hunter here."

"Detective Hunter, this is Theresa from the Children's Receiving Home. I have your name as a contact for Willow Larkin."

"Is she all right?"

"I hope so. She slipped out during the night. Willow's missing. She's not with you by any chance, is she?"

"No. She tell anyone she was leaving? You see what happened before she took off?"

"Nothing happened. Not that I'm aware of."

Emily glanced at Javier, who hooked a thumb south toward the children's home.

"We aren't far away right now. My partner and I will be there in a couple of minutes."

Theresa met the detectives on the front steps. They made introductions while they walked, and Emily learned Theresa was a former resident of the children's home and returned as a counselor after graduating from college.

In the room where Willow was last seen, Emily was taken at how bare and impersonal the space was. "Looks like a jail cell."

"We encourage everyone to make the room their own. Willow wasn't here long enough to make the effort."

Emily noted the second bed in the room. "No roommate, I take it?"

Theresa shook her head.

"Looks like she took everything with her," Javier said.

"Right down to the stuffed rabbit."

Theresa smiled softly. "She insisted keeping the ratty thing with her at all times. Meals, activities, and here in her room. Mr. Bunny was never far away."

"I understand her attachment," Javier said. "It's the last thing she had before her mom got hurt and her home was torched."

Emily looked under the mattress, behind the small hand-me-down bureau, and in the closet. "It's like she was never here. She took what she had with her." She pointed at the thin bare pillow. "Stuffed it all in a pillowcase, maybe."

"Huh, right? I didn't notice it before," Theresa said.

"I'd like to talk to a couple of the girls, Lida and Cyn," Emily said.

"They'd probably be in the dining room. Why talk to them?"

"Those two seem to have some interesting insights into girls who came from the camps."

Theresa led them to the dining room where twenty-plus girls fell into silence when they entered.

Emily felt the apprehension as she scanned the room. Most of these girls didn't have a positive experience with law enforcement. She spotted Lida and Cyn at the back of the room.

"Hey, Detectives," Lida said. "You find that perv, Bell?"

"Lida, that's no way to talk," Theresa said.

"She just being straight up," Cyn said.

"Actually, we did. We're still putting some things together. You might have been right about him," Emily said. "But we're here to talk about Willow."

"She gone, ain't she? Cult done took her. I told you."

"There is no cult, Cyn." Then to Emily, Lida said, "Girl was acting all strange last night."

"Strange how?"

"She was quiet, more than usual after dinner. She stayed off by herself with the stupid stuffed animal and didn't want to hang with any of us."

"Anything happen to make her split?"

"Didn't see nothing happen to her. No one was bothering her, if that's what you're thinking. Seems like a cool kid, just quiet is all," Lida said.

"She did say a weird thing last night. She said, 'They can't find out.' Don't know who *they* is or what they *can't find out*. I bet it's a cult."

"Would you stop with your cults?" Lida said.

"What was going on when you heard Willow say that?" Emily asked, getting the conversation back on track.

Cyn shrugged her shoulders. "We were in the activity room. The television was on. Wasn't paying attention to it. Now that you mention it, Willow was standing there with her rabbit. She saw some reporter talking about a dude they fished out of the river. I thought she was talking to the damn rabbit when she said, 'They can't find out.'"

"You think she saw something that spooked her on the news?"

Cyn shrugged. "Coulda. My money's still on a cult abduction."

"Wish someone would abduct you," Lida said.

"It could happen."

"They'd give you back."

"Thanks, ladies," Emily said.

Out of earshot of the girls, Emily asked, "Any staff member in the activity room while the news was on? Like to see if they can recall what was playing."

Theresa bit her cheek. "There should be someone in there, and we usually don't let the television play the local news. Too much of a chance for our girls to get re-traumatized—you know, see their family after some tragedy . . ."

"Thanks, Theresa. I think we've got what we need."

Outside on the sidewalk, Emily leaned on the Crown Vic, a few faces checking them out through the windows. "Willow saw something on the news, all right. A story about Pete Bell's body being found at Discovery Park."

"It means she knows what happened to him."

"And he was shot at the 7th Street homeless camp, not Discovery Park."

"Floated downriver."

"And Willow is a witness."

"We need to find her before Tommy Franklin does."

CHAPTER TWENTY-EIGHT

"If Franklin gets to the girl . . ." Emily said as she gripped the steering wheel.

"Where do you think she would go?"

"She's got no roots, no home, nothing, and no one familiar to run to."

"Just her and her mom," he said.

Emily made a quick left turn and shot down Broadway. "That's it. Willow is heading for her mom. The last place she saw her was at the hospital."

Emily slid the Crown Vic into a spot at the curb. She spotted a security guard and worried he'd stop them from parking there, but he must have sensed their urgency. He followed as they entered the hospital and caught up to them in the elevator.

"We're looking for a little girl, not a whisper over four feet tall, sandy blonde hair. Might be trying to get in to see her mother in ICU."

"Got a photo I can get out on the hospital network?"

"I don't."

"I do." Javier scrolled through his cell phone and found a photo of Willow when they first found her at the river. She was sitting on the bed of a pickup truck holding her stuffed animal.

"That'll do."

Javier sent the image to the email address the security man gave him and by the time the elevator doors slid open at the ICU nursing station, Willow's image glistened from multiple computer monitors.

"I said the girl is missing and at risk. I hope that's all right."

"It's perfect. Thanks for the assist. If you hear anything, please let one of us know."

As Emily approached the nursing station, the nurse put the phone down. "I was just calling you, Detective—Hunter, is it?" The nurse held a business card Emily had left with them.

"That's me. You didn't see our girl, did you?" Emily said.

She nodded. "Come with me."

The nurse led the detectives to the back of the ICU. Emily recognized Lisa and thought her coloring looked better. No respirator breathing for her. Curled up next to her on the bed was Willow, sound asleep.

"She wandered in about an hour and a half ago. Don't usually let visitors stay here in ICU, but this poor girl, I think she needed her mom."

"How is mom doing?" Emily asked.

The nurse nodded, her red ponytail bouncing in time. "The doctors are pleased. All her vital signs have improved. They think she may gain consciousness at any time."

"That would be good on a number of fronts. For her, for Willow, and I think she holds the key to understanding what happened out there the night this went down."

"So, you know, it's not unusual for patients to have limited recall of the events around the trauma."

"Amnesia?"

"In a way, yes. I'm not a neurologist, but the way it was explained to me is a traumatic brain injury like hers—at the moment of the injury, the nerve impulses in the brain are disrupted and a common result is memory loss. You've seen it before, like an accident victim who can't remember what happened. Part disruption of the neural signals, part the mind wanting to protect itself from the traumatic memory."

Javier circled around the bed and noticed Willow's stuffed animal on the floor. It must have fallen when the girl fell asleep.

"Girl's not let this thing out of her sight—"

He hefted the worn stuffed bunny and his brow knit. "Em, there's something wrong here. It's heavy."

The bunny went on a counter, and Emily leaned next to Javier.

"This thing's head is barely hanging on, see?"

Emily noted the broken, frayed stitching around the bunny's floppy head.

"There's a safety pin," Emily said.

Javier released the dull silver safety pin and the bunny head lolled off to one side. The stuffing long gone, leaving a hollowed-out husk of a plush toy rabbit.

"Was she using this to keep her secrets?" Emily asked.

Javier peered inside. "You could say that. Look."

He held the head back so Emily could get a look at the contents. She was right. There were a couple of baubles, but the weight came from a Cobra .380 handgun. The compact gun sported a blue and white frame and was less than six inches long.

"Holy shit. Our girl's been carrying a firearm along with her all this time?" Emily said.

Javier pulled on a pair of purple nitrile gloves from a dispenser on the wall and gently retrieved the weapon from its furry holster. He racked back the slide and out popped a shiny .380 round.

"A loaded gun. This girl's been carrying a loaded firearm. No wonder she didn't want anyone to touch her precious stuffed animal."

"So many questions . . ." Emily said.

Javier tilted the handgun, revealing the magazine well was empty.

"How did Willow get her hands on it?"

"We'll need to ask her."

Emily glanced over at the sleeping child. "We'll find out later. Right now, let's let her get some rest. Poor thing probably hasn't had more than a few hours' sleep in days."

"We need to get someone to sit on her until we get this sorted out. I'll start the paperwork on the recovered firearm and make a call to the Watch Commander to get someone detailed over here."

Javier gathered the firearm and the bullet and left the room. Emily tucked the bunny's head back in place and safety pinned the connection. The stuffed rabbit held one less secret. Emily tucked the animal under Willow's arm.

Emily and the nurse stepped from the room. "We're going to have an officer stationed outside this door. This girl is not to go anywhere. I don't care what excuse she comes up with. She's here until we can put all of this together. There may be a man who wants to get rid of her for what she saw out there on the river."

Emily sent a photo of Tommy Franklin to the nurse, who said she would make sure everyone knew who to watch for.

Two quick phone calls—one to Theresa at the children's home to let them know Willow wasn't missing any longer—and a second to Patty Thompkins at Child Protective Services updating her on Willow's wandering tendencies and link to the suspected shooter. Patty said she'd drop everything and get over to the hospital to sit with Willow after she woke up.

No sooner than she'd hung up with Patty, Emily's cell pinged with a new text message. Dr. Pixley was scheduled to start the postmortem on Bell in an hour.

A uniformed officer Emily recognized strolled down the hall. Traci Hernandez was a slight five-four woman who wore her dark hair tied up in a tight bun under her hat. Raised with four older brothers, she knew how to manage conflict. And if that didn't work, her black belt in Brazilian jiu-jitsu would. She tried to teach Emily a few techniques, but the younger, smaller woman only succeeded in throwing and arm-barring Emily into submission.

"Traci. Good to see you. Where have they been hiding you? This is my partner, Detective Medina."

Javier straightened up a bit, sucked in his gut, and nodded back. Emily rolled her eyes at him.

"I've been out in the Southside for a while. Was finishing up with my reports on a domestic and the lieutenant said you needed a body over here. Got an in-custody medical?"

"I'm not sure what we've got." Emily briefed Traci on Willow, her escape from the Receiving Home, the firearm she'd been packing around, and the possibility Tommy Franklin might come to find her.

Traci looked at the girl. "She must be all of eight? Ten? Girl's been exposed to way more than her share. Yeah, I got this. Anything comes up, I'll get at you."

They left Traci in the hallway and Emily whispered, "I'm telling Jenny you had impure thoughts."

"Oh, shut up."

He held a bag containing the cheap .380 handgun. "Remember, I'm armed."

"Let's go see what Pete Bell can tell us."

CHAPTER TWENTY-NINE

EMILY AND JAVIER found Dr. Pixley changing into a fresh set of protective garments after finishing an autopsy.

"Morning, Detectives. Right on time. We're set up in the private room."

Emily knew she meant the one autopsy suite reserved for homicide investigations.

Dr. Pixley bumped the door open with her hip. "Shall we?"

Pete Bell's remains lay on a stainless-steel table covered to his chest with a sheet. Skin gray green in spots with evidence of nibbles and chunks taken from his cheek by hungry steelhead trout, or salmon. Another reason Emily was not a seafood lover.

Dr. Pixley threw up an X-ray film. Two small bright white spots popped in the dark background of what was on Bell's torso.

"Looks like we have an entrance wound. Posterior upper left, struck the fourth rib, the bullet fragmented and the largest of the two punctured his heart. Here," Dr. Pixley said pointing at the image.

"That was a lucky shot," Emily said.

"Not for him." Dr. Pixley pressed a foot switch for a microphone. She recited the date and time, and who was present in the room. "We are conducting the postmortem examination of Peter J. Bell, identified from fingerprints verified by Livescan. Bell is forty-three years old, mildly obese at five-eleven and two hundred seventy-nine pounds. There is evidence of animal predation on the face and arms. Skin has sloughed mildly because of prolonged exposure and submersion in water."

She rolled Bell on his side and described the gunshot wound track. There were no contact or powder burns.

"Let's do this." Dr. Pixley lay Bell on his back and pulled the sheet down. She gripped a scalpel, hit the microphone foot switch once more as she sliced a Y-shaped incision from each clavicle, joining at the sternum, down to the man's flabby belly.

Next came the part Emily loathed. Dr. Pixley snipped away each rib with a tool Emily thought came from a home improvement store for snapping through thick tree branches. *Snap.* Followed by the sucking sound of the rib carapace pulling away from the chest.

"Aorta shows some degree of flattening." Dr. Pixley selected a long pair of forceps and probed the section of artery. "I was partially correct on what I thought I saw on the X-ray." She retracted the surgical tool along with a flattened chunk of lead.

"The bullet entered the victim's back, where it was redirected off the rib, sending a fragment into the aorta. The fatal wound." The microphone switch clicked once more. "The largest bullet fragment lacerated the aorta and came to rest against the victim's left ventricular chamber. Massive hemorrhage."

Emily held a plastic tray under the bullet fragment and Dr. Pixley placed the metal chunks inside. Emily sealed the container.

"What do you think, Javi? A .380?"

"Have to turn the nerd herd loose on that one. Seems near the right size. Hard to tell with a fragment. Hope we can run a ballistics match on these."

"We can turn over the handgun we found in Willow's things. I've seen this before. If the rounds are old, the lead becomes brittle. I'm hopeful they can put the two together," Emily said.

"How did that little girl get ahold of a murder weapon and hide it? Franklin drops it after he shot Stone, and she picks it up? It's hard to swallow," Javier said.

Dr. Pixley began the ritual of disassembling—it's what Emily called it when the pathologist removed one organ at a time, documented the weight and size, taking tissue samples, before wrapping all the bits, bobs, and pieces in plastic and stuffing them back inside the hollowed-out cadaver.

The doctor stitched the incision up with heavy gauge sutures. When she was done, she took Bell's left hand. The skin was pale and had sloughed from his arm as she pulled it up.

"Huh." She pulled on a set of magnifying glasses. Then turned to a computer terminal and tapped in a sequence, bringing up Bell's records. "The techs didn't scrape under his nails. Probably thought because he was found in the water, there wouldn't be anything to find. The nail on his left index finger is broken. Looks like he was one of those guys who liked to sport longish nails."

She took a small instrument and dug under the nail. When she pulled it out, a small whitish deposit clung to the tool. She carefully placed the instrument and the tissue sample in a container and handed it to Emily. "Might be some DNA in this sample. He scratched someone before he went in the water."

Emily took the sample and tried to recall if she saw a scratch on Franklin's arm. He'd been wearing long sleeves when they saw him on the work sites. This could close it. Franklin's DNA.

"I'll let you know if the tox reports come back with anything unusual," Dr. Pixley said after pulling off her gloves and disposable gown.

Emily thanked her as the doctor made a note in the computer and brought up the pathology schedule for the day. "Two down, six to go. Would you do something about that, Detectives?"

"We're trying, Doc. We're trying," Emily said.

Javier's phone buzzed with the muted refrain of the Pat Benatar song. He snagged it quickly. "Detective Medina."

He listened and locked eyes with his partner. "You sure about that? No listing at all?"

He paused and thanked whoever called, shoving the phone back in his pocket.

"Guess who was never registered as a licensed clinical social worker? In fact—never graduated from college?"

Emily's gaze turned onto the dead and ravaged remains of Pete Bell.

She felt the investigation shift, finally.

CHAPTER THIRTY

EMILY FILLED OUT the evidence forms for the bullet fragment and the tissue sample and printed them out. She waited for the whirring printer to finish.

"Javi, we have the registration, ownership data yet?"

"The Cobra .380 is registered to an H. Purlmutter. No DMV records matching that name and address. It's an old gun. We'll hopefully get a pop from NIBN on the brass we collected—that'll be icing on the cake. The weapon wasn't reported stolen, but it could've been and the owner never reported it. I've asked Mike Black to come and run the full package on the weapon. He'll need to do a test-fire to get a comparison slug. I'll get this to him for a side-by-side." Javier held the container with the bullet fragment extracted from Pete Bell.

"I'll fill out the lab request for the tissue sample. It'd be too much to hope it comes back to Franklin, wouldn't it?" Emily said.

"I ran Franklin while we were on the road. No hits, no wants, no warrants, and no prior history, apart from the bogus address he listed with the DMV. If he's not in the system . . ."

"We won't have a DNA sample in CODIS to compare against." Emily meant the Combined DNA Indexing System. "Exactly. And if we can't find him, we can't get a sample either."

"We could go back with a warrant and see if we can scrape a few hairs from his apartment."

Emily spun around in her chair and pulled the evidence forms from the printer tray. She spun around again and faced Javier.

"A defense attorney would claim we found no evidence of Franklin actually living there—and they would be right on that count."

Javier stood and grabbed the plastic disc holding the bullet fragment. "I'm gonna run down and personally hand this to Mike."

"Use your impressive skills of persuasion to get him to move this to the top of the pile. I mean, you are one of the city's most eligible bachelors." Emily said the last part louder than she needed to, causing a couple of other detectives to pop their heads up from their tasks like meerkats with ADHD.

Javier glared at Emily.

"Hey, Medina, that come with a sash and tiara?" a slightly built female detective called out. It seemed even more awkward as the detective was dressed in bright-red hot pants and a halter top as she and her vice team prepped for a prostitution sweep.

"Can it, Marci!" Javier leaned toward Emily. "I owe you for this . . ."

Javier slunk out of the detective bureau to catcalls from his fellow detectives.

Marci, the detective dressed as the lure for tonight's sweep, came over to Emily's desk. "Was he listed as a top contender in the singles scene?"

Emily rocked back in her chair. "Indeed, he was."

"Huh, he's kinda cute, I guess. You ever notice how you don't see someone until they're, like, in demand? He with anyone right now?"

"I don't know about in demand, but, yeah, I think he's involved currently. But you dress like that and you might have a chance."

"Yeah, that ain't happening," Marci said as Emily's desk phone rang.

"Hunter here."

"Hey, Emily, your girl woke up," Officer Traci Hernandez said.

"Is CPS there yet?"

"Yeah, no—not that girl. Her mom. The woman in the coma. She's awake."

CHAPTER THIRTY-ONE

LISA LARKIN SAT propped upright in the hospital bed, whispering to Willow when Emily entered the room. The curtain was drawn down the center of the space and Emily ducked around the curtain and found the other bed occupied by an old woman who seemed asleep.

Willow sat on the edge of the bed, her head downcast, a trait she must have acquired living in the camps. Don't challenge anyone, avoid dog-eyeing people who could hurt you, and make yourself as small as possible. Emily had seen these street survival skills before, but not in someone so young.

Emily sat in a chair near the bedside. She didn't want to come off threatening by looking down on the woman's bed.

"Nice to see you awake, Lisa. I'm Detective Hunter. How are you feeling?"

"I've been better. They're giving me the good drugs. I'll be fine." Lisa lifted her arm, dangling the clear IV line. "Willow told me you found her at the river and got her some nice place to stay."

Emily glanced at the girl, who nervously began kicking her legs back and forth.

"Willow should still be there. It's not safe for a young girl to wander around."

"I'm sorry. I had to see my momma," she said in a slight voice.

"I get it. How did you get here from the Receiving Home?"

Willow flicked her eyes toward her mom. "I got a ride. A lady with two kids drove me."

"Willow Marie, what have we said about strangers? You never, ever, get in a car with a stranger," Lisa said.

"I needed to—"

"You shouldn't have done that. What have I told you?"

"Don't talk to strangers. But—"

"No *buts*, Willow. That was very dangerous."

Lisa clenched her eyes shut and put a hand to the back of her head. Her fingertips grazed the patch where the emergency room doctors shaved her scalp to suture the head wound.

"Willow's here and she's safe and I'm sure she won't do something so reckless again. Will you?" Emily said.

Willow was quick to shake her head in agreement.

"Okay then. Lisa, I need to talk to you about what happened out there on the river. We have a handful of witnesses, but I'd like to hear your account. Let's start with, what were you doing before the camp was attacked?"

Lisa closed her eyes again. Emily couldn't tell if she was trying to visualize the events, or hoping to wipe them from memory.

"I—I don't remember."

"What's the last thing you recall?"

"Waking up here a little while ago."

"Back at the camp—what's the last thing you remember doing?"

"Willow and I had dinner. We had some cereal."

Willow's legs started rocking a little faster. The girl looked anxious and scared.

"What about right after that?"

Lisa's forehead creased and a pained expression crossed her face. "Nothing. I'm sorry."

"Don't remember who attacked you?"

"I don't."

"How about who set fire to the camp?"

Lisa shook her head. Willow's legs were rocking faster, Emily noted.

"When was the last time you saw Pete Bell?"

Lisa stiffened.

"We know something happened out there. Something between you and Bell." Emily recalled the initial contact with Willow when she admitted Bell and her mom were arguing.

"I can't remember."

"You know Pete Bell, though, right?"

Yes." The word came out as a hiss.

Willow's legs stopped their back-and-forth rocking and froze in place.

"Tell me about Bell."

Lisa fumed and remained quiet for a moment. Emily could sense the anger welling through the injured woman. Anger enough to kill him?

"Some people are saying Bell was a good man, working in the camps like he did. There's talk of a memorial—"

"He was an animal." The reply came out in a guttural outburst. "He's not who he said he was. All he ever did was hurt people. He could never make up for what he did by pretending to be a social worker in the camp."

"He ever hurt you?"

Lisa nodded and wiped away a tear.

"How'd you know he wasn't a social worker?"

"If you spent more than five minutes with the man, it was obvious. It was always about *him*—what was in it for *him*."

Javier ducked into the room and gave a nod to Emily.

"And that's why you shot him." It wasn't a question.

"Yes! Yes, I shot him and I'd do it again."

Lisa was wide-eyed and shaking.

Emily knew the spontaneous admission might not be admissible. She hadn't advised Lisa of her rights. Lisa wasn't technically detained, and Lisa's confession came without a direct question. A defense attorney would argue differently.

"Lisa, we're going to take this slow, all right? I'm going to read you your Miranda rights and want to make sure you understand you don't have to talk to me."

Emily took a laminated card from her jacket and read the advisement, word for word.

"What's gonna happen to Willow? Promise me she'll be in a good place."

Willow began to shake.

"Hey, Javi? Could you take Willow and get her a bite to eat?"

Javier held his hand out for Willow. "Come on. I know where they keep the ice cream in this place."

The offer of ice cream got her attention, and she hopped off the bed, sending her mother a reluctant glance. Lisa gave her a stern nod in response.

When the girl left the room, Emily settled back into the chair again.

"Do you understand the rights I explained to you?"

"Yes."

"Do you wish to waive your right to remain silent and speak with me without an attorney present?"

"Yes. I shot Pete Bell. He was going to hurt my daughter."

"You're not the first one to mention Bell cruising through the camp. Seemed to be looking for girls from the camp. He had his sights on Willow?"

Lisa nodded. "He was going to pay me to let her go. Buy my daughter like she was a thing. When I told him to get lost, he grabbed her and told me he'd do what he wanted and he'd be doing Willow a favor by getting her away from an unfit mother."

"What happened after Bell grabbed Willow?"

"I—I couldn't let him take her. He'd make Willow disappear, and I'd never see my girl again. I told him to stop, but he was taking her—so I shot him."

"Where were you and he standing when you shot him?"

She frowned for a moment. "Near the river. He and Willow were at the river and I was up the hill a little bit."

"How far away were you? Weren't you afraid you were going to hit Willow?"

"I was close enough."

"What happened after you shot him?"

She pursed her face. "What do you mean? I shot him. It was done. I pulled Bell out into the river and let him float off. Grabbed my daughter and we set back to our tent. If you're thinking about why no one mentioned the gunshot—no one cares, or if they do, they don't want to get involved. Even if they did, no one would blame me for shooting him."

"Tell me about Tommy Franklin."

She shrugged. "I don't know who that is."

"Was there anyone else around when you shot Bell?"

"No—if there was, it was people like me—camp people."

"You're a good mom, Lisa. I get why you did what you thought you had to. I'm going to have to arrest you for killing him though—you know that, right?"

She nodded. "I know. Will you make sure Willow gets to a safe place, maybe with a family? I'd like her to have a chance, you know? A chance I never had..."

Emily stood. "I'll do what I can. I'm not going to handcuff you to the bed. Officer Hernandez will be outside, and if you give her any trouble, she will shackle you up. Oh, one more thing. What did you do with the gun?"

"The gun?"

"Yeah, after you shot him, what'd you do with it?"

"I—I threw it in the river."

Emily nodded. "Yeah, I figured. All right, you rest up. A friend from Child Protective Services will make sure Willow gets taken care of."

"Thank you—for my daughter."

Emily nodded and stepped out into the hall. Officer Hernandez was standing against the wall, her eyes checking out all the movement in the corridor.

"Traci, keep watch on our patient in there. She confessed to shooting Pete Bell, the guy Javier and I found in Discovery Park."

"No shit? That little slip of a thing?"

"Nothing like a protective momma bear. But there's more going on and she's covering for someone. Tommy Franklin, the guy you have the photo of, I know he had a hand in the goings-on out there. Lisa's not telling me everything. I don't know why yet. But if he shows up here, don't take any chances with him."

"Understood. What about the little girl?"

"CPS is going to take her and get her placed."

Traci shook her head. "Tough break."

"She mention her stuffed animal?"

"Yeah, she did. She got a little overexcited when she woke up, and it wasn't exactly where she left it. Her mom got her calmed down after they talked a little."

Javier turned the corner with Willow. They both ate ice cream as they walked down the crowded hospital corridor.

The girl skipped into her mother's room and Javier leaned against the doorway, moving back to let a nurse get through with her rolling cart of medications and computer.

Emily joined him at the doorway and caught a quick interaction between mother and daughter. Willow nodded after her mother's words. Lisa stroked her daughter's face.

"Mom just confessed to shooting Pete Bell."

Javier almost dropped his ice cream. "I thought she might recant once she realized what was happening. Does explain the .380 shell casing in her pant cuff. How's she gonna explain that to her daughter? I mean, I know the girl saw the whole thing happen—but can Willow understand why her mother killed someone?"

"Willow's young and might not get the consequences of what her mom did. But the girl has some street survival instincts in her—she managed to slip out of the Receiving Home and run here."

"Still, at that age, to see someone killed. Makes you wonder what damage she's going to deal with when she grows up," Javier said.

Emily nodded and took in Lisa smoothing her daughter's hair. A simple, soft, and loving gesture. She didn't seem like a killer. There was a single slight tear tracking down the mother's cheek. Emily guessed if those you love were threatened enough, there were no limits to how far you'd go.

"She explain how Willow had the gun stashed away in her stuffed animal?"

"She did not. Claims she tossed the gun in the river."

Javier lost interest in his ice cream and tossed it in a waste can inside the door. "Willow doesn't strike me as a salvage diver."

"No, not quite. Mom's not telling me the complete story here. She admits shooting the man, but she lies about what she did with the gun. Why?"

"Why was Willow carrying around that old gun after the shooting? And where does Tommy Franklin fit in?" Javier asked.

Emily glanced in at Lisa and Willow. A confessed killer and a child victim—and they were both hiding a secret.

CHAPTER THIRTY-TWO

EMILY MADE ARRANGEMENTS to move Lisa to the hospital's secure ward for in-custody patients. The doctor she consulted with said Lisa's recovery was progressing well and she wouldn't require ICU level of care.

Patty Thompkins, the social worker from Child Protective Services, sat with Lisa and Willow. Now, the mother was awake, Patty was getting her up to speed on the placement Willow needed.

"You know we're gonna have to sweat the girl about the gun in the bunny at some point, right?" Javier said.

"Yeah, we do. This isn't the place. I need to talk to Willow away from her mom. The girl isn't talking about what happened out there."

Emily strode into the room and stood next to Willow trying to gauge her mood. The girl was quiet but glanced up at Emily with soft eyes—eyes that had seen too much in her short life. But there wasn't any anger or fear behind them. If Emily had to put a pin in it, she'd call it cautious.

"Lisa, I need to have a word with Willow,"

"What about?" The heart monitor connected to Lisa stuttered and clicked along at an increased pace.

"Just some loose ends. People she might have seen on the river that night, that kind of thing."

"She didn't see anything. I don't want my girl dragged into any more of this mess—my mess."

"I understand. I know. But I need to cover all the bases here. We're talking to everyone who was out there that night." A bit of a stretch, but no one else witnessed the shooting in the moments before the camp was set ablaze. "I'll have Patty with her when I talk with her."

"I want to be there. I am her mother." The heart monitor flashed at a more rapid pace.

"Normally, I would. But you've confessed to—" Emily glanced down at Willow. "And I need to make sure Willow can tell us what she remembers without—"

"No. I want to be with her when you question her. I have a right." Lisa was getting more agitated now and Willow stiffened up her small shoulders.

"Hey, Patty, would you mind taking Willow out for a bit?"

Patty nodded. "Come with me, little one." She held a hand for Willow and, with a glance to Lisa, the girl hopped down from the bedside, clasped Patty's hand, and left the room.

Emily squared to Lisa. "Okay. Here's the deal. I know you aren't telling me the whole truth here. You didn't toss the gun in the river—"

"Yes, I did—"

"We found the gun."

Lisa grew pale. "What? No, that's not possible."

"Willow had it. She hid it inside her stuffed animal."

"Mr. Bunny? Why would she do that?"

"Kinda what we want to find out, too," Emily said.

Lisa scooted up in the bed. The woman's calm disappeared, and her voice quivered as she spoke. "Please, please, leave my daughter alone. She's too young."

"We need to know how she came to have the gun in her possession."

Lisa put her arm out and grasped Emily. "It doesn't matter. I—I wrapped it up and hid it in the rocks by the river after I killed Pete. She must have picked it up. I did it. Nothing matters after . . ."

Lisa sobbed and her entire body quaked. She withdrew her right hand from Emily's arm. The burns from the fire looked painful. Her right arm was singed up to her wrist, which must have been protected under her body after she fell during the attack. Her neck and left arm weren't as lucky.

"Please leave Willow alone . . ."

"You need to rest and mend. Willow is going to need her mom in the months ahead."

Emily stopped a nurse in the hallway, asking where they could get some private space to talk with Willow. There wasn't much in the ICU to promote privacy. Curtains and a few glass panels were all the separation available in a space designed to manage chaos.

Javier waited with Willow and Patty Thompkins from Child Protective Services. He leaned against the wall and tipped his head toward Willow. The girl was rocking back and forth. Nervous anxiety flowed from her.

They found a spot near the elevator where a small sofa tucked into a niche in the wall. Emily sat on the surface and patted the seat next to her for Willow.

"Willow, I need to talk to you about something important."

The girl nodded and plopped up on the stiff sofa.

"I need you to tell me the truth. Do you understand what I mean? You can't tell me any fibs."

Willow's eyes widened a bit and her young mouth grew taut, as if preparing herself not to speak.

"Momma says it's not good to lie."

"Your mom's right. I know what you hid inside Mr. Bunny," Emily said.

Willow withdrew a little and leaned away from Emily. The girl said nothing in response, looking away to avoid the confrontation.

"Willow, I need you to tell me how you found the gun."

"I—I don't want to get in trouble."

"It's important to tell me why you hid the gun inside Mr. Bunny."

"I found it."

"When did you find it?"

"When my mom and the man were yelling."

"Then what happened?"

Her eyes clamped shut, telling Emily she witnessed the shooting.

"Okay, let's start before that. Where did you find the gun?" Emily took the girl's hands, hoping she would look at her.

"I found it."

"Where?"

"Mom got it from someone. She said it was to keep us safe."

"You know those things are dangerous, right?"

"I didn't want anyone else to get in trouble, so I hid it."

Willow looked down at the floor. Emily knew this was about all she was going to get from her.

The girl's hands were tiny. The unicorn Band-Aid on the web of her right hand drew Emily's attention.

She knew. Emily knew what happened that night on the river.

"Willow, why did you shoot that man?"

CHAPTER THIRTY-THREE

JAVIER STIFFENED AND Patty, the social worker, cleared her throat.

"Emily, maybe we should take a break."

Emily put a hand up. "Willow, why did you shoot him?"

"He was hurting my mom."

"How did you know what to do? With the gun?"

She shrugged. "We used to have video games in the before times."

Emily knew she meant before she and her mom had to live on the street and in places like the riverside homeless camp. Learning to kill someone from a video game? It was possible, she supposed. It was more likely Lisa had taught her daughter what to do if they were attacked. It was a different world with different rules. Lisa and Willow were survivors. But at what cost?

"Had the man hurt your mom before?"

She nodded.

"More than once?"

"A couple times. This time was worse. He grabbed her hard, and she was crying."

"Okay, Willow. I understand."

"Am I in trouble for lying?"

Emily patted the girl's arm. "We're gonna make it okay. I need you to go with Patty while we take care of your mom. You know she's okay now. I need you to make sure you stay safe, too."

"Am I going back to that place again? With the others?"

Patty rubbed her hands together and stood. "Did you have trouble there?"

"No. There were nice people there. It was okay."

"Promise me you won't run off this time? As soon as your mom is strong enough, we'll get you two back together," Emily said.

"Can I visit her sometimes?"

"We can do that," Patty said.

Emily tipped her head to the exit, and Patty took Willow by the hand and they waited for the elevator.

Once the two disappeared behind the sliding doors, Javier elbowed his partner. "She must be the littlest killer I've ever seen. Hate to think about what's gonna happen to her."

"There will be all sorts of legal red tape and wrangling. I'm certain the juvenile court will find she's too young to understand the difference between right and wrong. She's going to face years of therapy to help her cope with what she's done—when she's old enough to understand."

"How did you know, other than the gun in the stuffed animal trick?" Javier asked.

"Slide bite."

"Huh?"

"Willow's hand. She had a slice in the webbing of her right hand. You remember from firearms training. If you don't hold your hand the right way, that slide comes back and will cut the hell out of your hand. She had a slide bite. Her mom didn't."

"But her mom had a couple of scratches on her unburnt arm. Wanna bet they will match the tissue sample Dr. Sherman collected from under Bell's nails?" Javier said.

"Good catch, partner. You're like an idiot savant. With less idiot," Emily said.

He shook his head and chuffed. "Thanks, I think. Come on, we need to talk to mom again."

Lisa's eyes cut to the door the minute the detectives stepped inside. "Where's Willow? What have you done with my daughter?"

Emily sat while a nurse finished up taking her patient's vitals. A tired-looking man in his fifties slipped inside and made his way to the other patient's bedside. Glancing at the nurse: "Hi, Addie, any change with Mom?"

"She comes around every now and then. The doctor wants to keep an eye on her for another day or so to make sure she doesn't have another stroke."

He nodded and ducked behind the curtain. Emily heard him greet his mother and receive no response.

Shifting back to Lisa, Emily settled in the chair. "We know what happened out there."

"I shot him."

"We know you're trying to protect your daughter."

Lisa leaned to one side to lessen the pressure on the burns. She grimaced and glared at Emily.

"We found the gun. Willow hid it inside her stuffed rabbit."

Lisa closed her eyes and tipped her head back. "She was supposed to throw it in the river. It doesn't change anything. I'm responsible. I shot him. He was trying to take Willow away."

"Lisa, we know what happened. Willow told us. She shot him to protect you."

Tears streamed down Lisa's cheeks. "No, she didn't." The reply came as a stifled whisper.

"Lisa, I have to ask—where did Willow find the gun?"

"Did you arrest her? My God. My baby in jail?" She shook with sobs.

"No, we didn't arrest Willow. We got her back in a home where she'll be safe and cared for until you're back on your feet."

Lisa blinked and wiped the tears with the back of her hand. "You're lying. You took Willow away."

"Listen, I know who Pete Bell was—what he was. Bell was a predator going after young girls like your daughter."

Lisa stiffened. "He was going to take her away from me. He knew we couldn't fight back. I'd never see Willow again. He told me he'd kill me if I came after them."

"What was he doing out there in the first place? Why did he want Willow?"

"She was nothing to him. A possession. Something to control."

"Some girls from the camp say Bell was cruising through the camps looking for special girls. You ever hear anything like that?"

"I kept Willow hidden from him. I know he would talk parents into giving up a child, putting them in foster care. That's no way to live. I did it. I wanted to keep her out of that system. I guess I screwed that up. I didn't have a choice. He was going to steal my baby away. I know I'm a nobody. Bell said he'd have the state take her from me—because of what I am."

Emily knew what she meant. Ignored, discounted, and invisible. Emily experienced a small taste of what Lisa described when she was a rookie officer—the expectation was she would fail, be a burden to the other officers, all because she was a woman. In spite of what the knuckle-draggers like Stark did to get in her way, she'd established herself as a top investigator and had the case closure rates to back it up.

"The only people who think that are hiding their own insecurities," Emily said as much for Lisa as for herself.

Lisa fell silent.

"Now, how do we explain Willow having a gun in the first place?"

"She shouldn't have had it. I tried to keep it hidden. I was—assaulted—sexually, a few months ago. I wanted to keep us safe. I never thought Willow would . . ."

Lisa grew silent. Emily saw the resignation on her face. The gun. Her daughter. The terrible outcome. Lisa knew she was responsible for all of it.

"We have a question about this man." Emily held her phone with the photo of Tommy Franklin with Bell, Jensen, and the ex-mayor. She tapped on Franklin's image.

Lisa cradled Emily's hands, focusing on the photo.

"I've seen him around the camp before. He was there with him." Lisa pointed at another face on the screen.

The former mayor, and very much deceased John Stone.

CHAPTER THIRTY-FOUR

"THIS MAN? ARE you certain?"

Lisa nodded firmly. "I'm sure. It's been a couple of months, but that man was an ass. Kicking over tents, pointing at the river, and saying weird things. I think he was a little off his rocker."

"Saying what kind of things?"

"It was all weird. You know, like, how this was his land. He's gonna build here. Told us to pack up and leave. Go to some other city and beg for handouts. He kept repeating this was his legacy. What kinda legacy is a bunch of tents and a handful of city porta-potties?"

"And you saw him with this man." Emily pointed at Franklin again.

"More than once. Like he was the man's butler or something."

Emily cast a glance at Javier, who was tracking the conversation as well.

The pause made Lisa nervous. She balled her fists and looked from one detective to the other. "What?"

"The second man was killed, too," Emily said.

"No. Willow had nothing to do with it. I swear."

"We know. There were two deaths, and we're trying to find the connection."

"Where—where was he killed?"

Emily pursed her mouth, trying to recall.

"About two rows up the hill from your tent," Javier said. "It was covered with an orange tarp, I think."

"Orange? You're talking about Delila's place. She's kinda one of the OG camp leaders. She's been on the street better than twenty years. Knows everyone. She was good to me and Willow when we first showed up. Gave us a sleeping bag and some food. She's good people. I know she didn't have anything to do with anyone dying."

Emily pocketed her phone. "You're probably right, but she might have seen how it all went down. She could help us tie it together. You have any idea where we can find her, with the camp being taken down and all?"

Lisa shook her head. "I don't know where she'd go. She had this thing about being near the river. Claimed it had magical healing powers and such. I know it was all crap, but it made her feel good. She wasn't hurting nobody. Oh, she used to help out at Loaves and Fishes sometimes. They'd let her take back meals for the people who were too ill to make the walk from the camp to the soup kitchen."

Javier took out his notebook. "Delila have a last name?"

"Not one I ever knew. Everyone knew her, and I only heard them call her Delila."

Lisa was able to offer a description of the camp matriarch, and Javier jotted the details down.

A nurse came in with a medication cart.

Emily rose from the chair. "You get some rest, Lisa. Willow's going to need you."

"My girl—she's going to be all right?"

Emily nodded. "She will." Emily hoped it was true.

Leaving the hospital, Javier scanned his notes. "Franklin and Stone were buddy-buddy at the camp?"

"It kinda fits. The former mayor—may God have mercy on his soul—was the force behind the River Gardens project. I can't imagine the camp ever being referred to as a *garden*—but to make his vision come true, he needed one thing to happen."

Javier stopped and faced his partner. "Stone needed those camps to disappear. Franklin was the man to make it happen."

"And we have video evidence of Franklin chasing people out of the tents at one camp. But it was after Stone died. It's all coming together except who Franklin is working for now." Emily said.

Javier leaned on the hood of the Crown Vic. "If Stone was killed to get him to stop kicking people out of the camps, it backfired because there've been two camps eliminated since he died."

Emily grew silent. The murder of a former mayor was getting the most attention in the corner offices. The politicians wanted to lump Bell's murder in with a wave of homeless violence spawned in the camps. Her instincts told her the death of a small-time fake social worker might have a darker underpinning, despite Willow's confession.

She pulled out of the hospital lot and pointed the vehicle toward police headquarters on Freeport. They'd burned the better part of the day, taffy-pulling a confession from a mother and daughter. She couldn't see either of them being held criminally for what amounted to self-defense. Ultimately, it would be the district attorney's call. If it landed with the wrong deputy DA, two more lives would be flushed away—and they were already circling the drain.

Emily felt the psychological and emotional fallout from a case like this. She'd been able to keep her life compartmentalized—work at work and separate from her home life—until recently. The space between wore transparently thin.

After getting back to the office, both detectives stopped in their tracks. The mayor and Ryan Jensen stood in the detective bureau in what looked like a heated conversation with the lieutenant.

Lieutenant Hall's eyes shifted and caught Emily. It came with a subtle shake of the head. A gesture she interpreted as "Don't jump in and make this worse." Or better yet, "Don't let them see you and get out of here."

She took a half step back, but Javier didn't read the room and plopped into his chair with a loud sigh. Emily clinched her eyes closed.

The mayor glanced over her shoulder, spotted the detectives, and spun around on her heel.

"Speak of the devils," the mayor said in a tone with a bit of venom.

Mayor Carsten strode over to Emily and struck a defiant pose. "Where do you get off challenging my authority?"

"I'm sorry, Mayor Carsten. I don't know what you're referring to." Emily tossed her cell phone and notebook onto her desk.

"You and Detective Medina have ordered public works crews to stop cleaning my city's public spaces. I have an executive order in place to move us toward a city where we can return the parks and riverside access to the people."

It sounded like a prepared news release, and Emily tried not to react to the pompous look on the politician's face.

Emily rubbed her temples with her fingertips and took a deep breath.

Mayor Carsten took a step closer. Inches from Emily's face. "Well? What do you have to say for yourself? You've defied me and my office."

Emily put her hands on her hips and tensed her jaw. "Lady, back the fuck off. You have no idea what you're talking about. Returning parks to the people? What a crock. Who do you think lives in those camps? I've got news for you—they're people.

"No one 'defied'"—Emily used air quotes—"your authority. What we uncovered is a massive fraud scheme run out of *your* public works operation. Employees using city equipment and getting paid under the table to do private work on city time. And at least one of your city employees was involved in burning the camps.

"Excuse me if we exposed that the city doesn't care about the most vulnerable among us. We don't have that luxury. Every victim matters, even if they don't live next door to you in Land Park."

The mayor's face turned red, and she stormed out of the detective bureau. Ryan Jensen followed a few paces behind, but paused at Emily.

"Be careful, Detective. You're swimming in some deep waters here. Do you want to throw your career away for a few homeless camps?"

"Did you just threaten me, Mr. Jensen?" There wasn't any heat behind her question.

"No. There is much more going on behind the scenes here you couldn't be expected to understand. Be careful. Maybe you should spend taxpayer dollars investigating real crimes against real people." Jensen tilted his head and offered a polished smile.

"And what? Two murders aren't real crimes? Get the fuck out of here."

When the political flack left the offices, three other detectives stood and clapped their support.

Javier leaned into his partner. "I call dibs on your desk. You won't need one when you get reassigned to parking meter duty. You will have a snazzy golf cart, though."

"You two, my office," Lieutenant Hall said.

Emily and Javier followed the boss into his office and shut the door.

"Sit down."

Instead of the dress-down and reprimand Emily expected, a smile grew on Lieutenant Hall's face, followed by a belly laugh. "Emily, we need to work on your filters. You know, those little things that keep us from saying the things we really think. Sometimes those voices need to stay on the inside."

"I know—I know. That woman pushed my buttons. Pompous, entitled ass."

"That woman is the mayor."

"I didn't vote for her."

"Emily, I think what the lieutenant is trying to say is sometimes you have a tendency to go off on people."

"What is it with you two? Is this an intervention?"

"You can call it whatever you want," Hall said. "We have to do a little damage control before she runs to the chief."

"She won't."

"How can you be sure?"

"She knows I'm right. She can't go around whining to the chief when her own house is a mess."

"I hope you're right, Emily. Go write up what you have. I need to have it all lined up if she does come back at us."

She stood. "Will do."

Javier followed suit. "Oh, boss, I called dibs on her desk for when she gets reassigned writing parking tickets around the capitol."

"You'll be going with her. Someone has to drive the meter maid cart. You're responsible for her, Medina. Go. Now. Oh, and look contrite when you leave the office. I have a reputation to uphold."

They both returned to their desks under the curious glances from a few others in the office. Emily brought up her computer.

"You know, when I was going off on the mayor, a few things fell into place for me," Emily said.

"Like your willingness to self-destruct at a moment's notice?"

She threw a paper clip at him.

"No. Hear me out. The city is dirty. Look, the mayor's grand plan is to somehow round up and hide all the homeless so the 'real citizens' can use the parks and bike paths. Old mayor Johnny Stone had the River Gardens plan, which, by the way, needed the very land occupied by the homeless camps. In comes city employee Tommy Franklin, who burns the camps down, leaving them ready for the mayor's grand plan."

Javier nodded in agreement and shoved his keyboard away. "I'm with you all the way. The part I can't quite wrap my head around are our two murders. How do they fit into some city cleanup plan?"

"I'm not able to put my finger on it yet. It's right there. I can feel it."

They typed up their reports and saved them in the system. Emily spent extra time on the summary of the interviews with Willow and Lisa. Investigative reports were designed to be distant and objective, reporting the facts of the case. In this instance, Emily added the extra layer of Bell's searching for a "special girl" in the camp. His reasons for picking Willow were murky at best, and it appeared Willow killed Bell in self-defense. There were no witnesses to state otherwise. Emily also included a statement that, because of Willow's age, there was some doubt if she could understand what she had done, a key element in prosecuting a minor, mens rea, the ability to tell right from wrong. Lisa did admit disposing Bell's body in the river, making her an accessory.

What form of justice would be served by feeding Lisa and Willow into the system?

CHAPTER THIRTY-FIVE

SHE'D ENTERED THE last keystroke on her report when she sensed someone approach from behind. Officer Brian Conner, dressed in jeans and a polo shirt, came over to her desk.

"Ready?" he asked.

"For?" Emily said.

"I left you a couple of voicemails. You, me, your mom. We have an appointment at a new memory care facility."

Emily reached for her phone and knocked over a stack of case files. She flipped over the phone and saw three missed voice messages from Brian, two texts from Lucinda Medina, and a missed call from a number she didn't recognize.

"Sorry, I must have turned the phone on silent."

"You can still get away, right? I'm interested in seeing what this new facility has to offer."

"I don't know. We're right in the middle—"

"Go. I can follow up and make sure these get to the lieutenant," Javier said.

"Thanks, Javi."

Emily got up and grabbed her jacket.

"You two kids have fun. Don't stay out late," Javier said.

"Do we need to mention your most eligible bachelor ranking again?"

Javier didn't respond, but grinned and returned to his keyboard.

"Most eligible, what?" Brian said as he and Emily left the detective bureau.

Brian dangled his keys, signaling he'd be driving, which Emily figured was a good idea—not only because she shouldn't be driving a city vehicle on private business—the very thing she accused the mayor's staff of doing. But it would give her time to watch her mom and get a sense of her willingness to find a new, more secure, living environment.

Brian pulled his 1965 Mustang into the driveway at Emily's place. He shut off the engine and the *tick-tick* sound from the hot exhaust sounded outside the car.

He took Emily by the elbow. "Remember, this might be hard for your mom. She'll have trouble figuring out why she needs this extra care and won't want to be a bother. You know how it goes."

She nodded, and the front door opened as she reached for the doorknob. Lucinda was there with Connie, ready to go.

"She's been looking forward to this little outing all day," Lucinda said. "She's had all her medication and isn't due for another dose for four hours. We've had a delightful day."

"That's great. Thanks so much, Lucinda. Shall we go, Mom? Brian is going to drive us around in his fancy car."

Connie clasped her handbag and looked past Emily to the racy white Mustang. "We're going in that? That hot rod?"

"It's not a hotrod, Mrs. Hunter." Brian held the door open for her and helped her into the low seat.

"Emily, your father had a car like this when you were young."

Emily climbed into the back seat from the driver's side and leaned forward. "I don't remember that, Mom. I can picture a yellow station wagon we had."

A view of confusion crossed Connie's face, followed by an abrupt change of topic. "Where are we going again, dear?"

Brian took over and started the car and handed Connie a shiny, polished brochure. "Thought we'd take a nice drive this afternoon and maybe look at this place. It looks like it would be fun."

Connie wasn't reading the text, but scanning the photos of a bright, active adult community. Emily could read the slightest confusion starting to take root, so she deflected before it could overwhelm her.

"Mom, Brian and I thought it would be fun. You know how we used to go look at model homes and get ideas for my kitchen remodel?"

"Aren't you done with all that? It's not very ladylike."

Brian turned out of the driveway. "I don't know. I think it's kind of attractive."

Emily caught his eyes in the rearview.

"In my day, ladies would let their man take care of home repairs. They would be occupied with cooking and taking care of the children. There was no free time to fritter away with nonsense like plumbing and laying tile. Besides, a man likes to feel needed."

"Mom, as I remember, Dad wasn't too handy around the house. He had to call a professional to repair what he tried to fix."

A slight smile appeared on Connie's face. A glimmer of a memory there.

"How'd you find out about this place?" Emily asked.

"It was suggested by one facility I looked at for my mom. It's brand new, and they are expanding."

"Talk about taking advantage of the market. Everyone is getting older."

"Speak for yourself," he said. "Hey, could you read the address off the brochure? Should be up here somewhere."

Emily pointed from the back seat. "Senior Care Solutions."

"There. Doesn't look like a facility. It's an office building in a commercial district. Even if they converted it to condos, you want to bother?" Brian asked.

"Doesn't look like the brochure, for sure. Why not? We're here. Let's check it out."

The parking lot was nearly empty, and the silver mirrored doors prevented anyone from peeking inside. Brian took a slot near the door so Connie wouldn't have to walk far.

He ran around to the passenger side and helped Connie up from the seat.

"Don't worry about me. I'm fine," Emily said, crawling out from the back seat.

Brian held the door for them and all three stepped inside a slick-looking commercial office setup. Offices, drafting tables, large conference room tucked off to one side.

Emily got a timeshare vibe from the place, based on the vapid poster art and conceptual drawings of buildings and design schematics. The timeshare influence solidified when a twenty-something blonde stepped from one office and greeted them with an impossibly cheery tone.

"Welcome to SCS. Can I direct you to our model units?" Her tight gray pencil skirt and clingy white silk blouse were expensive designer quality.

"Here? Models here in this building?" Emily asked. *Other than you*, she thought. The lieutenant would be proud of her for keeping it to herself. Filters and all that.

"I'm Tiffany—"

"Of course you are. I—I meant to ask—you said model units. Where is the actual facility? I thought that's what we were looking for."

Tiffany leaned her head to one side letting her hair cascade over her shoulder. "The models are in this building and are the exact designs going into our new SCS condo towers."

"Where are the towers?"

"I can show you. Please come this way."

She shimmied on four-inch heels to a flat tabletop display. Emily elbowed Brian. "Eyes up, dude."

He turned red. "What is this we're looking at?" he said.

"SCS prides itself on planning for our senior population. Each of the four towers will provide varying levels of care available, which means as a resident's needs change, they will have access to the health care and supportive services they need. They don't need to look for another facility. It's very much a one-stop shop for all their needs."

"You said these towers *will* provide these services. *Will* as in they aren't built yet?"

"You have the perfect opportunity to select your model, lock in a price that will never change no matter the level of service need in the future. And you get to select which tower location you prefer."

Timeshare. *Trust your first instincts, Emily.*

Emily glanced down at the display table. Miniature models of condo towers were set against the city backdrop. Four separate but nearly identical tower complexes sat in scenic city locations—scenic river's edge locations.

Tiffany tapped one site on a river bend. "This will be the first tower constructed. It's all set. City planning approved and permitted. We start construction in less than a month. We're half sold. So, if you're looking to get your loved one in on the grand opening, now's the time."

"These locations, how did Senior Care Solutions come to build on them?"

A prickly feeling grew at the base of Emily's neck.

"Our executive team has been working with city officials for some time now. We were able to combine low-rise residential with light commercial to reinvigorate the communities surrounding our towers. We've invested in improving the infrastructure and local commercial opportunities."

Emily's eye drew to a small brass plaque on the bottom right corner of the map display. "Welcome to River Gardens Sacramento."

CHAPTER THIRTY-SIX

THE SIGHT OF the River Gardens name attached to these condo buildings niggled at the base of Emily's brain. It all made perfect sense. The push to move the homeless out of the area, burning the camps, and using city resources to do it. It was all a big land grab. A redevelopment scheme costing people their lives.

"Tiffany," Emily tapped on the River Gardens badge. "What can you tell me about this project? I mean, if we consider investing in one or more of these properties, we need to know who's behind it. You know, what they stand for and if there is a legitimate funding plan in place to guarantee the project will be built."

The saleswoman's face lit up when Emily said "invest in multiple units." She saw a commission on the horizon. There was a shift in Tiffany's tone, and her attention turned from Brian to Emily.

"River Gardens is the exclusive development from SCS. You won't find anything like it on the West Coast."

"Who's behind it? I mean, I don't want to invest only to find out some foreign corporation owns the property and will sell it out from under us."

Tiffany placed both of her hands lightly on Emily's forearm. She leaned in and, with a conspiratorial whisper, said, "River Gardens is locally controlled. The SCS executive board includes some very influential city power brokers. Come, let me show you."

Trotting as fast as her heels would allow, Tiffany motioned Emily to the conference room where Emily expected the real estate equivalent of a car sales closer to swoop in and finish the deal.

A long, polished table dominated the room and a squat plastic contraption on the center of the table marked a conference calling device.

Instead, the saleswoman gestured, with a flourish that would make a television game show host jealous, to a row of photographs—headshots of, if the brass plaque above them was accurate, the SCS board of directors.

Prominently displayed in the center of the display was Mayor Ellen Carsten.

Brian seemed to notice the look on Emily's face.

"Uh, Tiffany, could you give us a moment?" Brian asked.

He ushered Connie into a chair at the conference table.

"Certainly. I'll bring some water. Coffee anyone?" After getting no takers, Tiffany left the conference room.

Brian closed the door, turned to Emily. "Emily, what's—"

Emily put a finger to her lips.

She took him by the arm to the conference table and pointed at the conference call receiver. A single red light glowed on the top of the device. Someone was listening in. Probably the eager young saleswoman.

"These condominiums are a great investment opportunity." Emily pointed at the mayor's photo on the wall. "We need certain assurances the project has the green light from the city for all the building and environmental reviews that derail efforts like this at the last minute. And I need to know who will be providing the day-to-day management of the facility and services. These facilities open with grand promises and then sell to another corporate group with little thought about the residents."

Brian seemed to understand where she was going and ad-libbed his part. "If we're going to invest in this project on the scale we discussed, we'll need more than assurances. We'll need proof of concept, access to permits, and put eyes on the environmental waivers."

Emily slunk over to the board of directors' photo board. Five in total, including the mayor. She didn't recognize any of the old white men in the portraits.

Tiffany sashayed into the conference room with bottled waters and a file folder tucked under her gym-toned arm.

"Here you are. And I brought in some sample contracts, floor plans, and copies of the city permits and filings." She laid them all out on the conference table.

She had been listening in on the room.

Emily unscrewed the cap on a water bottle and handed it to her mother, who had grown unusually silent since they arrived in the offices.

"Mom, you okay?"

"Yes, dear. I'm waiting for this little tart to cut to the chase and show us some models. So far, it's been all smoke and no fire."

Tiffany rebounded quickly. Yes, yes, by all means, I can show you the model units.

"Before we do that," Brian said, opening a file folder, "these permits. They aren't final."

"They are the official filings with the city. This is a formality. The city said they'd rubber stamp all the approvals to get the River Gardens project shovel-ready."

Shovel-ready was another term of art that stuck in Emily's craw. In her mind, all it meant was a photo op for out-of-shape corporate desk jockeys digging in a sandpit with a golden shovel while the real construction workers sweated their asses off in the background.

Emily focused on one permit—an environmental waiver allowing the development in a protected watershed along the American River. The permit listed an address she recognized was the former location of the 7th Street homeless camp.

"This site here. Do you have a plot map of the project?"

Tiffany smiled, sensing a potential buyer. "I believe I have one in my office. Hold on a sec."

She tiptoed out of the conference room in her heels and Emily hit the off button on the conference call speaker.

"This is the homeless camp where Stone died. He was the one who first supported this River Gardens project. Someone got him out of the way."

Tiffany returned with a white cardboard tube. She popped open one end and slid out a roll of blueprint-looking construction plans. Emily knew how to read them from her own renovation work, and she also knew how long the city's permitting processes took. A remodel of her Victorian home couldn't begin until the city signed off on the interior construction, the waste management plan, the historic register analysis, the city arborist to make sure none of the town's famed trees would be harmed, and all of the signatures she needed took eight months.

Tiffany rolled out the plans and flipped the long pages until the plot plan came into view. She smoothed it out with the flat of her hand. "River Gardens One."

She pointed a lacquered nail at the sprawling complex, easily two acres in size. "These are the two condo towers. Can you imagine the river view from these units? The river-facing units include an additional premium. This is the community space where residents take meals, use the on-site library, enjoy spa services and a yoga studio."

"Have you even been in one of these places, young lady?" Connie said, interrupting the sales pitch.

Tiffany blinked.

"Do you expect old people to navigate a small city like this to have dinner, or get their hair done?"

"The community is self-contained. And we have a staffing plan to escort or drive our residents to their appointments. Like here, at our SCS brand pharmacy. Or access to our very own transportation hub."

Emily glanced at the bottom right corner. It bore the name of an architectural firm she'd never heard of and the date these plans were prepared over a year ago.

"Are these the most recent plans? Still, I'd like to actually see the city's stamp approving them."

"These are the approved plans, copies, but they were approved. Our executive team work from the originals."

"Can you give us some documentation showing there is some thread of city approval?" she said.

Brian double-teamed with, "I'd feel better if we could speak with your CEO. What's their name? We probably know them."

Tiffany's jaw dropped slightly before she recovered. "I think I might have some reassurance for you." Once more, she trotted out of the conference room.

Emily snapped photos of the plans, the architectural firm's information, and the preliminary permits Tiffany claimed were filed.

Tiffany rushed back into the room and handed her phone to Emily, along with a signed and stamped city permit to begin excavation at the site.

"Hello?" Emily said into a cell phone awash with a floral perfume.

"Hello, Tiffany tells me you're interested in an investment in River Gardens."

Emily stiffened. The voice. She knew it. She raised the permit Tiffany had handed her and her stomach turned to ice at the name.

"Hello? Are you there?" the voice called out. The same voice that had threatened her a few hours ago. Ryan Jensen.

CHAPTER THIRTY-SEVEN

TIFFANY LOOKED CRESTFALLEN when Emily made up an excuse to leave the SCS offices—for an appointment at another property management company.

Brian pulled from the lot as quickly as he could after loading Connie into the front seat.

"Jensen—he's the City Hall guy, right? The mayor's chief of staff?"

"That's the one. He picked up the reins of River Garden."

"Mayor Stone isn't even in the ground yet and he pulls this kind of play. I'm no detective, but isn't it kinda quick for Jensen to get all this together?"

"Those plans were a year old, or more. And the permit was signed off and approved six months ago. This has been in the works for some time. The current mayor is smack in the middle of it."

"Her whole clean-up-the-streets pitch," Brian said.

"You're making the connection, too, right?"

He drove Emily and Connie home, pulling the Mustang into the driveway behind Emily's faded yellow Jeep, one she rarely got to drive.

Brian shut off the Mustang's engine and trotted around to the driver's door to help Connie out.

Once inside, Emily got Connie situated in the living room. "I'll get you some tea," she offered

"That would be nice. I don't want to move to the place we saw today. I know I have to find a new apartment, but I don't like that young woman."

"Me either, Mom."

"She was too busy watching Brian's butt when she thought you weren't looking. And she ignored me altogether. I'm the one who'd be living there. Fat chance now."

Emily laughed, and Brian blushed. "I think we can cross this one off the list. We'll find the right place. You can stay here with me until we find one."

"I know I'm getting in the way here. And I know I need more help now than I did before. Lucinda helps me realize what I'm facing. The medication does help most days. Remembering to take them is easy when she's here, but I can't expect Lucinda to babysit me forever."

"She doesn't think of it that way, Mom. She's a friend."

"I don't want to be a burden to my friends, or to you."

"You aren't.

"Nonsense. You aren't getting any younger, Emily, and I'd like to see some grandchildren someday. With me hanging around, it's not going to happen." Connie glanced at Brian, who quickly found something to do in the kitchen.

"I'm not in any rush, mind you," Connie said.

"I'll go see about that tea."

Emily found Brian leaning against the counter laughing as quietly as he could.

"I'm so happy you think this is funny."

He grabbed her by the waist, pulled her to him, and whispered into her ear, "You aren't getting any younger, Emily."

She kissed him on the neck. "I'll have you know, I'm in my prime." She pushed off and turned the kettle on.

"So, Tiffany was checking out my butt?"

"Tiffany might find her car impounded tomorrow."

"Don't hate the player, Emily—"

Brian's cell rang.

"If that's Tiffany, tell her you're busy."

He shook his head. "I'll see what she has to offer."

She backhanded his shoulder.

"Hi, Lieutenant, what's up?"

Brian listened with an occasional "uh-huh" and finished the call with a "Thank you, sir."

"What's going on? You get called in?"

"Yes and no. He made me Acting Sergeant."

"No kidding, really? That's great! Where's he going to assign you? Del Paso? I heard there's a vacancy there."

"Watch Commander's office. First watch. I know, I know, it's the lieutenant's admin gopher, filling out watch rosters, patrol assignments, and fielding sick calls."

"And getting coffee for the lieutenant, fetching their dry cleaning—"

"I think I could learn a lot from Lieutenant Wilson. She's great."

"Sheila's the best, and she's had my back when it counted. I am worried about the job, though."

Brian's brow furrowed. "What?"

"If you're sitting down all shift long, you could ruin that perfect little ass of yours." She grabbed his butt as she brushed past to get the kettle.

"Tiffany didn't say it was perfect."

"I'm sure that's what Mom said."

"No, she didn't. You did, right now."

"You misheard me."

"I know what I heard," he said to an empty kitchen. Emily had taken the tea out to her mother.

Connie settled in with her warm tea. She turned on one of her favorite movies. "Have you seen this one?"

"A few times, Mom." Emily knew Connie watched this movie at least once a week.

Brian settled on the sofa next to Emily. He pulled a folded paper from his pocket. "Here are a few other places we could look into."

Emily unfolded the document listing four facilities under a handwritten title of Memory Care Facilities.

Moments like these were fleeting. Emily's closest souls were here, and everyone was safe, sound, and in Connie's case, living in the present. She wanted to tear up the list and pretend it wasn't needed. But she knew the dementia would rear its ugly, indiscriminate head again soon. It was only a matter of time.

She shook her head to get the negative thought out of the front of her mind. "When do you start the new job?"

"Tonight."

"Tonight, tonight?"

"As in a couple of hours from now." He squeezed Emily's hand.

"Oh, I thought we'd have more time."

"Yeah, me too, 'cause like Connie said, you aren't getting any—"

"Finish that thought and you won't be getting any, mister."

Emily stood, took Brian by the hand, and led him down the hall.

CHAPTER THIRTY-EIGHT

EMILY SAW BRIAN off two hours later as Connie was finishing up her movie. Emily felt like she was a teenager sneaking around while her mom watched television at the other end of the house. Emily had made sure all the locks were secured before she took Brian into her room.

They were good together. In every sense of the word.

Connie eyed her daughter as she kissed Brian goodbye. It was a deep, passionate kiss. And Emily didn't expect to see her mother standing there when she turned around.

Suddenly self-conscious that she wore a long T-shirt and little else, Emily tugged on the hem.

"In my day, a woman would wear something a little more feminine for special occasions." Connie wore a tight grin and turned to the kitchen.

Emily leaned against the front door, and even though her mother busted her sneaking Brian out, she felt something else. Was it happiness or contentment? She wasn't sure because, when it came to relationships, this one felt—she had trouble putting a label on it—different.

Emily strode into the kitchen and rinsed out the teacups before placing them on the drying rack.

"If you're up to it tomorrow, we can go check out a few new apartments," Emily said. She'd started using the term "apartment" instead of "memory care" or "assisted living." It sounded less clinical and didn't sound like Emily was tossing her mother into a "home."

"If you have the time, dear. Lucinda and I can go take a peek at them and get an idea of what they're like." She paused and glanced at Emily's bare legs poking out under her T-shirt. "Apparently, one of us needs a little more privacy with her boy toy."

"Mom. Between you and Javier, I can't catch a break. Both of you would have me living in a convent."

"The Sisters of Mercy would never survive."

"Come on, let's get you ready for bed."

"I'd say the same to you, but . . ."

"You're impossible."

"I love you, Emily, and I'm just happy to see *you* so happy."

With Connie safely tucked away in her bed, Emily wasn't sure she could sleep. She needed to remake the bed before she could get back in. She hugged her pillow tight and breathed in a faint lingering scent of Brian's aftershave.

She woke to her cell vibrating on the bedside table. A quick glance at the counter said it was five thirty, so she had managed to get some sleep, surprisingly.

The Watch Commander's number blazed on the screen and instantly cleared her head. Another new case?

"Hunter here."

"Sergeant Conner here."

"Well, good morning, Sergeant. Is this the booty call we talked about?"

"Don't I wish. No, this is a business call from the Watch Commander. She wanted you to know there is a disturbance at Camp Hope. Anti-homeless protesters are facing off with residents of the camp. Two protesters were taken to the hospital after a homeless woman tossed a Molotov cocktail into the crowd."

"They know who tossed the device?"

"She did it in full view of the officers we had on scene. Apparently, she's some self-appointed leader of the camp militia."

Emily's brain sorted out the details, and the conversation with Lisa in the hospital popped into her mind. "The woman who tossed the Molotov cocktail—was it Delila something?"

Emily heard Brian rustling paperwork in the background.

"Yeah, it was. Delila McDaniel. How'd you know?"

"I am a detective, Sergeant Conner. We have her in custody, I take it?"

"We do."

"Watch Commander need a detective out there? I know Javier and I are off the rotation until we tie up the Stone killing."

"Not the Watch Commander. Delila McDaniel. She asked to talk to the detective looking into the fires."

"What?"

"No kidding. She won't talk to our officers until she speaks to you."

"All right. I'll roust Javier and see if I can get Lucinda over here to sit with Mom. Where are they holding her?"

"Still on scene. You want me to have them bring her in?"

"No, I'll go out there. Soon as I can get Lucinda here."

"Okay. Hey, Em . . ."

"Yeah?"

"It's nice to hear your voice."

"You too, Sergeant."

She hung up and dialed Javier. He must have been getting ready for work because he picked up the phone on the first ring. He said he'd be there to pick her up in twenty and Lucinda would be with him.

Fifteen minutes later, a soft knock sounded on the front door. Lucinda used the key Emily had given her and came inside. She found Emily in the kitchen, downing a cup of instant coffee.

"You have time for me to make you a proper cup?"

"Thanks, but I need to get going. Is your son on the way?"

"He's out front. He drove me over in the police vehicle. He took it home last night."

"Thanks so much for doing this. Mom should be asleep for a couple more hours. She had a great day yesterday and was even talking about looking at memory care facilities."

"Good. Good. I'll see if we can't keep her busy today. It helps."

Emily hugged Lucinda and thanked her again.

She trotted out to the waiting maroon Crown Vic and jumped into the passenger seat. Javier backed out of the drive and pulled away.

"Camp Hope, I understand? I spoke to the new Watch Sergeant."

Emily felt the heat start to work its way up. "Yeah, his first night on the job. Hope you weren't too hard on him."

"You getting soft on me, partner? No, besides, I'm not about to give anyone a hard time who has the power to wake me up in the middle of the night with a callout."

"Camp Hope is the last big homeless camp in the city. All the refugees from the other camps have found their way there."

"From the sound of it, they organized their own security forces—for real this time."

"Yeah, they aren't going to get caught by surprise again."

Camp Hope was a sprawling collection of tents, tarps, broken trailers, cars, and a dozen rusted RVs, all gathered at Miller Park, south of Broadway. Emily knew it was also one of the locations claimed on the SCS map for a condo complex. How a private developer could stake a claim on government-owned public land was a puzzler.

The sunrise hit the camp at the same time they arrived. Six black and white police vehicles blocked the street and served as a barrier between the camp and fifty anti–homeless camp protesters across from the park.

Emily pointed to a space between the patrol vehicles and Javier guided their car to a vacant spot at the curb near the park. The closest police unit had a woman in the rear seat and an officer stood outside the vehicle.

The officer recognized Emily and waved.

"Hey, Yashi. How's it going?"

"Good, Detective. I hope you're here to take custody of this one. She. Won't. Shut. Up."

"She the one who tossed a Molotov cocktail at the protesters?"

"The one and only."

"Let's have a word with her."

Officer Yashimura opened the SUV's rear door. A slightly built Black woman with long braids peered out over glasses perched on her nose.

"Well, it's about damn time you got here."

"Delila McDaniel?"

"I am."

"I'm Detective Hunter and this is my partner, Detective Medina. I understand you wanted to speak with us."

"I seen you out here talking to us. You know what we're up against. People like them want to see us disappear, like we ain't damn invisible to them already." Delila shot her chin toward the protesters.

Emily regarded the crowd, and it looked like the same gathering that appeared at City Hall. Except at the City Hall confrontation, the Molotov cocktail flew from the protesters into the tents erected at César Chávez Park.

"Officers tell me they have you on video throwing a Molotov cocktail at these guys."

"Like I told them. Go look at the video. They threw it and it landed on a tent and didn't break, so I tossed it back where it came from. Return to sender."

"I'll see what they have. Still doesn't make it right. I guess it sent a couple of them to the hospital."

"They been sending us to the hospital, or worse, for months. We done. Ain't taking it no more."

"You used to live at the 7th Street camp."

Delila eyed Emily and sat back in the police vehicle adjusting the handcuffs behind her.

"The night the camp burned—tell me about it."

She focused to the left into the sea of tents making up most of Camp Hope. "The sun been down for a while and things was getting quiet at the camp. We had a couple of guys posted up as security, for what good it done."

"I heard they were attacked up by the road. Did anyone see where the attackers came from?"

"I didn't—but others did. Claim they were dropped off like kids at an amusement park. Pulled up in a black van that took off after they got out."

"A van? Could it have been a black SUV?"

"I don't know what you call them. Those big boxy-looking things the soccer moms are supposed to tool around in."

"What happened after they got out of the vehicle?" Emily asked.

"You know what happened. They burned the camp to the ground. The two guys who were supposed to be on watch were too busy getting high and one of 'em got smacked with a ball bat. The other just run and hid. Didn't even give no warning to the rest of us."

"Where were you when this was going on? I understand you had a tent with an orange tarp on top."

Delila's eyes narrowed. "I wasn't there. I was down at the river."

"So, you weren't with Mayor Stone?"

"I didn't kill him, if that's what you're asking. But I saw who did."

CHAPTER THIRTY-NINE

"I DIDN'T EXACTLY see who done it, but I saw it happen."

"Back that up for me. What did you see?"

Delila picked up on Emily's interest and sat up a little straighter. "Let me go, and I tell you what I know."

"No deal. You almost killed people out here tonight."

"You wanna know what I know—then you gotta do me right."

"What was the ex-mayor doing out there that night?"

She paused a moment. "All right, I'll give you a taste. John Stone was trying to make a deal."

"What kind of deal?" Emily couldn't picture the fallen mayor making a drug deal in the squalid camp.

"He was gonna let us stay on the river."

"Seems off-brand for him. Didn't he start the whole eliminate the camps idea—the thing the current mayor picked up and ran with?"

"I know, right? It surprised the hell out of me. Him and his crew been pushing and harassing us to leave—and all the sudden he has this come to Jesus moment. He was gonna let us stay if we did what he wanted."

"What did he want you to do?"

"Set up tents in front of City Hall and make life miserable for the current mayor. She can't ignore us if she has to see us every single day. Stone didn't like her and wanted to make her life hard."

Emily thought it sounded like the petty bureaucrat she knew Stone to be.

"Then what happened?"

"Never got a chance to find out. Stone didn't seem right in the head—all swaying and acting like he was drunk."

"Where was this?"

"Back up at the camp."

"Around your tent? Because that's where we found him."

She shrugged.

"Did you even see anyone with the mayor, let alone attack him?"

"You know I did. I'm not saying nothing more till you let me go."

"That's not happening. You know better." She started to slam the back door closed and stopped. "You see what happened to that social worker?"

"Bell?"

Emily nodded.

"I heard the gunshots. That man had it coming from what I hear."

"How's that?"

"He been rough with a couple of the moms in the camp. Making them show him their girls. Had a photo like he wanted to find one who looked like some kid he knew."

"You ever see the photo?"

"No. Just heard from people he bothered."

"He hassled Lisa Larkin and her daughter, didn't he?"

"You know he did, and you know how that ended."

"You know who shot him, don't you?"

Delila nodded. "I do, but it won't serve any sense of justice if you take her in. She did what she had to do."

Emily bit her lip. Delila confirmed her belief that Bell was pressuring Lisa to hand over her daughter.

Emily closed the SUV door. She'd have to come back to Delila and press her for the detail of both deaths, Stone and Bell. If she was connected as much to the homeless community as people believed, she knew everything that happened out there.

Emily spotted Javier talking to protesters who pointed across the street at the camp.

She glanced in the direction they pointed and waded into the encampment. A pair of men stood and thought about challenging her, but they sensed she wasn't about to be distracted and watched her pass.

Emily stopped near the center of the long line of tents and a nylon dome covered with a ratty orange tarp sat twenty yards down the path from the asphalt parking lot. Must be Delila's place. Emily recalled the signature orange tarp at the old location. She must have been able to salvage it from the last fire and pitched her tent back from the others so the parking lot floodlights wouldn't shine into her home at night.

The tent rustled, and the flap flew back. A man wearing a black hoodie bent to duck out of the tent. From the distance and shadows around the tent, Emily couldn't make out the man's face. The hood was drawn up tightly over his head, leaving a small patch of light-tinted skin reflecting the glare of the flood lamps.

He froze when he noticed Emily on the edge of the parking lot, before he darted down the embankment. He pushed over an old woman who emerged from her shelter.

Emily snagged her radio and told Javier she was in foot pursuit, fifty yards west of his position.

She ran toward where she last saw the hooded man, and as she passed the tent with the orange tarp, the glow of flames flickered through the thin nylon shell. Then she spotted another tent ahead engulfed in flames. And another. The man she saw leave the tent was lighting fires in his wake.

Other residents noticed the orange flames in the dark and began shouting warnings to the others who might still be asleep in their shelters. The trail of the man in the hoodie was quickly overrun with panicked urban campers fleeing their tents and cardboard condos.

Another tent burst into flames farther down the slope. Emily headed for the last flickering tent and spotted a dark mass running toward the river's edge. She took off and made a line to cut off his escape.

"Suspect, heading to the river. He's heading upriver—north," she called into her radio.

She fell in behind him as he ducked right into a small grove of trees. She slowed and drew her weapon. The darkened riverbank and the thick undergrowth in the trees made it difficult to see.

Snap. A branch broke to her right and a dark form barreled through the brush, shouldering her out of the way, and tore off along the riverbank. Emily slipped on the muddy soil and fell on her ass. She took aim at the fleeing arsonist and the sight picture was lined up, her finger moving into position, and she caressed the trigger when two teenaged girls ran out of the thicket and stumbled in her path.

The two girls were panicked from the fire and when confronted with a mud-slicked woman, they screamed and ran up the hillside. They completely obscured the man in the black hoodie.

She radioed an update and told units north of her position to look for a man in dark pants, black hoodie, about six foot, medium-build, running in their direction. Even she knew it wasn't enough of a description. The county sheriff didn't have a boat in the water at this time of morning either. She lost him.

Javier found her at the river, fuming at her failure to grab the arsonist. She didn't care about the mud caked to the back of her pants.

"You okay, Em?"

"Other than being royally pissed, I'm fine."

"You get a look at our firebug?" he asked.

She turned, facing the hillside and the camp. Six tents were fully engulfed, and five others smoldered with a nasty odor of humid, musty stench from dousing them with water.

"Dark. Had a damn hoodie pulled up tight. Couldn't get much else. He was fast though; I'll give him that."

The fire department was only a few blocks away from Camp Hope, and someone must have called it in the moment the flames became visible. The fire didn't spread throughout the camp.

"Anyone hurt up there? Get caught in the tents?" she asked.

"None. The guy only lit up empty shelters. Like he knew which ones to hit."

Emily knocked a clump of mud from her hip. "I had him. He's gone now. Dammit."

They started back up the worn trail to the camp. The panicked energy continued to run through the encampment, feeding more anger than fear now.

When they reached the asphalt lot, four of the camp's residents clustered before a news camera lens, telling their stories. "The city promised us we'd be safe here. They don't care none."

Emily pointed out the partially charred tent with the orange tarp. "Delila's place. That's where I saw him. He was coming out of the tent."

She took a step around a smoldering hunk of plywood and found a corner of the orange tarp spared from the flames. Emily pulled it back, and the burnt nylon tent stuck to it as she lifted it.

"Oh, God. Javi."

Trapped inside the tent was Tommy Franklin, a six-inch rock hammer spiked into his forehead.

CHAPTER FORTY

"HE'S HAD A bad night," Javier said.

Emily watched as the medical examiner's team finished up their work with the former public works crew supervisor's body. An hour and a half after they arrived, the mood around the camp grew malignant.

Anti-homeless protesters shouted to anyone who would listen. Another dead body in a homeless camp was all the evidence they needed. "The camps gotta go!" And "Not in our city!"

Additional police units separated the protesters from the line of camp dwellers, who set up a picket line in front of the undamaged section of shelters to the south end of the parking lot.

"This could go off if someone throws another bottle," Javier said.

Emily was focused on Franklin as he was zipped up into a black body bag. The medical examiner left the weapon in place because, trying to extract it here, in the middle of the burnt remains of a tent camp, risked compromising the potential evidence. Emily snapped a few photos with her cell to use until the crime scene techs forwarded their photos and video of the scene.

Dr. White backed away from the bagged and tagged body and snapped off her gloves, depositing them in a portable biowaste container.

"At first glance, I'm thinking you found the murder weapon."

"No kidding, Doc. It's buried in the middle of his forehead."

The doctor looked over her glasses at Emily. "You know what I mean, Detective."

"I know. I couldn't help myself. When can we know for certain if this is the same weapon used on Mayor Stone?"

"I'll extract it when we get back to the ranch. Based on the cast Dr. Pixley took, the probability is you've found it."

Emily looked at the last photo on her cell. It was a shot of the handle of the hammer, and it looked different from the tool she identified with the help of the criminalist at the regional laboratory. This one bore a shorter wooden handle with a crack down the latter third of the wooden surface.

"How old would you guess this tool is?" Emily asked.

"I'm not an archaeologist or anything, but it doesn't look new, if that's what you mean. The wood is weathered—probably why it broke. You must hit someone hard to sink the business end deep into a man's skull. There's a spot or two of what could be rust on the head."

"All of which will make running down any recent sale impossible."

"I'll make sure we preserve this thing for you. You might be able to pull something from it. Your lab geeks are pretty talented at that sort of thing."

Emily tried to recall if the man she chased wore gloves. The black hoodie, dark pants, even a smell—a combination of woodsy and medicinal—she got when he barreled over her. No memory of gloves or not. Hopefully, there were prints or DNA left behind.

"Call me when you're ready to work on this one?"

"You bet." Dr. White packed up her equipment and joined her team as they loaded Franklin into their van.

Javier stepped away and spoke with a pair of uniformed officers while Emily returned to the burnt remains of Delila's tent. Charred bits of cardboard, plastic, and fabric lay strewn in the dirt. An unburnt patch in the center marked where Tommy Franklin dropped.

Emily kicked a section of tarp with her toe, and spotted a folded wad of paper.

She carefully unfolded the letter-sized sheet. A short, printed message read, "Camp Hope. Tonight. Double usual fee." The quick, terse message was a printed copy of the same text the public works supervisor showed them. Paper—so Tannen wouldn't leave an electronic trail back to him. Did Franklin's partner turn on him and kill him, or was there someone waiting for him in the tent?

Emily tightened her jaw. She saw the black-clad man emerge from the tent and run. She didn't see him assault Franklin. Was he running from her or from what he found in the tent?

"We need to track down our shop foreman Tannen, see if he passed this message on to Franklin and his partner. We hooked him up at Franklin's place."

"Either he bailed out already or this was in play before we found him. He did mention a plan for a cleanup at Miller Park in the morning."

"We can hit him up if he's still in custody and take another run at Delila since Franklin was found in her shelter."

"You don't think she did him, do you?"

"I don't know what to think. But two men have died in her tent and she knows more than she's giving us."

Emily's attention drew to a pair of city dump trucks and a skip loader. Lining up to blow through the line of tents.

"Oh, screw this," Emily said as she strode off to the lead truck.

By the time she'd arrived, the remaining campers had formed a line in front of the heavy trucks, locking arms with one another. A human shield for what remained of their makeshift existence.

"Hey, lady, get these freaks outta the way. I got work to do," the driver yelled down to Emily.

"Who told you to come and work at the crack of dawn?"

"I just go where I'm told, and for time-and-a-half, I'll go anywhere."

"Who gave you this assignment?"

"Lady, I don't care. I got called by the head of public works to clean up this mess, so get them out of the way or I will."

"You threatening them?"

He crept the truck closer to the human chain.

Emily jumped up on the running board and reached in across the steering wheel, switched off the ignition, and pulled out the keys. Her legs were sticking out of the window.

The camp residents cheered when she hopped back down from the truck.

"You aren't touching this camp. It's a crime scene until I say different. You understand me?"

"I gotta call this in."

"Yeah, you do that. I'll be glad to talk to your boss."

Emily stepped back to the line of campers. "Listen, I don't know how long I can hold them off."

"It's all we got. This is the last camp in the city. They done burned all the rest of them down around us. We gotta make a stand, here."

"I get it. We'll do what we can. Anyone see what happened in Delila's tent before the fires started? I think we found one of the firebugs dead in there."

"D didn't have nothing to do with it."

"I'd like to believe you, but I need more. What did you see?"

"I seen a man looking for her. Wanted to talk, he said. D never came back to her tent on account of us looking out for the protesters over there."

"You didn't see who came with the man looking for D?"

A couple of people shook their heads.

The rumble of an approaching vehicle drew her attention.

The truck driver jabbed a thumb in her direction. "You wanted to talk to my boss? Well, here you go."

Ryan Jensen stepped from the passenger seat of the black SUV.

"Detective, I told you to watch yourself."

"Mr. Jensen, kindly tell your public works crew to back away from my crime scene."

Jensen strode closer in crisp blue jeans and a white, tucked-in button-down. The tan, unscuffed Timberland boots completed the picture.

"Detective, the mayor's executive order requires any encampment that poses a risk to public safety, or is a location of criminal activity, shall be removed." Jensen gestured to the smoldering remains and scattered debris. "This place clearly qualifies."

"Might be, but not until my crime scene is cleared."

"I think the mayor might have a different opinion. Why don't you and I go have a late-night dinner and talk it over while my people do what they're paid to do?"

Emily cocked her head, put her hands on her hips. "Did you just threaten and hit on me at the same time?"

"So, what do you say?"

"Does anyone ever fall for your bullshit? One of those trucks so much as moves an inch and I'll have the drivers arrested."

A shadow crossed Jensen's eyes. He wasn't used to being told no. Especially from a woman. Emily could see it in the curl of his lip.

"Why are you wasting time on them?" Jensen shot a finger out at the line of homeless people blocking his equipment.

"They have the right to live. This is the best they have right now. You have somewhere else for them? A shelter? Warm beds? Food?"

"Most of them aren't even from this city. They came here because the previous administrations were trying to placate their liberal base. They actually put some of those people on city advisory boards—like we need to hear from them."

"Weren't you part of the prior administration working for Mayor Stone? I guess you are quite the chameleon changing to match the background. You're like the rest of them—phony and superficial."

He got within inches of Emily. A vein bulged on his forehead. "You'll regret this. You're done. The mayor will have your badge."

He stepped back and left Emily with a hint of a woodsy medicinal odor in his wake. The same smell as the man who lit the fires in the camp. The hair on the back of her neck tingled. She'd have to walk this line carefully. Did he have time to light the fires and get back here? Where was he during the other fires?

CHAPTER FORTY-ONE

EMILY ASSIGNED A crime scene team to scour the tent where Tommy Franklin was found and the surrounding area for any physical or trace evidence to help identify his killer. She told them to be as slow and methodical as possible—the longer they took, the more time the camp residents had to figure out where to go.

She knew the demolition was inevitable, but she wasn't going to let the mayor run over her crime scene. Every one of these camp attacks was followed by a quick cleanup. It made sure any evidence of the attacks and attackers was obliterated. This time, the attacker became a victim.

Tommy Franklin's greed and willingness to club the homeless into submission finally took its ultimate toll. Was he taken out because he became too much of a liability after his role in the attacks was caught on video? Or was he found in the act by someone in the camp?

A last word to a pair of uniformed officers at the scene made sure the city crews didn't touch so much as a tent stake or discarded water bottle until the crime scene teams finished up.

By the time Emily and Javier readied to leave, the protesters had given up and disbanded. There wasn't going to be any showdown between the "haves" and "have-nots."

The jail was a ten-minute drive from Miller Park and there were too many unconnected threads between Stone's murder, the camp arsons, and Franklin's head-splitting.

"You want me to take Tannen while you hit up Delila? She seemed willing to talk to you," Javier said.

"I still think Franklin was the connection between everything. He could have told us who was paying him. Tannen knows, but he's thinking he's safe if he keeps his mouth shut. Gotta wonder if he knows what happened to Franklin."

"Could use that to get this dude to open up. A 'he could be next' thing."

The early hours at the jail were generally quiet. The inmates were all locked down in the cells or dorms. Delila was in processing. The jail deputies locked her in a holding tank until they assigned her a cell in a housing unit.

"I'll go start with her while you see if you can get Tannen to spill it," Emily said.

Emily spotted Delila, now showered and dressed in an orange jail jumpsuit, sitting by herself in a ten-by-ten room. The holding tank would get busier as the day wore on, with petty criminals using the single phone in the tank to call their lawyers and bail bondsmen.

Delila didn't seem bothered by the confined spaces. Emily knew some homeless suffered from extreme claustrophobia in the jail after living outside.

"Them vultures plow up everything?" Delila asked as the electric lock buzzed, letting Emily inside.

"We were able to hold them off for a bit. Long enough to let most folks grab as much of their stuff as they could. Sorry it came to it, but like they say, 'You can't fight City Hall.' They'll have the place bulldozed before lunch. Where are folks gonna go?"

"They done took all the places away—places where we could be on our own, not bothering no one. There's a few camps under the W-X Freeway and some open spaces away from downtown. It's gonna be hard. There's no place to go. If you are lucky to find a spot, it's only temporary because the city will come try to roust you anyway."

"How did you come to live in the camps?"

"Nothing special about my story. Lost my job during the pandemic. Couldn't pay my rent no more and no matter what they tell you, they ain't gonna let you stay for free. This was the only option for me."

"What kind of work did you do?"

"Housekeeping supervisor at the Capitol Park Hotel. They ain't bringing us back."

"I'm sure you looked around, right?"

"Until I got tired and gave up. This's my life now. Living out here—you can't ever get it off of you. It's like a permanent shame. Everyone looks at you like you're looking at me right now."

"I didn't mean to . . ."

"No, I get it. At least you talk to us. Most people try to pretend we're invisible. Or try to get rid of us—that's what the city's been doing."

"The city didn't burn those camps."

"You sure about that? I mean, I ain't saying the mayor herself lit them fires, but anyone who wanted to burn us all out, she was more than willing to dance on in and claim it."

"We found one guy responsible for lighting the fires."

"Good. He needs to pay for what he done."

"Might be a little difficult. He's dead."

Delila lifted her chin and locked eyes with Emily. "Who killed him?"

The response came out flat with no surprise or emotion tied to it. Sure, a veteran of the streets like Delila had seen her share of violence and death, even in the past week, but her reaction was troubling.

"Why don't you tell me. He was found in your tent."

"My tent? What the hell was he doing in my space?" A little more heat in this response.

"Hoped you could answer that. See, Delila, one dead guy in your tent we might be able to explain away. Two makes it a little hard to ignore." Emily stepped away from the wall and stood in the center of the holding tank.

"I didn't kill no one." Her eyes widened as the seriousness of her situation started to set in.

"We have you on video throwing an incendiary device at other people—people who had to go to the hospital for their burn injuries. Not too much of a stretch from there to killing someone."

"Listen, I only threw a bottle back where it came from. And I sure as hell didn't kill no one."

"I'm gonna show you a picture. It's kinda hard to see. We know this guy was one of the firebugs." Emily pulled up the most recent photo with the rock hammer spike embedded into Franklin's skull.

"Oh sweet mother of God."

"Did you meet with him tonight? Like you did with Mayor Stone?"

"No-no, I didn't."

"You ever see anyone with a hammer like this around the camp? It's called a rock hammer."

"Yeah, I know what it is. It's mine."

Emily didn't see that coming. "The hammer—the one sticking out of the guy's head—you're telling me it's yours?"

"Because it is. It got taken the night of the big fires at the 7th Street camp."

"The one where Mayor Stone was killed."

"It was gone after. Din't know someone swiped it, or it got lost in the mess that followed. But I hadn't seen it since."

"You didn't have it with you at Camp Hope."

"No. Like I said, it was gone."

"What would you use it for?"

"It was easy to use to pound in tent stakes and dig me some potty pits—small ones, you know?"

"Would anyone at Camp Hope have reason to steal your hammer?"

"There's a few people who don't know to keep they hands off things what don't belong to them."

"Anyone who'd wanna do this?"

"If they knew he was the firestarter? Yeah, they would."

"Would you?"

"I prolly shouldn't say."

"Where'd you get the hammer?"

"Picked it up at a camp more than a year ago. Had it ever since until it got took."

Emily pinched the bridge of her nose. "This isn't going to look good—you see that, don't you? The city is going to argue you killed him while he was doing his job cleaning up after the homeless. You know how it's going to go down. Any support the homeless community had will evaporate. The mayor's predictions will have become true . . ."

"It ain't what happened. You said yourself he was lightin' them fires."

Emily stared off into a corner as a thought swirled through her mind.

"You listening to me, Detective?"

Emily paced to the other end of the holding tank, where a message had been scratched into the wall. Emily leaned close enough to see the small letters. Neatly scripted words took Emily's breath away. *Who knew you'd end up here? Everyone you ever met.*

"Detective?"

Emily turned and strode to the door, knocking for the deputy.

"Who knew all this would happen, Delila? Everyone."

CHAPTER FORTY-TWO

IT CLICKED WHEN Emily heard her own words—the mayor's predictions had come true. Were they predictions, or carefully directed, targeted actions to make sure events unfolded as the politician wanted? As she left the booking area, she spotted a crumpled newspaper on a desk. It was the morning's paper, over four hours old, but the page where the reader left off was a short four-inch column and the headline stopped Emily in her tracks.

She picked the paper up, unfolding the broadsheet, revealing the entire article. "City Leader Has Higher Aspirations." A quick scan of the piece recounted Mayor Carsten had launched an exploratory committee for a run at the governor's office in the next election.

Exploratory committees were little more than a donation pipeline to test the electability of a candidate before they announced a campaign. The article lauded the mayor's accomplishments while in office, notably eradicating the homeless camps and redevelopment of underused city properties.

"Mind if I keep this?" Emily asked a nearby deputy.

"Sure thing. Left over from the last shift anyway. Hey, we keeping your camp bomber, or what?"

"I don't think she's going anywhere. She's got no one to bail her out."

Javier waited for Emily when she exited the booking area.

"Tannen got released."

"Already?" Emily said.

"The sheriff's been getting pressure to reduce the jail population, and since he was booked on a nonviolent offense, they cut him loose after booking. No bail posted, released with a promise to appear."

"He could have passed the message to Franklin—the one telling him to move on Camp Hope."

"If he did, then he's still in contact with the moneyman," Javier said.

She handed him the newspaper. "Makes you wonder where the money is coming from, doesn't it?"

"The mayor, her backers . . . Someone told us we were getting in some deep water here."

She glanced at her watch. "The lieutenant will be in soon. Should brief him before he gets a call from the chief."

"Great. I—" Javier's cell phone with the Pat Benatar refrain sounded.

"Hey, Mom. Everything okay?"

Emily tensed and watched her partner's face.

"Uh-huh, yeah. Think we should drive by?"

"What's going on?"

"All right, let me know if anything changes." He disconnected the call and shoved the phone in his pocket.

"Your mom woke up a little agitated and confused. Mom says it's not unusual to have episodes like this. She gave her some hot tea and sat with her for a while. She's calm, but still confused. Says she's waiting for your dad to come home from work."

Emily's heart sank. The roller coaster of emotions was taking a toll. One day, like yesterday, her mom was lucid, able to talk about a memory care facility, then a lapse into memories as thin as lace curtains. Dementia and Alzheimer's were insidious diseases, robbing people of the substance of life, leaving them isolated and alone in their own fragile minds.

"I should go check on her. Can you get the lieutenant up to speed?"

Javier agreed, and they split up, Emily reminding him she was a phone call away.

She felt guilty sending him to deal with the fallout from the recent attack on Camp Hope. A call from the mayor's office to the chief would be coming, she could count on it.

Emily got in her SUV and pulled away from the jail parking lot behind the structure and turned south on 7th Street. She thought about cruising by Miller Park, but two city dump trucks piled with tents, scrap wood, and garbage passed her at the light on Broadway. They'd taken the camp down—exactly as she thought they would. Hopefully, the small window she was able to give the residents let them take most of their possessions with them. Where they would go next was the big question. The mayor's policies made it clear—you aren't welcome here.

Emily pulled into her driveway and couldn't help but wonder what would face her inside. As a cop, she always anticipated the outcome of every interaction. This, though, felt completely different, and she couldn't prepare for it. There would come a time, Emily knew, when she would enter her own home and her mother wouldn't know who she was. A total stranger.

When she entered, she locked her weapon in the safe mounted in the entry closet. She followed the voices to the kitchen.

"Those aren't mine," her mother's voice called out.

"Look at the prescription bottle. Your name is on it," Lucinda said.

Emily found them sitting at the kitchen table with a line of prescription bottles between them. A weekly pill container, the kind with a pocket for every day of the week, sat overturned on the surface.

"What's going on, Mom?"

Connie snapped her head around and her eyes tried to focus on Emily. She refocused on the tabletop.

"These pills—they aren't mine. I don't take drugs."

Lucinda held one bottle to Connie. "See, here's your name. And the doctor who prescribed them."

"I don't know him."

"Mom, you've been taking these for a while now. Why don't you want them?"

"They don't belong to me. I don't remember taking them before." The uncertainty crept into Connie's voice.

Emily moved an orange prescription bottle and saw a note written in a shaky hand. "Look here, Mom, you wrote this note on the bottle. You said twice a day. Oh, and this one." Emily moved another bottle closer. "You wrote every morning."

Connie glanced at the bottles and pursed her lips. "I—I don't remember writing this. It's not mine."

"It is, Mom. They are. These are to keep you healthy. Lucinda and I have been helping you remember to take them."

"What are you doing here?" Connie changed the subject to avoid the memory pothole where the prescriptions were concerned.

"I wanted to come and check on you. Make sure you're all right and that you were taking your prescriptions."

"You don't need to babysit me, dear. I can take care of myself."

"I know, Mom."

Lucinda slid a glass of water closer to Connie, hoping the muscle memory of taking her medications would kick in.

"Why are you here, dear? Shouldn't you be busy?"

A little alarm bell sounded in Emily's brain. Her mom was filling in the blanks, a coping strategy she clung to when the gaps in her memory got in the way of understanding where and when she was.

"Where do you think I should be, Mom?"

With uncertainty in her voice, Connie responded, "I know exactly where."

"Where's that?"

A pause, followed by a weak, tentative response. "You won't graduate if you keep playing hooky, Emily. I don't want to get another call from the principal."

Emily sat back and her heart felt cold. She was losing her mother. She'd had episodes like this where she lost track of where she was, even believed her husband was still alive. But they were becoming more frequent and seemed deeper in the void of her memory.

"Mom, I've been out of school for a while now." Emily took a photo from the wall near the living room. It was at her academy graduation. Emily was in her dress blue uniform, a bright shiny new badge freshly pinned on. Next to her in the photo was Connie. "Remember this?"

Connie held the photo in her frail hands. Emily recognized the confusion etched on her face.

"This was a few years ago. Look how happy we were," Emily said.

"How did you do this?"

"Do what, Mom?"

She dropped the photo on the table as if it became too hot to touch. "How did you put me in this photo?"

Emily reached a hand and covered her mother's trembling one. "I didn't add you to the picture. You were there with me."

"I—I don't remember it. I'm sure I would—if I was there."

"It's okay, Mom. Sometimes you get a little confused—especially when you don't take your medication." Emily nudged the pill container a little closer.

Connie noticed the prescriptions slide in front of her and stared at them for a moment as if she was trying to process what she was supposed to do with them. Connie dumped the seven pills and capsules into the small of her hand and tossed them into her mouth, following it with a swig of water.

Lucinda's shoulders relaxed. She tipped her head away from the table, telling Emily she needed to talk.

"Let me refresh your tea."

Emily joined Lucinda at the kitchen counter. "What brought this episode on?"

Lucinda rinsed out the cup and left the water running to mask their whispers.

"I think she did too much yesterday. Going to the facility was more than she's used to. She knew what the idea was—getting her a new place to live—but it was hard for her to process. The medication should help, but she will need a permanent placement in a memory care facility soon."

Emily put an arm around Lucinda and pulled her close. "I know..."

A text message popped up on Emily's phone.

"It's from your son. Checking up on us."

"Tell him to get in touch with Jenny. Her parents are bugging me about him dropping the ball."

"I don't think you have much to worry about there. I think there's been some progress in that area."

"Really? Why didn't he tell me? Why didn't Jenny mention it to her parents?"

"I think they want to do this their own way."

Emily tapped in a response saying things at the home front were under control. She didn't mention his mom's concerns over his dating life.

Javier texted back telling her to call the lieutenant when she could—trouble brewing at City Hall.

Great.

CHAPTER FORTY-THREE

LUCINDA GOT CONNIE all settled in and Emily snuck off to her home office to make a phone call to Lieutenant Hall. Waiting for her on her desk was the trespassing cat, yellow eyes judging her.

"What are you doing in here? Scoot."

Emily spotted a wool scarf she had laid over the back of the chair was now wadded up on the seat and a generous layer of black cat hair now adorned the item.

"I see you've been here before."

The cat yawned in her face.

Emily scooted the scarf onto the desk and sat to make her call.

The lieutenant picked up on the first ring.

"How's mom?"

"Starting to get her settled. It's—it's a lot."

"I'm sorry, Emily. My husband's mother suffered from dementia. I guess she didn't know, so it made things a little easier for her. The confusion and isolation were the scary thing for her, I think."

"It is. The last facility had some problems, so I'm trying to find a new one."

"I wish I could help."

"Javier get you up to speed on the latest camp homicide?"

Emily could hear the lieutenant's chair creak as he got up and heard the thump of his office door. This didn't bode well for the discussion to come.

"The mayor wants me booted off the Stone homicide case," she said.

"She does, but it's not her call. The chief has your back; so do I."

Emily felt a ball of anger form in her gut.

"Lieutenant, I know I can't go off half-cocked making allegations against the mayor. I know. Every rock we turn over in this case leads back to City Hall and the mayor's office. There are some dirty dealings happening over there. They were pretty damn quick to call the chief."

"I'm with you, and like you said, until we have solid, irrefutable evidence, we can't risk a run at the mayor."

"You hear she's planning on announcing a bid for governor? Morning paper mentioned she has an exploratory committee up and running."

"It means she's gonna be on the offense."

"Then we need to put her on defense."

Emily ran down the River Gardens redevelopment plans with ties back to the city, the connection of city staff, Franklin and Tannen taking orders to burn out the camps and then clear them out, making sure trace evidence was obliterated under heavy equipment. All of it coordinated to support the mayor's policies to eliminate the homeless camps in the city.

"How does Stone's murder fit into this?" Hall asked.

"He was an early supporter of River Gardens—it might have been his idea in the first place. Why he was targeted, I'm still sorting out.

"We have three dead in the camps and a single homeless woman is tied to two of them.

"The mayor knew about the connection." Emily heard paper rustle in the background. "She's going to hold a presser today saying the homeless camp murderer is in custody and it's another example of why these camps and large gatherings of homeless cannot be allowed to overrun our streets."

"I know how it looks, but I don't like Delila McDaniel for this. She has nothing to gain from these killings. I don't buy the mental health angle. I've talked to her, and she's tough, streetwise, and damaged, but she's not a psycho-killer."

"Got an alternative?"

"I'm working on it."

"Then you better work fast."

Emily thanked him and hung up. She pulled up the online version of the morning paper she'd taken at the jail. Her desktop computer flashed to life and displayed the story, buried on the third page of the feed.

In the last paragraph, there it was, a mention of a press conference this afternoon in front of City Hall condemning the ongoing violence stemming from the camps and announcing the arrest of a suspect in the murders.

Emily stared at the digital page. It couldn't be right. She read it again and confirmed what she saw on the first read through. The arrest of a suspect was announced in the morning paper, hours before the body was found, hours before Delila was arrested, and hours before protesters provoked a conflict at Camp Hope.

Emily scrolled up to the article's byline. She recognized the reporter and had his number in her phone, not because he was a reporter, but from a couple of dates that didn't seem to go anywhere.

She pressed dial on Brady Collier's number. It landed in his voicemail. "Hey, Brady, it's Emily Hunter. I have a question about your piece on the mayor's campaign committee. Give me a call, would you?"

How would the mayor know there would be an arrest? Stage a protest and make sure Delila was singled out. Maybe by tossing a Molotov cocktail at her, hoping for a reaction. The distraction of the protests and fire-bombing gave someone dressed in a black hoody time to drive a spike in Tommy Franklin's forehead.

The entire event was staged.

Emily reread the article. A source close to City Hall was cited but not named. She couldn't help but think the mayor's finger-prints were all over this leak.

Her cell rang and the caller ID displayed Brady Collier's name. "Hi, Brady."

"I was kind of surprised when I found your message in my voice-mail. Call to apologize?"

"For what?"

"The fact you need me to list out the reasons for you speaks volumes," Brady said, with a playful lilt in his voice.

"I don't remember it that way. Speaking of remembering, your piece in the morning rag about the mayor's press conference . . ."

"You mean the puff piece for the mayor's upcoming bid for the governor's office?"

"What's up with that? She's been a mayor for a hot minute and now she's posturing for the statehouse?"

"The timing. For her, it's her best shot at a move up. The polit-ical wonks say now's the time to strike with the current governor making noise about a bid for president. He's got too much baggage to carry that off, but his ego won't let him see it. Mayor Carsten hasn't been around enough to get pegged as an establishment hack, and her approach might be viewed as fresh to some."

"She's made a mess of the homeless situation in the city."

"Might not be viewed that way by voters elsewhere. They are going to see a candidate who took care of her city—we know all she did was push the problem somewhere else."

Brady took advantage of the a pause in Emily's response. "Emily, what is it you want to know?"

"Your article mentioned the arrest related to the recent murders in the camps."

"It wasn't a question."

"Who told you about the investigation? I know we didn't."

"I can't reveal my sources, Emily. You know that. I attributed it to a source close to the mayor's office."

"Your piece didn't reveal the name of the person arrested."

"I withheld it until we could corroborate. It didn't take away from the story. The whole homeless camp cycle of violence thing."

"I can corroborate the identification of the arrested person." Emily wasn't giving up any confidential details here. The names of people arrested and booked into the Sacramento County Jail were public record.

"Okay. Not that I need it. The story's put to bed."

"I'm not sure it is, Brady. The woman's name is McDaniel, Delila McDaniel.

"It's the name I was given."

"The problem is, I hadn't arrested her when you ran the story. She wasn't a suspect when your article hit the streets. We hadn't even found the body at Camp Hope last night. And the dead man wasn't a homeless person. What I need to know is who told you she was the one responsible."

"Emily, the source is solid, I assure you."

"Your source told you about a crime we hadn't yet discovered. They could only know her name if they had some guilty knowledge of the events."

"You're implying this source was involved in murder? Highly unlikely. What possible reason would they have to do that? They have too much at risk."

"What's at risk are millions of dollars in redevelopment deals."

"Emily, I'm not following. What do development and murder have to do with one another?"

Emily heard his interest begin to pique.

"How reliable is your source? I mean, there's a planned redevelopment project called River Gardens. It depends on eradicating the homeless camps on the river. Massive condo developments with city-issued environmental waivers for construction near or on protected watershed. Sound like a connection now?"

"You're talking about a City Hall conspiracy to displace the homeless and redevelop the land?"

"I am. It falls in line with the mayor's policy goals—eliminating the camps, revitalizing downtown with new construction, bringing in new development partners. And it all hinges on her ability to get rid of the camps and the people in them."

"But murder, Emily? That's a reach."

"Is it? She needs this project to pan out to pave her path to the governor's mansion. She can claim to have made the city safer, brought in new development, and people who can say differently are dying."

"You can't connect a specific individual to these crimes, or I don't think we'd be talking right now."

"That's why I need to know who told you about the arrest."

The silence on the other end made Emily believe Brady was considering her plea.

A sigh on the other end, then Brady cleared his throat. "Emily, I cannot reveal my source. It goes against all the ethical rules we have. I am concerned about what you've told me, and I need to check it out. If my source is a party to the crimes, that's a different issue."

"Don't go poking into this, Brady. People are getting killed, and no matter what the mayor says, none of the murder victims was a homeless person. A social worker, a city public works employee, and ex-mayor John Stone."

"Stone? I knew he died, but in the camps? That's been kept quiet."

"He was."

"The palace intrigue just took a hard right turn. Stone was a problematic city leader for many reasons. One of the more out-of-the-box ideas was to build shelters for the homeless on city land. Some city land was grabbed up under eminent domain the last year of his tenure."

"Where were these properties?"

"I don't remember the details. All over the city, under bridges, vacant lots, and privately owned land near the rivers."

"Ever hear about River Gardens? It was Stone's plan to put housing in places you mentioned. I saw a blueprint of three condo and commercial complexes along the river in the exact locations the camps were terrorized."

"River Gardens? No, haven't run across the name. But, Emily, even if the city is connected to these new developments, what's the rub? Those camps are an eyesore and a public health concern. What's wrong with taking back city property and putting it to better use?"

"The problem is people are dying. Not to mention the city created those camps in the first place by getting rid of every other public option for people who live on the street. The mayor forced this level of violence and unrest by shoving all these people together with no medical, mental health, or social safety net."

"When did you become a social worker, Emily?"

"Yeah, maybe it was a bit much. But this week, a young girl witnessed a man die." Emily didn't mention the girl was the one who did the killing. "There's so much going on there and no one cares. No one with the power or ability to do anything about it cares. They don't or can't vote, so they aren't of any value to the mayor's next election."

"I get it, I do. I can't reveal my source. But, Emily, it isn't Mayor Carsten."

Emily felt her gut turn cold. She was certain the power-hungry political animal was the confidential source.

"But . . . you're close. I will say it's a source in the mayor's office."

Emily held her breath. She knew. Ryan Jensen was the only person other than the mayor to talk to the press. Jensen was the mayor's mouthpiece when it came to dealing with the media.

"Thanks, Brady. I appreciate it. Please be careful if you look into this. I don't trust any of them, especially Jensen. Watch your back around him."

"I never said anything about Jensen."

"You didn't have to. He's been the one making the most noise over there. He certainly drank the mayor's Kool-Aid."

"It is the nature of his job. I don't think you can read too much into it."

"Yeah, yeah. You be careful, Brady."

"You, too."

Emily cut the call off and put her head back, trying to make the connections in her mind. Brady was right. Ryan Jensen's job was to make sure the issues of the day got the right spin. Jensen, the mayor, or someone within City Hall was making payments to Tannen and Tommy Franklin. Franklin wasn't around to talk about it. Chances were Tannen would disappear, too, and with it, the last link to the people behind burning the camps down.

The mystery behind the push to burn the camps deepened, and she was no closer to finding out who was responsible for the murder of the former mayor, John Stone. Despite his death, Stone's legacy of River Gardens was on the launch pad, with nothing in the way to block it. Hours to go before the mayor's press conference and River Gardens became reality.

Unless . . .

CHAPTER FORTY-FOUR

EMILY PULLED THE keyboard close. She tapped in the secretary of state's website, the government entity responsible for registering corporations and—surely a project as large as a multi-site condo development would register as a limited liability corporation, or LLC. It was standard practice to protect the business and the key investors.

Emily tapped in "River Gardens" and hit ENTER. The screen immediately spit back two corporate entities with the name in their name. A River Garden Memorial Park in Escondido, and River Gardens Pet Sitting in Burbank. Neither of the Southern California businesses had any tie to Sacramento or condo construction.

Remembering the photo of the development blueprints, Emily pulled up the image on her phone and enlarged the photo capturing the architectural firm responsible for drawing up the plans. She tapped in the phone number listed on the plans and a recorded message said the number was no longer in service.

"Shit." A quick search on the secretary of state's website for the architectural firm came back with an entry the business had folded two years ago.

She was about to log off when she remembered the plans were prepared for SCS, Senior Care Solutions. Back on the website, Emily tapped in "Senior Care Solutions," and no business or corporation with the name was listed.

The initials SCS, though, revealed a pageful of hits, and clicking through twenty-seven similarly named corporations brought her to one called Sacramento Conservatory Society, SCS. The corporation documents were filed three years ago, and the business agents and contacts were listed: John Stone and Ryan Jensen.

Emily started jotting down the address listed for the business, and it wasn't City Hall. It was the SCS office she visited, thinking it was a memory care facility.

All the SCS board members had their portraits on the conference room wall. Emily was focused on the mayor's photo. She didn't notice Ryan Jensen, and John Stone's image would have been taken down after he left office in disgrace. But SCS hadn't updated their secretary of state filing to reflect the change, moving Stone out and Mayor Carsten in, if the portrait gallery was to be believed.

Emily printed out the secretary of state's page. It was too late to drive to the SCS offices. And she couldn't leave her mother alone—she'd had episodes of waking at night, confused as to where she was, and on one occasion, walked out the front door in her nightclothes to go home.

The fear in her mother's eyes brought Emily to tears. What an insidious disease. There was little chance of getting a good night's sleep. She felt like a new mother, listening for their newborn stirring. Except in this case, the roles were reversed.

Emily awoke with a pressure on her chest. Before she could panic about an impending heart attack, she picked up on the purring sound coming from the curled-up lump of black cat sprawled on top of her. She'd fallen asleep with her legs propped up on the desk and they tingled with pins and needles when she moved them, cupping the contented cat so she didn't slip to the floor.

The cat glanced up at her with narrowed yellow eyes and an expression of disapproval over the change of sleeping arrangements.

"Sorry. Didn't I let you out last night?" Emily tried to recall if she had but couldn't remember if she let the furry little trespasser out to go home.

Emily stood and placed the cat on the floor. Both of them shook out their legs to get the blood flowing. The cat followed Emily to the kitchen and waited while Emily poured a cup of food in her bowl. A few quick crunches, and she darted out the back door when Emily opened it for her. "Remember to give our B&B a good rating on Yelp."

The clock on the oven said it wasn't six yet, and Emily put on a pot of coffee. The aroma did more for her spirits than did the hot dark brew itself. She huddled over her first cup and noticed a note Lucinda left for her saying she'd be over early. And a reminder not to feed the cat. Because she'd done it before she left. Damn cat fooled her again.

She peeked in on her mom and the woman slept soundly, unhampered by her failing mind. A hot shower and a fresh change of clothes took away the smoke residue from the Camp Hope fires she didn't even know came along with her.

She was pouring another cup of coffee when Lucinda let herself in.

"Good morning," Lucinda whispered.

Emily held the coffeepot up.

"Yes, please."

"Thank you again for staying with Mom."

"If she's up to it today, I hope to go look at a couple of memory care facilities. If they look good and Connie seems okay with them, I'll let you know, then you can take a look for yourself."

"That's a tremendous help. I still need to get you the names of places Brian has."

"Don't bother. Brian and I compared our lists."

Emily eyed Lucinda over the rim of her coffee cup. "You've been talking with my boyfriend? Do I need to be jealous?"

"Please, the man is crazy about you."

Emily felt a little tingle at Lucinda's admission.

"You make sure he stays that way, okay?" Emily asked.

"I'll let you know if we leave to go visit the new places."

Emily poured another cup into a travel mug and blew a kiss to Lucinda. She'd started the car when her phone buzzed.

"Hunter here."

"Hi, Detective," Dr. Pixley's voice sounded over the connection. "Thought I'd try and catch you before you got caught up in the cops and robbers of the day. Can you swing by on your way in? I have the final death cert for Stone."

"I'm in the car now. I can be there in fifteen minutes. What's up?"

"Our John Stone case took an unexpected turn."

* * *

Emily found Dr. Pixley in her office, signing a stack of death certificates, one after the other. A parade of death without end.

"Thanks for coming over early, Detective. I wanted you to see this." She handed Emily a file with John Stone's name on the label.

Emily flipped open the pressboard cover and the document on the top was a freshly prepared death certificate.

Emily scanned down to the section listing the cause, usually a jargon-laden explanation like respiratory failure, cardiac failure, or, as on Stone's original certification, massive cerebral hemorrhage. The brain hemorrhage was still listed, but now there was a secondary cause of death listed. Acute fentanyl poisoning.

"At the levels found in his blood, fatal levels, he was going to die without intervention. The levels were even higher than we thought. As I mentioned in our prelim, he was unconscious when he was struck on the back of his head. Both were fatal."

"We did find fentanyl patches in his home."

"There was no residue from a patch, and at these levels, he'd need a half dozen of them plastered on. No, this was taken internally. Oral or injection. The tissue damage from the burns limits the inspection for injection marks."

"Good way to cover it up."

"Thought you might want to know this new detail on the level of toxicity. I can swear to it now. Might help, might not."

"Oh, it helps. Someone incapacitated him before plunging the spike in his head. Which means the man wasn't walking and talking like we were led to believe."

"I've run blood panels on the new guy Dr. White brought in last night. See if he was dosed, too. I plan on taking a cast from the weapon lodged in his skull to match for Stone's. I'm fairly certain they are one and the same. I'll let you know when I can get the cast to you."

"Javier or I will be here when you're ready. Thanks, Doc. This helps."

"All right then, go forth and detect, Detective."

Dr. Pixley grabbed another death certification and reviewed before she signed off. A sigh, followed by, "Ten years old. Accidental drowning."

She picked up the next death record and Emily slipped out.

On the way to her car, she called Javier. "You up and running?"

"I'm at the office. Early bird and all."

"I'll swing by in ten. We need to make a few stops."

Javier waited at the door when Emily pulled in. He jumped in and buckled up. "Where we heading?"

Emily gave him a rundown of Dr. Pixley's discovery and the secretary of state's filing information for SCS.

"We recovered fentanyl from Stone's medicine cabinet."

"Indeed, we did. I want to drive by and poke the widow Stone a little and see what happens. We need to ask her about the drugs and press her on what she knows about SCS. She had those files on her living room table."

The ex-mayor's wife didn't give Emily the impression her husband was a pill-popping opiate abuser. Then again, addicts were notorious for hiding their use until they'd ripped off every family member they could. Was that why they were selling the house, and it was never about right-sizing their lifestyle?

Pulling up to the home, Emily noticed a couple exiting the front door. They were in their early thirties and the woman was heavily pregnant. They spoke with a platinum-haired woman in a tailored navy-blue pantsuit. The younger woman rubbed her belly as a frown appeared. She hooked an arm around the man with her as they strode down the walk. The pant-suited older woman followed them halfway where she paused and attached a sale pending placard to the real estate open house sign in the front yard.

"That didn't take long," Javier said. "I knew property was moving in the city, but this was fast. I mean, Mrs. Stone had piles of boxes in there the last time we were here."

Emily got out and waved at the young couple walking toward her. She met them on the sidewalk.

"Are we too late?" Emily asked, pointing at the Stone residence.

The pregnant woman huffed and cut her eyes at the real estate agent trotting back to the front door. "So were we. Been on the market less than two days and there are five offers—all over asking. Two of them cash. How are we supposed to compete with that?"

"Was the owner there? I mean, you could make a personal appeal—you have a pretty compelling reason there. Congratulations, by the way," Emily said.

The woman rubbed her belly again, an unconscious reaction. "I don't think so. There was another couple looking. It was—I hoped this would be the one. Excellent schools and they take care of their neighborhood by keeping out people who shouldn't live here, and it's away from the inner-city crime problems. The people here are—"

"White?" Javier said.

The woman's eyes widened when she noticed him join Emily.

"You're with *him*?" she said with an emphasis on *him*, as if she couldn't understand why someone would be with a man not of the same race.

Emily snaked her arm in Javier's. "Yes, we are. Why?"

The pregnant woman tried to backpedal, and her companion came to her defense. "I think what my wife is trying to say is this might not be the right neighborhood for you. They are, how can I say it? Exclusive."

"I should hope so. We plan on making a cash offer today—way above asking. We wouldn't be here if we didn't think it was exclusive enough," Emily said.

The woman's face froze in a shocked expression at the thought of this interracial couple having enough cash to make an offer.

"You think the house is big enough?" Javier asked.

"We'll go take a look. It's comforting to know not everyone can live here."

"Something to be said for an exclusive neighborhood," Javier said.

The couple hustled off; crestfallen they weren't exclusive enough.

"Okay, that was a little fun," Emily said.

"What is it lately with all the bigots in this town?"

"I'm feeling for the baby growing up in that home. What do you think they're going to learn?"

Emily and Javier entered the open front door. The real estate agent was talking with another couple when she caught the detectives in the living room.

"Please feel free to look around. I'll be with you in a moment."

Emily leaned to Javier. "Looks like Mrs. Stone managed to get rid of all the boxes."

"And the files, too,"

The house was professionally staged. Out was the Stones' older, dated furniture, replaced by more modern, neutral pieces. The slight whiff of paint meant a touch-up to cover the dark accent wall. Gone were the photos of the former mayor with athletes and dignitaries.

Emily wandered down the hallway to the left, past a bathroom bigger than her kitchen, and a guest suite, to a wood-paneled room with a built-in bookshelf and a desk in a dark exotic wood. The ex-politician's home office.

The built-in desk drawers were empty, as were the closet and bookshelves.

"Hey, get a load of this," Javier said as he pushed a panel on a bookshelf and a two-foot section unlocked a magnetic catch and pivoted open. A whiskey bar with six bottles and crystal tumblers arranged on a silver tray. "I want one of these in my next place."

"Redbreast 21, Pappy Van Winkle—he's got some expensive stuff here. What I don't see is any sign of hiding pills or paraphernalia an addict would have."

Emily found another hidden compartment, empty with dust lines where the outline of a tabbed file folder had rested.

"Wonder what this file was? Politician's dirty deals? Whatever it was hadn't been touched in a while."

The real estate agent found them in the office. "Quite a nice setup for remote work, wouldn't you agree?"

"Is the owner around?" Emily asked.

"No, we generally ask they find themselves busy elsewhere while buyers look about. Some find it intrusive and saddening. Is there a question you have about the place? I could make a phone call."

"Did you know the Stones?"

"Oh, you're aware. Yes, I'm a friend of Mrs. Stone. Shame about Johnny."

"What did Mrs. Stone tell you about what happened?"

She glanced over her shoulder to make sure potential buyers didn't hear gossip to send them running out the front door. "Janet told me he was killed—murdered at a homeless camp. Just dreadful. I can't imagine what he would be doing there."

"You know about his position on homeless camps while he was in office? He was opposed to them, right?"

"Of course. Which is why I found it especially odd that he was found in one. I can't imagine what would draw him to a filthy place like that."

"You were close to the Stones?"

"With Janet, mostly."

"She ever mention her husband's drug problem?"

A hand flew to her chest. "Heavens no. I can't even imagine. Johnny would never."

"Like Johnny would never be caught dead in a homeless camp—until he was," Emily said.

"What's with the interest in John and Janet?"

Emily pulled back her jacket to display the badge on her belt. The agent's shoulder fell not from the fact they were police officers, but she'd lost a prospective sale. "I understand you have some offers on the place?"

"Two point seven."

"Million?" Javier said.

"Fifty-five thousand over asking. These properties don't come on the market often. Janet picked the right time to sell."

"Lucky for her Johnny died then, isn't it?"

The agent didn't respond, but her reddened cheeks told she agreed.

"Where can we find Mrs. Stone?"

"I don't know."

"You must have a way to contact her and let her know she has offers on her place."

"I have a phone number."

"What is it?"

"Don't you, like, need a warrant for that?"

Emily glared at her. "No. I don't."

"Fine." The agent stepped away to get her phone.

Emily noticed Javier suppressing a smile. "What?"

"No warrant?"

"I don't need one if she gives it to me."

The agent returned with a bejeweled cell phone and held the display to Emily, who jotted down the number.

"Thank you."

"Now, if that will be all. I have a couple interested in making an offer." The agent tugged on the hem of her jacket and left to join the couple in the living room.

Emily and Javier followed. The couple looked anxious when they spotted them. Emily figured they thought she and Javier were competing bidders, no doubt a seed planted by the real estate agent.

As Emily passed, she said, "Shame about that death."

The eyes of the woman beside the agent widened. "Death? What death?"

"There wasn't a death here."

"Why would they say death? Who are they?"

"Nothing to worry about. Police officers."

The agent cringed as soon as she said it.

"Police officers? A death? Honey, we're out. I'm not living in a haunted house."

Emily grinned as they stepped out the front door ahead of the couple who couldn't leave the place fast enough.

"What day is it?" Emily asked.

"Saturday. Don't tell me I have to worry about your memory, too."

"I know where Mrs. Stone is right now."

CHAPTER FORTY-FIVE

IN THE CAR, Emily asked Javier to look up the address of the auction house. "Estate and Heirloom Liquidators."

"Would it be easier if I drove?"

"I'd like to get there before she leaves, Miss Daisy."

"You saying I'm a careful driver? Nothing wrong with that."

"Whatever. What's the address for the auction house?"

Javier looked up the name of the auction house—the one Emily recalled from the earlier visit to the Stone residence.

The auction house was in a downtown warehouse near the rail yards. The past three mayors had tried to develop the old Southern Pacific rail junction into commercial or residential space, but it always hit some roadblock. The toxic waste cleanup alone cost millions and left the hundred acres pockmarked with holes. Countless steel barrels were trucked out for storage in waste containment yards.

The auction house was on the northern end of the rail yards, close to the foster care and adoption office where Pete Bell worked.

There were a dozen cars parked in the lot at the auction house. Emily didn't know which one might belong to Janet Stone.

Inside, the house was arranged like an art gallery. There was no audience raising numbered cards to place their bid. Emily counted six people she pegged as buyers holding clipboards, and she spotted a man placing a red sticker on an oversized mahogany armoire.

A young woman who couldn't have measured five feet in her four-inch heels approached the detectives. "How can I help you? Are you here for the day's auction?"

"Sure," Emily said.

The young woman handed her a clipboard. She tucked her long brown hair behind an ear with five earrings that Emily counted.

"The item descriptions and minimum reserve amounts are listed here for you. If you want to place a bid, put your purple sticker on the item and write down the amount on your list. We'll come to you and take care of the purchase."

"Thanks," Javier said.

"I'm Sierra, like the mountains. Let me know if I can help you with anything." She caressed Javier's arm as she passed them.

"Easy now, partner, or I'm telling Jenny."

"What? I didn't do anything."

"It must be the almost most eligible vibe you give off."

"Shut it. There she is, up there in the corner, talking to the two guys in suits."

The widow Stone was chatting up two men who each held a clipboard. Emily didn't peg them as potential buyers. They were more upscale types who would have their underlings poking about a warehouse for auction items.

"Go ask your new girlfriend who those two guys are."

"She's not . . . fine."

Javier made a line over to Sierra, who brightened when she spotted him.

Emily took an indirect route to the back of the display space, keeping Mrs. Stone's back to her. She hadn't noticed the detective yet.

Emily tried to listen to the conversation, but another young auction worker stepped in between them. "Hi, what can I help you with?"

The auction worker was tall, lean, and had a smile that would melt a glacier. Emily felt his glance flick up and down her body.

"I'm Chad. What are you interested in today?"

The first thought Emily had was that young Chad was offering more than appeared on the auction list.

"What can you tell me about these pieces?" Emily turned and gestured to a pair of brass coatracks.

"They're coatracks."

"Thanks for the clarification, Chad."

He smiled back at her. "Let me know if you need help with anything."

The same line Sierra worked on Javier.

Chad backed away as his glance swept over Emily once more.

Javier joined his partner. "I see you made a friend."

"What is it with this place?"

"Sierra's nice."

"Are they selling more than furniture out of this warehouse?"

"You're so jaded you don't even know what friendly looks like."

"Shut up. What'd you get on these two chatting up Mrs. Stone? Or did you forget to ask the girl?"

"Unlike you, I actually had a conversation with Sierra. Those two aren't buyers—at least she hadn't seen them here before and they haven't put in a bid yet. The entire time, they've been hanging with Mrs. Stone. She heard they were business partners."

Emily took a casual glance over her shoulder at the widow's interaction with the two men. Mrs. Stone was laughing at something the taller of the two men said.

"Business partners? What business is that?"

"Sierra didn't say."

Emily tilted her head to the conversation and tried to pick up what they were saying, but the cavernous warehouse space made it impossible. She kicked herself for not digging into Mrs. Stone more. What line of work was she in? One way to find out.

She turned and strode over to the small gathering and inserted herself between the two men facing Mrs. Stone.

"Detective? What are you doing here?" Mrs. Stone said.

"I'm looking for a few pieces for the restoration work I'm doing."

The taller man cast a dismissive glance at Emily, and his partner said, "Restoration? What are you looking for?"

"I'm rehabbing a Victorian, here in downtown."

"You might find a few things here. Janet has a good eye for that sort of thing. If you're looking for structural elements, glazing, exterior doors, trusses, and period trim work, we work with some developers who come across special, one-of-a-kind items from time to time."

"It is getting harder to find the original pieces. Do you have a card? I might follow up with a wish list if your people run across some things I'm missing."

The shorter man didn't hesitate and pulled a silver-plated case from his breast pocket, withdrew a thick laminated card, and handed it to Emily.

William Turlock, chief operations officer, Sacramento Conservatory Society. The SCS corporation she'd searched for in the secretary of state's database. She had a tangible face to associate with SCS. She couldn't recall if Turlock's face adorned the wall in the SCS offices.

"Conservatory Society? What sort of conservation are you into?"

Turlock ran a hand through his expensive razor-cut hair and leaned in. "It's all about conserving our way of life."

"And what way of life might that be?"

"It all begins with making the most of what we have around us. Take this city, for example—there is so much unrealized potential here with the natural environment, the rivers, and protected woodlands. Yet, it's all at risk with unchecked and unregulated occupation by the homeless. You know what I'm talking about, Detective. You've seen it firsthand."

"I've seen what happens when people don't have anywhere else to go."

"Your own mayor seems to have a rational plan."

"Declaring the camps illegal without resources to shelter and care for the people who're displaced isn't a plan."

"From an interested business investor, it tells me enough."

Emily glanced over to Mrs. Stone, who listened to Turlock with a tight jaw. Emily got the sense it wasn't from what he said, but from Emily's presence.

"Mrs. Stone, I needed to ask you something. Might I have a word?"

"Concerning?" she said with a less than friendly tone.

"Your husband."

Mrs. Stone let out an exasperated breath. "Fine. What do you need?"

"Perhaps we can talk somewhere—a little more private." Emily tipped her head off to a space, away from the two business associates.

Mrs. Stone rolled her eyes and agreed, stalking off some thirty feet to a quiet corner. "Will this take long?" Mrs. Stone kept looking back at Turlock.

"Your husband—seems he had a significant amount of fentanyl in his system when he died. Any idea how he might have gotten the drug?"

Mrs. Stone's shoulders sagged. Almost like it wasn't the question she was afraid of. "He had a prescription. But you know that, Detective."

"The level was higher than the medical examiner expected."

"Let me ask you a question. How well did you know my husband?"

Emily squinted at the idea. She knew him as a pompous, arrogant, skirt-chasing political hack who would do whatever it took to get what he wanted. "Well enough, I suppose."

"Then you know he was prone to excess in all things. Drinking, women, and lately, drugs. You asked me before why he was hanging out in the camp? That's where he was buying the drugs his doctor wouldn't prescribe."

"Why didn't you mention it before?"

"Out of respect for what we once had, I suppose."

Emily felt the insincerity laden in the remark.

"How long do you think your husband was—"

"An addict?" she interrupted Emily. "Johnny had an addictive personality. He injured his back not long after he left office. He quickly became dependent on the pain pills and even his doctors realized what was happening. They cut him off the oxy and gave him the patches instead. Johnny was not happy about the little kink in his supply. I think it's when he started going to where he knew he could find what he was looking for."

"In the camps?"

Mrs. Stone nodded.

"What about his interest in cleaning up the camps and moving the unhoused into shelters? The Stone Plan?"

"You've dealt with more drug addicts than I have, Detective. What I saw was everything else faded away and all he cared about—was consumed with—was the search for where could score his next hit. Nothing else mattered."

Emily felt Mrs. Stone's energy abruptly change. She stiffened and her gaze focused back on the two SCS men—except a third had joined them. Ryan Jensen.

CHAPTER FORTY-SIX

"How do you know those guys?" Emily asked."

"I must go now, Detective. I trust you will keep my husband's secret. It will do no one any good if it gets out. He was a complicated and troubled man. He deserves to rest in peace."

Mrs. Stone strode off toward Jensen, Turlock, and the taller SCS man. Within a few seconds, all four strode out of the warehouse. Jensen gave Emily a stern glare before he followed the pack out of the building. Emily felt the look was somewhere in between a warning and assessing the threat she posed to his boss, the mayor.

Javier had snuck off to talk with Sierra once more. He caught Emily's eye and signaled for her to come over.

"Sierra, tell Detective Hunter what you just told me."

The young woman put a hand on her hip and looked around, checking who was within earshot. "That man is here all the time, and it's not for the auction."

"Which man are we talking about?" Emily asked.

"Jensen. Ryan Jensen. He comes here and meets with those people, the men and Mrs. Stone, like once a month. They never bid on anything. Today was a little different because Mrs. Stone was putting some of her pieces on the floor."

"You ever hear what they talk about?"

She shook her head. "No. This time was different because when Jensen came in, he saw you with Mrs. Stone. He came up to me and handed me a hundred-dollar bill to tell him what you were talking about."

"What'd you tell him?"

"I said you'd come in, got an auction list, and started talking with the guy in the dark blue suit."

"What did he want?"

"I don't know. I told him you were looking around until you started talking with the other guy. He told me to call him if I hear you asking about some place called River Gardens."

"Really?"

Sierra nodded quickly. "I have no idea what he was talking about. I've never heard the name before."

"I have."

Javier slipped Sierra his business card and thanked her.

After Sierra gathered their clipboards, she padded off to greet a potential buyer who'd arrived.

"Did we stumble upon the people behind SCS?" Emily said.

"I'd like to think we found it because of our superior detecting abilities. It sure fits, though. The political angle, the moneymen, and I think Mrs. Stone is hanging onto her husband's coattails on this one. They paid Tannen and Franklin to tear down the camps."

When Emily and Javier unlocked the Crown Vic, she paused. "Okay, if Turlock and the SCS bankrolled the River Gardens project, they wouldn't do it without some assurances, right? I mean, they'd have to know all the permits and clearances were in place before they invested. Who would make those promises? Jensen? He's not the one with the clout," Emily said.

"You're not thinking—"

"Her honor, the mayor."

"Emily, you better be dammed sure about this."

"Sure enough to know we need to go have a talk with her. Now's the time with her watchdog, Jensen, busy with his SCS friends. I don't think the mayor plunged a spike into John Stone's head, or Tommy Franklin, but she might know more than she realizes."

The drive from the warehouse to City Hall passed a new homeless camp at the edge of the rail yards, in the shadows of the William Jefferson Clinton federal building. The camp took advantage of the canceled construction project in the yard after the excavation and roads were completed. The result was a camp with the characteristics of a Middle East refugee center, with tents, tarps, and makeshift shelters set up in neat rows along the newly paved streets. A community trying to make a refuge in a sea of hostility.

"Must be what's left of the Camp Hope people," Javier said as they passed through.

"They have to go somewhere. The city keeps bulldozing camp after camp. Now they're up against the ropes. If the city crushes this camp..."

In the outer offices in the new City Hall, Emily asked to see the mayor, and no, she didn't have an appointment. She handed the young man her business card and said it was important and it had to do with the homeless camp fires.

Emily thought the mayor might pass her off to an underling or have her grow roots in the lobby while she waited. Instead, the junior staffer returned. "The mayor will see you now."

Emily was ushered into the chambers, where she found Ellen Carsten seated at a conference table in her well-appointed office. The mayor had her jacket removed, glasses perched on her nose, and she had a stack of files and documents spread on the table before her.

A sharp glance up from the work. "Detectives, here to harass me again?" The mayor seemed exhausted. Emily noted the usually polished city leader was wearing the same clothes she wore when they had their "discussion" at the detective bureau.

"No, ma'am, but I have some questions," Emily said, standing at the table.

"So do I," the mayor said.

Emily caught an expression on the mayor's face and followed her eyes to the spread of documents on the table between them. One stood out plainly. A plot plan for River Gardens—the same one she'd seen at the SCS offices.

"River Gardens," Emily said.

"It was Johnny Stone's pipe dream. Or I thought it was just a dream. After our . . . encounter at police headquarters, I needed to make certain you were full of yourself and making unsubstantiated allegations about my administration's handling of the camps and my policies surrounding the city's unhoused."

"Mayor, we know a private developer paid city employees to burn the camps."

"SCS?"

Emily nodded. "Did you know?" Emily didn't expect a response but wanted to put the question out there to have the mayor off balance. Instead, the mayor responded.

"I didn't until now. SCS is the only one who gains from these actions. Lawlessness in the camps, scores of homeless victimized. It's behavior we expected. It's born in these squalid camps. But not at the levels we're witnessing. I couldn't put it together—looking at what you claimed. I was ready to rub your face in it. Then I found these." The mayor pulled a file open and tossed the documents on the table's surface.

Emily picked up a city form, like countless others in typical government operations where a form was needed to sharpen a pencil.

"What you're looking at are city public works requests. Work orders. There are forms for the expedited cleanup for the homeless camps after the fires, for the 7th Street, 18th Street, and Camp Hope."

"Tracks with what Tommy Franklin and Walt Tannen told us. There was approval from the director of public works to clear out the camps."

"Except there wasn't. My public works chief had never seen these requests and never approved them."

"You trust him on that count?"

"As much as anyone in my administration. I don't think he knew about them."

"Someone did because Franklin and his crews were on cleanup duty. Granted, Franklin knew about the camp cleanups because he was there starting the fires."

"The part that stood out to me was this." The mayor pointed at a line on the form. "The request was submitted the day before the fire. Each and every time. It's as if they knew the camps were going to burn. See here—it even says public safety cleanup."

Emily checked three of the forms and confirmed the mayor's assessment. "Why would someone go through all the trouble to fill out a form? We know they were trying to get rid of any evidence of the arson they might have left behind, but why leave a paper trail behind?"

"If city equipment, fuel, or crews move, there are forms to document their use. It's part of our labor agreements with the unions to prove we aren't using non-union workers and paying them less than city employees."

"You're saying the city knew and approved these projects?"

The mayor removed her glasses and tossed them on the tabletop. "I'm not saying that at all. These projects were never approved by my public works chief. The paper trail was used to make sure the union stewards didn't think we were paying for scab labor. They wouldn't ask questions as long as their members were being paid."

"Then who approved these projects, if public works didn't know about them?"

The mayor handed Emily another form and tapped a finger on the last line. The project was approved by Ryan Jensen.

CHAPTER FORTY-SEVEN

"Jensen. Would he normally be in the approval process for city work crews like this?"

The mayor shook her head. "No. Ryan shouldn't have had any involvement in these work orders. He's a policy guy. A position paper writer, and frankly, a hand-me-down from John Stone. He's trying to ensure the former mayor's legacy lives on."

"Like River Gardens . . ."

"Like River Gardens. Here, take a look at these." The mayor led them to the large plot map unrolled on the table. "These condo developments were approved and permits issued in the days before I came into office. Environmental waivers, local zoning exemptions, all filed and rushed through. All they needed was the land."

"These parcels are on city property, right? How can a private firm like SCS build on land they don't own?"

"Typically, they can't." The mayor fussed over a stack of documents. "One of these, ahh, here it is. This is a city council resolution for a fifty-year lease of three parcels of city property—property which happens to be where the homeless camps were."

"The council approved this?"

"Not yet, they haven't. It was supposed to be on this afternoon's council agenda. I pulled it."

"Have any idea who prepared the resolution and put it on the council calendar?" Emily asked.

"That would be in Ryan Jensen's job description. It's part of his job to put the council agenda together. Looks like he thought he'd be slick and hide it in the council's consent items agenda, which means there wouldn't be any discussion or review. Those items are typically passed without comment. The little weasel. I don't need him. I'm not John Stone who had someone like Ryan Jensen to pick up after him, get his dry cleaning, cover up after his affairs, and do his dirty work."

Emily rested her palms on the table and leaned over the plot map of the new River Gardens development projects. She'd witnessed dozens of proposed projects wither and die in the city over the years. To reach this stage—where plot maps, surveys, permits, and sales offices were opened—testified that this project wasn't an overnight creation strung together with bubble gum and bailing wire.

"How much would it cost to get a project to this stage?" Emily asked.

The mayor shrugged. "Millions. Developers with projects like this take a risk to be in a position to make a competitive bid—except—"

"Let me guess, there was no competition."

The mayor frowned, making the fine lines around her mouth deepen. "I'm trying to find the details, but it looks like another waiver."

"Signed by Ryan Jensen?" The hair on the back of Emily's neck began to tingle.

The mayor tossed a document across the table. "He's not authorized to approve this."

Emily examined the document, and, like the other permits, Jensen was the signatory authorizing the contract with SCS. She noted the date was six months before Mayor Stone left office, losing the election in the wake of the corruption scandal involving his dirty campaign money from donors with close ties to criminal organizations.

"This says the contract was five million dollars," Emily said.

"For the first year," the mayor said.

"You mean the city funded SCS efforts to develop the proposal? Other developers don't get this kind of break, do they?"

"Absolutely not."

Emily pushed away from the table. "I think it's time we talk with him. We spotted him with two guys from SCS and the former mayor's widow a little while ago."

Mayor Carsten narrowed her eyes and strode across her office, snatching up the phone on her desk.

"Get me Ryan."

"Well, where is he? He should be prepping for the council session this afternoon."

She listened to the response, and her jaw tightened. Her eyes cut to the detectives before she slammed the phone down.

"He's not in his office, and they have been pinging him, and he's not returning their texts. They don't know where he is."

"Mind if we take a look at his office? I mean, I can go get a warrant—"

"Not necessary. This is a public house, and as far as I'm concerned, you can have access to all of it. If you find that little weasel, tell him not to bother coming back."

Emily and Javier headed for the door when Emily paused and turned back to the mayor.

"Your Honor, could you do me a favor?"

"It depends."

"Keep the resolution on the city council agenda, would you?"

"Why would I do that?"

"Someone will be there to make sure their interests are pro-tected, wouldn't they?"

"Typically . . . but if this is on the consent calendar, there wouldn't be any public comment." Her eyes hardened. "Unless I move it to the public session. Jensen will have to show up and defend his interests."

Emily nodded. There was a little respect growing for the politician. She had to be royally pissed Jensen was using her—undermining her—to feed lucrative contracts to his SCS buddies. Mayor Carsten was not a woman to be trifled with, and Emily imagined her ripping Ryan Jensen apart in a public forum.

The mayor's chief of staff warranted a nearby suite of offices, close enough where Ryan Jensen could respond quickly to urgent issues, and far enough away where visitors, donors, and the more than occasional disgruntled constituent wouldn't accidentally run into the mayor.

Emily pushed inside where a young woman occupied a recep-tion desk. Her long brown hair was pulled tightly back, and large dark-framed glasses magnified her worried eyes.

Javier approached the woman, Kait, if the nameplate on the desk was accurate, while Emily's attention turned to a photo display on the wall to the right.

After showing Kait his badge and identifying himself, Javier asked if she had heard from her boss this morning.

"No. We haven't. It's so unlike him. Mr. Jensen is always in the office before anyone. His calendar didn't show an off-site this morning."

"We ran into him earlier at an estate auction. He mention going to one?"

"Not at all. He'd never be out of the office on the day of a council meeting. It's all-hands-on-deck to prepare for the session."

"He was meeting Janet Stone, the ex-mayor's wife."

Kait's wide eyes hardened for a moment at the mention of Mrs. Stone. Her lips tightened. Whatever her feelings, Kait swallowed them down.

"Hey, Javi," Emily called. "Come here for a sec."

Emily faced the photo wall, and it wasn't the usual assortment of ego shots featuring some potbellied politicians with influencers and well-placed donors. This collection featured Jensen in locations all around the city, engaging in events and highlighting what the city has to offer. Indoor rock-climbing walls, the capitol rose garden, kayaking on the river and in nearby Lake Natoma, and a series of shots with Jensen decked out in a helmet, elbow pads, holding a skateboard posing in front of a local skate park ramp.

"Where was this taken?"

Kait rolled her eyes. "Oh, that one. I took the photo. Ryan thought it would make him seem cool—relevant, I guess. He was worried his image working for the former mayor might rub off. So, there was a push to get him out in public, 'with the people,'" —Kait made air quotes— "and position him as in tune with what's going on in the city."

"How'd that go?"

"Well, like this one—he kinda stood around and didn't interact with anyone. Sorta posed as a skateboarder. He didn't even drop in on the ramp. We had to pass out tickets to Kings' games to get people to pay attention."

"When was this?"

"Maybe six months ago at the new skate park in North Natomas."

"We need to take a look in his office. The mayor said we could."

"I know. She told me to give you anything you need. She sounded angry. She doesn't get that way often. Is Ryan in trouble?"

"That's what we're trying to find out." Emily slipped a business card on the desktop in front of Kait. "Call me if you hear from him."

Ryan Jensen's inner office wasn't what Emily expected. It was small, dark, and commanded a view of the portable toilets installed in César Chávez Park. No wonder his photo wall was outside the office. There wasn't enough wall space in his office to display them. The single bookshelf across one wall was jammed with binders, some upright, others stuffed on their sides. Stacks of papers poked out from the shelves, and this disorganization made Emily's slight OCD tendencies begin to itch.

She approached his desk and every single surface was covered with files, city council meeting transcripts, and all the paper needed to fuel a city.

On top of the pile of official bureaucratic pulp was a handwritten note. The script was hurried and sloppy. Emily recognized the address, and a chill gathered at the base of her spine.

Lisa Larkin Med Center room 232. Willow Sacramento Children's Receiving Home.

The address was scrawled below.

"We gotta go. He's going for Lisa and Willow."

CHAPTER FORTY-EIGHT

EMILY AND JAVIER pushed through the hospital doors and waded into the crowded waiting room. A quick elevator ride landed them in the ICU where Emily rapped a knuckle on the counter at the nurses' station. All it got her was a stink eye from the charge nurse.

"What room is Lisa Larkin in? 232?"

"The nurse glanced up again and recognition showed on her face this time.

"She's not here anymore. We discharged her."

"Discharged? How is it possible?"

"This ain't a prison ward, Detective. Didn't you tell us we didn't need to get her locked down? If a patient wants to leave, they may. We tell them all the reasons they shouldn't. But it's up to them in the end. That's why we call it discharge against medical advice."

"Why'd she go?"

"I don't know. That's not my responsibility."

"Did you hear her say where she was heading?"

The nurse paused for a moment, leaned on the counter, worn from another long shift. "I didn't hear what she was doing. She was in a hurry. The woman wanted out. She left so fast the guy picking her up got here after she split. You barely missed them—maybe ten minutes ago."

"Guy?"

"Yeah. A guy came in saying he was here for her. Wasn't happy when he found out she was gone. Like he made the trip for nothing. Funny, though, he didn't seem her type."

"What type was that?"

"Lisa was a no-frills kinda gal, you know. I mean, I know where she came from. Life has a way of beating some people down. Lisa was one of those. Anyway—this guy—he was more the fussy, hair-product-loving kinda guy. Right down to his woodsy cologne—probably never been in the woods in his life—"

"Woodsy?" Emily remembered the woodsy medicinal cologne the masked man running from Camp Hope wore when he sent her sprawling in the mud. The same scent Ryan Jensen wore.

"Hey, take a look at this for me. Recognize anyone?"

The nurse took no time pointing Ryan Jensen out in the ever-popular photograph while she took a phone call. "That's him," she said.

Emily turned to Javier. "Jensen—again."

"And Lisa didn't stick around to get a ride. Makes you wonder, doesn't it?"

"She was running from him. Somehow, she knew he was coming. Must have gotten word."

"Jensen wasn't coming here on some humanitarian gesture," Javier said.

"Nope. He's tying up another loose end. Lisa knows what happened that night—and she held it from us. If she's on the run, Lisa's gonna snag her daughter and disappear."

Emily knew Lisa wouldn't abandon Willow. She'd get to the facility and take her. She had no means to drive there and probably didn't have resources for as much as a bus pass to get her to the Children's Receiving Home. They could beat her there.

Jensen, though, was a wildcard. Did he know where Willow was? Would he try to grab the girl as leverage over her mother?

"What does Lisa know that's got Jensen chasing her down?"

"Whatever it is, she's got Jensen spooked. Let's go sit on the Receiving Home and see if we spot her. The only other option is she'll lure Jensen away from Willow. If she does, we might lose her."

The detectives hurried from the hospital ward and headed toward the Receiving Home. It wasn't far, and they kept a close eye on the sidewalks on the way. Lisa would likely take the straightest, most direct route to the facility. She knew where the facility was because the CPS case worker gave her all the paperwork detailing the placement information.

"She can't have gotten far. She only had a few minutes' head start," Emily said, scanning the street as they drove.

"Unless she panicked and ran. If she was spooked by Jensen coming to the hospital, she might have run off."

"Not without Willow. Lisa wouldn't risk leaving her behind. Whatever Lisa knew, so did her daughter."

They pulled into the Receiving Home parking lot without a glimpse of Lisa. The woman would still be in a great deal of pain, with severe burns on her back and arms. Every step she made would be excruciating. Even if she was able to grab a handful of pain meds on the way out of the hospital, they wouldn't deaden the sensation of thousands of exposed nerve endings firing off signals to her brain.

Emily and Javier entered the Receiving Home and the attendant at the desk directed them to the activity room. According to the schedule, Willow would be in the room with her group.

Three clusters of kids busied themselves in the activity room. One watched a cartoon on a video screen, another group of six huddled over drawings, and a third made some paper, glue, and glitter mess on another table.

Willow wasn't among them.

Emily approached the staffer working with the craft project group. "The attendant up front said Willow Larkin was supposed to be here. Have you seen her?"

"Oh, yeah. Willow said she wasn't feeling well and wanted to go lay down." Then to one of the younger girls at her table: "Tammy, don't put the glitter in your hair."

"Where is her room?"

"Second floor, on the left, room 4—Timothy, don't you dare eat that paste."

Emily whispered to Javier, "I'll go check her room. You hang here and keep an eye out for mom, or Jensen. He's got to know Willow's here."

She headed upstairs and Javier took a position in the hallway where he could watch the entrance and the door to the activity room.

The second-floor landing was occupied by a group of girls parked on the stairs. Among them were the two girls Emily met the first time she visited.

"Hey, Detective. Catch any bad guys today?"

"Working on it. You see Willow around?"

The girls exchanged a look between them. Emily recognized it as a shared secret, one their young, streetwise faces couldn't quite cover.

"What? Spill it? What's going on?" Emily said.

"Willow ain't here."

"She's not in her room?"

"Nah. She got a call from her moms and split."

"A call? How'd she get a phone call?"

The taller girl slid her leg to the side, exposing a slim cell phone tucked under her leg.

"Where'd she go?"

The taller one shrugged. "Said her mom wanted her to meet up."

"Where?"

"I don't know. It's not like I stood there listening. Gawd."

"But you did," Emily said.

"Whatever. Alls I know is Willow's mom didn't want to come here, but told her to meet her."

"Where?" Emily asked again because the girls knew, and they were covering for Willow. "Listen, there's a man who's looking for Willow and her mom. I think he wants to hurt them. If you know where Willow went, tell me, because we can't let bad things happen to them."

If there was one common experience among this group of girls, it was they knew hurt. They knew pain and all the various ways it was delivered. Loyalty to Willow was one thing, but keeping their new friend safe from harm overruled everything.

"She wanted to know the directions to some park," one of them finally said, followed by shushing sounds from another.

"What? If Willow's out there and this guy finds her . . ." the girl said.

"Willow said don't tell," another girl said.

Emily looked the last girl in the eye. "You want to live with knowing you could have kept Willow and her mom from getting hurt, but you didn't? All because you wanted to keep a secret. She's only eight years old."

"Brunswick Park. She wanted to know how to get to Brunswick Park."

Emily exhaled. The photo in Jensen's office—the skate park dedication. Ryan Jensen knew the park, too.

CHAPTER FORTY-NINE

"WHAT'S LISA TRYING to do?" Javier said, as they sped toward the city skate park.

Emily slid the Crown Vic around a corner, the back wheels slipping out in the water from a clogged storm drain. She punched the accelerator and pulled through the skid.

"She knows what happened the night John Stone was killed. She and Willow both. They were quick to cop to the shooting of Pete Bell. But there's more to this."

"She knows Jensen. Bottom line. She lied when we asked her if she knew anyone in the picture with Jensen, Stone, and Bell. She knew all of them," Javier said.

"Are you suggesting Lisa killed John Stone?"

"She and her daughter are wrapped up in one murder. It's an avenue we need to look at. It's not like she'd have to struggle with the guy. According to the tox screens, Stone was off his gourd on a fentanyl high. She coulda walked up and whacked him with the hammer Delila claimed was in her tent."

Emily pulled into the park lot and, for an early afternoon, the city green space was active. A few of the tables were occupied, the jogging trail was in use, but most of the activity was around the skate park, which to Emily's eye appeared more like a misshaped backyard pool. There was a competition happening, with onlookers huddling at the edge of the pool, and music blaring from tinny speakers.

Javier got out of the sedan, and Emily grabbed his arm.

"There—Lisa's sitting on the picnic table over there."

The table was off by itself, away from the bustle and frantic energy of the skateboarders. It was also in the open where she could see anyone who made an approach.

Lisa twisted and glanced behind her and jolted. Emily grunted in sympathy. The twisting motion would be torture on the burn injury, tearing at the semi-healed skin.

Emily caught Lisa stiffen and peer off to the right, behind the skate park. She waved her hand and stood.

Her gaze fell on Willow in the crowd around the rim of the swimming pool. Lisa rose from the picnic table, letting her daughter spot her without making a scene.

Emily and Javier stepped away from the Crown Vic, and Lisa spotted them from her perch near the picnic table. Lisa put her hand out, warning Willow, urging her to stay where she was. The girl saw the signal from her mom and stepped backwards into the throng of spectators. Willow faded from view.

Across the park, Lisa grabbed a paper bag and a rolled hospital blanket and strode toward the detectives.

"What are you doing here? Following me? I only want to get my daughter and go. Never want to see this town again."

Lisa grimaced as she spoke and positioned her arm bent in front of her to lessen the tension against the burn scarring. The clothes she wore were ill-fitted. Emily figured she snuck into another patient's room and borrowed the sweatpants and baggy polo shirt.

"You should be in the hospital," Emily said.

"I can't. It's not safe. For us."

"What's not safe is making Willow run around out here. Listen, I know you weren't telling me the whole truth about what happened that night at the camp. Whatever you and your daughter saw—there's a man who wants to make sure you never tell. You know that. You were here before when he was posing for the press, weren't you?"

"I—I don't want anything to do with this. Don't you understand?"

"It's way too late for that, Lisa."

"I just—I just want to get a fresh start for me and Willow."

Lisa raised on her toes and glanced over Emily's shoulder, looking at the gap in the crowd where Willow disappeared.

Her eyes widened. "Did you bring him?"

Emily turned. "Him, who?"

Lisa jabbed a finger at the left of the skateboard crowd. "Him."

Ryan Jensen strolled across the lawn. He stopped mid-stride when he noticed Emily and Javier. Their eyes locked for a second before he cut to his left into the thick of the crowd.

"Stay here," Emily told Lisa before she and Javier took off after Jensen.

Emily shouldered her way into the clutch of bodies lined up to watch the boarders throw tricks in the cement depression. Shouting came from up ahead, and Emily ran to the source, while Javier cut a wider path hoping to encircle Jensen.

At the lip of the pool, Emily caught Jensen running across the depression, knocking down a skateboarder. The spectators jeered at the interference, yelling at Jensen.

Emily hopped into the skate park and chased after Jensen. He climbed out of the far ledge and into the crowd. She pulled herself up the ledge and knew she was close behind from the woodsy medicinal smell he left behind.

A scream sounded ahead. Jensen grabbed a girl and gripped her in front of him.

"Get lost, Detective," Jensen said with a guttural tone.

His human shield wasn't any girl. He'd found Willow.

Emily drew her weapon.

"Willow and I are going to go for a little drive."

"Not happening, Jensen."

Emily noticed a glint in his right hand. He held a short blade to Willow's slim neck.

Jensen was shuffling backward, putting distance between him and Emily's gun barrel.

Javier approached from the side and drew his weapon. Those who hadn't noticed Emily and Jensen were now all aware they were caught in a moment of drama.

A skinny man wearing a tie-dye orange and blue shirt got between Emily and Jensen. Thick scraggly beard and wild gray hair, he seemed like a throwback to a sixties hippie.

"Hey, man, your weapons of war have no place in the people's park."

"Police officer. Back off."

Emily sidestepped, and the peacenik mirrored her, blocking her from Jensen.

"Sir, you're interfering. Back off."

"It's you and the police-industrial complex who are interfering with our right to assemble."

Another bystander joined the spontaneous protest, then another focused on Javier.

"Defund the police. Stop the militarization of the police."

Jensen used the distraction to pull Willow farther back from Emily.

Emily pressed forward, and the protester drew closer and rested his bony chest on the muzzle of the gun barrel.

Jensen yelled and grabbed his hand. Willow had bitten him. The scream panicked the tense crowd and people ran for cover. Emily shoved the Jerry Garcia look-alike aside and ran to Willow.

"Are you all right?"

She nodded.

Emily searched the mass of people running from the skate park for Jensen, but he slipped away using the fleeing crowd as cover.

Javier joined Emily and Willow.

"Em, I lost him. I couldn't see which way he went."

"Me either. Dammit."

Javier got on a knee in front of Willow. "Smart girl."

She tucked her chin up in response to his praise.

Lisa ran over and pulled Willow up in a bear hug. It had to hurt her healing burn scars. But at this moment, the hug was all that mattered.

Emily patted Willow on her back. "That was really brave. Did that man say anything?"

Willow raised her chin to meet Emily's eye. "He said he was going to hurt my mom."

"We won't let anything happen to you or your mom."

"I'm sorry—I didn't mean for this to happen. I don't know how he knew to come here. I didn't tell anyone but Willow."

Emily wondered how Jensen knew. One of the girls at the Receiving Home, maybe? It was their phone that was used to connect with Willow's mom. Or the hospital? Someone could have overheard.

"Let's get you out of here and somewhere safe. Hey, Javier, where's that scraggly hippie?"

Javier grinned. "He ran off like the others. Good thing for him. I think you were about to go medieval on the guy."

Emily wanted to cuff the guy and book him for interfering with a peace officer, but it might only bolster the creep's street cred.

Getting Lisa and Willow away to somewhere safe was more important. It was time for Lisa and her daughter to spill what they knew. And Emily knew how to make it happen.

CHAPTER FIFTY

IN THE DETECTIVE bureau interview room, Emily slid a coloring book and crayons over to Willow.

Javier opened the door and brought in a bag of In-N-Out burgers and milkshakes. The aroma of still-hot fries filled the room. He plopped the bag on the table and passed everything around.

Willow held a french fry in one hand and a yellow crayon in another as she filled in the spaces between the lines. She was careful and stuck her tongue out between her lips as she worked.

"She's never had her own coloring book. I guess I haven't been a good mother," Lisa said.

"You kept her safe, and it couldn't have been easy out there."

Emily took a pull from her milkshake. "Eat up. After hospital food, you need it."

"Actually, it wasn't too bad." Lisa unwrapped a burger and took a big bite. She rolled her eyes back and let out a sigh. "Okay, maybe it wasn't that great. Thanks for this. Is this how you get confessions? With carbs?"

"Sometimes," Emily said around her own mouthful.

Lisa unwrapped Willow's burger for her.

"Why don't we start with what happened at the camp the night you got hurt? Ryan Jensen went after you and Willow today—it has to tie back to that night."

Lisa sighed. "It does. I didn't tell you everything from that night."

"I kinda figured."

"I have seen him. The man, Jensen, you called him, before. He was at the camp—before it all happened."

"Tell me what you remember."

Lisa glanced down at her hands and seemed surprised they were shaking. "Willow and me were getting ready to eat, and him, Jensen, was arguing with John near Delila's place."

"John?"

"Oh, yeah, John—used to be the mayor."

"John Stone?"

"Yeah, I guess. We all called him John."

"What was he doing in the camp?"

"He'd been hanging around more and more. Used to say stuff like he was wrong and sorry for things he'd done to make it hard on us. It wasn't like he was the one pushing us out or spraying us with water hoses. Anyhow, John would bring food, blankets, and what he could for us in the camp."

"John Stone was sorry for trying to push the homeless out of the city? Did you believe him?" Javier asked.

"I think he meant it. The more time he spent with us, he got to know who we were. Sure, we've all done things we shouldn't have done to get by, but he didn't judge us for it. He was saying he had a plan."

"The Stone Plan," Emily said.

Lisa shrugged. "Don't know what that is. John said he had a plan to have the city set aside a place near the river where they would set up some of those tiny homes—you know, the little cottage things—for us—all of us. He called it River Gardens."

"River Gardens? He called it that?"

Lisa nodded and took another bite.

"John and Jensen were arguing?"

"Yeah, Jensen was angry. Started pushing John, screaming at him."

Emily leaned in and grabbed a french fry, trying to keep the conversation casual.

"What happened next?"

Lisa scrunched up her face. "John might have been drunk. He started getting kinda wobbly-like. Seemed like he was having a hard time standing. Then he flopped right over. Fell flat on his face. Jensen looked around and dragged him by his feet into Delila's tent. He came out a second or so later. Had some claw hammer thing in his hand. I swear it had blood on it. It was shiny and dark red."

Lisa hugged herself, reliving the memory.

"Could you hear any of what they were fighting about?"

"Not much. Bits and pieces. None of it made sense. Like, 'This wasn't the plan,' and 'You're ruining everything.' What they meant, I don't know."

"I think we have an idea. What happened next, after Jensen came out of Delila's tent?"

Lisa swallowed hard. "Jensen saw me and Willow. We weren't but thirty feet away. He shook the hammer thing and came toward us. I didn't know what he'd do. He pointed it at me. Told me if I ever said anything, he'd find me and Willow and take care of us—I knew what he meant. Said he'd have his people throw me out like the trash I was. I didn't deserve to have a daughter, and she'd be better off without me. Then he left—fast. Up the hill to the road."

Lisa's eyes watered, and she reached over to rub her daughter's back. Willow leaned in and kept coloring. The girl was used to shutting off the evils of the outside world. A thin protective shell. Emily couldn't help but wonder how many fine cracks were in Willow's protective layer.

"All this happened before the camp burned and you were attacked?"

"Maybe two hours before. I had to go look, and I saw John face down and a huge hole in his head." She reached back and touched her own skull near where the pick had crushed the former mayor's head. "I know I shoulda called someone, or done something, but he told me to keep my mouth shut."

"I get it."

"Then Pete shows up, wants to know what I'm doing in Delila's place. He was looking for Willow. I pushed him aside and told him to leave us alone. He grabbed me by the arm and shook me. I screamed. I was scared. Then he says he was going to take Willow from me—claimed he'd be able to give her a better life.

"Willow saw it—saw the argument and thought Bell was going to hurt us and take her away like Jensen said. Then . . ."

Lisa leaned over and kissed the top of Willow's head.

"It's not her fault, Detective. It's mine. If I never had the gun . . ."

Emily knew Lisa meant it. She was sorry for what happened and the position she put her daughter in. How could Willow recover from taking a life at such a tender age? Who could?

Willow was coloring away while her mom told the story. The only evidence she heard what was said was that the colors turned darker after Lisa began recounting the night's events as they unfolded. Her scribbles were denser and not as carefully contained in the lines. The residue of pulling a trigger lay deep inside.

Emily's phone sounded. She checked the caller ID—Brian.

"Hey, Brian—can I call you back? I'm in the middle of something."

"I thought you'd want to know. I'm parked out near Jensen's place."

"You see him?" Emily sat up stiffly.

"Not him. A woman. She pulled up in his drive—thought she was going to hit the garage door she came in so hot. Ran out, had a key to the place, and ducked inside. Ran back to the car carrying two bags.

"I ran the plates, and it comes back to your murder vic, John Stone."

"Could be the wife. They've been palling around lately."

"That's what I figured. She's pulling out now. Want me to stop her?"

Emily paused. "Follow her. I'd bet she's meeting Jensen. If she packed a bag for him, they're taking off together."

"Not that kind of bag. Two black trash bags."

"He sent her to clean up. Follow her, but don't let her destroy those bags."

CHAPTER FIFTY-ONE

EMILY CONVINCED LISA to stay at the police department headquarters until Jensen was located. He tried to take Willow once, and he was becoming more desperate as his world fell around him. An EMT from the fire department next door came and checked on Lisa's burns after she refused to go back to the hospital.

"Thank you, Detective. It's been a while since anyone even looked at us, let alone cared. We both thank you."

Willow handed Emily a hand-drawn picture using the crayons she'd given the girl.

"Thank you," Emily said before she glanced at the child's image.

The crayon-hued drawing captured a moment in time. A moment at the riverside homeless camp. A crudely formed man stood in the center of the picture, wearing black clothing, but carrying a hook-shaped object in his hand. The threatening object was dripping red. Emily knew what it was the second she laid eyes on it. Jensen with the rock hammer as he emerged from the orange tarped tent.

The image of Jensen was crude and wouldn't serve as identification in a lineup, but Willow witnessed him in the moments after killing John Stone. Emily felt the anger swell within. A child shouldn't have to hold these images inside. Jensen did this to her.

"Thank you, Willow. The man will never be able to hurt you or your mom again. I promise."

Emily knew better than to make promises she couldn't keep. But Willow needed to begin to feel safe.

Javier got off his phone and whispered to Emily, "The Watch Commander gave us three units. Where do you want them?"

"Let Brian—Sergeant Conner—tell us where he needs them."

Lisa and Willow moved from the sterile interview room to a break room. Emily noticed Lisa grab a magazine from a table and plop Willow in her lap, reading her a story—even if it was an article from a *Police 1* magazine.

Brian called in and gave an update. Janet Stone was driving in circles in the north part of downtown. She made a stop and tossed one of the bags in a dumpster behind a hotel.

"Please tell me you grabbed it," Emily said.

"I have it."

"What's in it? What did Jensen have her get rid of?"

"I didn't open it. I couldn't risk losing her. I pulled it out of the trash and tossed it in the back seat."

"Still have a visual on her?"

"Now heading north on 12th toward Arden."

"Not heading to the airport," Javier said.

With one last glance back at Lisa, Emily hoped they'd recover from their ordeal—trauma, if she was honest about it. They might be on the path, but it was going to be a lifelong journey. Some things you never forget—they become part of who you are.

Javier drove while Emily stayed on the phone with Brian. They crossed the river and merged onto Interstate 80, eastbound.

"Think she's headed to Reno? Making a run for the border?" Javier said.

"Not yet. Jensen was last seen on foot. Unless he jacked a car or stole a city vehicle. We would have heard about it by now."

A crackle over the phone speaker. "She's getting off on Arden Way, heading east. Slowing down. Turning. Turning into Cal Expo."

The state fairgrounds were quiet this time of year. Emily figured Jensen would look for a place where he could hide in a crowd. There was a large shopping mall across the street, one familiar to Sacramento police activity from Black Friday crowd stampedes and gang shootings.

"Wait. I know where she's heading. There's a homeless camp behind Cal Expo—on the river like the others. It was on the map for the River Gardens project."

"She's stopping, parking. Getting out of the car with the bag. Emily, she's heading toward the camp. Want me to take her down?"

"We're almost there. Keep her in sight. We need her to lead us to Jensen."

Javier took the exit off the interstate. "Two minutes out."

Emily noodled over Janet Stone and what she had to gain by helping Jensen. Then it hit her. It wasn't so much helping him as helping herself. She wanted to hang onto her dead husband's legacy. River Gardens would repair all the financial ruin John Stone brought down on them. If she was a part of SCS, and the way she cozied up to the two corporate types at the estate auction made it appear she was, River Gardens would make her rich.

"Hey, Brian—watch her. She could be planning to burn the camp."

Javier pulled into Cal Expo's massive blacktop parking lot. "You think she's capable of arson?"

"For the amount of money at stake? She is."

Javier slid the car next to Stone's and the unmarked Ford Crown Vic Brian drove.

"Brian, we're here. What's your 20?"

"Three hundred yards from the car, in the tree line straight ahead."

Emily and Javier trotted to the tree line using the well-worn path from the parking lot to the homeless camp. Trash, discarded clothing, water bottles, and condoms littered the brush along the path.

Brian turned and pocketed his cell when Emily appeared.

He pointed straight ahead. An uncomfortable, out-of-place-looking Janet Stone in her designer pantsuit watched where she trod to avoid soiling her silver ballet flats. She struggled with the heavy black trash bag.

"She's really not dressed for the part of an arsonist," Javier said.

"No, she isn't. Don't think she'd wade into the camp if she was going to burn it down. She's meeting Jensen to give him whatever she has in her bag."

"Jensen? Hiding out in a homeless camp?"

"How the mighty have fallen. He's got nowhere else to hide."

Janet Stone kept on her path into the camp. She knew where to go. Emily figured Jensen told her where to bring whatever was in the bag from his place.

"She's a duck out of water and not one person has tried to move on her," Javier said.

Emily snapped back to Lisa. "They all want to live and be left alone. Jensen's counting on it."

"You think Jensen is here, hiding?" Brian said.

"There he is." Emily pointed about fifty feet in front of Mrs. Stone.

Mrs. Stone ducked inside the tent and Jensen disappeared with her.

"Come on, time to move," Emily said.

Emily led and Javier peeled off to the left, cutting a wide arc around the tent. If Jensen were to make a break, he'd find his escape routes cut off.

Ten feet from the tent, they heard Mrs. Stone, and she didn't seem happy about her stroll through the squalid homeless camp on the outskirts of the city.

"I did what you asked, Ryan. I don't like it—not one bit."

Jensen sounded like he was trying to convince her it was going to plan. "We're almost there. River Gardens is happening. One little bump in the road—that's all. Here, hand it over."

Emily heard the thud of the black trash bag land and a rustle of plastic.

"This isn't enough. Where's the rest?" Jensen's voice hardened.

"It's all I could get my hands on. You're going to have to make do."

"Dammit, Janet, if we're going to pull this off, we need to make sure it's done—there aren't any second chances. Get SCS to—"

"SCS is done. They're pulling out. The police finding Franklin's body at Camp Hope was one bridge too far for them."

"It's taken care of. They got what they asked for. The riverside property is clear now—except for this one and—I'll take care of it tonight myself."

"The properties are crimes scenes. They never agreed to that."

"The hell they didn't. They knew we'd have to force those squatters out, and I delivered. I even got this mayor to give us political cover. It's all ready to cash in."

"They don't see it that way. There's too much attention—and not in a good way—on the way the camps were cleared. Not to mention people died making it happen."

"You know very well that's not all on me."

Emily signaled Javier and Brian to close in.

"I think I've heard enough," Emily said as she jerked two of the fiberglass tent poles away from the dome structure. It flattened on Jensen and Janet Stone. The pair flailed about, searching for the opening, and when they crawled out, their eyes widened at three guns aimed in their direction.

CHAPTER FIFTY-TWO

EMILY LET JENSEN and Janet Stone stew in separate interview rooms for an hour. The widow Stone was the first to show signs of stress. She couldn't sit still, paced the small confines of the locked room, and started biting her nails.

Through the video monitor, Jensen appeared less concerned. He sat still, hands in his lap, and glared at the camera lens. He had to know he was toast when it came to grabbing Willow in the park. But he seemed smug about it, like he was sure he was going to get away with everything else.

Emily and Javier entered the room with Mrs. Stone. and the widow started in. "You've got no reason to detain me like this. I've done nothing wrong."

"Park it, missy," Emily said, pointing to a chair.

Mrs. Stone was putting up a defiant front until Javier placed a clear evidence bag on the table.

"Still willing to talk with us and waive your right to an attorney?" Emily asked.

"I've got nothing to hide."

"Know what this is?" he asked.

"No, but I suppose you're going to tell me."

She tried to appear disinterested, but her eyes kept flicking back to the bag with wadded fentanyl patches and a syringe.

Emily tapped the table with a fingertip to get her attention. "Let me tell you a story. This begins with a woman trapped in a loveless marriage with a man who seemed bent on self-destruction. This man once held power and prestige, only to squander it all away. It made his wife angry. She'd put up with his drinking and skirt chasing for years, but then one day he threatens to pull the rug out from under her world and give away everything they'd worked for."

"Where is this going, Detective?"

"When I say 'worked for' I mean he worked for, because the wife didn't contribute a dime. When this man gave everything away, the wife came up with a plan to get him out of the picture and take what he'd worked for."

Emily pushed the baggie of wadded fentanyl patches closer. "Recognize these?"

Mrs. Stone flicked her eyes at the drug patches. "Should I?"

"Yes, you should. You picked up a prescription for your husband the day before he died. There are six used patches in there—way too many for him to use in less than twenty-four hours."

"You knew him, Detective. He was an addict—about many things."

"There was no adhesive residue on his body from using these patches, and he wasn't wearing one when he died."

"So?"

"So, these patches were soaked to leach out the fentanyl. The liquid was drawn up in this syringe and mixed in with your husband's insulin. The insulin bottle was empty, but there was fentanyl residue inside—along with the syringe. Guess whose fingerprints are on them?"

Mrs. Stone turned white. Her lips parted, and the words failed to follow. She swallowed hard, then said, "That bastard was going to leave me with nothing."

"Tell me—was this your idea, or Ryan's?"

Emily thought she would jump at the opportunity to throw Jensen under the bus, but her response surprised her.

"Ryan said he was going to talk to Johnny and get him to come back to his senses. I needed to get him 'receptive' to listening. Johnny was going to throw everything away."

"So you drugged him?"

"He drugged himself, actually."

"But you put the fentanyl into his insulin?"

She paused for a moment, raised her chin, and said, "I think I want to talk to my lawyer now."

"That's probably for the best," Emily said.

Emily pushed back from the table, glanced down at the widow Stone. "It seems your late husband spent his last days trying to make amends for his war against the homeless. He was going to turn River Gardens into a safe shelter zone for the unhoused in the city. Quite a sudden shift."

"All on account of Ryan pushing too hard. The camp burnings were too much for Johnny. He couldn't be a part of it."

Javier picked up the evidence bag, and they left Janet in the interview room.

In the hallway outside, Javier hefted the bag with the patches and syringe. "Wanna tell me where this came from?"

"The medical examiner did find fentanyl in Stone's tox screen. You found a used patch and his insulin. She did pick up a new prescription for another set of patches, and they were nowhere to be found. And there was drug residue in the syringe you recovered. We know she dosed him."

"But these aren't the items we found at the house."

"No, they aren't. The lab geeks were happy to make a prop for us with what it would have looked like. She took the bait. She thought she cleaned up after herself—and she did a good job of it."

"Remind me not to piss you off."

"I never told her those were from her house."

"The fingerprints? What fingerprints?"

"I only asked whose would be on it."

Javier shook his head. "Does Brian know you have this devious streak?"

"Shut up and let's go get Jensen locked down."

When they entered the interview room, Jensen acknowledged their presence with a turn of the head. Nothing more.

Emily and Javier took seats across from him.

"Mr. Jensen, you've been advised of your rights. Can I ask you a few questions?"

He shrugged.

"You and Mayor Stone developed the original River Gardens plan, isn't that right?"

"It's a matter of public record. You know we did."

"The only thing standing in the way were hundreds of homeless camped out on the land you needed for the project."

He shrugged. "I wouldn't expect you to know about planning and development, Detective. Projects like River Gardens take years. What's going on today—homeless camps, for example— won't be the reality when the project is ready to begin."

"I get it. Must have made it hard to attract investors to a billion-dollar project when all they can see are fields of tents and human waste," Emily said.

"Most see it for what it is—a temporary issue. Mayor Carsten and her policies reclaiming public land gave investors confidence to lay down their cash."

"Except these weren't the mayor's policies, were they? You prepared them and delivered the talking points for her."

Jensen sat back and cut a glare at Emily. "It's my job, Detective. I craft the policy points, white papers, and speeches that get people like Ellen Carsten and John Stone elected."

"You make it sound like you see yourself as a puppet master. Must have made you angry when John Stone decided to change course on River Gardens."

A vein popped on Jensen's forehead. A moment of rage shone behind his eyes before absorbing back into the depths. "John was no longer relevant in the project. His drug and alcohol use became a problem. Everyone saw it. He was written out of the project's leadership months ago. He could say whatever he wanted. It had zero impact."

Emily flashed back on the documents she saw in Stone's home when she first told Janet Stone of his murder. The River Gardens paperwork she spotted was a change in the corporate leadership—removing John Stone and adding her.

"Replacing one Stone with another doesn't change a thing."

"The investors saw the advantage of keeping the Stone name in the project, but without John's political and personal baggage."

He confirmed what she suspected had been hidden in those documents.

She changed the direction of the questions to keep him off balance.

"Why did you grab Willow, the girl at the skate park?"

"I don't know what you're talking about." He avoided eye contact and tried to look disinterested, but he knew he was vulnerable on this point.

"Cut the shit, Jensen. We have a dozen witnesses, and cell phone video of you holding the girl with a knife to her throat. You know some of the girls from the camp were talking about a guy hanging around the camp. All this time I thought it was Pete Bell."

"What? I don't know what Bell was into. He was always at the camps. I thought, at first, it was for his social worker gig, but there was more to it. He was looking for someone."

"Looking? What for?"

"Beats me."

"But you and Willow? I mean, what other reason could you have for grabbing a young girl like her? I think I can have the district attorney make a case for sexual assault. You know what happens to child molesters in prison?"

"I didn't molest her—or anyone."

"You haven't convinced me otherwise. Do you have another reason?"

He stewed in his chair, flop sweat starting to show on his brow.

"I'll give you props, though, she is a pretty girl."

"Bullshit"

Emily cut to the night of the fire. "You know, there was a witness who saw you and John Stone at the camp. How did you know he'd be there?"

"No one can say they saw me do anything to John. He was drunk or high again. His wife told me he'd been out in the camps. I found him and told him to go home."

"That's not what Janet said. She told us you were going to talk some sense into John because he'd been making noise about getting the city out of the River Gardens project."

"He was a drunk. He was always shooting his mouth off. That was part of what got him ousted."

"This time, his mouth put millions at risk. If SCS felt like the ground was shifting, they'd pull out of the project. That would leave you and Mrs. Stone high and dry."

"I'd put too much into the project—years of work setting the stage— and John Stone was putting it all at risk."

"So, you killed him?"

"I'm not answering that."

"See the cut on your right hand? There on your palm."

Jensen glanced at it and held it under the table.

"I know where you got it. You left blood behind on the handle when you hit Tommy Franklin so hard it cracked. You couldn't pull the spike out of his forehead. Musta whacked him pretty hard."

Jensen fell silent.

"Oh, we do have a witness identifying you dragging Stone's body into a tent and coming out seconds later with a bloody hammer in your hand. You killed him. You killed him to keep him quiet. He put your potential payday at risk. That's two murders."

"What? A homeless woman? That's all you got?"

Emily smiled.

"That's all we need."

CHAPTER FIFTY-THREE

SIX MONTHS LATER

JAVIER PLOPPED A coffee on Emily's desk after a late night at a crime scene at the Sacramento River. The floater was caught up in tree limbs and river debris in the middle of the flow. Yolo County on one side and Sacramento on the other, and this one drifted toward the Sacramento riverbank.

Sheriff's department boat crews retrieved the body and the gashes to the man's throat meant Emily and Javier were called out.

Emily scrolled through screen after screen of gang tattoos, trying to get an identification of the dead man.

"Today's the day, right?" Javier said.

"Jensen's trial begins this morning in Department 7. He's looking at two counts, first degree murder, three counts arson with great bodily injury, and a dozen counts of assault with intent. Heard the jury selection went fast. The deputy district attorney said he felt good about the panel makeup."

"What do you think? Jensen is a slick bastard. Smooth talker and he got a high-profile attorney from Los Angeles who loves to get her face on camera."

"We'll find out in a couple hours. We're both subpoenaed. So are Lisa and Willow."

"You've been keeping in touch with them? How have they handled all this attention?" he asked after a sip of his coffee.

"The last six months have been a life changer for them both. Lisa got a place in a facility for moms with kids—everyone there has a past they are trying to put behind them."

"The new shelter off of Lemon Hill?"

"That's the one. Willow has kids her own age and Lisa said it's made a big difference. She has Willow in counseling sessions a couple of days a week. Unpacking what she saw and did will take years to overcome."

"If ever. Shooting a man who you thought was hurting your mom—at her age—I can't even imagine what's going to haunt her dreams in the years ahead."

Emily cast an eye to Javier's coffee cup. The side bore a red "S" drawn in marker. "Are you drinking your stevia stuff again? I thought you swore off the artificial stuff."

"I need my sweetener. It's a natural substance. It's low calorie—" Javier stopped in mid-sentence. He'd said too much.

"Low calorie? Are you fighting off a middle-aged pooch?"

"Oh, eff-off with your middle-age. I have a trip coming up with Jenny. We're going to Cancun, and I want to be bathing-suit ready."

Emily rolled her eyes. "Ain't nobody want to see that."

"Hence the artificial sweetener." He took another sip. "Ahhh."

Emily's phone rang. She glanced at the clock and it wasn't quite seven. "Hunter here."

"Hey, Emily. It's Ken Liton from the DA's office. Glad I caught you. We won't need you today."

"Another continuance?"

Javier sat back in his chair, listening.

"Plea deal."

"Jensen's going to cop a plea? You have a strong case. No need to let him walk."

"He's going to plead guilty to two counts murder first, twenty-five to life, concurrent. We take the arson and a dozen assault charges off the table. In exchange, he testifies Janet Stone conspired to drug and kill her husband. Her prosecution was going to be the tougher of the two. This nails her down."

"Jensen will cop a guilty plea on Stone and Franklin? Did I hear you right?"

"Yeah, we're still looking at how to prosecute Tannen for his involvement in the arson-for-hire schemes, if we ever find him. It's more complicated and the witnesses are a bit transient."

"I get that."

"Since you are one of Jensen's assault victims, are you okay with the plea deal?"

"Gets him gone—I'm good."

"I need a favor."

"And the favor would be?"

"Can you reach out to Lisa Larkin and her daughter? Let them know, and I want them to be okay with this plea. Lisa's testimony at the prelim was a big reason the defense took the deal."

"Yeah, I can go talk with her. I'm not going to try to convince her. This animal took her daughter and held her at knifepoint."

"Exactly. If she's not on board, I'll pull the deal off the table. I don't care if the defense wants to paint her as an unreliable witness and dredge up the homeless, negligent mom bit. I think she'll blow them out of the water. But she needs to know what she's up against."

"Okay—okay. I'll go meet with her."

"I need to know by ten."

"I'll call when I hear what she has to say."

Emily hung up and stared at the phone for a moment. Was it over? Weeks of investigation, wading through the city's homeless camps, and it's over?

Jensen wasn't getting off. He was going to prison for the rest of his life. Granted, it wouldn't repair the trauma left in his wake. As flawed as John Stone was as a man, he didn't deserve to end up with a spike in the back of his head and left to burn in a homeless camp. In the end, it was all about greed. Stone's reversal on his riverside development project was the last straw for the ex-mayor's wife. She'd had enough of his self-destructive ways, womanizing, and they were on the brink of losing everything. She needed the River Gardens project to regain the life she once had. Was Ryan Jensen her willing tool to make it all happen?

Emily wasn't sure if it mattered now. They'd both face years in prison for their parts in the killings.

"Wanna take a ride?" Emily asked her partner.

"The DA needs you to get Lisa on board?"

She nodded as she shrugged on her coat. "He's giving her the final say if Jensen gets a plea deal or not."

"That's a lot for her to shoulder." Javier chugged another mouthful of coffee.

"It is. I think the DA feels the case is solid and wants to make sure she's not going to make a lot of noise when the deal goes through. Lisa has gotten some press attention—her and Willow—and maybe this is the way the DA tries to keep everything quiet."

Javier held the door for Emily. "Maybe. Can't help but think what's in it for Jensen?"

"Whaddaya mean? He's going away for life."

"There's no guarantee there. You've seen enough examples of sentences getting commuted. Lifers get cut lose all the time."

Emily unlocked their Crown Vic. "You think Jensen has that kind of political clout?"

Javier buckled up and woke up the dash-mounted computer. "In the circles he and John Stone ran in, I'm just saying it's a possibility."

Emily backed out of the parking stall. The radio crackled to life. "All units, reported 415 at 2371 Lemon Hill. White male threatening resident."

"Lemon Hill? Isn't that the address for the shelter Lisa and Willow are at?" Javier said.

Emily punched the accelerator, shot out of the parking lot, and headed east toward the Lemon Hill address.

Two black and white units were on-site when Emily arrived. A code 4 "suspect in custody" call sounded over the radio and additional units were canceled.

Emily recognized the officer in the closest patrol unit. "Hey, Miller. What's happening?" she called out.

"Hiya, Detective. We got this handled. Some yahoo broke in and started threatening one of the residents. Didn't go well for him. She ended up popping his ass with a fry pan. We gonna run him to the med center before we book him."

"Got an ID on the guy?"

Emily got an itch as soon as the address sounded over the radio.

Officer Miller flipped the pages in his notebook. "Tannen. Walt Tannen."

"You got to be kidding," Javier said. "Was the RP Lisa Larkin?"

"The reporting party was." Miller flicked the notebook pages again. "Yep, Lisa Larkin. What, you guys deal with a domestic disturbance with these two before?"

"Sort of," Emily said. "The Larkin woman still inside?"

"Yep. Tannen's parked on the curb waiting for an ambulance ride."

"Thanks, Miller," Emily said.

"You got it, Hunter. Anytime."

Emily and Javier cut across the street to the women's shelter and, as Miller described, Tannen sat handcuffed on the curb. Blood dripped from the side of his head where a two-inch gash gaped open.

"You wanna take Tannen and I'll go talk to Lisa?" Emily said.

Tannen wasn't so injured that he didn't tighten his jaw when the detectives approached. "This ain't what it looks like."

"It never is," Emily said as she kept walking to the front door.

The facility was a residence, repurposed to serve a modest number of women and children. Only a small brass plaque above the doorbell gave it away.

The front door was still ajar, and Emily stepped inside and spotted another uniformed officer sitting with Lisa on a worn, but clean sofa. Lisa's eyes flicked to Emily as she came into view. A slight relief crept onto her face.

"Hey, Detective, finishing up with Ms. Larkin," the officer said. "We called in a Code 4. Don't think we have anything here for you."

"Yeah, I heard. I have business with Ms. Larkin when you're through."

"Oh, okay, then." The officer closed his notebook and handed Lisa a card. Emily recognized the blue and white logo from a domestic violence support organization. An unsettled feeling crept in.

Lisa held the card in her fingertips, rubbing the raised logo. "All yours, Detective."

Emily glanced down at an empty coffee cup. "You wanna refill?"

Lisa nodded. "I could use one. You?"

"Always."

Lisa rose from the sofa and Emily followed her into the communal kitchen, dominated by a long table. Another woman was putting a bowl of cereal in front of a blonde girl about Willow's age.

Lisa fished another mug from the kitchen cabinet and poured a cup for Emily.

Emily leaned back on the counter cradling her hot mug in both hands. "Wanna tell me what happened and how you know this guy?"

"Walt was a friend of Willow's father. Hadn't seen him in five years."

"When's the last time you saw her father?"

A dark shadow crossed behind Lisa's eyes. "Willow was two the last time we were together. She doesn't have any memory of him. Probably for the best. We got married, but after Willow was born, he got dark. I don't know what happened. Maybe he felt he wasn't getting enough attention, or whatever. He made sure he got what he believed he deserved."

"He abused you."

"Yeah. At first, I didn't blame him. I wasn't a great wife. Willow was my universe. After a couple of emergency room visits for a busted nose and a broken wrist, it got worse. He threatened to take it out on Willow. That's when I left. I couldn't put her at risk for my stupid decisions."

"You've been on the street since?"

"Mostly."

"Lisa, it's not your fault. You know that, right?"

"That's what they tell me. I know I played my part. I could have been a better—"

"Stop. None of this is on you."

The woman at the table who had pretended not to listen piped up with, "Amen."

"How did Tannen know you were here?"

"It was chance. He didn't know it was me. He was told to come, and he did as he was told—'Get the bitch to back off and refuse to testify.'"

"Testify? Against Jensen?"

"Yeah. You should have seen his face when he realized the woman he was coming to threaten was me. He saw Willow at the table and made a move toward her. Well, he didn't get too far."

"How's Willow?"

Lisa sighed. "There's only so much of this she can take before she starts believing violence like this is normal. I don't want that for her. I've had so much of it in my life. It's like it follows me. Willow can't follow in my footsteps—but it seems she's destined to do just that."

Willow poked around the corner and brightened when she saw Emily. She ran over and hugged the detective.

"Sasha, it's time for school," Willow said to the other girl at the table. Together, they skipped down the hallway.

"They have an in-house school here. It's pretty good. Willow can make up for the time I made her miss."

"Sounds like you didn't have any other option. You protected your daughter the best you knew how. And you still do. You're a good mom, Lisa."

The woman's eyes welled.

"I have news from the district attorney's office. You and Willow won't have to testify."

"What? How did—They dropped the charges, didn't they? People like him always snake out from under—"

"No, no. Jensen's attorney agreed to a plea deal that'll put him behind bars for twenty-five to life."

"Really? And Willow won't have to go through it all again?"

"Looks like it."

"Why do I feel there's a *but* coming?"

"The charges relating to the camp arsons, Jensen grabbing Willow, and all the trauma he caused—they want to drop those."

Lisa mulled for a moment and bit her bottom lip. "No."

"No?"

"Jensen can't get away with what he did to all of us. There were hundreds of human beings caught up in his bullshit. People. They lost everything—what little they had, and the DA wants to pretend they don't matter? No. I won't be part of that. Jensen's afraid. He sent Walt to threaten me, and I won't be bullied—not anymore. You take that to the DA."

"You sure?"

"As sure as I'm standing here on my own two feet. I'm not going to be someone's victim ever again."

CHAPTER FIFTY-FOUR

IN THE THREE months that followed, Emily made a mental note never to play poker with Lisa Larkin. The woman didn't bluff. When news got back to the defense attorney that Lisa was not buckling under the witness intimidation, Jensen's lawyer quit. A court-appointed defense attorney quickly made a new plea deal on behalf of his new client. A guilty plea on the two murders, a count of witness intimidation, and three counts of arson causing bodily injury. Jensen would never see the light of day as a free man again.

Emily attended the sentencing hearing two months ago. Jensen never looked up from the floor and he showed no reaction when the judge imposed the fifty-to-life prison term. Lisa was there to witness the final act in Jensen's story. He never made eye contact with her as he was led from the courtroom.

* * *

"Emily, where do you want this?" Brian asked as he lugged a cardboard box through the door.

"Let's put it in Mom's bedroom."

It was moving day for Connie. She'd found a brand-new memory care facility during one of the visits with Lucinda. The place was small enough for the residents to have individualized attention to their needs. Forty residents lived in the facility with their rooms surrounding the common spaces. An enormous fireplace was in the center of the open area, with comfy sofas and recliners. Connie had made new friends and seemed open to the move from Emily's to the River Gardens Memory Care Facility.

The SCS corporate structure fell apart after the scandal broke involving Jensen and the former mayor's widow. A new company recognized the potential in offering service to a growing population of older folks who needed additional support when their memories began to fail. The company bought out the name and long-term lease of public lands on the river. While the all too familiar River Gardens name gave Emily some heartburn, after thoroughly vetting the facility and the staff, she felt comfortable allowing her mother to live there.

Still, there was a part of her that felt like she was throwing her away—putting her in a home. But as Lucinda reminded her, this was the care Connie needed now.

Brian returned to the apartment living room, where Emily was shoving a small sofa with her hip.

"That look okay?" she asked.

Emily reconstructed the living room to resemble her living room, where Connie had been living for the past eight months. There was a great deal to be said for the comfort of familiar surroundings. The slight bit of deception was worth a smooth transition into the new surroundings. Brian was right about that.

He'd been right about a number of things, and it was infuriating. Beyond all the decisions she needed to make to get her mom safely tucked into the new memory care facility, Brian was right—for her. The realization she was no longer all alone was comforting, but unnerving at the same time. Emily enjoyed being in control and, with Brian, she could put it aside and just be.

As if he sensed her thoughts, Brian wrapped his arms around her from behind and hugged her, resting his chin against her ear. "Feels good to me."

"You're impossible," she said as she pressed into his embrace.

"Ahem," Javier said from the door, lugging another box. "When I said for you two to get a room, I didn't mean here."

Emily felt the heat rise in her chest.

"Shut it. That goes in the bedroom. Her closet."

Jenny trailed after Javier with clothes on hangers. "We'll get it all set."

"Thanks, Jenny. Oh, and keep my partner from rummaging through my mother's unmentionables. He has priors."

"I do not. Good Lord, Emily. It was one time," Javier said with a huff.

Jenny's eyes widened. "I think this is something I need to hear." She trotted off to hang the clothes in the bedroom closet.

"She is so out of your league," Emily said.

"Tell me about it."

"So, what's this about? Javi's dirty little secret?" Jenny said, as she returned to the room.

"There's no secret. Emily's exaggerating again. We were searching a house, and I had the master bedroom. I searched through the dresser—"

"The lady of the house had a lingerie dresser," Emily said.

"Oh, one of those tall cabinets with the narrow drawers?" Jenny said.

"Exactly. Javier hadn't seen one before—I don't think he'd seen a collection of 'unmentionables' like the things in that cabinet either."

Javier started to blush. "You gonna let me tell it?"

"Oh, please, by all means."

"What we didn't know at the time was the lady was a 'professional' and I was looking through her—work attire—I guess you could call it."

"He was holding it up to the light. Tilting his head like a confused little puppy. Like he didn't know how these things worked."

"I was not. I searched in a professional manner. But I did wonder how long some of her stuff took to get into, with the straps and garters, and see-through corsets."

"You spent a long time 'searching' that room."

"I was thorough."

"More than usual . . ."

Jenny grinned. "I'll make sure your mother's things aren't violated."

"You, too?" Javier said. He marched back out the apartment door in a pretend huff. Jenny followed with a high-pitched giggle.

"They're good together," Emily said.

"So are we." Brian hugged her tighter.

The warm embrace was broken by her cell phone chirping.

"Hunter here."

"Hey, Emily. You near a television?" Lieutenant Hall said.

"Umm, yeah. What's going on?" She pointed at the television and Brian turned the set on.

"Turn on the local news."

"What am I looking for?"

"You'll see it."

The television blossomed to life. A breaking news banner scrolled on the bottom of the screen. "A federal grand jury indicted Ryan Jensen, a former political consultant, on fifty-two counts of civil rights violations, and conspiracy. A federal district court judge ordered the indictment unsealed and by our quick reading of the document, the allegations involve a series of arsons designed to drive the city's homeless out of the camps in some of the most desirable real estate in the region. Corporate board members of an organization called SCS were also indicted for their roles in the conspiracy to acquire access to these public lands once the homeless were driven out."

"Are you hearing this, Emily?" Lieutenant Hall said.

"Yeah. How did the Feds get on this?"

"I got a call from the lead FBI agent this morning. They had a confidential informant in the camps. Someone you met."

Emily's mind reeled off the possibilities, and no one stood out—which was what you'd want from an informant.

"Who?"

"Remember Delila McDaniel?"

"Her? She was the informant?"

"Apparently so. She turned the Feds onto the key witnesses."

The live television report switched to a second location in Sacramento City Hall, where Mayor Carsten was in the middle of a briefing.

"With this dark chapter now behind us, it's time to announce the realization of my predecessor Mayor John Stone's effort to establish a safe location for our citizens who need temporary shelter and supportive services to get them back on their feet again. The River Haven community will provide one hundred tiny homes in the undeveloped rail-yards property. The community will be safe and close to city resources."

"She's walking a thin political line on this one, boss."

"The mayor knows there is a vulnerability there. Her chief of staff is doing prison time for this, and the best way she knows to distance herself from the blowback is to embrace the River Haven—whatever this iteration of the Stone Plan is."

"Think people will buy it?"

"People hear what they want to hear. Notice how she's trying to play both sides with the protect the homeless and keep the streets safe?"

"What's the FBI need from us? I'm assuming they didn't call you out of the goodness of their little dark fed hearts?"

"See? That's why you're my favorite detective. They are looking into the murders in and around the camp. Stone, Franklin, and Bell."

Emily grew cold. Stone and Franklin were officially solved and in the bag. Jensen was hopefully rotting away behind prison bars for these crimes. Bell, though . . .

"They want our case files and look to take over the investigation?"

"No. They're asking if we have any intention on prosecuting Pete Bell's murder. They have enough on Stone and Franklin, and those two counts are included in the grand jury's civil rights indictment. On Bell—they want to know if it's worth pursuing. They are willing to take us at our word. If Bell was a random act of violence in a homeless camp, they aren't going to put effort into the case."

Emily paused. The Feds poking around at the Bell killing would eventually come around to Willow. She didn't deserve to get pulled into a new nightmare. She had nightmares of her own.

"Let me go back through the case notes on Bell. When do we need to get back to the Feds?"

"Let me know by tomorrow morning."

"Will do, Lieutenant."

Emily hung up the phone and was relieved to know the lieutenant wasn't going to dig his heels in on the Bell killing. There had been enough suffering. She hoped Willow could overcome a single deadly night.

*　　*　　*

Connie and Lucinda strolled into the apartment and took in the carefully arranged furnishings. Lucinda gave Emily a wink.

"This looks lovely, dear," Connie said.

"We hope you like it," Emily said.

"I know I will." Connie focused on the television. "I remember her."

"The mayor? She is on television a lot."

"No, no. The small brown-haired woman to the far right." Connie pointed a gnarled finger at the screen.

Emily leaned in and searched for the figure her mother had mentioned. At the far edge, Lisa Larkin stood with the other supporters. She was dressed in a blue business suit. Emily pointed to her. "This one? This woman here?"

"Yes. I remember she was in one of my classes—when I taught fourth grade. Terrible age—not children, and not quite grown up yet. She was different."

"How so?"

"Well, I didn't get a whole lot of time with her."

"How come?"

"I don't remember all of it. I do know she was taken away after her parents died."

"What? What happened to them?"

"Never got an official account, mind you, but what we heard at the school was murder-suicide. Father lost his job and took it out on the family. That girl—at first they thought she killed her parents. Nonsense. She was just a little girl."

Brian elbowed Emily. "Poor girl never had a chance."

"I hope Willow can break the cycle of violence." The hair on the back of Emily's neck tingled.

CHAPTER FIFTY-FIVE

A FEW HOURS after getting Connie safely tucked into her new apartment, Emily begged off and said she needed to head back to the office.

"Need my help on something? You were kind of quiet after the lieutenant's phone call. Everything all right?" Javier said.

"Yeah, yeah. I think so. The boss wants a status report on where we left off with the Bell case. The Feds want to know if it's worth pursuing."

"The lieutenant knows the girl killed Bell, right?"

"He does. We didn't hide anything in the reports. I don't see what would be gained by dragging a vulnerable kid like her back through this again. She's just now starting to get her life together. Her and her mom. It's . . ."

"It's what?"

Emily glanced over her partner's shoulder where Lucinda and Jenny were busy moving knickknacks at Connie's direction.

"You've got a good one there, Javi. Don't screw it up."

"It's only a matter of time until she realizes she could do so much better." He turned and caught a sly smile from Jenny.

"I dunno. Looks like she might have bought into that most eligible thing."

"We can hope the illusion continues. You need me to help you with something on the Bell case?"

"No. I got this. You go take Jenny out on a proper date. I'll get Brian to take me to the office."

Brian carried the last of the empty boxes outside to a recycle bin. "I overhear you needed a ride?"

Emily got in the passenger seat of Brian's Mustang. She bit her lip and fell silent.

"What's got you brooding? Jensen? He's going away forever."

"No, it's not him. He's done. It's Bell. Something Mom said is bothering me. Lisa Larkin may have killed her own family."

"And you think she might have killed again?"

"Maybe. Or got Willow to do it for her. I need to check out a couple of threads and see if I can find out where they go."

Brian dropped her off at police headquarters, and she saw the lieutenant's office light was on. She knocked on the doorframe. "Hey, Lieutenant, got a minute?"

"Emily, sure. What's on your mind? Mom get moved in and settled?" Lieutenant Hall said.

"Moved in, yes. Settled, the jury is still out on that count. I wanted to bounce something off you."

Hall closed the file in front of him and leaned back in his chair. "Shoot."

"The Bell homicide. I thought we put that to rest."

"Now the Feds want to see if it's worth their time to prosecute. Anything change since you closed the case?"

"No. Yes. I'm not sure, maybe . . ."

"That's the decisive detective I've come to know. Lay it out for me."

"We know Willow pulled the trigger on Pete Bell. We have the slide bite on her hand and the lab reports had a trace of her blood on the gun. That's not in question."

"What's got you twisted up, then?"

"The *why*."

"We said it was self-defense. The girl believed she was protecting her mom as Bell was assaulting her."

"And I still think that's what Willow believes. She killed that man."

"But?"

"I learned that Lisa Larkin was once thought to have shot and killed her parents."

"Like mother—like daughter. You're thinking mom may have set her up to do it?"

"I'd like to run it down. It doesn't change the end result. Bell is still dead. But why it happened is out of focus for me."

"All right. Chase it down. Let me know if we need to tell the Feds anything. We have till morning."

"Thanks, LT."

Emily plopped at her desk. Not sure where to begin, she powered up her desktop computer. While she waited for the monitor to blossom to life, she grabbed a notepad and tapped a pen on the blank page. Emily jotted, *Lisa Larkin juvenile record?*

She typed Lisa Larkin's name into the search field in the department's system. Nothing came back before she was caught in the homeless camp fire. A deeper dive didn't reveal a juvenile record—or the existence of a sealed one.

Maybe Mom got it wrong. It could have been a faulty memory caused by the invisible demon short-circuiting her life. Her mother was once a vibrant, energetic teacher. Emily remembered how much she cared for the students under her charge, and could recite birth dates, names of siblings, and the kids' favorite books.

Emily grabbed the phone and tapped a number, twirling the pencil as she waited for the connection.

"Brady Collier," the reporter said when he came on the line.

"Brady, it's me, Emily. I need your help."

"What's this about, Emily? Last time we spoke, my source turned out to be a multiple murder suspect."

"And you got a front-page, above-the-fold article out if it."

"Now you're calling in a favor? What does one of Sacramento's most eligible singles need?"

"Most what?"

"The year's list releases next week. Congrats."

"How did—when—wait, is Javier Medina on the list?"

"Who?"

"That's all I needed to hear. Hey, I'm trying to run something down. A double murder, twenty-five to thirty years ago."

"That's not much to go on. Isn't that something you should have in your records?"

"You've got all the media and press clipping in that LexisNexis database of yours and I don't have the victims' names. What I do have is the victims were husband and wife and the sole survivor of the event was a girl between eight and ten years old. Her name is Lisa Larkin, but I'm thinking she might have taken that name after the murders."

"Lisa Larkin? The same Larkin?"

"Yes."

"If I help you on this, and if there is a story here, I get the exclusive."

"Fine by me."

Emily repeated the details as relayed by her mother. The murder, the surviving child, and the approximate time the crimes may have occurred. "The woman is thirty-five now. This happened when she was in fourth grade, so nine to ten years old. Twenty-five years ago . . ."

"Okay, okay, hang on for a minute. Let me check the paper's archives first."

Emily heard the tapping sounds of a keyboard in the background.

"There were a lot of murders in Sacramento in the late nineties. Can you give me anything more to narrow the field?"

"I don't think so—oh, wait. At the time, it was thought to be a murder-suicide."

"That might—yes, got it. I have one murder-suicide article published twenty-five years ago. Harold and Mary Purlmutter were found shot to death in their Curtis Park home. Investigators believe the deaths were a murder-suicide. It mentions a nine-year-old girl witnessed the killings. Doesn't reveal her name. You think that's Lisa Larkin?"

"The fact pattern fits. Thanks, Brady. I owe you one."

"If this goes anywhere, I get that exclusive."

"Yeah, yeah, I gotta run with this. Thanks again."

Emily hung up and entered Harold and Mary Purlmutter into the department's system. She hoped this was one of the case files digitized in recent years.

"Dammit." The case file wasn't available in an electronic format. Emily jotted down the case number, ripped the page off the note-pad, and set off for the department's records storage. She needed to get the Watch Commander to send someone to open the locked storage room.

While she waited, Emily mulled over the life Lisa experienced after the death of her parents. Foster care, exactly as she claimed. Then by her own account an abusive relationship at the hands of Willow's father. The woman hadn't lived an easy existence and it came to a head in the homeless camp.

"Hey, Detective. The lieutenant tells me you need to pull a file from archives."

"Cortez, I wondered where you went." Theresa Cortez was a sergeant Emily worked with right after graduating from the academy.

"Got the relief job backing up the Watch Commander, filling in on Brian's RDOs. I don't know what witchcraft you worked on that boy, but he is smitten, I'll tell you."

"Glad to hear the spell is still working."

Sergeant Cortez unlocked the records storage and flipped on the light, revealing box after box of files on wire racks. "You have a case number?"

Emily waved the notebook page.

"Have at it. Log it out and lock up when you're done."

Emily strode down the rows of boxes and checked the case numbers against the one she'd jotted down.

She'd checked all but the last row, set aside for cold cases, the unsolved investigations where all the leads dried up over time. There were detectives assigned to these cases and they'd regularly check for new threads, but most would stay entombed in these boxes until the paper turned to dust.

On the cold case shelf, Emily found the matching case number and the name Purlmutter printed on the box. She pulled it down, logged it out, and took it back to the detective bureau, away from the ghosts of other dead files.

She opened the box and removed the case files, setting them on her desk. The last summary was a terse accounting of the crime scene. Two victims, one male, one female, both shot at close range. Originally believed to be a murder-suicide.

Originally?

Emily kept reading. An uncommunicative Lisa Purlmutter was found at the scene and was taken to the hospital for evaluation and turned over to Child Protective Services.

Another yellowed report in the file from the precursor of what was now the forensics arm of the department documented the slugs removed from the victims were .380 caliber.

An electric twinge hit Emily.

The weapon was never recovered at the scene.

No . . .

The gun in Willow's stuffed animal. It was registered to an H. Purlmutter. Lisa had the gun the entire time.

A photo of a nine-year-old Lisa faced the camera. She looked scared in the harsh black-and-white photo. Blood spatter pockmarked her light-colored sundress. A small droplet dried on her cheek. What drew Emily's attention was a small bandage on the web between her thumb and first finger on her right hand.

Slide bite. Lisa had murdered her parents.

CHAPTER FIFTY-SIX

EMILY CLOSED THE file after reading about several police encounters at the home. Harold Purlmutter had a temper and officers responded to domestic violence complaints five times in the months before Harold and Mary were found dead in the home. Investigators questioned Lisa but she wasn't able to tell them who shot her parents. They immediately discounted the nine-year-old as the shooter. The detectives at the time worked two theories, the first being a murder-suicide in keeping with Harold Purlmutter's abusive history. Then there was the troubling fact of the missing gun. There was only one other person in the home—Lisa.

She turned to her computer and brought up the Bell homicide files. She already knew the caliber of the bullet was the same. An entry into the file came in after the case had been closed. The Bureau of Forensic Sciences, the state lab charged with running many of the DNA samples submitted by law enforcement, filed a report on the case.

Emily didn't need the DNA from the gun, because they'd already tied Willow's blood to the weapon.

Clicking on the report, Emily scanned the science-envy jargon until she froze on one line. DNA sample from Subject 1 is a familial match to victim Bell.

Emily's vision faded, and a chill wrapped around her spine.

Subject 1 was Willow. A familial match meant one thing. Willow had killed her father.

Emily stabbed the number of the Lemon Hill shelter into her phone. The woman who picked up told her Lisa and Willow had slipped out last night without saying a word.

Emily sat back and all the pieces started coming together. The .380 brass shell casing in Lisa's rolled-up pant leg, the weapon registered to her long-dead father, hiding it in Willow's favorite stuffed animal—it all gelled. Pete Bell wasn't cruising the camp to prey on young, vulnerable girls—he was looking for his daughter. A daughter Lisa had kept from him.

Emily snatched the phone from her desk, dialed Javier, and put her jacket on while the call connected.

"Em, what's up? Everything okay?"

"You need to drop whatever it is you're doing and meet me. We've got this all wrong."

"What?"

"Willow didn't kill Pete Bell."

"What are you talking about? We heard what she told us. The slice to her right hand from the slide bite."

Emily told him where to meet and hung up. She ran from the detective bureau and, slipping into her Crown Vic, tore out of the parking lot.

Javier pulled in next to her and rolled his window down. The burnt aroma from the ash heap that was once a homeless camp remained a sour pungent memorial.

"Tell me what's going on, Em."

"Pete Bell was Willow's father—"

"Whoa. But—"

"Wait, it gets better. The gun—the gun Willow was toting around—was used in a double homicide in the nineties. Lisa's parents. Purlmutter, remember? Lisa Purlmutter, at nine years old, was suspected, but the detectives just didn't figure a little girl could pull the trigger. The shell casing we found in Lisa's pant leg. There's no way that could have come from the gun when Willow fired, from behind Bell."

"But Willow's confession and the cut on her hand. She pulled the trigger."

"Yes, she did," Emily said. "When I spoke with Delila, she told me she heard the gunshots that night, Javi. Gunshots, plural. I didn't put it together until now."

"Willow missed and Lisa finished the job. That explains the shell casing in her pant leg," Javier said.

"Bell wasn't a perv looking to score—he was trying to find his daughter. Lisa absconded with her."

"Holy shit. She counted on us not wanting to prosecute a nine-year-old for murder, so she had this all planned—her quick confession, knowing we'd find the gun in Willow's bunny. Then Willow would tell her story about how she shot Bell because he was hurting mommy. We'd think she was such a great mom, trying to take the rap for her daughter. How devious is that?"

"Right? She figured it worked for her when she was Willow's age—why not do it again now?"

"My God, that is some messed-up shit right there. Why are we waiting here at the burnt-out camp?"

"One thing Lisa said was she would hide things in the rocks. She's taking off and she's gonna grab anything else she had before she splits."

"Good thinking. Unless she's already in the wind."

A gray Toyota Camry pulled into the far side of the lot and parked. The white Uber sticker stood out in the front window. Seconds later, Lisa Larkin and Willow stepped from the sedan. Lisa leaned in and spoke to the driver.

She must have told him to wait, because the Uber driver shut off his car while Lisa and Willow trotted down the trail to the river's edge.

"Come on, Javier, let's finish this."

CHAPTER FIFTY-SEVEN

LISA WADED INTO the icy river water. The current pulled at her legs and she bent her knees to remain steady in the cold pull of the flow.

"Momma? What are you doing?"

Lisa glanced over her shoulder. Willow stood on the muddy bank, in the very spot she waited before the camp burned.

"I'll be right there, sweetie. We have a bus to catch."

Lisa unwrapped the fabric bundle she'd hidden in the rocks. She pitched the missing magazine of .380 rounds into the deepest part of the river. The fabric also held a photo of a two-year-old Willow with Bell and Lisa, taken a lifetime ago. The faded picture she'd taken from Bell's body bore his blood stains. She remembered the look of disbelief on his face when Willow tried to shoot him. She grabbed the gun from her daughter, and Bell tried to run, but he only got a couple of steps before she fired. Pete Bell fell face-first, and she was disappointed he didn't suffer. It was over quick—too quick.

Lisa nearly believed his line of bullshit—she was unfit. The girl would end up selling herself on the street like she did, if he didn't get her out.

Lisa saw Willow creep up behind Bell with the gun in hand. She didn't stop her. She locked eyes with her daughter and nodded. Girl would have to do better next time.

Well, she got Willow out. Who's the terrible mom now?

She ripped the old photo—the only link to another life—and spread the pieces on the water. Willow would never know they'd killed her father. It would break her. Lisa wasn't sure if the cycle of violence that had plagued her since childhood could ever fade away. She rubbed the old scar on the web of her right hand as she wondered at the price her daughter would pay for what happened one night on a dark riverbank.

Once the last bloodstained scrap vanished, Lisa waded to shore and took Willow by the hand.

"Remember what I said?"

"Yes, Momma. We never let anyone hurt us."

Lisa turned for the riverbank and found Emily and Javier standing behind Willow. Three uniformed officers stood farther up the bank.

Emily stood with a pair of handcuffs. "Let's go, Lisa. It's over."

ACKNOWLEDGMENTS

The inspiration of *River of Lies* goes back to my parole days. I was with some of my regional parole staff as we walked through skid row in Los Angeles, then the largest homeless camp in the nation. We had to come up with strategies to monitor parolees who lived in the camps in response to politicians who wanted to ignore this population or thought they could legislate the social issues away. Huge credit to the parole agents and administrators who never gave up.

When writing *River of Lies*, I thought about that and other homeless encampments I'd witnessed. What stories, tragedies, and long-kept secrets were hidden in the tents and cardboard shelters?

A novel like *River of Lies* might be written in isolation but can only come to life with a fantastic team pulling together. I'm forever grateful to Bob and Pat Gussin and the team at Oceanview who brought Emily's story to life. Thanks to Lee Randall, Faith Matson, and Tracy Sheehan for their help getting the book into your hands.

Thanks to Elizabeth K. Kracht of Kimberley Cameron & Associates for not giving up and finding the perfect home for this series. Thanks, Liz, we did it again!

A special thanks to my advance readers, especially Jessica Windham, Janis Herbert, and Megan Cuffe, who are never shy about telling me what works and what doesn't.

The book community is incredible, and I appreciate the support of independent bookstores like Face in a Book (Tina Ferguson and Janis Herbert) and Book Passage (Kathy Petrocelli and Luisa Smith). They make a bookstore feel like home.

Sometimes it's words of encouragement that came when they were most needed. J. T. Ellison, Wendall Thomas, Karen Dionne, Baron Birtcher, Bruce Coffin, Alison Gaylin, Rachel Howzell Hall, Wendy Corsi Staub, and Shawn Reilly Simmons, I thank you endlessly. A special shout-out to my 2:00 a.m. ThrillerFest road crew and my fellow Capitol Crimes Chapter of Sisters-in-Crime members for the love and support.

Thanks to my kids: Jessica, whose snarkiness may have influenced Emily's character, and to Michael—I love you guys.

I wasn't always alone at the keyboard, and I owe Emma and Bryn the corgis extra treats for all the plot points they helped me work through on countless walks. The corgis aren't happy they didn't make an appearance this time—I've promised them I will fix that grievous oversight. Then there's #NotMyCat who now demands extra catnip because of her newfound celebrity. The book would have been done months earlier if not for her walking on my keyboard.

A special thank-you to Ann-Marie L'Etoile for tolerating my nonsense over the years. You let me disappear behind my keyboard and still love me when I come up for air. Love you.

And finally, thanks to you, dear reader. It's only possible because of you.

NOTE FROM THE PUBLISHER

We hope that you enjoyed *River of Lies*, the second in the Detective Emily Hunter Mystery Series.

The first in the series is *Face of Greed*. Each of the novels stands on its own and can be read in either order. Here's a brief summary of *Face of Greed*:

Detective Emily Hunter and her partner, Javier Medina, are called to investigate a brutal home invasion and murder. At first, it appears a crime of opportunity gone horribly wrong, but soon she finds herself immersed in the shadowy world of gang violence and retribution, where she has to identify the killer—without becoming the next victim.

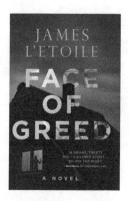

"In *Face of Greed*, James L'Etoile gives us a Sacramento rarely seen in crime fiction. In a city without an identity, L'Etoile's Sacramento bursts with good cops and crooked cops, skinheads and tweakers, bad men and femme fatales. This helluva page turner has hella heart!"

—Rachel Howzell Hall,
best-selling author

Face of Greed is the first appearance of Detective Emily Hunter—tough as nails when investigating a murder, and deeply compassionate when caring for her mother with Alzheimer's.

We hope that you will enjoy reading *Face of Greed* and that you will look forward to more Detective Emily Hunter novels to come.

For more information, please visit the author's website:
https://jamesletoile.com.

If you liked *River of Lies*, we would be very appreciative if you would consider leaving a review. As you probably already know, book reviews are important to authors and they are very grateful when a reader makes the special effort to write a review, however brief.

Happy Reading,
Oceanview Publishing
Your Home for Mystery, Thriller, and Suspense

BOOK CLUB
DISCUSSION QUESTIONS

1. Emily Hunter is a smart cop with a strong moral compass. What do you think she's had to sacrifice and compromise to succeed in a male-dominated profession as a police detective?

2. Emily's mother, Connie, and fifty million people worldwide rely on caregivers and facilities to help with family members suffering from dementia. What do you believe Emily thought about when she found her mother unattended in a facility?

3. *River of Lies* deals with the homeless camps in and around Sacramento. What do you think are some of the root causes of homelessness?

4. Political types make promises to deal with people living on the street. Mayor Carsten makes similar statements. What's driving her decisions?

5. Redevelopment and gentrification are often cast in glowing positive terms. What negative consequences does Emily

uncover? Can you think of examples where political pressure was used to redevelop property where you live?

6. Emily's relationship with Officer Brian Conner blossoms in *River of Lies*. What drew them together, and what challenges do you foresee in their path?

7. Relationships are challenging for men and women working in law enforcement. What problems or obstacles can you think of that may create difficulty in this kind of relationship?

8. Javier Medina is a great partner for Emily. What are some of the reasons why you feel their partnership works?

9. Lisa Larkin is a single mom living on the streets. What do you think Lisa has had to do to survive and protect her daughter, Willow? How will these choices impact Willow as she grows up?

10. *River of Lies* looks at the generational cycle of domestic abuse. Lisa Larkin has experienced violence in her life since childhood. What can she do to prevent Willow from following in her path?

11. Investigations involve a mix of physical evidence, observations, and information from witnesses and informants. Which do you believe are the most important? Which would carry the most weight in front of a jury?